FALCON'S prey

C. Lymari

FALCON'S PREY

C. LYMARI

Falcon's Prey Copyright © 2020 by C. Lymari. All rights reserved.

No part of this book may be reproduced or transmitted in any form or by any means, electronic or mechanical, including photocopying, recording, or by information storage and retrieval system, without the written permission of the publisher, except where permitted by law.

This book is a work of fiction. Names, places, characters, and incidents are the product of the author's imagination or are used fictitiously.

www.clymaribooks.com

Editors: Sandra, One Love Editing

Cover Design: TRC Designs

Proofreader: Carmen Richter from CPR Editing

Also by C. Lymari

It's Not Home Without You Hoco #1 -Available Now

(Second Chance/ Forbidden)

The Way Back Home Hoco #2- Available Now

(Friends-to-Lovers)

You Were Always Home Hoco#3- Available Now

(Enemies-to-Lovers/ Second Chances)

HOCO#4- Coming Soon!

(Quincy's & Jessa's story.)

Standalone

For Three Seconds- Available now

(Forbidden/ Sports Romance)

Authors Note

I'm not a fan of trigger warnings. I feel like they take away from the reading experience, so if you need one, this book is probably not for you. The hero is a jerk, and the heroine is a bitch, and they are bound to clash. If you love twisted, fucked-up shit, then buckle up and prepare to get mind fucked.

Playlist

"Do I Wanna Know"- Artic Monkeys
"Why'd You Only Call Me When You're High?"- Artic Monkeys
"Mala Santa"- Becky G
"Bad Guy"-Billie Eilish
"You Should See Me in a Crown"- Billie Eilish
"Solider"- Fleurie
"Seven Devils"-Florence + The Machine
"Nightmare"- Halsey
"Born To Die"- Lana Del Rey
"Salvatorre"- Lana Del Rey
"Everybody Wants To Rule The World"- Lord
"Mi Mala Remix"- Mau y Ricky
"Dollhouse"- Malanie Martinez
"Show & Tell"- Melanie Martinez
"Devil Devil"- MILCK
"NBK"- Niykee Heaton
"The Wolf"- PHIlDEL
"A Little Wicked"- Valerie Broussard
For the full Spotify playlist
https://bit.ly/Falconplay

To everyone who is afraid, but still puts on a brave face. This one is for you.

He was her dark fairytale and she was his twisted fantasy. And together they made magic.

Part One

"You cannot burn away what has always been aflame."
- Nikita Gill, "Witches" from *Wild Embers*

Prologue

The heady smell of sex filled my senses as I lay in a bed fit for ten. My body stayed unmoving, my legs open, and my arms held on to the man who once promised me everything.

It was all lies.

Lies I once believed.

"Fuck," he groaned in my ear. "You feel so fucking good."

I closed my eyes and let the sensations take over, to see if I could shut my brain off from everything that was trying to overtake me. What we were doing was wrong and fucked-up —yet it felt right. He got off on fucking my body, and I fed from the pain it brought me.

His hand roamed my leg, all the way to my pussy, where he was thrusting inside me. His fingers made their way to my clit, and I closed my eyes tightly. Years of giving myself to him, and he knew my body better than I ever could. His fingers circled my clit, and I moaned. Part of me was repulsed, but the other sick part of me only felt the pleasure.

"That's it, baby, give it to me." He kissed my neck possessively as he fucked me harder into the bed.

His fingers worked faster to the rhythm of his thrusts, and I couldn't help it when my body started to convulse around him. I bit my lip until I tasted blood. My orgasm came fast and hard, and he came with me.

When he was finished, he rose above me. I didn't have to open my eyes to see what he looked like. I had him memorized. He had jet-black hair that almost seemed blue, a devilish smirk on his face, a baby-smooth face with a square jaw, and the darkest eyes I'd ever seen. He was handsome, and he knew it. He could have had anyone in the world, yet he only wanted me.

At one point, that made me feel special. Now, I only felt sick.

"I wish I could stay longer, baby, but I have to go."

He kissed me, and it was like poison: toxic and sweet, killing me slowly each time. His tongue ran over the blood and licked it off my lips. I kept my eyes closed and just lay in bed, spent.

I heard the noises he made as he got changed.

"I'll let you know when I'm in town again." And with those parting words, he walked out of my guest room and closed the door behind him.

I took a deep breath and finally opened my eyes. Once upon a time, I wanted him. I relished the way he made me feel—special, consequential, like I was someone worthy of love. Until I realized how fucked-up we were, and what we had was nothing to feel good about.

Now I was stuck in a cage, and he had the key. Closing my eyes was the only way I could temporarily be free.

Even if you closed your eyes so you couldn't see the things he did to you, you sure as fuck could feel them.

When I didn't hear any noise, I sat up. I swallowed back the vileness that threatened to come back out when cum started to leak down my thighs. Once in my room, I went straight to my laptop. I opened the program I had downloaded a while ago but never had the guts to open.

I'd asked around. Usually dumb questions that people laughed at, but it led me to the page I was looking for. My hand holding the mouse shook for a second. Looking up at the ceiling, I did the sign of the cross, aware that God would not approve of what I was about to do. So many options and I didn't know which one to pick. In the end, I went with the simplest one.

The screen turned black as soon as I clicked on it, turning into a chat room.

No names. No personal information. I don't need to know the why, just the who.

My heart beat frantically as the words appeared. I'd done a lot of stupid shit in my life, but this one definitely took the cake.

If the why was bullshit, wouldn't that affect the who? I found myself typing before I thought better of it.

I got green-colored glasses. I don't give a fuck about the rest.

I held my breath considering if this was what I wanted to do.

Just tell me who, they typed again, and my heart skipped a beat. **No more fear.**

It was tempting. So tempting.

You'll be free.

I bit my lip, because I had no idea how that felt. I was about to put in the information, and all my problems would be solved, but at the last minute, I had a change of heart.

Thank you, but your services won't be needed anymore.

I felt like a dumbass typing that, since whoever was on the other end of the screen wouldn't care. I was about to log off, but words started to appear, as did a sinking feeling in the pit of my stomach full of dread.

If you say so.

There's a reason you came.

A reason why you were ready to get dirty and lie in blood.

My palms started to get sweaty, and my breathing got shallow. I was about to close the laptop, but they wrote more.

Until we meet again.

I turned off my laptop quickly, my heart racing faster than when I was getting fucked a couple of minutes ago. My life was already a fucking mess; I didn't need to add blood on my hands.

The asphalt crunched under my Giuseppe Zanotti heels as I made my way through the parking lot of the club. The line was long, which was expected because this was the hottest club in town. When people spotted me, they started pointing at me like I was some sort of zoo animal.

Hello? I was a fucking person. Just because my life was publicized, it didn't mean they had to act like I was less than human.

I was taught from a young age to be unbreakable like a diamond. To withstand the pressure that came with my last name. Uncut and rough, but still shiny. I was used to the glitz, glamour, cameras, flashlights, and whispers. The taste of lies for breakfast and deceit for dinner was something I'd learned to acquire. I didn't really trust anyone.

People were good at two things: fucking you and fucking you over. It was better to have fun in the meantime.

Once I made it to the front of the line, I flashed a smile to the bouncer. That was all it took for him to let me in, bypassing everyone who had been waiting for hours.

"That's not fair!" some girl whined. "We've been here for an hour."

I turned around, grinning at the girl while she glared at me. To drive the point home, I opened my Alexander Wang clutch and pulled out a pack of cigarettes. I lit my death stick, took a puff, and turned to her, blowing the smoke in her direction.

"It's the way of the world, kid. Life. Is. Not. Fair."

I walked in while the bouncer shook his head. I heard the girls call me a bitch, and without turning around, I stuck my middle finger out. Once inside the club, I made my way to the VIP section. I didn't come here to make friends. I didn't have any—life at the top was rather lonely. Perhaps stupid, but honestly, I didn't care.

"What a surprise," David said.

He'd been a bartender here for a while, and since I was a regular, he knew me pretty well. And by saying David knew me, I meant that he knew my moods and what kind of drink I preferred. He knew when I was wired, high, or just plain pissed at the world.

"Oh, cheer up, Davie. You know you'd miss me if I didn't come."

"Where's your goon?" He smirked at me.

I grabbed some cashews from the tray nearby and threw a few in my mouth. "I ditched him."

David made a face. "Is that wise?"

"I'm a big girl. I can take care of myself." I smiled at him. "Now, give me a tequila sunrise."

As David went to work on my drink, I turned my head with the nagging feeling that I was being watched. It had been happening since that day I'd almost made the biggest mistake of my life, but I was sure I was just being paranoid. When I scanned the club and didn't notice anything, I turned back to the bar. Of course people were looking at me; it came down to my name.

THE NEXT MORNING, I WOKE UP FEELING LIKE I HAD A LITTLE person in my head doing renovations. I groaned and sat up.

Fuck me. I'd forgotten to take my aspirin and water last night.

"Hey, Siri," I shouted.

"Good morning, Ember. How may I assist you?"

The surround sound was to the max, and I shrieked. My head was sure to explode now.

"Text Dr. Wozniak."

"What would you like to text him?"

"Come now, exclamation point, exclamation point."

I waited while she repeated the text to me and then sent it. Dr. W would come with a banana bag, and I would feel so much better. I laid in the dark for a few more seconds, and then I got up, went to my nightstand, and blew out the white candle I'd lit before leaving the house last night: *Angel de mi Guardia*, my guardian angel candle that I got from a little Mexican flower shop every time I went. The lady said it was for protection. Angels didn't play where demons went to prey, but that was just my opinion. Still, like clockwork, I kept going back for more candles. Before I left my room, I went into the bathroom to brush my teeth. I was still in last night's barely-there dress and makeup.

"Oh good, you're up," came Sammy's, my dad's head of security, cheery voice as I made my way down the stairs of my three-floor penthouse.

I loved Sammy. When I was young, he'd been my bodyguard. He'd taken care of me, and when I went through my rebellious stage, he hadn't judged me. He still didn't. Sammy was the best, and my father knew it, since he'd made him head of the whole family's safety. The bad thing about that was, when he'd made Sammy head of security, he'd taken him away from me.

"Barely. Is Dr. W here?"

"Not yet. Come here, kiddo," he said.

I rolled my eyes but followed the sound of his voice to the kitchen.

"I'm sorry about yesterday, but as you can see, I'm safe and in one piece," I said to him as he came into view.

Sammy gave me a disapproving head shake and took a sip of his coffee. "Well, he's fired."

I sat on the stool of my breakfast bar and scrunched my nose when my maid, Karen, put food in front of me.

"Ewww, take that away," I groaned.

She immediately did as I asked.

"Sorry, I guess. I mean, it's like, he should have known I would ditch him," I told Sammy.

"Your safety, Ember, is no laughing matter."

"I'm safe and sound. No harm, no foul."

Sammy ignored me and motioned for someone to come in.

"Don't tell me you got another poor schmuck to watch over me already?"

Sammy gave me a *you should know better* look.

"Ember, meet Ren Falcon. Falcon, meet your worst nightmare."

I didn't have the energy to turn around, but I did it anyway.

Fuck. Me. Sideways.

I'd had good-looking bodyguards before. I'd let them guard my body real well, if you know what I'm saying, but none of them looked like the man in front of me. For one, he was not in a suit. I let my eyes trail up from his black combat boots, to his dark jeans, gray V-neck, and leather jacket. His chest looked hard and defined, and from what I could see of his arms, they weren't too shabby either.

He had a lovely neck, not too thick or thin. I wasn't one to stare at throats, but then he swallowed and his Adam's apple bobbed, and don't ask me why, but I thought it was hot. He had a full beard, neatly trimmed. Blond. I'd never had a thing for blond guys—until now. His hair wasn't too short, but not too long, and was slicked back without looking greasy or grimy. It just looked...hot. His face was hard and rugged. Even though his jaw was covered in facial hair, I could still see how sharp it was.

Once my eyes made contact with his, I forgot to breathe for a quick second. Either that or I still had junk in my system and was about to OD. He had gorgeous blue eyes, like the sky with no clouds. I quickly averted my eyes from him without registering the look he was giving me.

I gave him another glance. My new bodyguard was the definition of masculine beauty, and he was looking at me like he hated me.

"He'll be gone by the end of the month." I turned around to Sammy, dismissing my new security.

Sammy shook his head. "I hope not."

Just then, my bell rang and in came Dr. W.

"Finally! I felt like I was about to diiiiiiie," I told Dr. W, aware that Sammy and Ren were looking at me. I got up from my stool, waltzed to my couch, and extended my right arm for the good doctor.

"You would feel much better if we didn't do this every other day, Miss Remington."

"Look, I pay you, you come, and it's a win-win for both of us."

Dr. Wozniak didn't say anything more. We'd had this argument loads of times before. It was a moot point.

"I'll see you later, kiddo," Sam told me.

I turned my head as he gave my new guard an *I'll be watching you* sign.

When Dr. W was getting ready to put the needle in my

arm, I turned around. I hated to watch the needle pierce my skin. It reminded me that no matter how thick my skin was, it was still easily ripped.

"You know the drill," my doctor mumbled, and then he left.

I stood there for five minutes, my body soaking up the nutrients I was getting from my bag. The controller for the television was across the room, so I did what I'd always done and started to push people's buttons.

"Hey, new guy," I called out.

I didn't turn to look at him but knew he was still standing in the same spot he had been earlier, right by the door. I had one of the penthouse suites in my building. The only escape was the elevator door.

"Did you need something, Miss Remington?" he said in a hoarse, sexy voice.

Even though the sound of his voice was a sex phone call jackpot, I could still hear his disdain for me.

He didn't like me.

"The controller is right over there." I smiled brightly at him and even helped him out by pointing to exactly where it was.

His jaw got hard again, and his eyes looked like it was going to storm. They got dark and, frankly, a little scary, yet he did as I asked.

"Thank you." I took the controller from him. "Now take a seat. We have to lay down a few ground rules."

He gave me a tense nod and sat across from me. His legs spread, and looking at that did something funny to me. His elbows came to his knees, his undivided attention on me.

"Speak," he grunted.

"Karen!" I shouted for my maid, and she came running.

I didn't know why she did that. I wasn't a bitch to her.

"Yes, miss?"

"Can I have some oatmeal?"

"Of course. I'll have it ready for you shortly."

I dismissed her with a nod.

"Do you get off on it?"

"What?" I turned to look at Ren, and again, I found it hard to look him in the eye.

"To have people cater to your every whim?"

I smiled at him. "It actually takes me a bit to get off."

Ren gave me a disgusted look. "Listen, darling, I'm here to protect your body and nothing more. I'm not your maid. Next time you want something, get off your ass."

"Wow," I said in amusement. "The help has jokes." Then I got serious. "You are nothing. You got hired to protect me because, unlike you, *I am* somebody. So let this be the last time you speak to me like you and I are on the same level."

My headache was still there, and this asshole was making it worse. The damn bag in my hand was making its way through my system painfully slowly.

"Don't bite off the hand that feeds you."

He sneered at me. "Listen, diamond *princess*. Your daddy signs my checks, not you."

"Out. Of. My. Sight."

"With pleasure." He rose to his feet and left me alone.

For the first time, there was someone who didn't drop to their knees for my so-called beauty.

Ren

I GOT OUT OF THE LIVING ROOM LIKE IT WAS ON FIRE. IT WAS either that or blow this job before I even had a chance to start. This was on me—I'd wanted to take the job. I wanted more for myself for the first time in my life. I just didn't know that more entailed *her*.

Ember Remington.

Her name was at the top of my file description. She wasn't supposed to be my job, but the security guy had last night fucked up. I had stellar references and was a no-bullshit type of guy. Sam took one look at me and told me he had the perfect job for me. And here I thought that my long-term plans were coming together much quicker than I had expected. The universe must have laughed at me today.

My first week was spent in what Sam liked to call "headquarters." That was where the Remington offices were located. It was where they kept *the vault*. The Remingtons came from a long line of South African heirs to the diamond trade. Some of their familial ties were in their homeland, while others were in Rome, France, London, and New York. Michael Remington was a visionary and deviated from the norm. So far off the norm that he'd married a Mexican oil heiress. I'd researched the Remingtons, and there wasn't much on Michael and Maria's relationship. From the few paparazzi shots I'd found, they seemed like a happy couple.

Maria Sofia Escalante was a beautiful woman who'd loved her husband. Too bad that love got her killed. There were complications during birth, and when it came down to a choice between her life or her daughter's, Maria decided to save her daughter's.

This was the only public knowledge of Ember until after she went to college, where she pulled a little stunt and set a building on fire. Her dad did an interview and talked about how hard it was to raise a girl on his own. Honestly, I thought it was all bullshit; the girl could have used a good dose of discipline. I bet her father left her to her nannies, and he went away doing business as usual.

So to go back to earlier today, I was not expecting to be standing around the penthouse and watching Ember Remington walking down the hall in a dress too small for her frame, looking like shit, yet at the same time completely alluring. She didn't notice me, and that gave me the advantage of watching her. Sam obviously adored her; it was clear in the way he looked at her and talked about her, but also when he told me I had an important job.

"You can't keep all your treasures in one spot," he'd said.

Now here I was, babysitting a spoiled brat. This was not what I had signed up for at all. I was rounding the corner, trying to get to the control room to make myself familiar with the place, when the maid came out, holding a long black velvet box.

"Hey," I told her.

She stopped and gave me a wry look. Looks of fear or contempt, I was used to. I wasn't an approachable type of guy. I didn't wear a smile on my face. I wanted people to stay out of my way, but I did have compassion, somewhat. Sometimes.

Karen looked at me and gave a nod for me to keep going.

"I'm sorry for the way she treats you."

"Miss Ember is hard as a diamond, sure, but the more you stare at her, you'll see all the different angles, and all of them are beautiful because even a defective diamond still shines."

"If you say so," I said as I kept walking to the control room.

Once inside, I made myself familiar with the cameras. The whole place was covered, even her room, but the cameras went all around, leaving her bed hidden. I sat down on a chair and found the camera I was looking for. Ember was in the living room, the television was on, but she was texting, and she still had the IV in her arm.

"Is she okay?" I had asked Sam before he left.

Maybe, just maybe, the diamond princess had a reason to be mad at the world.

"It's a banana bag. It makes her hangover disappear." He clapped my shoulder and left.

Of course; rich people had the means to solve all their problems. Money gave you doctors at your beck and call, and with that, they didn't have to suffer like the rest of us poor fuckers.

Ember threw her phone aside and grabbed the black velvet box. I'd seen a lot of shit in my life. It came with the territory when you grew up in the system. You always bounced around from one place to the other. But I had never seen anything as I had right then.

"Unfuckingbelievable." I gave a humorless chuckle.

The girl had a fucking glittery bong. Still, I watched with avid fascination as Ember took a hit, then threw her head back and closed her eyes as if she wanted the world to disappear.

She was one fucking train wreck, and all of a sudden, it felt like I'd just walked myself on board the crazy train.

Just then, my cell phone pinged with a text from Pam.

Pam: So, how'd it go?

Pam and I were old associates, you could say.

Me: I'm in.

Pam: Don't fuck it up.

Pam knew just like I did what it felt like to be the dirt beneath people's shoes. We'd grown up together. Well, as together as two orphans could. We'd fought, lied, and bled our way out of the gutters.

Me: I won't.

Ember Remington was just another stop to my endgame.

"Daddy?" I called after my father.

We were new in this city. Well, I was new. Since I could remember, we'd lived in my father's country, until a few weeks ago when he'd packed us up and brought us to New York. I had yet to start school and make friends; I was lonely. My dad was all I had, and he was away more than he was home.

"My little diamond." He turned around and smiled at me.

I was seven, but still, I knew his smile never reached his eyes.

"Where are you going? It's Sunday. I thought we were spending the day together?"

"I'm sorry, baby. I have to take care of some business."

"Can I come?"

My dad gave me another smile. To his credit, he looked remorseful.

"Not today. But soon. I will be hiring new security for us, and then you can go out."

I can go out. Not we. Me and whoever took care of me.

"Okay." I gave a nod and started to turn around.

"Love you, Ember."

"Love you too, Daddy," I said without bothering to look back.

As children, we do we love our parents unconditionally, even if they don't deserve it.

I woke up covered in sweat, despite the chilly weather in my apartment. I hated when memories came to me in my sleep. I was glad this was one of the better ones…if having a neglectful father was better.

Dad had been in and out of my life since I'd moved out of the house. A text here and there, a random call, or a personal visit if I did something extremely scandalous. Earlier today, while I recovered from my hangover, I got a text from him. He wanted a family dinner. I had a sick feeling of dread because we weren't the family dinner type of family. When we did get together, it was a business talk or to drop bombs.

Since there was no way I was going back to sleep, I removed the covers, grabbed my robe, and went to the kitchen for a cup of water. The hallway was dark, and the only light came from the floor-to-ceiling windows in the living room. I didn't much mind the sun, but I preferred my curtains closed. Karen insisted on letting sunlight in, except in my room. No one dared to move my black curtains.

I was used to the darkness; it didn't scare me. Not even when I was a little girl. I would wander around at night with my dolls, not scared of monsters. Because some monsters thrived in the sun, so what was the point of being afraid of the dark?

Grabbing a cup, I filled it with ice and pulled a water bottle out of the fridge. My bong was still on the couch where I had left it. I grabbed that too, then opened the sliding door that led to my terrace.

The air was chilly, and my skin was still damp; it caused me to shiver. I threw my head back and closed my eyes.

"What the fuck are you doing?"

Lazily, I turned my head and then opened my eyes. Ren Falcon was standing a few feet away from me in jeans that rode low on his hips, the top of his boxers peeking through, washboard abs that looked Photoshopped, a gun tucked into his waist, and a cold stare on his gorgeous face. Fuck me, he had a tattoo. A half sleeve that went from his elbow to his wrist. It was too dark, but I could see shading and swirls. For a second, I imagined his inked hand running over my naked body.

He probably knew how to fuck like a god. Probably a selfish lover too. Definitely the latter—he looked like a selfish prick.

"I'm sunbathing." I rolled my eyes at him. "What does it look like I'm doing?"

"It looks to me like you're reckless," he spat at me.

"I'm in the penthouse suite. No one is getting to me." I dismissed his anger.

It had taken him five minutes for him to make up his mind about me. Well, fuck him. Ignoring him, I started to put the ice cubes I'd brought into my bong, and I added some water. I was about to grab some bud when he stood right behind me. My heart accelerated, and my hands got clammy. He leaned over the sofa I was lying on and grabbed my face in his palms. Not rough, but with enough force that I couldn't move. He turned my head so I could look across the street to the other building and did the same to my other side. We were surrounded by skyscrapers.

"You're rich, darling," he said.

"No, really? I hadn't noticed," I sassed.

He ignored me and kept going. "The type of rich that requires a security team for you and your family. Now I don't know about you, but I'd say with that comes with threats on a different scale than your average coked-out thug."

Ren let go of one side of my face and brought his other hand to grip my chin.

"You see that building?" he asked as he pointed to it.

I obviously saw the building. He turned his face toward me, his nose grazing the shell of my ear and making me shiver.

"Someone could stand right there and blow your pretty little head off."

My heart thumped, and I was sure it had nothing to do with the imagery he provided.

"Now that would suck for you, wouldn't it? You'd be out of a job." I tilted my head, making him lose his grip on me.

Our gazes collided, and it became a stare-off to see who would give in first. My eyes traveled down to his neck and his chest. Someone was cold.

"Get inside now," he demanded. "It's cold."

"If you're so cold, maybe you should go in." I reached for my black velvet box and grabbed my pick of weed for the night.

Ren was still behind me, and he gave a dark chuckle once he got a good look at the contents of my box.

"You have no regard for your life," he stated.

Ren did not leave; he walked around, making sure it was safe, then took a seat across from me. I pretended he wasn't there while I broke down my bud and packed it.

"Jesus," he muttered.

"What?" I asked.

"You don't need glitz to get high?"

I held up my bong, admiring the handiwork the people at Remington Diamonds had done. "It's made out of crystal and our most luxurious diamonds."

Ren shook his head. "People are starving and you do some stupid shit like this?"

I heard the disgust in his voice.

"Am I not allowed to have things that make *me* happy?" I said.

He didn't need to know about the charities I gave to. That was none of his concern.

Placing the head of the bong to my lips, I lit the bowl and took a hit.

The thick smoke instantly relaxed me. I threw my head back, closed my eyes, then released the smoke into the starless night. I liked sitting outside, amidst all these buildings.

"Great, now that you're high, can you go back to bed?" Ren got up.

I untucked my feet from my Indian-style seated position, and Ren looked at my bare legs.

"You're not wearing socks or even shoes."

"Neither are you," I said.

He took a step toward me.

"What are you doing?" I put a hand up to stop him.

"Listen up, darling. I'm here to protect you, and if that means that I have to fucking carry your ass inside because you were too stupid to wear shoes, then that's me earning my money."

The weed must have gotten me high fast, because I burst out laughing. Maybe what he said wasn't hilarious, but I found it funny.

"Fuck, you're high," he muttered.

"I'm fine," I said and pushed past him. "We are not doing the whole Whitney Houston thing right now."

Ren was hot on my heels. I felt his presence behind me like a shadow.

"Trust me, darling, if it weren't for the fact that I was getting paid to be here, I would never bother with the likes of you."

Ouch. That hurt. It picked at a wound that I'd had for a long time, but hell if I'd let him know.

"Don't worry, bodyguard," I spat. "You'll be out of a job soon enough."

I took a step to walk away, but Ren was there, grabbing

my arm and forcing me to turn around to face him. He looked like a bull ready to strike. His face was easy to read. I didn't know if he did have a poker face, or maybe he ran on anger, but I could understand him. Perhaps his emotions mirrored my own.

The mint from his breath hit my nostrils, and it smelled intoxicating.

"You trying to come up with a way to get me fired?" he asked, his face getting closer to mine.

"Either that or I might get killed," I replied, not giving much thought to my words.

Ren swallowed, and he looked at my face, his blue eyes blazing with fire. He dropped his hold on me and walked away.

"Asshole!" I yelled after him.

I sat on the sofa with everything dark around me, lost in sweet oblivion. It was around five in the morning when I got a text.

I miss you. I need you.

Not wanting to deal with the emotions it made me feel, I grabbed my velvet box, took out a vial, and snorted part of my problems away.

"WHAT THE FUCK?!" I SHRIEKED, THE SPLASH OF COLD WATER waking me up.

Ren was beside me with a bottle of water in his hand. "Sorry, making sure you didn't die on me."

I wiped the water off with my hand and glared at him. I grabbed my stuff and made my way to my room. I was bored, angry, and restless. It was Friday and I knew just

Falcon's Prey

where to go party. I went into my walk-in closet and picked an outfit for the day.

I grabbed a ruby-red silk tank top that looked more like a sleeping undergarment and paired it with a black corduroy skirt and black high-heeled booties. My father had sent our new collection of diamonds a couple of days ago, so I figured I could kill two birds with one stone and showcase them as well.

I was Daddy's walking billboard, something I had made peace with a long time ago.

There was a pendant, some rings, bracelets, bands, and a necklace, but like always, I went for my diamond choker. It used to be my mother's, one of a kind. My father hated that I wore it, but I didn't give a fuck. I had no mom; the least I could have was her necklace. Maybe my dad didn't want me to wear it since I was the one who killed her.

Once ready, I went straight to the control room. I knocked and waited for an answer.

"Marcus," I said when I saw the man who opened the door.

"Ember." He gave me a sad smile.

Marcus had been my security guard when I was nineteen. He was nice. Back then, he was twenty-four and wanted a job in law enforcement, but that didn't happen. Instead, he came to work for us. Safe to say, I used him.

Right after I fucked him and he professed his love to me, I kicked him out of my life. I felt terrible thinking he would lose his job, so I'd made sure he kept it, but since then, he never wanted to be near me. Not that I could blame him.

"Is Ren here?" I asked.

"He got called into headquarters. That's why I'm here."

"Cool," I said, trying not to grin.

"Ember." There was a warning to Marcus's voice.

"Hmmm?" I played innocent.

"You are not to go anywhere without him."

"I know," I said. "I'll be on the terrace. You're more than welcome to keep me company."

Marcus made a horrified expression, and then he shut the door in my face. Walking back to the living room, I saw Karen, who shook her head at me.

"Two-minute window is all I ask for," she said.

Ren

It was useless to try to go back to sleep when I was feeling wired. Instead, I went to the control room. From there, I made sure everything was in order, then focused the bigger monitor on the living room. Ember was high off her ass, sitting on the couch, just staring at the wall.

This girl had everything at her fingertips, yet she treated her life like it was nothing. I grew up a charity case, bouncing between foster homes because my mother was a junkie whore, and my father was a drunk con man. They only got their shit together enough to get custody back and cash a few checks. From a young age, I had to fend for myself. Learn how to survive on the streets because it was either I became street smart or ended up dead.

Drugs? I didn't touch them. There was already enough shit that could kill me. I didn't need to add a useless habit to the list.

Around five in the morning, Ember's phone lit up. I wondered who would text her at this hour, especially since she stared at her screen for a few minutes. Her face was devoid of all emotion. Throwing her phone aside, she walked out of the living room back outside. I quickly grabbed my phone and turned off the alarm. I wasn't sure if she was aware of it or not, but her personal bodyguard got a notification after the doors were locked for the night.

I was prepared to get up again and tell her to come back inside when she walked back in carrying her bong box. I seriously thought I'd seen the stupidity humanity had to offer, but then I'd sat across from the diamond princess taking a hit from a bong that probably cost more money than I would see in my life. I sat back down, preparing myself to watch her take another hit, but instead, she grabbed a vial of white powder.

The image was almost too familiar as I watched her cut the lines and inhale them. I remember watching my father do the same. Ember lay on the couch turned the television on, then fell asleep. I went to the living room to do one more thing while she was passed out, then went to my room and slept.

It felt like I had barely gone back to bed when my phone rang.

"Hello?"

"Falcon," the authoritative voice spoke, and I immediately got up at the sound of Sam's voice.

"Sir."

"I need you to come to headquarters," he stated.

"Sir, I can't leave the girl alone."

"Her name is Ember," he spat at me, and I bit my tongue. "I'm sending someone to cover for you. This won't take long."

"Sounds good."

As soon as the line disconnected, I opened the camera feed on my cell, and once I saw Ember was still passed out in the living room, I threw my phone on the bed and changed. When the guard posted at the entrance of the building texted me to let me know my replacement was here, I left my room. The first thing I did when I walked out was to check what Ember was doing. Not surprisingly, she was still sleeping.

Before I left the house, I went to the couch and stared at Ember. She looked peaceful, with an almost angelic face. When I noticed still some powder on her nose, I poured some water on her face.

She was nothing like I thought she would be.

The penthouse had two exits. The front door led to a hallway with an elevator and fire exits. This was only accessible to Ember. The penthouse on the other side was this one's mirror. My replacement, a light-skinned African American, was already in the elevator lobby waiting for me.

"Ren." I nodded.

"Marcus," he replied. He took a step toward the door but stopped. "What is she doing?"

"She just woke up," I said as I walked into the elevator door and closed it.

It took me about twenty minutes to make it to headquarters. Here I was, an orphan from the streets getting around in a company Maybach. Talk about wasting money on unnecessary shit for employees.

"Here I am," I said as I walked into Sam's office.

He wasn't as tall as I was, but he carried himself with an authority that came with years of experience. He spoke to all his men in the same hard tone, unflinching except when he talked to Ember. That's when you saw the hard man soften a bit.

"Take a seat." He motioned for the chair across from him.

Doing as he asked, I waited to see what he would tell me next. He didn't say anything; instead, he pulled out a folder and handed it to me. My blood chilled the minute I opened the contents of the envelope. It was all cut-out pictures of

Ember. Some were of her walking down the street, getting into a cab, at clubs, in alleys with guys.

"Normally, I don't make it a habit to show her security this information." As he said those words, I felt pride that he saw something different in me. "But things have escalated, and I can't keep you in the dark, so for my sake and hers, I hope you last."

"I don't see myself quitting anytime soon," I told him.

He gave me a look, but didn't comment.

"Listen, kid, this job won't be easy. Ember's the kind of girl that makes you work double. Until we find a way to end this, I need to know that you will make her a priority in all things."

"What do you mean?" I was already making more than enough just protecting this girl.

"I mean, you are her shadow. You basically don't have a life outside of hers."

This complicated things with Pam. I would figure it out, though.

"I don't have much outside this job." That wasn't entirely a lie either. "May I ask why you're concerned now?"

Sam took a deep breath and looked at the wall. "She's always had a target on her back. She's an heiress to the second-largest diamond distributor in the world. That kind of money doesn't come without a price. Around her nineteenth birthday was when we received the first photo. We tried to trace it, but there was no way to do it. We assumed she had a stalker, so we added more security without her knowing. Her father has had a hit on him. That's why he doesn't want to be in the same place as her for long. If her target and his come from the same person, it would make it easier to get both of them."

"Why is this happening?"

Sam looked at me now, and if I were a lesser man, I would have flinched. "Money. Power. Take your pick."

I gave an understanding nod.

"You may go. Stay vigilant; you see anything out of the ordinary, report it. I don't give a fuck how insignificant you might think it is."

I moved to stand up. "Why haven't you notified the authorities?"

"Boy, in this world, everyone has someone in their pocket."

That was the damn truth. With power came corruption. I started to walk out when I remembered he hadn't answered my other question.

"What happened that made you take this seriously?"

"Ember had long hair. Beautiful, shiny hair. A couple of weeks ago, she cut it."

"Okay," I replied slowly.

Sam opened the cabinet behind him and pulled out a clear bag full of hair.

Shit.

"We tested it. One hundred percent match."

"I won't let you down, sir."

He didn't reply right away, so I took that as my cue to leave. Just as I was walking out the door, he called after me.

"We'll see about that."

I had the car door open when I got a call on my phone. "Yeah?"

"Ember took off," Marcus replied.

"What!" I yelled. "How could you let that happen?"

I got in the car, putting the phone on speaker and opening the app I had installed on Ember's phone. Every iPhone came with a Maps app, but Ember did not need to use hers. Last night when she passed out, I went to the living room and swiped her finger on it. Seriously that was the stupidest shit ever invented. I deleted that app and downloaded a maskable tracker app so she wouldn't notice what I'd done.

"You're new, so you don't know how Ember gets," Marcus replied.

I didn't bother with an answer and instead hung up on him.

Following the tracker, I saw her on the move a couple of blocks from where I was. As I drove to catch up to her, I cursed her name. This was my fucking job, and she had no regard for anyone but herself.

THIRTY MINUTES.

That was how long it took me to catch up to her location. I parked on the side of the street. I figured that if the car got towed, the Remingtons wouldn't bat an eyelash at paying the fee.

I was new to the city, so I didn't fucking know where I was going. The alley seemed seedy as fuck, and a part of me was praying to God that I didn't find Ember Remington dead. I came to a stop when I saw I was by the lake. On the horizon, there was a boat.

"Fuck. Me." I gripped my hair.

How did you save someone who didn't want to be saved?

I went back to the car and asked the first person I saw directions to the harbor.

I swore this was the last time this spoiled bitch made a fool out of me.

Ember

"Do you want to tell me why you're so quiet?" Lilah, who lived in the same building as me, asked me as I looked across the water.

I got lucky that Lilah had an Uber already waiting downstairs, and with the extra cash we gave the driver, he took off like the hounds of hell were after him.

"Ho, I'm talking to you." Lilah snapped her fingers in my face. "Is it the Marcus thing? 'Cause you got to let go. You fucked him once, and it's not your fault he went and caught feelings."

"It's not that," I told her.

Lilah was the closest thing I had to a friend. We'd grown up in the same circles and did drugs together, but whenever she wanted to go out of state, I had to decline. My father was paranoid and barely let me out of my protective bubble. She knew everything about me, knew all my truths except those I didn't want to admit to myself.

"Your mom's birthday is coming up," she said in a softer tone.

The last thing I wanted was to talk about my mother. I remembered the day I asked my father why I didn't have one. I didn't know if he explained it wrong, or if he'd intended to say it the way he did it, but all I got from it was that I was responsible for my mother's death. I'd been a screwup since the day I was born. Yay me.

Not wanting to talk about this, I changed the subject.

"I think I might like blonds. You know, other than you."

Lilah snorted. "No, you don't. You like Charlie Hunnam, and Tim Austin, that's about it, and yet you argue that their hair color is brond and not blond."

"I do not," I told her.

"Do too."

"I hate you," I said with a smile.

The yacht had circled the lake for longer than I expected. A little part of me felt guilty for doing this; the other part didn't care. I mean, it was my life, and I was allowed to do what I wanted, when I wanted. For years I begged my father to stop with the ridiculous amount of security. I got it. We were rich. But come on! It was like we were the first family of the United States. My dad exaggerated things.

"Here." Lilah handed me a glass of champagne.

"No, thanks," I said.

Lilah shrugged and sipped from that one as well. I smiled at my best friend. One thing she loved was her wine and champagne.

"You didn't touch the booze, you said no to the joint that was being passed around, and didn't even grab a party favor."

"I'm not in the mood," I told her.

My head was not in the right place. And I wasn't completely irresponsible. I didn't touch party favors unless I knew where they came from. I got my weed, coke, and molly from a top-notch dealer—no cut-down shit for me.

I sighed with relief when I saw the yacht making its way to the pier. I could finally go home and relax. Lilah was tipsy, and I was sober; it was a rare night, that's for sure. Grabbing Lilah's hand, I dragged her down to the pier with me.

"Excuse me." I pushed people out of the way. "Coming through."

"Damn you, Ember," Whitney shouted when her champagne spilled on her dress.

"Sorry. Send me the bill."

What was everyone's hurry to be the first out? I was so annoyed, I just wanted to be alone. Once my heels made contact with the pavement, I sighed in relief. We were walking toward the street where we could hail a cab when I saw him.

I felt a chill run through my body.

Ren Falcon did not look happy.

He was leaning on a pillar; his jaw was set, and even from here I could tell how pissed off he was. Something like dread stirred inside of me. I was used to looks of disappointment from my father and Sammy, and anger from my uncle. Usually, my bodyguards acted more like I was a hindrance than anything else.

Ren pushed off from the pillar, making his way toward us, and I wanted to go back onto the boat.

"Ember, Lilah, you two are going to the after-party, right?"

I turned my head to look at Zeke, our host. He loved having Friday parties and games on his yacht.

"I don't think so," Lilah said as she patted his cheek.

"Yeah, I'll pass," I said as I tried to pull Lilah with me.

Zeke grabbed Lilah's other arm, dragging her to his body.

"You two sluts never say no to a party."

"Let me go." Lilah started to push him off her. One thing we hated was being called sluts.

"Zeke, don't be stupid now. Let her go," I seethed.

He smirked at me and pushed Lilah off him. As I took a step to get her, he grabbed me.

"If you wanted me to grab you, all you had to do was ask," he mocked in my ear.

Before I had a chance to tell him to let me go or he'd regret it, someone else did it.

"Let. Her. Go," Ren said through gritted teeth.

He was standing a few feet away from us, one of his hands behind his back. I might have thought he looked at me with hate before, but it was nothing compared to the look he was giving Zeke right now.

"Who the fuck are you?" Zeke mocked.

So far, Ren didn't dress like my other bodyguards with a black suit and the diamond pin all our workers wore. It was a symbol showing who they served. He wore his boots, with jeans and a leather jacket.

"Let me go, Zeke, before you get hurt," I said in a bored tone since I wasn't afraid.

Zeke, however, didn't let me go. Instead, he smirked at Ren.

"Listen, I'll give you five hundred bucks. Take it and buy yourself something nice."

Ren laughed. He then took his arm from behind his back and pulled a Glock and aimed it at Zeke's face. I bit my lip to stop myself from grinning. Finally, a guard that wasn't a pussy.

"How about if I shoot you, then you can take your money and shove it in the hole to try and stop the bleeding?"

Zeke might not have shown it, but I felt the moment his body went still against me.

"You'll end up in jail," he said with fake confidence.

Ren gave a wicked grin. "You want to find out?"

I rolled my eyes at both men trying to prove each had a bigger dick than the other. Having guards all my life and an absentee father showed me that I needed to learn to take care of myself. Bringing my heel down to one of Zeke's Hermès loafers, I dug in until he howled with pain. Then I pulled my elbow back with force until it hit him in the ribs.

I stepped out of Zeke's embrace, and Ren was already grabbing on to my wrist, pulling me away. Lilah kept pace with us.

I turned around. "Maybe next time you should bring your guards! You're a pussy who can't take care of himself!"

Zeke glared at me.

"Shut up," Ren growled. "I had to run around all over town because Daddy's little diamond went missing."

I tried to pull my hand from his hold, but I think the only way I would get out of his grasp was when he wanted to let go or break my wrist. Since I was fond of my bones not being broken, I decided to let him be—for now.

Ren had the Maybach with the hazard lights at the entrance to the harbor.

"Get in the car now." Ren all but shoved me in. "Who the fuck are you?" He turned to Lilah, finally taking notice of her.

"She's with me," I said from inside the car, arching a brow when he turned to look at me.

"She can find her way back home."

"Contrary to what people think, these boots are not made for walking." Lilah pointed to her thigh-high Louboutins

"She lives in our building," I said.

Ren stepped aside so Lilah could get in. Once she was seated, he slammed the door, making us both flinch.

"He's angry," Lilah whispered.

When I turned to face her, we both laughed. Getting comfortable in the car, I pulled out a water bottle for Lilah and some aspirin. After years of coasting through life drunk, I was more than prepared. Lilah took the aspirins, then turned to me with a mischievous grin.

"Hey, you. Mr. Gunman."

"His name is Ren," I said, pretending not to care that my so-called friend was talking to my bodyguard. I tried to hide my satisfied smile when Ren kept driving without answering her.

Lilah, however, didn't let that stop her. "Has anyone ever told you that you have a lovely shade of brond hair?"

My eyes went to the front of the car, where my gaze collided with Ren's through the mirror. I couldn't read him. And that bothered me more than I wanted to admit to myself.

Since I was young, I'd developed an instinct for reading people. My life was a revolving door of fake friends and conquests. As I got older, it got easier to tell why someone was in my life. The answers were always the same: influence, drugs, sex, money. Ren might work for me, but there was something he was hiding. I could practically smell it on him.

"It's like blond but not too blond, you know?" Lilah's question snapped me out of staring at him.

Ren didn't bother to answer her; instead, he put up the partition.

"Rude!" Lilah screamed so Ren could more than hear her.

I turned to face her silently, glaring at her to not say more.

She smiled. "I like him."

Of course she did.

"Lilah." I leaned into her, careful to not be heard. Lilah did the same. "You aren't allowed to fuck him."

The ride to Hill Hotel was silent. Ren parked in my private parking. Once there, he opened the door to Lilah's side of the car even though I was behind him.

Whatever.

Ren and Lilah took off in the opposite direction of my entrance. I got out of the car, slammed the door, and started walking to my elevator entrance. I needed a drink now that I was home. Maybe a line or a blunt. Remembering that I had hidden a tin with blunts in the phone box, I grabbed that first. It took me a minute to light up. Once I took a hit, I pressed the button to go up.

"Ember, hold the door!" Ren shouted.

You know what I didn't do? I didn't hold the fucking door.

Ren

"You're doing a stellar job of protecting my friend," the leggy blonde said as I walked her to her private entrance.

"Marcus is on cameras; if your friend had been in trouble, he would have paged me by now."

"Hmm." Ember's friend made a face.

"What's that supposed to mean?"

"Marcus used to be Ember's bodyguard. There's a reason they've removed him."

No wonder the fucker lost her in the five minutes she was in his care.

"I'm pretty sure you know the way to your place from here." I pointed toward her elevator door. It was a few steps away when I left Ember's friend and took off running in the other direction. Ember had a blunt in her fingers as she pressed the elevator button.

"Ember, hold the door!" I shouted.

Ember looked up, her brown eyes dark and intense. She smirked at me and pressed the button, closing the door before I could reach her.

"Son of a bitch."

I'd grown up in the streets. The only person who'd ever mattered was myself, and now I was in charge of one of the most self-centered women I'd ever met.

By the time I walked out of the elevator door, I was fuming. It shouldn't have taken me nearly ten minutes for the elevator to go down. Marcus was waiting for me in the lobby with a smirk on his face. "She spent ten minutes opening and closing the elevator doors. "

Of course she fucking did.

Marcus patted my shoulder as he passed me to go into the elevator. "An ember may be the last thing burning in a fire, but this Ember, she's the blaze."

I removed my shoulder so he would stop touching me, then walked into the penthouse. Ember was already on the kitchen island, dropping champagne into the bong and packing it.

"Didn't you just smoke? The elevator reeked."

"I put it out after a hit of it. I didn't want to hotbox it," she answered without looking at me.

"I looked everywhere for you today," I said through gritted teeth. I watched her inhale and exhale the drugs in her system.

"Congratula—" She started to cough. "—tions."

I took a step toward her, mad as fuck that I needed to be reduced to a glorified babysitter. My whole life, I'd been trying to make my way out of the gutters to stop people making me feel inferior, and this bitch did it on day one.

"Congratulations? Are you serious right now? I chased you around town, trying to make sure you were okay." There was an edge to my voice.

Ember jumped down from the kitchen island. "I'm a big girl. I can take care of myself."

I stepped toward her. I towered over her; even in her heels, she was tiny. Breakable.

"Yeah?" I purred my words. "If I hadn't been at the harbor, what would your *friend* have done?"

"Zeke is a dipshit." She glared at me as if her so-called friend manhandling her was my problem.

"Well, dipshits are usually the ones who end up on the news for raping women," I growled.

To her credit, Ember didn't flinch or react. Instead, her eyes went vacant.

"Real monsters don't get caught," she mumbled, leaving me too dumbfounded to say anything else.

I watched her leave and didn't say any more. Once she was gone, I went over to where she'd left her box and looked through her belongings, not able to hide my disgust. She had the world at her feet, and she was here tempting death.

The next day I was still in bed, contemplating if I needed this job, when the bedroom door opened. Ember walked in wearing a short dress and heels, her lips blood-red.

"Ah, look, you're happy to see me." She smirked at me, looking at my morning wood.

"I was hard, but then you walked into the room and killed my vibe," I replied.

What the fuck was wrong with me, resorting to childish games?

Ember rolled her eyes at me. "I need to leave, so get let's go."

"No."

When she smiled, I waited to see what would come out of her mouth.

"I'm sure the first thing they teach you in dog school is to obey your master." She pointed a finger at me. "You, dog." Then one at herself. "Me, master."

The blood that was in my dick earlier boiled all over my body.

When she snapped her fingers, I forced myself to keep my face impassive.

"Let's. Go." She walked out of the room without looking back.

I dressed quickly, grabbing my guns, and when I came out, Ember was smoking a cigarette in the lobby. I got close to her, and the only thing I could smell was tobacco. Since she was going to make me do everything, I pressed the elevator button while I stared at her nose in the elevator reflection. No sign of cocaine, but who knew?

"Are you telling me where we're going?" I asked her.

"Does it fucking matter? You do as I say," she told me as we stepped into the elevator.

I smirked at her. "It matters in the way that if I see someone trying to kill you, I'll stop them or not. Then again, a little spilled blood never hurt anyone."

Ember stared at me, and I took the cigarette from her lips and took a drag from it just as the elevator opened again.

I got in the Maybach, waiting for her to come in. Since I didn't open the door for her, she glared at me.

"This is the part where you tell me where I'm taking you."

She didn't answer me. Instead she typed an address on the GPS. I drove around the city, trying not to stare at her; she looked so different than she did on my screen when I'd researched her. Still, she was dumb and naïve.

"Are you fucking serious right now?" I said when the GPS took us to McDonald's.

Ember ignored me. "Park right there."

I did as she said, surprised the diamond princess was

going to get out and not use the drive-through. Not even a minute later, workers started to come out, holding Happy Meals in boxes.

"Thank you." She waved goodbye.

She then put in another address, and I followed the directions until we were in the underground parking for the biggest children's hospital in the state.

Once out, Ember grabbed her purse, and she gave me a smile that didn't reach her eyes. "I'll be on the twentieth floor."

Then the bitch walked away, leaving me with all the fucking food. I stood there watching her go when I pulled my burner phone out.

"Yeah?"

"It's me," I said.

"Took you long enough, asshole," Pam said.

"I know. Things are going to be harder than I thought."

When Pam didn't answer immediately, I knew that wasn't a good sign.

"It better not be because you have a hard-on for that little bitch, because I swear to God—"

"You swear what, Pam?" I growled. "Don't forget where we stand. Just because I have a soft spot for you, it doesn't mean—"

"I'm sorry. Yeah, look, be careful okay, asshole? There's a reason why everything is so shady, and I'm worried."

"I got to go. I don't have time for your sentimental bullshit."

I hung up, then took all the boxes to the twentieth floor.

When I finally made it to the correct floor, the staff helped me. I had one box when they led down the hall. The room was big with a bunch of kids, all of them sick, but they were smiling. In the center of them all was Ember, and she was smiling at them. The light hit her, and the choker at her neck seemed like it glowed.

I'd done more than my fair share of research on Ember, and not once did I come across her visits to sickly kids. Fund-raisers to raise money for bullshit events for other rich people, yes, I'd seen her plastered all over, but this I didn't have a clue about, which made me curious, and I wondered if I should pull in a favor.

I walked toward Ember, and I got to listen to the conversation she was having with a little boy.

"Tell you what—you don't give up, you keep strong, and I'll get you a dog as a gift." When Ember smiled, the little kid got twinkles in his eyes.

"Do you have dogs?"

Ember cast me a side glance. "I have one. It's not all that great, Dion, but nothing I can do about it."

"Sometimes it's not the dog but its master. Dogs know when their master is a fraud, a failure; they can smell weakness, and let me tell you something..." I leaned close to her ear and whispered, "You reek of it."

Ember stopped breathing for a second, her hands going to the diamonds at her neck, and then she walked away. Everyone loved to point out flaws until it was their own.

Ember

"Daddy, please let me come with you," I begged my father when he came to kiss and hug me goodbye before his trip to Africa.

He gave a sad smile. "I'm sorry, princess. I wish I could."

Right. He always wished he could.

I waved goodbye to my father.

"It's okay, Ember. I'm keeping you company," Uncle Silas said.

He wasn't much older than me, just five years. I was eight, and he was thirteen. My grandparents had adopted him a few years back, but now Grandma was sick, and Grandpa was leaving with my dad on his trip.

"You think my daddy loves me?"

"How could anyone not love you?"

In my twenty-four years, I realized that love was also a weapon in the game of life. People used it, lied for it, stole for it. Some even killed for it. But in the end, it was a weapon nonetheless.

I reached for my nightstand, trying to find some joints, when my hand touched the cold surface of my laptop. Instantly, there was a chill in my body. The last time I'd touched it was when I made the mistake of logging into places I had no business being in.

Since I was in skimpy shorts and a tank top, I grabbed a long robe before I made my way out of my room. The hallways were dark, but for the first time, I felt an icy feeling go down my spine. I looked around, but found nothing. Shaking my head, I made my way outside. Once I was there, I grabbed the lighter and lit up my joint. I walked all the way to the edge of my building, dragging a chair with me. The fence was a little high for safety measures. I stood on top of the chair and looked down at the world. The people down below couldn't see me, and they didn't matter to me.

I exhaled smoke, and when I turned around, I found Ren standing by the door.

"If you jump, there's no way in hell I'll jump after you," Ren said in a lazy drawl.

Tomorrow was my family's dinner, and I was feeling reckless. I turned around, sliding down to the chair, aware that my robe was now hanging open at the sides. Slowly I started to bend one of my legs, and Ren followed the movement. It wasn't cold, but it was chilly, and I knew my nipples had pebbled.

Ren knew it too. His eyes raked over my body, stopping at my center, and I could feel myself get wet. I wondered if he could see it through the satin cloth.

"Inside. Now," he demanded in a gruff tone.

Instead of answering, I took another hit, then threw my head back and let out the thick smoke. The stench of marijuana and blueberry was in the air. When I brought my head back down, I opened my eyes and saw Ren had taken a seat on a chaise.

There were a million things I could have said to him, but instead, I went with the truth.

"You ever wonder what would happen if you died? Like if you were to die tomorrow, what would the people around you do? Would they cry? Be shocked? How long would they mourn, and how quickly would they forget you?"

Ren leaned back on the chair, his gaze leaving me and

scanning the area around us. "Are you afraid of being forgotten?"

Something in my chest tightened like it was trying to suffocate me. It was probably my insecurities. Those bitches loved to taunt me.

"How can you forget someone you barely know exists?" I mused.

In my mother's culture, people started praying immediately for your immortal soul after death. They prayed for nine days, then for the next nine years on the anniversary of your death. When I died, who would pray for me? Who would even remember me?

Ren stayed quiet, and I started to feel uncomfortable with my overshare. There was something dark and alluring about him that I wanted to reach and maybe be consumed by. After all, darkness would be welcome to the invisible shackles I found myself in. In the dark, no one gave a fuck what was right or wrong.

"I'm surprised you aren't bitching at me about getting killed," I said, mainly to try to move past my verbal diarrhea from earlier.

"Your back is to the fence, so no one can get you from behind. From this point the only one who can kill you is me," he rasped.

For a second, I contemplated his words, wondering if he was capable of doing that to me.

"You need to relax," I told him.

"I relax, you end up dead."

I rolled my eyes at him and got up from my seat. He was starting to be as paranoid as my father.

"Tell you what. You take a hit, and I'll go to bed like a good little girl. Just relax," I said.

Ren gave me a questioning look, but ultimately he

nodded. He extended his hand so I could pass the joint, but instead, I took it, which surprised him. I moved to him and watched the way his body stilled as I straddled him. I wasn't stupid, and I knew that if he wanted, he could have stopped me at any given moment. There was a part of him that wanted me.

They always did.

"What are you doing?" He looked straight at me, and not at my body, or the way that I had yet to sink into his lap.

"My Kush, my rules," I whispered as I sank into his lap.

He. Was. Hard.

And I fed off that kind of knowledge. My pussy was on his dick, and I leaned back to take a hit, then rolled my hips, making my eyes flutter, but glad I didn't moan. Ren's chest rose and fell. His blue eyes looked like the ocean—beautiful, but deadly. I lowered my mouth to him, and Ren opened his. We didn't kiss, but our lips touched, and I felt that graze of our mouths straight to my core. I pressed my face closer to his, and I shotgunned the smoke into his mouth. Ren inhaled it, then threw his head back and let it out.

I was mesmerized by his beauty. It wasn't prim and proper; it was rugged, lethal, and dirty. Once again, I was attracted to his throat and the way his tendons flexed. He lowered his head and wordlessly took the joint from me. He brought it to his lips, inhaling, then throwing the joint away. His hands came to my waist, his fingers digging into my hips. He got up, and before I could wrap my legs around his waist, he laid me on the chaise. He took my hands and lifted them above my head, then thrust his hips into my pussy, and when I moaned, he put his mouth on me and blew the smoke.

I started to cough, feeling like I was choking.

With his hard dick still pressed against my now obviously wet pussy, he whispered in my ear. "Are you always this easy, princess?"

I glared at him, my throat still burning from the smoke.

"Your little pussy is drenched, and I barely touched you." He smirked at me. "I'm not going to fuck you."

He then walked into the house, not looking back at me. My cheeks flamed, and I was glad for the night because at least it felt like I could hide my shame in the darkness.

I was annoyed, pissed, but mainly horny when I made it to my room. The first thing I did was check my phone, and I wished I hadn't.

In two days, you're mine.

Wasn't I always?

I felt that sick feeling in the pit of my stomach, the one you get before a big test—well, no, that was a lie; I never gave a shit about mundane things like that—as I pressed call on the number.

"This is a lovely surprise," he mused. "You never call anymore."

"What's so important about this dinner?" I questioned.

"Can't we just see you, baby girl?" Silas questioned.

"Don't call me that," I bit out.

"I'm well aware you aren't a little girl," he chuckled.

I didn't answer him; instead, I threw my phone across the room and lay awake until the early hours of the morning.

When dawn broke, I couldn't take it anymore. I got up and headed to my closet. Ever since I was little, I knew we had money, but as I got older, I realized people didn't build empires without bloodshed on the way. Remington's diamonds weren't clean, not when blood was spilled continuously for our products.

This building had gone through renovations before I moved in. You see, as absent as my father was, he knew he has enemies, and he put in a fail-safe. I didn't bother with my phone and walked to my walk-in closet. I pushed my coats to the side and found the small door and opened it. Once I was inside the short tunnel, the sensory lights turned on, which made finding the door handle easier. I pushed the door to the side, and it opened to an undisclosed hallway.

The other side of my penthouse belonged to Ashton Hill, the heir to the hotel, and he was the only other person with access to this hallway. I sat there on the top stair just grateful that I was away from cameras. If I could, I'd make it to the bottom of the stairs where it would take me to the primary hotel elevators, but I didn't want to go out. Instead I sat there thinking about my fucked-up life.

It was my seventeenth birthday, and my father was nowhere near our home. I didn't know why I was surprised about it. There was always a deal, a new merger, the mines, a new line, everything, and everyone came before me. Our immediate family had shrunk once again. Grandma had passed away, and Grandpa was slowly losing his mind to Alzheimer's. Why they adopted when they were old as shit was beyond me, but I was grateful.

Silas was the only person who gave a fuck about me. My dad's room felt cold; he barely even lived here. I went to the back of his closet and found the velvet box, which he used to keep my mother's things. I dug through her stuff, trying to find a connection to the mother I never knew. She was beautiful. I couldn't deny that. Black hair, golden skin, and the darkest brown eyes, they almost looked black. I looked a bit like her except a shade lighter. I pulled all the stuff out when I found a diamond choker with intricate designs on the back rather than the front. Maybe it was a way to say, "Fuck you, Dad," or maybe I just wanted something of my mother's.

Silas was on the couch, drinking some scotch on the rocks. He had celebrated his twenty-third birthday a few months back, and I was sure he had better things to do with his time than spend it with me.

"He's not coming, is he?" I asked him.

Silas turned his attention from the television toward me. He was handsome. I was sure he had a girl or two waiting at home for him. He was tall, lean, with hollowed cheekbones that made him look refined. Black hair, fair skin, and honey eyes that lacked warmth.

"I'm not leaving you alone on your birthday."

He stood up, enveloping me in a tight hug. My skin prickled when his arm snaked around my waist a little lower than I was comfortable with.

"Happy Birthday, Ember," he whispered against my ear.

With my hand in his, he led me up to the rooftop of our building. There were fairy lights all over, with a picnic set up and a fancy spread all around.

"Love you, Ember." He kissed my cheek.

My heart thumped like a wild beast inside the confines of my ribs. I could taste the wrongness of it all in the air, breath in the vile, and I didn't care. All my life, I had to share my life with the spotlight, my father to his work, and my mother to death. Silas was the one person who loved me, and I was holding on to that love like a crutch.

"What are you doing?" I said as soon as we both were sitting on the blankets. I was many things, but stupid was not one of them.

"I love you, Ember," Silas said, his hand coming to my nape.

"I do too," I said because that's what you said to family.

Silas came closer, rising to his knees. "You're not my blood, Ember, and you're not my family—"

Hearing him say that hurt. It cracked pieces of my soul enough to make me angry, and with my anger came selfishness. I glared at Silas, ready to tell him he was nobody. A poor little orphan boy who got taken in to our dynasty. Before I could say more, Silas kissed me. His lips were cold and brutal. He kissed me with hunger and dominance.

"But you are *mine."*

My lips trembled. It should have been intrusive, it should have felt wrong, but all I felt was the warmth I'd been denied all my life.

"I love you, Ember."

He kissed me again, and I let him. I basked in the sin of his love. In the dark, I let him do to me things I might not have done in the light. I wasn't a virgin, far from it, but I let Silas have my innocence—and he did.

He did me sweet, with peppered kisses on my skin.

On my knees, telling me it was always going to be him and me.

Licked the wrongness of my release while he smiled at me.

We fucked, him and me, and all I could think was finally, someone loved me.

Ren

My dick was rock fucking hard.

I couldn't remember a time where I'd lost control of my body like I did last night. I was used to keeping all my feelings in check; it came with the job. I'd learned to anticipate people's moves before they even knew it themselves.

All that didn't matter with Ember. Not since I'd started to develop some sort of sick obsession with her. When I watched her, I thought she was going to be one thing, but the reality of her had a stench. She reeked of desperation and loneliness, submerged in darkness and covered in selfishness.

Ember Remington was beauty wrapped in sadness and sealed with hatred. Yet it was all the ugly in her that called to me. Something so pretty and refined was one breath away from shattering.

Now that was something I wouldn't mind seeing. I liked seeing people when they got to their breaking point—the delirious line between life, death, and fantasy.

I reached for my phone and checked the cameras. There was no sign of Ember. She must have still been sleeping. The first thing I did was hit the gym and work out, then shower.

When I came out, I noticed that Ember still had yet to leave her room. It wasn't that I was worried, but if she'd overdosed on my watch, well, shit would get hard to explain to her daddy.

"Are you dead?" I shouted as I knocked.

There wasn't an answer, so I tried to open the door, but it was locked. Well, I guessed that meant she was in her room. She was probably still pissed about yesterday. Shaking my head, I made my way to the control room. I absently watched the cameras as I thought of the way her little satin shorts were wet. It would have been easy to fuck her yesterday, if I'd wanted to. But, then again, easy was never my style.

I looked at the clock again, then went to my room and grabbed my lock-picking kit. It took a minute to open her door. The pit of my stomach sank when I saw she wasn't in her bed.

Son of a bitch.

I ran to the bathroom, not giving a fuck if she was there naked and wet. The place was empty. I brought my phone up and started to scan all the cameras, and there was no trace of her in the apartment.

There was probably a protocol of what I should do, but I'd be dammed if the spoiled little bitch made a fool out of me. I was ready to go out and search for her when the lobby door opened.

"Well, don't you look happy to see me?" Marcus joked as he walked into the penthouse.

"What do you want?" I barked.

"Sam sent me here. Protocol for when the family meets. We usually send Ember with two guards."

"What meet?"

"With her father and her Uncle Silas," Marcus explained. "Didn't she tell you?"

I said nothing.

"Of course she didn't," Marcus mumbled.

"I need to run an errand real quick. Stay in the control room," I said before I started to track Ember's phone.

It made no sense because it showed her in the building. So the little bitch left her phone. Frustrated, I grabbed a smoke and made my way outside so I wouldn't be here feeling more useless and stupid than I already was.

◆

To say I was pissed was putting it mildly. I was fucking furious. The blood in my veins boiled, and I wanted to throttle Ember. It would give me sick satisfaction to watch her face pale by the lack of oxygen.

When my phone rang, I debated letting it go to voicemail.

"You can stop looking for her. She was at Lilah's place. She's making her way up now," Marcus said on the other end of the line.

"Do. Not. Let. Her. In," I gritted out, then hung up. It made no fucking sense. I'd checked the feed, and it never showed her going anywhere. I was in a fucked-up mood by the time I made it back to the building.

The ride back up to the penthouse was excruciatingly slow. The only pleasure I got was watching Ember on my phone screen as she flicked off the camera because no one came to let her in her own house.

It was about time someone showed her that harsh reality of life. By the looks of things, that someone was going to have to be me. There was a sarcastic smile on my face when the elevator door pinged. Ember turned around, pissed as hell, and that made my grin grow.

"Motherfucker!" she screeched as she ran toward me.

Her arms started to pound on my chest with more force than I expected her to have. "Learn your place, you piece of shit!"

Grabbing one of her wrists, I twisted until her back was pressed to my front. I walked us to straight to the wall underneath the lobby camera. It wasn't a blind spot, but Marcus wouldn't exactly see what we were doing.

"I'm already sick and tired of you," I greeted her.

Ember kept trying to move, but I wasn't letting her. "Then find another job, asshole!"

"I don't think so, darling," I growled in her ear.

"Wait until I tell Sammy about this!"

"You could," I said casually, aware that she could call my bluff. "The thing is, I'm sure you won't. How many times does Sammy have to hire a new guard, huh? Don't you think he's disappointed every time you act like a spoiled little bitch?"

She stayed silent, her body going taut. However, I didn't stop.

"One thing you should know about me, darling, is that I'm not a pussy. I'm going to give it to you straight because you're a fucking idiot who thinks nothing is ever going to go wrong with their life."

I pressed closer to her, inhaling the scent of her mint shampoo. It wasn't fruity and annoying like most women I knew.

"The next time you get a wild hair and run around loose might as well be your last. I'd rather report to your father that you are safe and sound than telling him I'm waiting for 911 to get your splattered brains off an alley. So from now on, you are going to do what I say." I pressed into her more until our bodies were flush. "Are we clear?"

"I can feel how hard you are." Her voice came out hushed and gravelly.

This only made me smile. When was the last time I did that? Who the fuck knew? I brought my right hand down next to her waist and trailed it up her body, careful so that only my knuckles grazed her. Ember's breathing stopped. When I reached the top of my abdomen, I pulled out my Glock. I didn't give a fuck if *that* touched her, and I glided it between her body. I let the object trace down the curve of her ass down to where the hem of those skimpy shorts started. I wedged the Glock between her legs, causing her to shiver and her back to arch. My piece was between her legs, and I'd bet that if I wanted, I could have moved it back and forth and made Daddy's little diamond come all over it. I pulled my hand higher, making her shorts pull up, knowing it only added to the sensation she was feeling in her pussy. I pushed my hand as high as it went, my knuckles touching her ass, and the neck of my Glock aligning with her pussy lips.

"Don't flatter yourself, darling. I've seen teenagers with more tits and ass than you," I hissed in her ear.

Just like I knew it would, those words pissed Ember off. She brought her head back, ready to slam it against my nose.

"Careful, Ember. I'm not Zeke," I warned her.

Because I was an asshole, I moved my piece back and then forward again, not missing the inhale of breath from her.

"I bet your pussy is as wet as it was last night," I mocked before I let her go.

She walked up to the door and raised her middle finger to the camera. We heard the buzzing sound of the locks being disarmed. Ember walked in, not acknowledging anyone, and went straight to her room.

I walked to the kitchen and found Karen cooking. She looked at me apprehensively. Must have been the grin I was sporting.

"Is everything all right, Mr. Falcon?"

"Everything is perfect," I replied, heading for a water bottle. "I don't think she ate, so take that for her."

I left the water bottle on the counter for Karen, then walked out to the control room. Marcus opened the door as soon as I got to the door.

"I told you. No one can handle her," Marcus mocked.

"You don't know what I can or can't handle."

Marcus rolled his eyes at me. "You think you have her under control?"

I didn't bother answering Marcus. I'd show them that I was better than all of them.

"I need a quick smoke break. I'll be back," Marcus said as he walked out. Before he left, he turned to me. "Ember will always do what's best for *her*. She doesn't give a fuck who she hurts in the process."

Closing the door in Marcus's face, I didn't bother to answer him. The difference was, I wasn't a pussy. I was lethal, and if I had to make Ember kneel before me to keep my job, I wouldn't hesitate.

◆

AFTER TALKING TO MARCUS, I CHANGED INTO A BLACK SUIT just like the rest of the security team, something I hadn't bothered doing before. Everything was black, and before I left my room, I grabbed a pair of black leather gloves for later.

Marcus and I were in the living room, waiting for Ember to grace us with her presence. I knew she'd walked out of her room the moment Marcus sucked in a breath, and I wanted to punch him in the face the moment I noticed the way he looked at her.

There was heat in his eyes and longing but also hurt. My jaw felt rigid because I was pretty sure at one point, Ember had fucked him. With anger coursing through my veins, I turned to look at Ember, and I had never felt bloodlust like I did at this moment.

Her raven hair shone, and her eyelashes looked fitted for a whore, but they worked for her. Her lips were blood-red, and I could picture the red smeared all over her mouth after choking her with my cock. Then I got angry at the thought. Her dress was burnt red like dried blood, with a plunging V that barely covered her nipples, and a slit on the side that went below her hipbone. On her neck was the choker she seemed so fond of, and on her middle finger, she wore a ring that had the outline of a heart with a barb of thorns in the middle and a small cross. The dress was made up of a bunch of little jewels and beads, and there was no doubt in my mind they were Remington gems.

"Let's go," she said after she swallowed.

"A little early, isn't it?"

"Silas doesn't like to be kept waiting," Marcus mumbled.

Silas Remington was the poor orphan boy who got adopted into the family. Ember's grandfather had taken him in when the boy's parents passed away. It seemed odd that an older couple would adopt a kid a few years older than their granddaughter, but as was the way with rich people, no one questioned it.

The ride down to the elevator was quiet, and I could feel the unease that was rolling off Ember in waves. Her posture was stiff, she kept fidgeting, and I bet that if I touched that delicate vein in the arch of her nape, it would be strumming.

Interesting.

"Excited to see your father?" I asked once we made our way to the car.

"Sure." She shrugged as she walked ahead faster.

She stopped by the door of the car, waiting for me to open it. Once I did, I touched her naked back and nudged her in. Since Marcus was with us, I let him drive.

As we made our way to the restaurant, both Marcus's and my cell phones pinged. We looked at each other and then at Ember, who was oblivious to the change in atmosphere.

I pulled my phone out while Marcus kept driving.

"Change of plans," I said as Ember turned to face me. "Your father and uncle have been in an accident."

Ember

THERE WAS A NINETY-NINE PERCENT CHANCE I WAS GOING TO hell. Why, might you ask? Well, the first thought running through my mind should have been worry or sadness, not fear of who the hell was going to run Remington Enterprises since I was a fuckup, and the only thing I was good at was being a billboard on legs.

"Are they dead?" I asked.

Ren looked at me quizzically. His brows furrowed like he was trying to figure something out. I didn't look at him; instead, I looked at Marcus through the mirror.

"Sam didn't say," Ren replied.

I nodded my head and closed my eyes as I let the guys take me to whichever hospital my father and Silas resided at. The city lights passed in a blur, and I kept my mind blank, not wanting to think about what was happening. Hoping for the best but preparing for the worst.

"Stay calm," Ren's deep baritone voice whispered in my ear soothingly, easing me a little, while his hand went to my knee that kept bouncing up and down.

I felt his cold palm like a million small nerve endings finding current and igniting me. I turned to look at him, and for the first time since I met him, I got lost in his eyes. They were like an endless abyss full of secrets that I wanted to reveal. Ren Falcon wasn't a great guy—hell, he wasn't even a good guy. He was an asshole, but he was worried about me.

I could count on one hand the number of times people

had worried about me. I wasn't a girl everyone liked; I knew that. I was an acquired taste, and that was my own doing.

"I'm fine," I told Ren after I blinked back tears.

Marcus kept driving, and Ren kept his hand on my knee. I wanted to feel something other than the dread that had crept up on me. Slowly, without looking at him, I started to lift my leg, causing his hand to glide down lower. I felt Ren's hot gaze on me, but I kept looking straight. I rested my leg in the middle, aware that if Marcus fixed his mirror, he would be seeing a lot more of me.

My heart stopped the moment Ren leaned up and grabbed a water bottle that was in the little fridge compartment by me. For a second, I feared he would stop, and I would be forced to face my emotions. Instead, he used the opportunity to move his hand to my apex. I opened my legs a little and let him feel the arousal he had created. When his fingers finally reached my pussy, the feel of his skin caused me to bite my lip. I wanted him. I made no secret of my want; I just didn't think he would have given in so quickly.

Ren leaned close. I had a feeling he wanted to tell me something, so I made it easier for him. His finger kept teasing my entrance, not moving just caressing.

"You're that much of a slut that you'd get wet at a time like this?" His voice was soft, but his words cut.

Grinning, he removed his finger and made a show of pouring water on it and wiping it clean.

Marcus turned at that moment and gave him a questioning look. "What the fuck are you doing?"

My heart stopped for a second to see what he would say. I'd felt humiliated a time or two in my life, and I hated the way my stomach churned. I didn't look at Ren, but I heard his response.

"I touched something nasty. Wanted it off my skin."

I heard the mocking in his tone, and I was glad I had a fucked-up childhood that I was able to control my reactions. Shortly after, Marcus parked at the front of the hospital. I didn't wait for Ren to open my door; I got out and ran inside.

"Where the fuck do you think you're going?" Ren barked, holding on to my arm.

"I don't know? To see if I'm finally an orphan," I spat.

Ren didn't say more, and his hold on my arm lessened but not by much.

When we got to the front desk, upon hearing my name, the nurse sent us to the VIP wing of the hospital—you know, only the best for my family. When the elevator doors opened, my stomach dropped when I saw Silas. He was pacing the hall, looking undone. There was a gash on his head, but other than that, he looked fine, albeit nervous. I stopped walking, and so did Ren. The hand that was gripping my arm now rested on my bare back, and he pushed me gently as if he was giving me strength.

I looked at Ren, still mad at him for what happened earlier, but a part of me wanted to ask for help. For what I had no idea. With everything going on—the nerves over seeing Silas, then the accident—I hadn't gotten a good look at him. He was in a suit, and I supposed he looked handsome, but he didn't look like himself; he looked more like every other guy I knew.

My gaze collided with his, and for the first time, there wasn't disdain staring back at me.

"Ren." I whispered his name like a prayer.

His nostrils flared, and his eyes swirled like a thunder in the day.

"Ember." I heard my name.

My lip trembled, and I slowly turned toward Silas. He stood there looking between my bodyguard and me. I was aware we had eyes on us—not just that of our detail but staff. Doing what was expected, I ran to him. I reached him with tears in my eyes, not for him or my father, but for me.

"Fuck, baby. I'm right here. I'm okay," Silas whispered in my ear as he comforted me.

I cried because, for a second, I wished he were dead. That was when I noticed my father was not with us.

"Where's my dad?"

Silas pulled back and fixed his fucking tie. His jaw clenched a bit, and he looked anywhere but me.

"He's in surgery. The fuckers who hit us ran."

"What do you mean, ran?" Ren said, coming close to me again.

I closed my eyes when I felt his heat at my back.

"Exactly what I said. Do you need me to spell it out for you?"

"I need a moment," I said as I ran away to the women's bathroom.

I sank behind the door, and I cried. It didn't matter who I was or who I pretended to be; I was a spineless little piece of shit.

Moments like this, I wished I had real friends. Someone to share my burdens with. Truth be told, I never let anyone close for fear they would see all the ugly shit I hid. I was all about being on a surface level. Like the tip of an iceberg, you never knew how much damage it would do until you collided with them.

"Ember." Ren's voice sounded worried on the other side of the door.

"Just a second," I called back.

I got up from the floor and fixed my makeup. Still, there was no hiding that I'd cried. When I pulled the door open, I was met with Ren's chest.

"What have I told you about running out on your own?" he asked in a soft tone.

"So, just because my dad might be dying, you're going to be nice to me?" I spat at him. I think he knew I needed a distraction.

A smile spread across his face, and my stomach dipped. I'd seen him angry, frustrated, but not happy. Well, not that he looked happy, but pleased.

"What?" I asked, touching my face.

"Nothing. Come on, let's go." He pulled me out of the bathroom and dragged me back to the hall where Silas now stood with a doctor.

We made it there in time to hear the doctor tell Silas my dad would pull through. That the internal damage was controlled, and he had high hopes. I felt so relieved that I leaned into Ren, letting myself grow slack in his arms.

"Your father's going to be fine," Ren said. "You can go back to being a thirsty little slut for my dick tomorrow."

I pulled back from him and walked away to the room where my dad was lying unconscious.

Silas was fucking me, and I should have felt ashamed, repulsed. Instead, I was dripping wet. I'd had sex before, but not like this—not like him. He kept worshiping me and kissing me—he loved me.

"Fuck, baby, I knew it would be explosive with you," he whispered against my jaw.

"Silas," I moaned when he circled my clit.

"Yeah?" he groaned.

"Never leave me," I pleaded.

He pulled back, his eyes obsidian and wild. "I'm never letting you go." He thrust in me hard, then pulled back and flipped me. "You're mine." He slammed into me again. "You're fucking mine, Ember."

He always got like this since I'd left for college two years ago. It was like he was scared I would leave him. We'd had a family dinner, and to no one's surprise, my father had to leave for some important business. As soon as he was gone, Silas cleared the house, then led me to his room.

"Silas," I moaned when he refused to let me come.

He chuckled and then pulled out and lay on his back, letting me ride him.

"Fuck, Ember. You don't know how much I hate not being able to tell everyone you're mine."

I was his.

When we were skin to skin between these four walls, I was only his. I stopped fucking around. I stopped having dates. I had Silas, and he had me.

I put my hand on his chest and started to move, finding a rhythm and taking pleasure in it.

"I love you, Ember," he said through greeted teeth.

"Me too," I replied.

Once we were both spent, I pulled away from Silas, walking over to his drawer and pulling out a bag of cocaine. I always got this feeling after sex. Not during and not before, but after, and I needed to numb it. Ever since I went to college and got a taste of the real world, my beliefs started to shift a bit.

"Ember," Silas said.

I did the line first, then looked at him.

He brought his finger to my cheek and stroked it.

"You need to change your security."

"Why?"

"He was asking questions."

My heart thumped.

"About what?" I asked him.

"Me, you, and how close we are." Silas sat up, and he reached for my hips and brought me to his lap.

My heart was beating like crazy, and I knew it wasn't only the coke.

"Can't he be moved?"

He gripped my chin, forcing me to stare at him. His eyes had gone cold; he didn't look like my Silas anymore.

"Either you get rid of him, or I do."

IT WAS SAFE TO SAY I HAD BEEN GETTING RID OF THEM ALL this time.

"What?" I said when I felt him staring at me.

Silas was in the room with me, and he watched me with his penetrative gaze. He walked over to where I'd been sleeping on a chair and pulled me up. He then sat down and brought me to his lap. The first thing I felt was his hardness, and I closed my eyes.

"Who is he, Ember?"

"Who?" I played stupid.

Silas's hand came to my throat, choking me. "Don't play stupid."

"He's my new bodyguard," I spat, removing my face from his grip.

"I don't like him."

"Well, too fucking bad. I just got rid of the last one. You have to give me a few weeks unless you want Sammy to be my new shadow." The lie came easy and flawlessly. "He's tired of my shit."

Silas stayed quiet, and I prayed he believed me. It took a

minute, but his arms wrapped around my waist, pulling me tightly against him.

"I hate sharing you."

I let out a humorless laugh. "Share me with who?"

"With every fucking asshole who crosses your path."

Yeah, after being faithful for a few years, I started to fuck everything that moved, hoping Silas would tire of me and let me go, but that didn't work. Instead, he just fucked me harder to remind me who really owned me. He got off on it, knowing that while everyone else only got me for a night, I was his forever.

"Fuck, I missed you," he said as he inhaled the skin behind my neck.

I felt a shiver run down my spine, not from arousal but dread.

"Silas," I whispered.

"Damn, you know what hearing my name does to me," he groaned.

I closed my eyes because I wasn't in the mood for his games today. I was over them, but right now, I didn't want to do anything with him.

"Silas, stop," I begged, something I swore I wouldn't do.

It never helped.

The moment the words left my mouth, I felt Silas's fury. The taste was bitter on my tongue and heavy on my heart. His arm came to my neck, gripping it and controlling my air intake.

"Ember," he warned as his other hand started to cup my pussy, making me arch up from the pain. "Did you forget what happens when you don't remember who owns you?"

"S-S-Silas," I managed to hiss.

He didn't answer; instead, he brought his hand to under my dress, moving my thong aside and touching my pussy. I closed my eyes tightly when he chuckled because I knew I was wet—just not for him.

"You say you don't want me, baby, but your body doesn't lie."

"Stop." I held back tears as he inserted a finger in me.

I looked straight ahead, where my father slept motionlessly, and I knew I had hit a new low. Some days, I wished someone actually tried to do something to me. I had so much protection, and all for what?

"I told you what would happen if you defied me." Silas bit my earlobe. I held back a whimper. "On. Your. Knees."

I got up only because he allowed it. "Someone could walk in."

"I locked the door. Told the staff to gives us a moment as a family," he smirked at me.

My chest was rising and falling as I did what he asked of me. I sank to my knees and didn't say a thing. I didn't need him at my back—not right now. If he wanted to mistake my hatred for lust, that was on him. It was amazing how we as humans could mentally check out when we did things we didn't enjoy doing. Like doing a grocery list, thinking of what errands to run, or even contemplating murder. My thumb pressed against the thorns in my flaming heart ring, feeling the pressure as I broke my skin. This was a better outlet for my pain.

Silas groaned as he came in my mouth. As soon as he was done, I got up, went to the bathroom attached to my father's room, and spat his release out. I probably rinsed my mouth five times before I went out of the room. Silas wasn't around, and for that, I was thankful. He'd gotten what he wanted from me, and for now he would be content.

Ember

I REFUSED TO FEEL VIOLATED. I HAD MADE MY FUCKED-UP BED, and now I was lying in it. I left my father's room in a hurry; shame didn't allow me to say goodbye to him. For all I knew, this could be the last time I'd see him.

Marcus and Ren came to me as soon as they saw me round the corner.

"Is your father okay?" Marcus asked.

"Yeah. Can you please stay with him?" I pleaded with Marcus, using that weakness I knew he had for me. I know it was wrong, but at the moment, I didn't care.

"Yeah, you don't even have to ask," he said, his voice soft.

He started to reach for my face, but Ren pulled me away before Marcus could get his hands on me. Too drained to care, I let Ren drag me toward the elevator so we could head home.

"You fucked him," Ren stated as the elevator door closed.

For a second, I froze, wondering if he knew my dirty little secret.

"What?"

"Marcus," Ren growled.

I relaxed and leaned against the rail. I felt too tired of today—of life.

"I've fucked a lot of guys, Ren," I admitted.

I didn't dare look at his face. Not when I was feeling like shit.

The ride down was slow, the tension thick. I was starting

to suffocate—at least it felt that way. Not able to stand it anymore, I looked up only to find Ren's gaze on me. There was no emotion on his face, just an empty stare.

"I know what you think of me," I said; he raised a brow. "I know what the world thinks of me too."

"Is this the part where you tell me you're trying to fill a void?"

I glared at him.

"No, this is who I am. I make no apologies for it. I make my decisions, and I live with them."

"So, if I had left you with Marcus, would you have gotten your lipstick ruined, fucked him, and called it grief?"

His words killed, but I'd be dammed if I let him know that. I'd be dammed if I let the world know my weakness. When the elevator door dinged, I was more than happy to walk out.

Fuck him.

Fuck Silas.

Fuck my dad.

Too bad for me, there was no shaking my bodyguard at this time. Ren was there, opening my car door for me. I took a step to go in, but stopped.

"My lipstick doesn't smear, so if I kneeled to suck dick, you'd never know," I spat at him before going in.

The door closed with a loud thud, covering how fast my heart rate had gotten. As soon as the car turned on, I pressed the button for the partition. I couldn't look at Ren now. I didn't want to give him another excuse to judge me. Digging through the compartment in the middle, I sighed in relief when I found a little vial.

You see, I wasn't your typical addict. I didn't yearn for my next hit. I didn't go crazy thinking about my next high. I did it to suppress the emotions when they became too much because I'd been disappointed my whole life, so I could control it.

REN

There was a hunger in me that kept growing; unlike Ember, I was the one looking to fill a void until my next hit. My addiction didn't get fed easily, and I'd learned to curb my appetite. As I drove back to the penthouse, I tried not to think about everything that had gone down tonight.

Number one, Marcus had it bad for Ember. The fucker was in love with her, and she knew it. She used his affection toward her and manipulated it to her advantage.

Number two, I didn't like Silas. There was something about him that made me get twitchy fingers, but I couldn't put my finger on it.

Number three, this was no accident, so whoever attacked Ember's father and uncle wanted to send a warning or kill them.

Number four—probably the one I didn't want to admit —was the fact that the spoiled little bitch was growing on me. I should have known she would. The first time I saw her, she intrigued me, but meeting her in person? Well, that had worked against her. Yet underneath all her ugly was a soft spot I could see but not touch—and that fucked with me.

Deciding that Ember didn't get to hide from me, I pulled down the partition.

"Ember," I called her name in a warning.

She turned to look at me, her eyes high and full of mischief. I didn't smell anything, so she'd either popped a pill or inhaled it.

"Ren." She brought up a flute of champagne to her mouth.

"What the fuck did you take?"

"I just wanted to feel happy again." She gave me a soft smile that was all wrong.

I hated that look on her. The grip I had on the steering wheel got tighter.

"Why don't you like me?" Ember looked at me through the mirror, our eyes meeting, and I could see the hurt in them.

"You're a fucking mess right now," I told her.

She laughed and tipped back more champagne. I hated her like this, the way she numbed herself. She thought she was strong, but the weakness in her reeked, especially with the bullshit she put in her system.

"Why don't you want me?" Her voice was gravelly, and I felt her glare through the glass. "Everyone wants me." Her voice dropped to a throaty moan.

I heard movement in the back, but I was focused on changing lanes, so I didn't look right away.

Fuck me.

Fuck *me*.

Fuck.

I looked at the road and then back at Ember again. Her head was thrown back in ecstasy, her lip between her teeth, and I could see her chest rising and falling as her hand moved too far for me to see from this angle.

With my hand on the wheel and one on the mirror, I moved it until it gave me the perfect view of Ember fucking her fingers. My eyes alternated from the road to watch her fingers dip into the entrance of her pussy, gathering moisture before bringing them to her clit. Her glistening pink folds taunted me. I wanted to be the one to touch her.

Earlier, I'd lied—it'd taken everything in me to stop myself —but now...

Fuck, we were going to crash if she kept doing that.

"Ember," I groaned, as I watched two fingers dip inside.

"Ren," she moaned.

Fuck me, it stirred my dick to life. I knew I could get pussy when I wanted, but sometimes I only fucked if it was convenient. Just a release that was lacking, and it never took the edge off. Only one thing did. I was thankful to pull into the parking lot of the penthouse just in time for the show to come to an end. I didn't turn to look back once I was parked. Instead, I adjusted the mirror and fixed my hard dick in my pants.

"You're picturing me, aren't you?" My voice came out thick with desire.

Ember didn't reply, but she didn't have to, not when she started to work her fingers faster, and I could see her pussy get wetter.

"Fuck three fingers," I growled.

To my surprise, she opened her eyes and looked at me. They were still hazy from whatever she'd taken, but her lust for me was right there. Slowly, she opened her legs more, giving me a perfect view. She inserted her fingers one by one and started to move her hips. The sound of her fingers and wet heat caused my dick to grow painfully hard.

What was she doing to me?

"Ren," she moaned again, and I wanted nothing more than to have her bouncing in my lap as I thrust into her. "*Ren.*"

She threw her head back, and I knew she was close to coming.

"Look at me," I demanded.

The mirror worked as a barrier; it was enough for both

of us to look, but not close enough to see each other's soul. Ember looked at my reflection as she came, her mouth open to a silent moan, and I wanted to hear her scream. My chest was rising and falling I held on to the steering wheel, watching her as she leaned up to me.

She didn't say anything, but she gave me a playful smile. I was about to ask her what she wanted when she shoved her three fingers in my mouth.

She tasted phenomenal. I grabbed her wrist and sucked her fingers, aware I had crossed a line with her.

"Here, let me wash the nastiness out of your mouth."

I started to turn to see what the fuck Ember was up to when cold champagne hit my face.

"Fucking bitch," I murmured.

Ember got out of the Maybach and started to run toward the elevator. She was smiling, starting to flick me off, when I used all my strength to make sure the door didn't close in my face.

Ren

My heart spiked up like it did when I unleashed my darkness. It was something that had never happened before, certainly not with a woman I wanted to fuck. Right now, I wanted to fuck Ember, but I also wanted to hurt her. I could practically hear Pam telling me I needed to chill the fuck down.

I grinned when I made it through the elevator door. Even in her fucked-up state, Ember knew she was in trouble. Fucking with her was half the fun. I undid the knot in my tie as I cocked my head to smirk at her.

"What have I told you about underestimating me?"

Ember stayed quiet. She bit her lip, then tilted her chin and looked at me defiantly.

Oh, she wanted to play it like that? Fine by me. I removed the tie that I was forced to wear for tonight's special dinner. I stalked to her and smiled; she had nowhere to go.

"You're weak, Ember," I said and saw fire behind her eyes.

She didn't like to be reminded of it. She knew it, and it drove her crazy with rage.

"You're like a scared little girl."

Her chin lifted, and she gave me a smirk. "You didn't

seem to think I was a scared little girl when you were sucking on my fingers."

One last step and I was right in front of her. The air crackled with rage, violence, and lust. I reached a hand to grip her hip, testing her barriers, and stopped myself from grinning when she allowed it.

"You act out in hopes people will notice you." One of my legs came between hers. "Some attention is better than no attention." I leaned in, my face almost touching hers. "You are so weak, Ember, you get off on the smallest amount of affection."

She was just about to respond when I shoved the tie that had been at my neck in her mouth. The black silk tie was in a nice little ball, and Ember gagged on it. With one hand in her mouth and the other on her waist, I picked her up and set her on my thigh and started to move her. I could still feel her wet pussy from earlier.

"I bet I can make you come like this," I whispered as I shoved the tie deeper. She started to get red from the lack of oxygen and the orgasm that was threatening to come.

I turned my head to see that we were almost at the penthouse. In one second, I removed the tie and let her go. Ember dropped to the floor, holding on to her throat as she took in a breath. When I felt the sway of the elevator, a signal that the doors were going to open, I threw the wet tie at her feet.

"Probably tasted better than your fingers."

When the elevator dinged, I stepped out and waited by the door for Ember to do the same. She had composed herself and passed me without a backward glance. The entrance to the penthouse opened when I nodded toward the camera. Standing in the foyer was Sam, and for a second, I felt unease thinking he might have seen what had happened in the elevator. It was reckless on my part, but when I was in a rage, I couldn't think straight. That would fuck with my plans.

"Sam." I broke the tension.

Sam looked at Ember, who just walked straight to her room without a word. Playing things off, I shrugged. My ability to lie was uncanny. To be honest, it wasn't hard when you hardly gave a fuck.

"What happened?" Sam eyed me, and I couldn't tell if the look was suspicious or not.

I shrugged, still testing him out. "Must be the drugs."

Sam nodded, like he understood why she did what she did. "I'll send Dr. Wozniak a text."

Right, 'cause that was what Ember needed: a doctor to make sure she didn't overdose so she could go back and do it all over again. No my problem, though.

"Any update?" I asked as I went for water.

"It wasn't an accident," Sam said, like I hadn't already come to that conclusion myself.

"What makes you say that?"

"The light had turned green sixty seconds before Michael and Silas drove past it."

Running a red light wasn't uncommon. Running a red light one minute after the light had turned red? Now *that* was uncommon.

I walked around the kitchen island counter to where Sam had the tablet. "You have the footage?"

Sam handed me the slick device, and I played the recording. Figured they had the information in a heartbeat. I watched the black-and-white traffic light tape and saw a car floor it the moment the limousine with the Remingtons started to cross the intersection. A job like this was detailed, and it was thought out to the very last second.

"You have any suspects?"

"We're working on it," Sam said and took the tablet away from me.

I started to walk away when Sam called my name. My hand tightened on the bottle before I turned to look at him. "Yeah?"

"You can have your day off tomorrow. I'll be at the hospital with Mr. Remington, and I'll have Marcus watch over Ember."

"Perfect," I managed to say through gritted teeth.

This time when I left, Sam didn't stop me. Before I thought better of it, I took the servant stairs to the second floor to where Ember's room was. I knocked on the door and waited for an answer, but I didn't hear one. I tried to open her door, but it was locked. I stayed there for a second, staring at the large gray doors, before I turned around back to my room.

Making sure that my door was locked, I went to my bed and went through my messages—nothing I could do about those for now. After that, I started to search the Remingtons. Something I probably should have done sooner, but arrogance was a downfall. I couldn't find much, which was frustrating. All I found was the company's website and pictures of Ember walking around displaying diamonds like a whore. Pictures of her father and uncle. It was all galas, parties, and shows, but nothing that could help me.

I was starting to lose my shit. A couple of pages in, I found pictures from another party. I found myself clicking on it because Ember was smiling. Now that I thought about it, I couldn't remember if I'd ever seen her smile. Gloating

Falcon's Prey

and smirking, yes, but not a smile. Ember was a lot younger; her face still had the softness and roundness from her teenage years. Her hair was long, her dress strapless but not revealing. She was standing in between her father and uncle. Her father didn't touch her, and her uncle had a hand across her waist. I did think much about it until I came across another picture that looked like it was the same event, but a few years later. In this picture, Ember looked older, her eyes sharper, and there was no longer a smile on her face as she stood between her father and uncle. If anything, she looked vacant. I could tell she was biting the inside of her cheeks by the hollow look in her jaw.

"What made you angry?" I asked the empty room.

After more searching and coming across more useless shit, I did what I should have done since the beginning and used Wiki, where I found out more useless shit.

Their original name wasn't even Remington. Ember's great-grandfather had changed it when they came to America. Redelinghuys was their original name before they Americanized it. Since all that Wiki gave me was that the Remingtons originally had a partner, but after a mining accident took him out, they became sole heirs since there was no more family, I decided to call it quits.

There were two things I was now sure of: first, I needed to find whoever was targeting the Remingtons, because they were making my job more difficult. Second, I was going to need Pamela's help, after all.

◆

THE NEXT MORNING WHEN I WOKE UP, I HEADED STRAIGHT FOR the gym. I had some pent-up aggression, and it would be the only thing to give me a release. The first thing I heard were grunts, and my first thought was that Ember was fucking someone in the weights room. Murder before breakfast wasn't my favorite. I walked deeper into the gym facility as I took off the safety on my gun. There was no guy, and Ember wasn't even naked. She was wearing black joggers and a pink sports bra, and the grunts were because she was "hitting" a punching bag. She didn't have gloves; she just had her hands wrapped.

"You're only going to hurt yourself if you keep doing that."

"Go away." Her response was immediate.

"Look, I don't want to be responsible if you break your wrist in a fit," I mocked, knowing it would make her angry.

Ember stopped hitting the bag, then turned around and glared at me.

"What part of get out of my fucking face don't you understand, dog?!" she screamed before she came at me, hitting me.

Fuck, her technique was all wrong, but that shit still hurt.

"Stop."

"I hate you!" She punched my chest. "I hate you." My stomach. "I hate you!" My jaw.

"That's enough," I gritted out before she lifted her foot to kick me.

Before it could make contact with my body, I grabbed it and lifted her heel, making her lose balance. My other hand was at her waist before she could tip over.

"Are you done acting like a bitch?"

"Fuck you," she spat.

She wiggled, trying to kick me, but all that did was align

my hard dick to her pussy. The moment she noticed, her eyes burned up, not with lust but with hate.

"Get. Away. From. Me."

I smiled at her. "You're still mad because I wouldn't fuck you?"

Her hand came to my face, but she didn't slap me—the bitch started to scratch me. That fucking pissed me off. With her leg still in my hand and my other arm around her waist, I walked us until the bench press was behind us, and I threw her on top of it. She didn't have enough time to get up before I was on top of her, grabbing her arms and pinning them above her head.

"It kills you, doesn't it, princess? That I won't touch you," I taunted her.

When she just glared at me, I smirked at her and then put my mouth to her jaw, trailing soft bites down to her chin. Ember's chest rose and fell, but she had yet to move or tell me to fuck off.

My face was right in front of hers. I could see the purple bags under her eyes, and her bloodshot eyes that I had a feeling weren't due to being high, but from crying. She was delicate, despite her tough exterior

"Are you done, dog? I have shit to do," she said in a blasé tone that made me seethe.

Instead of getting off as I should have, I bent my head to hers. I was so close I could taste the mint on her lips mixed with desperation. With my lips, I grabbed her lower one. She wasn't sweet, but she was still addicting. Her eyes grew wide, and her mouth parted. That's when I removed my lips and used my teeth. When both of our breaths were labored, I did what I'd wanted to do since the beginning. I bit her hard until I drew blood. Her back arched as I swallowed her pain. The coppery taste of her blood hit my taste buds—now that was sweet.

"You're weak, Ember. You know that, and deep down, it kills you," I spat in her face.

"I. Hate. You."

I smiled. "You hate that I won't fall on my knees for you."

I pushed off her and walked away, still tasting her blood on my lips.

Ember

Anger lit a fire under my veins. It fueled the hatred in my heart, and it still wasn't directed at Ren, as much as I wished it could be. Looking at my lip in the mirror, I knew it was a problem.

My father was in a goddammed coma; it had been four days since the accident and nothing. My lip was busted, and I was summoned out of my castle into a meeting. Things were rocky with Silas right now, so I needed to find a way to cover up my bruised lip so it wouldn't raise suspicion. Maybe the guilt was only on my part.

Right now, I was an heiress with no fortune, like a princess with no crown. I was useless.

My mother's choker was on my neck a little too tight, suffocating me, a reminder of her death. I wore a strapless black leather dress with a black jacket and black combat boots. On each boot, I added a necklace instead of shoestrings.

In these meetings, the council liked to remind me how useless I was to the company. I loved proving them wrong. Whatever I wore sold. I was their biggest asset despite the fact that I was what they called a liability. That was the main reason why I didn't have my trust fund. My every move was monitored, down to the drugs I bought. My dealer took my diamonds. I took his drugs. They didn't trust me with much cash or credit cards, so I traded what I had.

Poor little rich girl.

The nude lipstick was thick enough to cover the bruising. My lip still hurt, and it was a reminder that I was weak. But one thing Ren got wrong was that I hated myself way before he got in the picture. Before I left my room, I grabbed a spiked collar Lilah had dared me to wear on Halloween.

"Dog!" I yelled as I came down the stairs. "Let's go. Time for your walk."

Ren appeared from somewhere in the living room, walking toward me. He wore his usual dark jeans and T-shirt attire.

"That's all you got, Ember? Your whole 'dog' bullshit is getting old."

I threw the collar at him. "Here, Fido, got you some accessories."

His face became stony the moment he caught the spiked collar. I walked past him smiling to myself. Before I could close the elevator door, he was there.

Bummer.

"Where to?"

"Headquarters."

The ride to Remington's headquarters was quiet on my end. Not that Ren tried to engage me in conversation.

I knew how things worked, and with my father in a coma, the board would make a move for temporary control over our assets. Even when something was yours, it was still conditional. Men craved power, and they seized opportunities.

Once Ren parked the Maybach, I got out and smiled because I knew this close to downtown, someone would always be watching.

Ren gave me a funny look. The doors to my family's empire opened, and the employee there greeted me.

"Good morning, Miss Reming—"

"Fuck off," I told him as I made my way to the elevators.

"You're a delight this morning," Ren commented.

When the elevator to the top floor of headquarters opened, I walked in like I owned the place. I was used to the looks—you know, the ones jealous people give you. The whole "she was born into this, she didn't deserve it" bullshit. Well, I believed I'd paid for my entitlement—every day at the cost of my life or when I kneeled for my family. There were things I did that they had no idea about.

"You can come into the room, but you have to stay in the back. Do not talk," I told Ren without waiting for his response.

I pushed open the doors to the meeting room and strutted inside. The men at the oval table looked at me, some with disdain, others with lust, all of them with hate.

"You're late," Mattias, the head of the board of trustees, said as I walked in.

"Sorry. While you were too busy sitting here contemplating a way to remove my father from power, I was out there making the snake necklace a best seller. You know, the one I said was too basic and you shouldn't produce in the first place?"

His jaw went hard, and he sent a look toward Silas, who was sitting at the head where my father should have been. But right now, he was too busy *almost* dying.

"Please sit down, Ember," Silas said between gritted teeth.

Rolling my eyes at him, I did as he said and took a seat next to him.

"So, what's your big play?" I directed my question toward Mattias.

"Remington's annual gala is fast approaching, and with your father indisposed, we need to move fast before investors sense weakness. We took a vote, and for all of our best interest, we decided that while your father recuperates, I should take the lead for the company."

I looked over to Silas, who was eerily quiet.

"Excuse me," I said in a sweet voice. "But I think I missed the part where your last name was Remington."

"You may carry the name, but don't forget this company would be under if it wasn't for the shareholders," Mattias said as others silently agreed.

"First of all, that was a long time ago. Don't sit there like you haven't made back your investment five times over already. Second of all, we have the mines in South Africa, Canada, and Brazil. Let's not forget we have the Ember. So if we were to part ways, guess who wins?"

"That's enough, Ember!" Silas yelled.

I sent him a reproachful look. It was like he didn't care.

"You're right; this is enough." I got up, not sure why I'd bothered to come in the first place. "You're all going to do whatever the fuck you want either way."

I started to walk away, but got pulled by my arm.

"You're causing a scene," Silas said in a calm voice, but his eyes told a different story. I would pay for this later.

"Take. Your. Hands. Off. Me. *Uncle*." We were in a staredown, neither of us wanting to back down.

"Let her go," was said in a lethal tone beside me.

I closed my eyes. Ren just fucked up.

"You don't tell me what to do," Silas growled.

"I do when you're hurting her." Ren pulled me away from Silas's hold and dragged me out of the meeting room.

Actions had consequences, and mine were taking me straight to hell.

Once in the hallway, I pushed Ren away. "What part of 'don't say a word' didn't you fucking understand?"

"He was hurting you," Ren stated, like that was answer enough.

People were staring at us, or more at him.

When we were alone in the elevator, I said, "You hurt me too."

"The difference is, your pussy gets wet when I do it."

I kept my mouth shut as the elevator went down, counting down the floors before we got off.

When the door pinged, I turned around, finding Ren right behind me. He looked down on me, his blue eyes bright. The shape of his lips invited me to repay him for what he'd done to mine. We were so close already; this was perfect. My knee went up fast before he could register my move. He bent with a grunt, holding on to his balls.

"Now, *that* made me wet." I walked away with a smile.

"*Fuck*...you're a bitch."

Only when people push me to be one. As soon as I stepped outside, I felt raindrops on my face. I had barely tilted my face toward the sky when I heard questions being fired my way.

"Is it true your father is in critical condition?"

"Was this an attempt on his life?"

"Can you confirm this was no accident?"

"How are you handling the news?"

I couldn't see past the reporters and their flashing cameras. The one thing I knew to do since I was old enough to go out on my own was evade reporters, and I froze. I was trying to find my way out when an arm wrapped around my waist, and I was pressed against a chest. Not just any chest—Ren's. I closed my eyes as I pressed closer to him while he led us away from the reporters. We walked until I was sure the headquarters were long behind.

"No thanks?" Ren said once we stopped walking.

"Do you need me to praise you for doing your job?" I mumbled against his chest.

Ren didn't say more, but he also didn't let go of me nor push me away. The rain was starting to pick up, and with my eyes still closed, I tipped back, enjoying the sense of washing away my sins, if only just temporarily. When I opened my eyes, it wasn't the azure of the dark sky staring down at me, it was Ren's penetrating gaze.

In ways, he was so close when he still was too far away. My lip was sore, but I wanted to know how he kissed, without the pain of his teeth. With my eyes, I begged for him to do what I would never do with words. His mouth opened, and his tongue peeked out as he licked his lower lip. The air got thick, and the water started to come down faster.

Falling for Ren was dangerous, and I wasn't that much of a bitch.

I smiled up at him. "Now I *am* wet."

Something flashed in his eyes as he stared at me, but he didn't comment. His lips did tip in a small grin, though.

His hand shot up, and my belly dipped, wondering what he was going to do, but when he pulled away, I noticed he called a taxi over.

"I'll send someone for the Maybach later."

Nodding, I followed after him, letting him guide me home. The cab ride was quiet and cold.

When the cab arrived at Hill Hotel, I took out my black card to pay. The machine in the back gave me the answer I should have been prepared to receive since my little outburst. Denied.

Ignoring Ren, I started to take off the snake necklace from my shoes.

"Here, this are real diamo—"

I didn't finish my sentence because Ren took the diamonds away. He handed the cabbie a hundred and pulled me out.

Great. He was pissed now. Probably because he had to pay.

Ren

My long strides were too fast for Ember to keep up at a comfortable pace, but I didn't give a fuck. There were a lot of things about today that pissed me off. None of them had to do with the way Ember had acted toward me.

"The car is at headquarters; make sure someone picks it up," I told one of the guys who guarded the lower level.

"Look at you, bossing around."

"Shut up," I snapped.

Ember rolled her eyes at me but didn't say more. When we got to the elevator, she went to the phone, where she pulled out a pack of cigarettes. She put the carton to her mouth, grabbing a stick with her lips. Then she proceeded to try and light it. All she got were sparks, not enough to make it burn. I took the cigarette from her, put it in my mouth, then snatched the lighter up. Once it was lit, I took a drag, trying to calm myself down. These feelings were unwanted. Once I was done, I put the cigarette to Ember's lips.

"Does that happen often?" I asked, keeping my voice calm.

"What? The paps? Yeah, my—"

"No. Cutting off your cards."

The elevator door opened, and Ember walked out. She

didn't talk until she got to the living room. She took off her jacket, grabbed a blanket, and wrapped herself.

"It's the oldest trick in the gold-spoon book. Cut off the money, make them fall in line."

I took a seat at the table in front of her. I cocked my head and stared at her. I could tell it made her uncomfortable because she started to fidget.

"How many times?" I wondered.

"I don't know...more than I can count with my fingers. I mean, they did it because once after a meeting, I stormed out and threw my cards around and told people to have fun with them."

I snickered. Of course she did. When I noticed she was shivering, I told her to go shower and change into clean clothes. I went up to my room and did the same. Grabbing my burner phone from under the bed, I brought it to the bathroom with me and waited until I turned on the water before making a call.

"I was starting to get worried about you. When's your day off?"

"Soon," I lied. "Listen, I need your help."

I got straight to the point. Pam let out a bunch of Spanish curses.

"What is it?"

"I need you to dig deep into this family. I want everything. Something isn't adding up."

"You want me to go dark?" she asked.

"Pitch-black," I told her before I hung up.

Jumping in the shower, I tried to figure out the easiest way to get what I wanted, but the easiest way involved Ember, and she got to me like no other. She was like lava under my skin, waiting to erupt. Once out of the shower, I wrapped a towel around my waist and stepped out of the bathroom. I was starting to feel restless. This job had its perks, but I didn't like to feel caged.

When I heard my door opening, I grabbed the Glock from my nightstand, ready to shoot.

Ember didn't even bat an eyelash. She stood in the entrance of my room in a thick black robe, fuzzy slippers on her feet, her hair still dripping with water, but the thing that got to me was the purple bruising around her lower lip. *I did that.*

"I need you to set up the fire pit for me."

"Don't you have staff for that?"

She shook her head. "It's their day off."

"Can't you do that?"

"Most people don't want me near fire since the whole college incident."

"Out. Now."

I needed her to get out before she noticed she was getting my cock hard. It would be so easy to pull her into my room, push her against the wall, and fuck her so hard and deep she'd never forget me.

Ember gave me a carefree smile, and fuck me if that didn't do something to me.

"Drop the towel, bodyguard."

I smiled back at her, a real one this time. "Darling, you couldn't handle me."

"Drop the towel, and we can find out," she teased.

Without a word, I closed the door in her face.

She screamed, and fuck my life that sounded like a fucking challenge. One thing was for sure: something was wrong with that woman. One second, she was fire; the next, she was ice. Shaking my head, I got ready, and instead of trying to figure things out, I decided I would use her mood change to my advantage.

Ember was outside, sitting on a chaise, a bottle of water in one hand and her bong in another. While she broke her weed, I got to work on her fire. Everything was neatly set up; I knew she'd have no problem doing this on her own. She was humming a song while her head nodded from side to side. It hit me then that she was lonely.

"Is that all?" I asked once the fire was blazing.

"Aren't you going to sit down? Make sure my body is protected and all that bullshit?"

Letting her think it was her idea for me to stay, I sat on the opposite side of her. I let her take two hits before I began to ask questions. Mellow Ember was better than the bitch one.

"When was the first time they cut you off?" There were probably a few questions I should have asked instead of this one.

"I was nineteen. They wanted me to endorse a partnership we had with a fashion line, but the fashion house was big on furs, so I told the director of said house to fuck off there for disgracing my family. It was close to the holidays, so I was stuck at school."

"What did you do?" My voice was low. Controlled.

"Diamonds are an easy trade." She shrugged it off. "My turn." I should have expected this. Even high, she was sharp. "Why haven't you quit?"

"You don't scare me, princess." I leaned back and gauged her. "Why are you not being a bitch?"

Her shoulders sagged. "I'm tired, okay? Silas, Mattias, the board, you—I don't have to the energy to fight the whole world today."

"Any word on your father?" I pretended to look at the fence when I was observing her, trying to figure out why she wasn't at his side every day.

"Nope. His body is still recovering. Who knows how long that will take. Maybe by the time he wakes it will be too late... When's your day off?"

Jackpot.

"It was the day after the accident—"

Ember's eyes locked with mine, and I had the urge to pull away. "You stayed home with me."

My chest rose and fell. Hell if I know why I stayed home that day. She didn't bring her bloody lip, and neither did I.

"The whole deal with the board?" I asked in a docile tone. My body was relaxed, or as relaxed as I could make it appear to be. "If you don't mind me asking, how does that work?"

"Checks and balances. Back when the depression hit, we struggled. Jewelry was a luxury, one not many could afford. My great-grandfather managed to secure connections, some through marriage, most through his cunning. Remington Diamonds stopped being family-owned and instead became incorporated. Fast-forward through a lot of bullshit and a few losses, Remington Diamonds own fifty-eight percent, the board forty-two."

Ember took another hit, and I waited for her before asking more questions.

"My great-great-grandfather was on some Costa Nostra bullshit." She shrugged, and I snorted. "We get our trust funds when we turn twenty-five."

"How old are you?" I interrupted her.

"Twenty-five."

"Then why are they still cutting you off?"

"Let me finish. We get our trust funds at twenty-five unless you are a liability."

Which she was, but that still wasn't fair to her.

"That's not even the part that makes me angry. I'll wait

five more years, whatever; I'm sure Mattias will find a way to not give me my money."

"Is he in charge of your money?"

Because if he was, he just got to the top of my shit list. Ember licked her bottom lip and tried to bite it, but winced. The action had my dick getting hard.

"Yep." She laid down and stopped looking at me. "As I said, my great-great-grandfather was on some mafia shit. The president position goes to the firstborn of the family and gets passed down."

"You should be president right now, shouldn't you?"

"Should, could, but won't because between my legs is a pussy and not a dick, so moot fucking point."

"You like it, don't you? The diamonds and all that shit?"

"Do you know anything about diamonds?"

I shook my head.

"Let me enlighten you, bodyguard. Colored diamonds are expensive, as long as they're not artificially dyed. Whenever we run across them, they are sold before we get them processed. Yellow diamonds are your basic bitches more commonly found, but also more in demand, since they cost less. Green and orange diamonds are at the bottom of the rare pool. Pink diamonds are in high demand and the ones that get the most invested on, which brings me to number two on the rarity scale—the blue diamonds. It's always a battle between pink and blue, but pink is a little more basic."

I smiled as I watched her speak with a passion I didn't know she possessed. "And the rarest diamond?"

Ember yawned. "The red diamonds. Once upon a time, people believed that red diamonds didn't exist."

"There are red diamonds, darling."

She shook her head. "You're such a commoner; you're probably confusing them with rubies."

I shook my head, so she went on.

"Those are a purple red or brownish red; the rest are man-made. There is only one red and two that come close. The Moussaieff Red, and the Hancock Red, which looks reddish to the naked eye."

My body stilled as I waited for the next part.

"The Remington Ember, or more commonly known as the Ember, is the only dark red there is. The color is dark, but the cuts shine, making it appear lighter from where the sunlight hits, giving it a burning look."

"Your parents named you after your own diamond?" I laughed it off to change the subject.

Ember gave me a sleepy glare. "My family is on some old-school bull. When my great-grandfather discovered the Ember, he put a stipulation clause so only our family line could use it as a first name. The right belonging to a male firstborn...so here I am."

I gave her a nod and waited a few more minutes so she could fall asleep. "Why are you nice to me?"

When she gave me her answer, I almost wished I hadn't asked.

"Because pretty soon, you're going to leave me too."

Ember

My place always felt cold, not at all like a home. I sat on the sofa covered in a blanket, and I realized you could pluck me out and put someone else in and you'd never realize I'd ever lived here. The place was lovely, the decorations modern, but none of them were me. My father was still in a coma. It was fucked-up that him being chained to a bed was the only way I'd see more of him than I had my whole life.

My bong lay lonely on the ottoman. Let out of its cage, it was now just another diamond artifact that I owned. I asked all my maids, and none of them had seen my drugs. I had my suspicions, but it was a battle I didn't have the energy to fight.

Ren was walking down the stairs, his hair a little wet, his black T-shirt fitting perfect against his muscular frame. Suddenly I was thirsty and not for water.

"Did you fall off the bed?" he said without looking at me.

I didn't know if it was the fact that he felt sorry for me, but we had called a temporary truce. I didn't sleep; it was one of those rare nights when dread filled the air, and in those long dark hours between midnight and dawn, you contemplated every lousy choice that made you feel like a fuckup.

"Do you want to get fired today?" I responded.

He shook his head and went to grab a water. He was

always drinking water; no pop, juice, or beer for him. When he ate, he always had non-fatty foods—all bland-looking and flavorless. He took care of his body. And oh boy, did it show.

"I can feel you staring," he said as he sat with his back to me at the kitchen island.

"I'm hungry," I said.

"Good for you. Eat something."

"Everyone is off today," I reminded him.

"Then, do it yourself."

"I need to run a few errands. Be ready to leave in forty." With the blanket still wrapped around me, I left to take a scalding shower, hoping that would help wash away the shitty night I had.

Once I was showered, I dressed in some jeans and a T-shirt. No fancy shit today.

Money made people treat you different. Some because they felt inferior, others because they thought you were equals, and most because they wanted to use you. It was rare when you found people who treated you like you were normal.

Maybe that was why I liked my kids at the hospital. To them, I wasn't Ember Remington. I was just Ember, the girl who made their day a little brighter. I loved, yet hated, going to the hospital because I got attached, and not all stories had happy endings. Even with all the money in the world, I never felt as helpless as I did when I lost one of my kids. Donating my time and money seemed like the least I could do to help out.

Putting my checkbook in my purse, I walked out of the room.

"Let's go, dog. I want to get food on the way..."

The words died as I said them when I came down to the

stairs and saw a plate with food for me. Ren was nowhere in sight.

Something warm stirred inside of me, a different emotion I'd never felt before. It made my eyes water and my throat clog. *Fuck*, I was going to cry.

There was a grilled cheese and bacon sandwich on the plate.

My mouth watered. I was starving, and the art of cooking was one I didn't know anything about. The only baking I knew how to do was my makeup.

"You're ready?" Ren came out, tucking a gun into his waistband as I finished off my food.

"Thank you," I said.

"For what?" He passed by me, dismissing me.

Well, if that was how he wanted to play it, that was fine by me.

Once in the Maybach, I gave Ren the address to the flower shop.

People did a lot of things for their parents, and in trying to know my mother, I'd found her religion. Not that I went to church often, but my father, riddled with guilt over his wife, had me brought up Catholic. I assumed it was what my mother would have wanted.

One holiday intrigued me, in particular. *El Día de los Muertos.* Day of the Dead. As a society, we feared death because we feared the unknown. A holiday dedicated to celebrating it fascinated me.

"What are we doing here?" Ren scanned the area, looking skeptical about getting out.

People were walking down the street. Someone was selling corn on the corner, and kids play with a soccer ball in the empty parking lot. I thought the place was bursting with life.

"I'll be quick," I told Ren as I got out of the car. I was about to get the door open when he grabbed my elbow.

"How many times do I have to tell you that you don't get to run away from me?"

"Wait in the car." I turned around and crossed my arms, glaring at him.

"Either I go in with you, or I carry your ass back to the car."

He stared me down. The harder I glared, the more I could see the laughter in his eyes.

"Don't say a word." I pointed a finger at him.

He raised his hands in mock surrender. Seriously, sometimes I didn't get this guy. He ran hot and cold, but I guess he could say the same about me.

The place smelled like flowers. I liked the fresh smell; it was pure.

Mrs. Rosales came from the back and greeted me. "Niña."

"Hóla," I greeted her, making my way to the counter.

"I see you have another one," she mused at Ren.

"This one is annoying," I told her.

She looked at Ren and then at me, and she smiled. "Está guapo."

Yeah, not going there. I was going to pretend like I didn't know what she said.

"I brought donations for the festival, and Jorge told me my stuff was ready."

I could feel Ren staring at me, but I ignored the heat of his gaze. I would rather he never knew this about me, but he was like a thorn in my side.

"Jorge!" Mrs. Rosales yelled.

"Sí, abuela."

Jorge came out. He looked taller than the last time I'd

seen him. He was tan with dark eyes, skinny, but now with a little muscle.

"*Brasa.*"

I gave him a look. He got a kick out of saying Ember in Spanish. He came up to me, ready to give me a hug, but Ren pulled me back.

What. The. Hell?

"Let me go."

Jorge just shrugged it off. "So, now that I'm nineteen, will you go on a date with me?"

"Hor-hay, boy. Eighteen, nineteen, thirty, I'm not the girl for you. You need a good girl." I told him the same thing I'd been telling him since I met him. He thought I was joking, but I wasn't.

"Denied again." He shook his head but had a smile on his face. "I'll get your stuff."

While Mrs. Rosales helped him, I put my wallet on the table and wrote the check. I needed to make sure I laid low and didn't get the board pissed at me so it could clear.

Ren whistled. "That's a lot of cash."

"It's a donation for the Day of the Dead."

"Do you fund the whole thing?"

I ignored him. Some of the money went to the parade, the rest for local charities in this community, but I didn't handle those.

When I heard the steps coming back, I turned to Ren. "Open the trunk."

Jorge came carrying stacks of thick Mexican blankets, while Mrs. Rosales brought a huge pot.

"Gracias," I told her.

"No, mi niña, gracias a ti." She thanked me and gave me a kiss on my cheek. I turned around and left.

"See you at the parade," she called after me.

I didn't turn around but said, "You know I'd never miss it."

As soon as Ren and I were alone in the car, he moved the mirror so he could look at me. "Are there drugs in those blankets?"

I laughed. "Do you think I'm some kind of mule?"

When he didn't answer, I knew he wouldn't put it past me. That hurt a bit, but like with all other disappointment in my life, I shook it off.

"Drive back home," I said, putting the partition up.

The drive back home was uneventful.

As Ren made his way to the hotel, I told him to take a turn into one of the alleys. He brought the Maybach to a halt when he saw the tents all around the end of the aisle.

"Are you here to score drugs?"

"No!" I was appalled. "I can get my dealer to deliver those."

"Then why haven't you?" He regarded me with a weird look.

"Because you have them."

When he didn't admit nor deny anything, I tried to get the door open, but he'd locked it.

"I want you at my side at all times," he demanded.

When I nodded, he opened his door, then came to mine. As soon as I was out, his hand came to my back. It was hot and felt like it burned. I had never been more aware of someone's touch in my life. I could tune them out during sex. Focus on other things and pretend like no one had their hands on me. With Ren, that seemed impossible.

"If we get mugged, I'll kill you," he whispered as people started to come our way.

"You're kinda dramatic," I told him as I motioned for him to open the trunk.

"And you have no regard for your life."

I went to the side of the car to grab the pot Mrs. Rosales had given me.

Ren didn't say anything more as we handed people blankets and tamales. He kept giving me weird looks that made me feel self-conscious. Once the last blanket was gone, I turned around and went to the car. Ren still stayed five more minutes, talking to the homeless. By the time he came into the car, I had put the partition up.

I think he got the feeling he knew I didn't want to talk about what had happened today. Pretty soon he would stop feeling sorry for me and I would go back to being a bitch and he would go back to being an asshole I couldn't get rid of.

Except it was those small acts of kindness that made their way to your heart and didn't want to let go.

Ember

THE LAST FEW DAYS HAD NOT BEEN KIND TO ME. WHATEVER sort of truce Ren and I had fallen into was now gone. He was short clipped when he talked to me, barely around only when I really needed him. If I stayed home, he would lock himself in the surveillance room and ignore me.

Silas had sent me one text message.

I want him gone.

And I knew Ren's days were limited. With that in mind, I knew the chance to get him in my bed was diminishing by the second. I was being nice for that whole purpose alone, but nice wasn't working.

Last night Ren had to go out. Who the fuck knew where he went or what he did.? Poor Marcus was stuck with me, and since he didn't bitch or moan, he just did the job. I went to the club, and when I got there, I realized it had been a while. When I got home, I could have sworn Ren was pissed, but he didn't come directly at me; he just yelled at Marcus.

Now my head was pounding, and one thing I knew for sure was that Ren Falcon was going to fuck me and fuck me over before he left me—and I was okay with that. What was one more mistake in my long list of fuckups?

My hair was a mess from last night's party, and my mascara had run a bit. I'd learned a long time ago to just run with the look; it gave me an edge. There was no one in the living room or kitchen, and I knew Ren would be done with his workout soon. While he got done with that, I went to the fridge, then sat my ass on the kitchen counter and waited.

It didn't take long for Ren to emerge. He was wearing sweatpants that low rode on his hips—and damn. I didn't know what that V was called, but I knew it was like arrows pointing straight to getting the D. I wanted the D, and I wanted it bad.

"What are you doing?"

"I'm having a mimosa," I said.

"Where's the orange juice?"

I took a sip of my champagne glass, then answered, "We ran out."

"So basically you're having champagne for breakfast," he stated in a judgmental tone.

"A mimosa sans the juice," I corrected.

He didn't say anything; he just kept looking at me with his icy stare.

Grabbing another bottle, I handed it to him. "Can you open this for me?"

"No," he snapped

"Excuse me?"

His response ticked me off.

"You. Work. For. Me." I glared at him.

He really was handsome, by far more attractive than all the men who came before him. He had a good five to six years on me. His hair was not too short, but perfect "pull me while I eat you" type.

"My job, darling, is making sure nothing happens to your body, and that's it."

I got chills whenever he said *your body*. He looked like he could give my body a good time. Manly hands, muscles in all the right places, not too thick, but not thin. I would sleep with him soon because time was running out. I hadn't pushed the issue because when I fucked someone, it was, "Thank you. Next," and I didn't want to let him go.

I crossed my legs, relishing when he followed the movement of my exposed flesh.

"Nothing is going to happen to my hot little body," I said in a breathy tone. "Nothing ever does."

That seemed to anger him; I could tell because he had very expressive eyes. The blue became icy.

"You change guards faster than you do underwear. You don't think people notice this shit? It leaves you vulnerable."

"I don't wear underwear," I replied casually. "And the way I see it, I could get hurt with the cork of this bottle. It can hit me in my eye and blind me, and then you will have failed in protecting my body, *bodyguard*."

I stretched my hand at him and smiled when he made his way over to grab the bottle.

"I'm glad you could see things my way." It was hard not to gloat.

Ren didn't answer. He snatched the bottle from me with more force than necessary, then went to the kitchen and opened it. He came back and put the bottle on the table instead of in my outstretched hand.

I was about to take a sip when he spoke again.

"You're such a bitch. That's why no one likes you. Not even your *daddy*."

He hit a nerve with the last part, but like hell if I would let him see me flinch. "You have no right to talk to me like that."

Ren smirked at me, and for a second, it was like looking at a different person, not the one I had gotten used to these last few weeks.

"I don't think you'll fire me for that, princess, or else you would have done it already. Newsflash: the world doesn't revolve around your spoiled ass."

He thought I didn't know pain, but he had no idea. I also had friends. I didn't see them often, but they were there. I just didn't want my bullshit to affect their lives, so I stayed away. Except for Lilah—she got that life in the spotlight wasn't all that it was cracked up to be.

When I didn't answer him, he smirked at me and walked away while I sat there drinking on my own. I drank until the last of the champagne was gone. While I was under the effect of alcohol, I realized that I didn't give many fucks about what people thought of me, except now I cared about Ren's perception of me or if he even remotely cared. I turned my body to face the nearest camera knowing full well whoever was in the surveillance room with Ren was still in there since no one had left. *Let's see if he was watching.*

I lay down on the marble countertop, my legs facing the camera. I ran my hand through my hair, down my neck, over my breast, and then cupped myself between my legs. My back arched a bit at the feeling. I closed my eyes as I let my hands wander back to where my robe was tied. Once open, I ran my hands over the lacy cups of my bra while I kept my legs crossed.

I tried not to smile when I heard footsteps.

"Goodbye, Miss Remington," the voice said in a rush.

Slowly I started to part my legs when I heard the door close. I spread them, letting my hand come to the top of my panties. I dipped one finger in, imagining it was Ren who had come down here and finally caved. One wasn't enough, so I added two and started to fuck myself in front of the surveillance camera. Feeling bold, I removed my underwear so that Ren could see every little detail. The two fingers I was fucking, I brought them out and glided them up to my aching clit, where I started to rub myself faster. I could feel my orgasm coming, but it wasn't enough.

Fuck this shit.

Sitting up, I looked straight at the camera as I licked my two fingers clean. Leaving my undies there, I jumped up and walked away.

"Open the door, Ren!" I screamed as I tapped the door to the surveillance room. I knocked and knocked until he opened.

"What do you want?" He looked angry.

"What do I want?" I mocked him. "You don't get to ask me those questions."

I pushed past him. The room was not very big, and it made me feel like I couldn't breathe. I didn't do well in small spaces. I fucking hated them. Smalls spaces didn't leave room for me to hide.

"I'm busy," he said through gritted teeth.

I was horny and frustrated and angry. I didn't care about his own anger. I let my eyes trail from his pissed-off face down to the top of his unbuttoned jeans.

"You'd think I'd made your life easier by bringing my body to you." My voice dropped to a sultry tone.

His eyes flashed as he sucked in a breath. I wasn't in heels, so he towered over me by a lot. I gulped, and for a second, fear stroke through my body. I really didn't know anything about him. Not that I thought it would matter. Ren was emitting waves of rage that made me want to get out of this confined space. I took a step back, but the door was already closed. Ren put his hand on either side of my face, and I waited to see what his next move would be.

"You seemed to think you can treat me like you did all those other fools who had the job before me."

He had my number, but I was never one to shy from a

fight. I brought my leg up, exposing it. My robe parted up to the apex of my thighs. I got up on my toes and then wrapped one leg around his waist. Both our breathing got heavier. His nostrils flared, and I smiled.

"Some of them did their job *really* well," I whispered.

In an instant, his hands came to my waist, holding me up. My body seemed to spark to life. He brought his hand to my foot, where it was wrapped around his waist, making sure it was secured before he grabbed my knee and glided up to my thigh. I was heaving at the sensation. My pebbled nipples poked against the material of my nightgown. I thought he would have stopped, but he kept moving his hand farther up. My center started throbbing.

"Unlike you, Ember—"

His hand reached my pussy, and he stroked it with his knuckles, making my hips buck. Then he turned his hand over, gliding two fingers over my wet folds.

"—I have standards."

His tone was smoky and hoarse as he rubbed my clit forcefully, enough to cause me pleasure mixed with pain. I held on to his arms for support because my whole body was shaking. I looked up to see Ren's jaw tight as he looked at where his fingers were touching my pussy. Without warning, he roughly inserted two fingers inside me, causing me to writher in pain before he stroked a part in me that made me moan.

"I wouldn't fuck you if you were the last woman on earth." He was lying because, at that same moment, I put my hand to the imprint of his hard dick.

"You're fucking soaked, Ember," he growled as he buried his face in my neck.

"Ren," I moaned when I felt myself getting closer.

He smiled against my neck.

"You like that, don't you?"

I was so lost I nodded.

"You like the way I fucking hurt you." He took his fingers out to pinch my clit, causing my body to burn up.

He pulled his fingers out of me so fast I almost fell. He tipped my head back, then put two fingers in my mouth until I could feel them down my throat, causing me to gag and my eyes to water.

"Hmmm, shame you lied." His tone was now calm and icy, nothing like the loss of control from earlier.

He backed away so fast I lost my balance and fell to the floor.

"You can't make me fuck you. Nice try, though." He then walked away, slamming the door in my face.

Maybe because I was an only child or because I was rich and spoiled that hearing the word *no* made me want it more. Having something forbidden made for quite a thrill. Trust me, I knew. And it was past the time for Ren to go.

Ren said he didn't want me, but his eyes told a different story.

They consumed me.

Followed my every move.

His eyes shone with hate, and I wanted to make him eat his words, for him to give in, and then I could kick him to the curb.

I'D BEEN WAKING UP EARLY AS FUCK TO GO DO YOGA WHILE Ren worked out. My back was turned to him, but I always felt his hot gaze on my skin. It only made me get up early the next day and do it again. However, I was getting tired. I looked at my phone and the reason for my need to get Ren out of my system, my life and in my bed. My cell phone was still turned off after the text I received from Silas.

It's been too long, my love.

It wasn't long enough.

Some sins didn't wash away with water and prayers. They became imprinted on your soul, casting a dark shadow so you'd never forget what you'd done.

Before I could back out, I changed into spandex shorts and a matching sports bra.

I made my way out the door, surprising Karen on the way out.

"Miss Remington, is everything okay?"

"Yeah," I said slowly.

"I'm sorry. It's that you are never up this early."

She had a point.

"Dr. Wozniak called to make sure you are okay. He said it's been a few days, and you've not sent for him."

"Ren stole my stash. I haven't gone out for more. Tell Dr. W I'm not dead," I said to her as I walked away.

I made it to where the gym was located. The space was dark since Ren wasn't much for having the blinds up. I heard the noises his fist made against the punching bag.

I stopped at the entrance just to take him in. He was shirtless in a pair of gray sweatpants, with a gleam of sweat covering parts of his skin. Why did he have to wear those pants today?

Squaring my shoulders, I walked in and picked up the remote for the gym. I walked back to where I usually did yoga, but this time, I pressed the button for the pole to come out. I didn't have to turn back around to know Ren had noticed because he stopped punching.

I didn't turn around; instead, I turned on the surround sound and put on "Gods & Monsters" by Lana Del Rey and got down to it. I put my hand on the pole, took a step on my tiptoe, then did a twirl on the pole for warm-up. When I landed, I held on to the pole with both hands and shook my hips, gliding them down to the beat of the music, then back up. I did another twirl. This time when I landed, I put my hands as high they went and twirled, lifting myself up, feeling the burn in my body. I opened my legs and put the pole between them, then let go of one hand and straightened my body. I was slowly spinning, and he was right there watching me. He stirred on the press bench, not doing weights, but staring at me.

I lifted up again only to put the pole behind my knee, and I let go. My eyes met his as I was semi-suspended through the air, and the intensity almost caused me to collapse. I kept working the pole like I'd never worked it before, dancing to the beat of the music. Once the song was coming to an end, I climbed up to the top, then crossed my legs, my body in a sitting position. I didn't look at Ren as I opened one of my legs so I could let go. At the same time, my body started to drop. I heard him shout my name. I ignored it. I crossed my leg a few feet before my body hit the ground, and my body came to a halt, stopping me from falling on my ass, which, judging by Ren's shout, he thought would happen. I was breathing heavily as I touched the floor again.

Ren was right there in front of me, his body tense. I think he was scared I could have gotten hurt. I took a deep breath and looked into his icy eyes. I took a step toward him, and he didn't move.

"Are you going to tell me that's your gun?" I cocked a brow at him, referring to the bulge between his pants. It was long and thick, and sooner rather than later, it was going to be between my legs, pounding me into oblivion.

One second I was in control, the next Ren was. He reached out, putting his arm behind my head, pulling me closer to him.

"Do you always dance like that?" he asked with an edge to his voice.

I shrugged it off. "When the mood strikes."

He didn't say more, and I was feeling bold, so I reached out to touch him between his legs. The proof that no matter what he said, he wanted me as bad as I wanted him. I barely grazed him when he yanked my head back.

I groaned and not from pain.

"Kneel," he commanded.

I smirked at him and did as he asked. My knees dropped to the floor in a heartbeat. I went for the waistband of his pants.

Ren pulled my hair again, signaling for me to stop.

Once I did, he brought my face to his crotch.

"Suck."

The word was low. I got the feeling he was trying to keep his cool. So I did as he asked. I sucked through the thin material of the sweatpants. I heard his soft inhale as I did it, leaving a wet mess in the cloth. As I worked my way to the tip, I was yanked back, and I fell on my ass. I glared up at Ren.

"You want my dick, Ember? You have to earn it." Then he walked away, leaving me panting on the floor.

"I hate you!" I screeched after him, having the last word.

He was making this harder than it needed to be. He would either leave by my hand or Silas's, and I'd rather it was mine.

Ren

Ember Remington was like lava under my skin, slowly rising and boiling, but I couldn't let it erupt. It would be a clusterfuck if I did. All she saw were the half-truths and lies I'd fed her. I usually didn't care what women knew about me, but with Ember, I wanted her to go in with eyes wide open—and that was the problem itself. I couldn't scare her without telling her the truth, and in saying the truth, I'd be condemning myself.

Storming out of the gym facility, I made my way outside to the terrace; that way, I could keep an eye out in case she tried to leave the penthouse. When my eyes fell on top of the kitchen island, I remembered what Ember looked like touching her body. At that moment, I'd never hated a job more than I did right now.

People liked to run from their demons, but I chased mine. Now here I was stuck in limbo for a cause I wasn't sure I believed in anymore.

Pam had fucked up, and I needed to fix her shit.

Ember

Hell descended on earth when you least expected it.

Three days after humiliating myself, I woke up to a string of text messages from my friends. All of them congratulating me, yet demanding to know why I hadn't told them about my new boyfriend.

As soon as I read those words, my stomach dropped. Opening the browser app on my phone, I searched my name and waited for the results.

Fuck me; I was going to be sick.

My body shook as tremors worked their way through my body as I stared at the picture on my screen. *How could I have been so reckless?* Closing the browser, I checked my text messages and my missed calls. I didn't know if I should be relieved or scared that there were none from Silas. Immediately I called him, and it rang twice and got sent to voicemail. I felt like I was going to throw up.

I opened the browser app again, and I stared at the picture once more as if that would make it disappear.

Diamond heiress showcases a new boyfriend.

The caption was enough to cause attention, but pictures did say a thousand words, and *that* picture was saying all the wrong things. It was the day of the board meeting when Ren had held me before he hailed a cab. I was in his arms, looking up at him with a smile on my face while he stared down at me.

Pathetic.

Weak.

Hopeful.

I gazed at him with stars in my eyes like he was my salvation. While he glared at me with hate in his eyes as if I was his damnation.

One thing I was sure of now was that Ren Falcon had to go.

Throwing my phone aside, I put on jeans and a T-shirt so I could run errands before tonight's gala. Of all days for that picture to surface, it had to be today. I laughed to myself; it didn't matter if my father was dead or alive, it wasn't like he'd ever protected me anyway.

Some days you fucked the world, but most of the time, the world fucked you over, and today was one of those days. Putting my mother's choker on, I held my head high before walking out of my room. I might be all broken pieces on the inside, but I'd be dammed if I let my cracks show. Fake it till you make it.

Ren was drinking bottled water while he checked his phone. He didn't even look up when I walked down the stairs, and in a way that made me feel more foolish and stupid than I already was.

"I need to get a few things before tonight," I said, and he looked up to stare at me.

His expression was blank, and he gave me a nod.

"Marcus will accompany me. You have the day off."

His eyes flashed, and if I wasn't looking at him, I might have missed it.

"Marcus is a pussy who wouldn't know the first thing to do if someone tried to attack you."

Maybe he expected me to throw a tantrum because that's what desperate old me would have done. I didn't answer; I shrugged and walked out. The elevator ride was quiet, and he kept looking at me while I ignored him and typed on my phone. We made it to the Maybach when he broke the silence.

"Are you planning to tell me where we are going, or am I supposed to guess? 'Cause if I have to pick what we do, you probably won't like it."

I finished typing my text and sent it. "I just sent you today's itinerary."

I didn't look at him as I spoke, and I could feel his anger as I put the divider up. Did he honestly think I'd ever take yesterday's defeat with my head bowed? There were parts of me the world did not see—*he* did not see. Everyone only saw surface-deep and never dug into the wounds of others. No one ever saw the wounds I'd carried or the scars that had never healed. People saw what they wanted because that's just how they dealt with unsavory events.

My unsavory event clung to me. I looked at my phone, and still radio silence on Silas's part. My uncle. Once my lover. My blackmailer.

Who knew having friends made a difference in how you saw the world. Lilah was much like me—rich, spoiled, and alone. Except she wasn't fucking her uncle. We talked about anything and everything, but I could never bring up Silas.

Then came Lexi and Aubrey, and with them, I learned more about what love and family meant. Maybe I knew it all along, and I didn't want to see it, or I wanted to hurt my father like he had hurt me all these years, and taking his little stepbrother to bed was the easiest way. Fuck my hate into someone he considered his flesh.

Maybe I was just a victim, or I was a willing player in this filthy game. Well, it was time I ended it, because I didn't want to do it anymore. I was tired of it, and to be frank, I was beyond angry with Silas. He said he loved me, yet he was okay with the board cutting me off during the holidays.

Daddy Dearest was on a trip to Africa; he didn't have a clue. What did Silas do? Tell me I shouldn't have mouthed off to the hand that fed me. What did I do? I fucked someone else since the first time we started our affair. Because it was an affair; the person we were hurting in the process was my father.

When I landed in the city, I'd taken a cab straight to Silas's condo. I rode the elevator all the way up to his floor, feeling lighter—feeling free. It was early enough that I could do this. Break things off, then go home, get high, and forget about ever fucking him.

When I made it to his condo, I put the security code and let myself in. I wanted this done and over, and I didn't think when I went in search of him. When I made it to his room, I felt nothing, and that right there should have clued me in on my feelings.

Silas was leaned against the headboard while some blonde bimbo sucked him off. I wasn't jealous, nor hurt, I just felt stupid for going along with this in the first place.

"Hi, Uncle." I smiled at him and waved.

He looked at me with a blank face. I turned around and walked to his office. I smiled to myself, feeling better because this was actually easier than I thought it would be. I was standing by his desk when Silas walked in with no shirt, his pants pulled up, but the zipper opened, revealing his happy trail. Well, happy for blondie who was in his room. Seriously, I felt such relief right now, knowing we were on the same page.

"I actually came here to talk—"

My cheek turned from the force of Silas's slap. The sting of his hand burned on my skin. I glared at him. This was nothing like the Silas I knew.

"Did you think I wouldn't find out?" he seethed.

I took a step back, but he was right there holding on to my throat.

"You fucked Enzo Toscano."

"Y-y-you fucked..." It was hard to get words out. Part of me couldn't believe Silas had hit me.

"Yeah, because you're a slut, but you know what, Ember? You are still mine. So go fuck Enzo—hell, the whole fucking world—but at the end of the day, I'm the one who owns this." His hand came to my pussy, gripping it with force, making me howl in pain.

"Stop!" I howled, my heart pounding hard against my ribs. "Get off me!"

I tried to push him off, but instead, he pushed me back until I hit his desk with my back painfully. He then turned me around and bent me over the desk.

"Enough, Silas! Let me go!"

He had me trapped, I couldn't move at all, and that was when fear like I had never felt before ran through my body. People always said my name was fitting because I was full of fire, but at this moment, I felt like my veins were freezing over. My body started to shiver. The pit of my stomach felt like it had a hole that was an endless void. Bile made its way up my throat.

"I tried this your way. Now we do this mine."

Silas grabbed my long hair and wrapped it in his hand. He pulled it so tight my scalp burned. He brought his arm on top of me, and he leaned his weight on me so I couldn't move. I felt his erection press against my ass, and for the first time in my life, I prayed.

Silas turned his computer monitor around and dug through files hidden amongst files until he played a video for me.

Every. Single. Time. I'd given my body so freely to him, and he'd recorded it. My eyes burned with unshed tears, my throat felt tight, and under my tongue saliva pooled. The video he showed me was manipulated to his liking.

"Stop... Ember, stop... Goddammit... I said, stop." Silas's voice sounded pissed.

In the video, it looked like I was in his lap trying to seduce him. I remembered that day. It was during fashion week; he'd hated the dress I was wearing because it was too short. When we made it to his apartment, he wanted to fuck me. He was begging me not to make him come yet, not for me to stop.

"Please." My breathy moan made me flinch. "Please. I've waited so long for this."

I sounded like a wanton slut who wanted to seduce her uncle. I watched as the screen showed my face buried in his neck before I kissed him. My eyes blurred as I kept watching. This was all wrong. I was referring to the fact that he had fingered me on the ride home without letting me come, not what the video implied. While my face was buried in his neck, he was telling me he loved me. The footage showed Silas throwing me to the side on the couch as he looked distressed, when in reality, he did that so he could fuck me into next week.

"Why?" I croaked as the footage turned to another clip that looked like it was from the same day, but I knew it wasn't. I was on my knees, sucking Silas off with a smirk on my face.

Silas gripped my hair, forcing me to keep watching.

"Not one time did you tell me you loved me," he hissed. "I was prepared to make you my queen, Ember, and you proved to be a backstabbing bitch, just like all of them."

"Silas, this is wrong," I pleaded as I closed my eyes so I wouldn't have to look at the screen.

He laughed. "Wrong? You sure as fuck didn't think that when your pussy would get all wet when I fucked it. You did this to yourself, Ember."

"Silas, let me go...please." My *eyes were still closed, and for the first time in my life, I was begging.*

He brought his lips to my ear and kissed behind my neck. My skin crawled.

"Never. I can't. I am never letting you go."

"I'll go to the police, asshole!" I screamed, trying to break free.

"I will release that video and more. You seduced me. You came to me. Who do you think they'll believe? You, the drug addict, the party heiress who is always on the tabloids for reckless behavior, or me, the orphan boy who got a new chance at life and has won humanitarian awards? I'm a man, and I can only take so much."

He stopped talking and started to pull my pants down.

"How could I resist..."

I closed my eyes tighter as tears wanted to spring free.

"...What was so freely given?" Silas spread my legs with his, and he plunged into me.

It burned.

My body was not ready for his penetration. Pain spread through my sex and my lower stomach. I wanted him gone, but he was right. These were my sins, and now I was paying for it. I closed my eyes tightly, thinking of better and happier days. The funny part was that I didn't have any of those. I didn't have happy memories with my mother because she was dead. My father had never been in my life. His empire was more important than his daughter. And the one person who said they loved me was—I couldn't think the word. It made me feel dirty, and it wasn't true. Not when I'd wanted it in the first place.

My pussy throbbed in pain by the time Silas grunted in pleasure. I held my tears at bay and didn't make a sound as I heard him zip his jeans up.

"Fuck who you want, Ember. Just know that at the end of the day, I still get you. With or without your cooperation. Tell anyone and that video will make news."

When he walked away, I stayed in the same position for about twenty minutes, telling myself it was my fault.

Our bodies can handle almost anything, and mine had. Silas had turned me into what I was today. I adapted the only way I knew how. Mentally, I hated what he did to me, but physically I'd learned to like it. As humans, we wanted to survive, to cope, and it didn't matter what kind of depraved things you did, telling yourself it was normal. My body was forced to like the pain.

After all, it wasn't rape if you got off on it, right?

Ren

My hands wrapped tight against the steering wheel as I drove to the location Ember had sent me. This was what I'd wanted since the beginning: not to have to play babysitter. But now that I had it, I missed her smart-ass fucking mouth. That day in the control room, I almost snapped and gave in. Hell, before she came in, I was ready to jack off to the footage of her touching herself. Ember in the back seat of the Maybach fingering herself was one of the hottest things I'd ever seen.

Which brought me to my shit mood because she put the partition up, obscuring my view. Since I had been in her employment, I had done nothing but humiliate her and reject her advances, so I didn't see why this time had to be any different. If anything, she seemed to get off on them. The more I hurt her, the more she pushed back at me.

Ember wasn't beautiful like a flower; she was beautiful like flames of a fire. Something that looked stunning, but you knew it was dangerous to touch. Inviting enough to want to get close to the warmth, but once you were close, hot enough to burn. And lately, I was itching for it.

The GPS took me to a warehouse in the trendy part of town. Before I was fully parked, Ember was opening her door.

"Hey." I pulled at her arm. "You can't walk out like that."

"Let me go."

I did, only because she looked alarmed, scanning the streets. Something wasn't right, and I cared that I was bothered by it. Once inside the warehouse, I realized it was some sort of fashion warehouse. There were clothes everywhere, but it wasn't laid out like a store.

"Miss Remington." A tall blonde with more plastic to her than Barbie appeared. She smiled brightly at Ember and then gave me an appreciative look that I ignored. "We are honored you chose us to dress you for tonight's gala."

"I heard you have the most exquisite black silk dress," Ember purred.

Plastic Barbie smiled and led Ember away from the entrance, and I followed. They took us to the top part of the building, where the whole wall was floor-to-ceiling windows.

"Please take a seat," Plastic Barbie told me as she grabbed me by my arm and led me to a couch. I sat on the fancy chair, waiting while they offered me something to drink.

"Water's fine," I replied, dismissing the girl who had come up to me.

When the chick came back, she handed me the water but stayed. Her eyes trailed over my body valiantly. I raised an eyebrow at her.

"You know..." she said, her hand coming to my arm. "...if you ever want a *real* woman..."

I stopped listening to her talk. The comment pissed me off. Sure she had more tits and ass than Ember, but she wouldn't even come close to satisfying me. Before I could respond, Ember walked out of the room as Plastic Barbie carried a black bag behind her. Ember's eyes went to me, then to where the chick in front of me touched me. I bit my lips when I saw anger in them, but just as quickly, she masked it.

"Let's go," she said as she passed me.

"My offer stands," the chick said.

I got up, putting me chest to chest with the chick in front of me. "Would you do anything I want?"

Her breathy "yes" was instant.

"I think I'd get more thrill from a blow-up doll than you." Then I pushed past her and went after Ember.

Ember was about to open the door when I threw my hand over her shoulder. "Where to next?"

She stiffened.

"Let me go." She shrugged off my hand, then ran into the car.

I took a step to follow her, but before I could do that, a man came running toward me with a bag like the one Ember carried.

"We have the perfect suit for you. Our house would love to dress Miss Remington's new boyfriend."

New what?

I took the bag and left before Ember could do something stupid. When I got in the car, I had to bite my tongue to stop myself from screaming obscenities. The partition blocked my view, but she would be able to hear what I said. I would not be giving her that satisfaction.

Driving back to the Hill, my phone started to ring. My stomach dropped when I saw the unknown number. No one unknown should be calling me, especially since this was the company phone.

"Speak," I said.

"*Idiota!*" Pamela's voice was easily recognized.

"Please tell me that you didn't just call me on this line," I barked.

I'd given her the number for emergencies for when I couldn't be reached at my burner. I still had to find out if our company phones were bugged.

"It's a fucking emergency when your fucking face is plastered all over the fashion section of the newspaper."

Shit.

That defeated the whole purpose of keeping things lowkey. I didn't bother to say goodbye to Pam; I just ended the call. She was starting to get on my nerves, making me regret everything I'd done in her name. When we stopped at a red light, I typed Ember's name in the search bar.

The result made me freeze, until the car honking behind me made me snap out of it. My head turned, surprised Ember didn't say shit to me. I didn't know how I knew, but this was the reason she was suddenly treating me like I had leprosy. The thought had me smiling.

Once at Hill Hotel, I parked the car and pulled Ember's door open.

"Please tell me the whole boyfriend thing is not why you're acting so strange today?"

When her face fell and her eyes widened, I started to laugh. "Shit, Ember, if I won't fuck you, what makes you think I'd date you?"

"Get out of my way." Her tone was missing the fire she usually carried, and she walked away, leaving me the bag in the backseat.

I grabbed it along with my own and trailed after her. Watching her backside, I was reminded of the feel of her pussy, the tightness around my fingers, and imagined how tight it would feel around my cock. She was so fucking tiny, I would destroy her, and I would enjoy it too.

The ride up was silent with Ember still giving me the silent treatment. Did I care? Only that my face was plastered everywhere, but not particularly. I mean, I was with her at all times, and probably kept her on a tighter leash than those before me. But Ember? She seemed almost rattled. She took the bag from me and walked up to her room. An hour later, someone was in the lobby.

I called the guy that was guarding the private entrance. "Did you let someone up?"

"Oh, yeah. Miss Remington's stylist."

Dipshit.

I waited by the door as the stylist walked in. He was young and skinny with bleached hair that looked white, bigger lips than a Kardashian, and eyeshadow that was neon blue.

"Whoa, you are even hotter in person," he mused.

"Do you want to die?"

"*Ohmigod.*" He threw his head back on a loud moan. "You're bossy."

Shaking my head, I walked away to the control room.

MY HOLSTER WAS ON, TWO WEAPONS ON EACH SIDE. I HAD A knife strapped to my leg and a small scalpel in my pocket. Going to my bed, I grabbed my tuxedo jacket, and I caught my reflection in the mirror. I didn't even look like myself, in a black designer suit that fit me like it was made for me with shiny fucking shoes on. My hair was left messy—no way was I going to style it for this fucking event. Opening the door, I fixed my bow tie as I made my way to the living room.

"That's it, bitch. Work it, baby. You look so fucking hot!" I heard the makeup artist's voice sing praises.

The fall of great men wasn't because they were weak. It was because they didn't understand their limits. Fortunately for me, I'd danced with my demons for a long time, and I knew what they wanted. Ever since I had stepped foot in this place, mine had been begging for Ember, but I'd been too stubborn to hear their call.

Right now, she looked beautiful, like a dark angel. Slightly frightening, ethereal, capable of bringing a man to his knees, but not me. If anyone were kneeling by the end of the night, it would be her. She wore a black ball gown that looked like the top of a heart over her tits and made her waist look tiny, and then it flared out. She looked like a princess; all she was missing was a tiara. Her face lifted, and she turned to look at me. Her eyes were dark and smoky with her lashes fanned out, her lips dark red. On her neck, as always, was her choker.

"Come on, boyfriend, take a picture," the makeup artist said.

"Not my boyfriend." Ember walked toward the elevator.

As I followed her and the boy, my cell phone rang.

"Hello?" I answered, noticing it was Sam.

"Falcon, I need you to stop by headquarters."

"Why?"

"Marcus and Gio will come with you. In honor of Ember's twenty-fifth birthday, she's wearing the Ember."

"You can't spring something like this before arriving at the fucking event." I gripped the cell phone, knowing full well I shouldn't have lost my cool.

"She will be perfectly fine," Sam said before he hung up on me.

Once the elevator door was open, I looked at the makeup artist. "Leave."

"What the fuck!" Ember spouted. "You don't feed, fuck, or finance me, so you get no right to treat my guest like that."

"We can take care of one of those. Right here, right now," I said, looking down at her.

She rolled her eyes and shook her head. "I'm tired of this shit. I want to go, show my face, come home, and forget it ever happened."

"When's your birthday?" I held on to her elbow as I started to drag her to the car.

"I don't see how that's relevant to keeping me alive."

"Ember," I warned.

"Next week." She finally shook her head. "I'm turning twenty-five."

And she wouldn't be getting her inheritance, but her family was still going to parade her around wearing a thirty-million-dollar diamond while there was a fucking price on her head.

"Get in the car." I opened the door for her, then made my way to headquarters, but on the way, I made a stop.

At the nearest drugstore, I parked illegally, but right now I didn't give a fuck about that. I got out of the car and opened one of Ember's doors. She was confused, looking at me with wide eyes. Before she could speak, I pulled out one of my Glocks and showed it to her.

"Anyone who isn't me tries to come in here, shoot them." My voice was lethal; she didn't argue.

I slammed the door and went into the drugstore. Making my way to the chicks' section, I grabbed one of those thick elastic headbands and then some grabbed some double-sided tape just in case. Once that was bought, I went back to the car.

Ember handed me the gun wordlessly. I put it back in the holster before I put the bag in her lap.

"We're going to stop by headquarters, where Marcus and Gio will join us. With them will be the Ember."

At that, her mouth parted.

"You will be wearing it."

She let out a humorless laugh. "They won't give me my trust fund, but trust me with millions for a night?"

"Face me," I commanded her. "This—" I pulled out the scalpel that was in my pocket. I pulled the cap off so she could see the obsidian steel. "—is fucking sharp. One swipe of this in a major artery is near fatal." As I taped the scalpel to the headband, I started to instruct her. "In case you haven't noticed, princess, you're guarded more than the fucking president. I think it's bullshit that your family won't tell you this...so I am. Someone wants you dead."

She let out a soft gasp, and her eyes went wide with shock.

I ignored it. "I want you to wear this tonight."

In her eyes was something that had every part of me wanting to recoil. Fuck me, she trusted me.

"Something happens, you hit major arteries. Neck, wrist, left side of the chest. If you're down, try to go for the tendon behind the ankle. Not only will it hurt like a motherfucker, but cut off the ability to walk."

Ember swallowed, but ultimately nodded.

"I'm going to hide this. It will be our little secret, okay?"

When she didn't say anything, I brought both my hands under her dress.

"What are you—"

Her words trailed off the moment my cold fingers made

contact with her bare leg. Her skin was smooth like silk, no scars tarnishing her flesh, making my makeshift holster glide with ease. I felt her skin shiver beneath my fingertips, making my cock grow hard. When I made it to the top, Ember was looking at me with wide eyes and a parted mouth. I heard a car honk, but I ignored it. Putting my hand higher, I cupped her pussy.

"Tonight, I own this."

Ember

There was a fucking knife between my legs. Someone wanted me dead, but all of that didn't matter at the moment. Right now, I was savoring the fact that I had finally brought Ren down to his knees.

If I was being honest with myself, it didn't surprise me that someone wanted me dead. It did scare me, but for now I was going to enjoy this small victory. I mean, the timing didn't get more perfect than this. I fucked Ren, and he was gone, and Silas's threat would remain at bay. Then I would worry about whoever wanted me dead.

Wars were won through cunning and intelligence, and sometimes it was easier to lose a battle, no matter how devastating it might be, than to lose the war. So my battle with Ren was coming to an end. He could think he won and he owned me, but everyone knew a woman could never be owned. She could be kept, or possessed, taking away her fight, making her hide within herself or cower, but owned? Never.

So, I tried to calm myself with the fact that tonight I would have one less problem to worry about. Before I knew it, we were parking at Remington's headquarters with Marcus waiting outside. He opened the door in a suit, not as fancy as the one Ren wore, and slid in next to me.

"How are you holding up, Em?" he said, the nickname he used to call me with casualness and ease. What he used to call me at a time I'd lashed out and seduced him, taking out my rage on him.

"I'm okay," I said without meeting his stare.

My father was in a coma, and I had yet to see him. What was the point? I was used to him not being there; this was nothing new.

When I turned my head to the company doors, three guards came out with the one in the middle carrying a briefcase that was cuffed to his wrist. Gio was one of Silas's preferred bodyguards. He was tall and beefy, and his morals were questionable, but he was a loyal dog to his master. He saw me the day I left Silas's place with a red cheek, my hair a mess and a limp to my walk. Sam had never made a comment, which meant Gio hadn't reported anything to him.

He took a seat next to Ren, and we finally made our way to our annual gala.

Ren parked in a side entrance, since I would not be coming through the front. Instead, I would arrive once everyone was seated and descend the stairs with a rock of fire around my neck.

The car that was behind us came out first, flanking Gio to make sure the Ember was protected with Marcus following behind them. Once they were inside, Ren opened my door. I took a deep breath and took the outstretched hand he offered.

Emotions were a weakness, a disease really once you started feeling it spread until it touched your chest, and that right there was one hell of a way to make it go away: broken heart or a dead body. You felt too deeply, or you felt nothing at all, and my perfectly crafted world had tilted the moment Ren Falcon stepped foot in it.

The moment he held on to me, I knew my life was in his

hands. He could be my savior, or he was just here to make my time pass while I waited for hell.

We walked quickly inside, and the quiet made my skin crawl. I was about to put on a show. The back hallways were empty; just Gio, Marcus, Ren, and me. Everyone watched Gio as he worked the combination to the safe. Millions of dollars hung off his wrist.

My hand went to the back of my neck to remove the diamond choker. Before I could remove it, I felt Ren at my back like someone would feel death looming. His presence was strong and near suffocating. I asked myself if I wanted to go down this road tonight, then turned my head to look at him. His blue eyes shone with mischief, and my answer was yes. Everyone always did stupid things for a pretty face.

"Let me," he said.

I turned to look forward, not meeting Marcus's nor Gio's eyes. "Can you guys make sure that the hallways are empty before I make my way down?"

Marcus nodded and walked away, giving Ren and me one last look.

Gio looked at me. "I'm in charge of the Ember."

I extended my hand for him to drop the red diamond, which he did.

"Now get the fuck out of my face," I commanded.

Ren chuckled as he finished unclasping the choker. I turned around to face him. Even in heels, I barely reached past his chest. I tilted my head up. His fingers came to the imprint the choker had left on my neck from the intricate design it had on the inside.

"Looks like stars," he mused, his finger tracing over the three little dots, then going for the single one and the four that were aligned.

Before he could keep tracing, I pulled away. I started to

walk away, putting my family's jewel around my neck so it rested above my chest. All valuable things came at a price, and ours was dipped in blood and covered in betrayal, a fact no one liked to talk about.

"If you lose my mother's choker, I will castrate you," I said as I walked, not bothering to look at Ren.

He let out a dark chuckle.

"Give a girl some steel, and she thinks she's a warrior."

Before I could tell him to fuck off, we had made it to the top of the staircase. They curved down to the ballroom, so I wouldn't be able to see anyone until the midway point. I looked down at my chest to where the Ember sat as a beacon of our wealth, and all I could see was the symbol of something I could never have nor achieve. This piece of jewelry was adored, studied, immortalized, and famous for just existing while I was infamous for the same thing.

"Are you okay?" Ren stepped next to me while he fixed the button on his wrist.

He looked at it like it was of utter importance, and I was glad he did because if I looked into those deep blue eyes, I might have blurted the truth.

"One thing to know, *dog*, is I'm always okay. No matter what."

I took a deep breath, letting the stale air filled with hatred and arrogance give me the strength to put on a show. I descended the stairs with my bitch face on as I scanned the ballroom full of tables and people seated, all with their fine attires and fake smiles. At the bottom was Silas waiting for me, as the devil would welcome a new soul into hell. His eyes raked over every inch of me, and I looked everywhere else, pretending like I couldn't feel his gaze burn and make me want to come out of my skin.

He stretched out his hand to me, and everyone smiled at

how loving my *uncle* was. I turned to my right and looked at Ren, maybe with pleading, as I took Silas's hand. He looked at where my hand and Silas's joined, but he didn't stop me; he just let me go.

"You look beautiful," Silas whispered in my ear as he led me to our table.

All I could feel was the knife between my legs. It begged to be used, and I knew just where to place it.

Ignoring Silas, I smiled at the people who were seated at our table. Silas took his seat, and as I went to grab mine, I noticed Ren was there pulling my chair back. The people at our table couldn't stop staring at my chest, and for once, it had nothing to do with my tits. I was wearing a piece of jewelry; all of them would never know how it felt rested upon their stupid little hands.

My eyes crossed with Mattias, and he had his same loathing look. I smirked at him as I played with the Ember and polished the stone with my middle finger.

"I'm sorry to hear about your father, Miss Remington."

I smiled at the old man. Mr. Sheppard was old, came from old money, lived for a good gala, young pussy, and donating money to important things, and adored his three kids most of all.

"My father is a strong man, so I have hope."

I didn't need to add what everyone at the table knew. The longer my father stayed in a coma, the slimmer his chances were of ever waking up.

The food came and went, and I was dying for a smoke. Something to take away the edge I was feeling at the moment. The mindless chatter, the fakeness, it was all getting to me, and I wanted to scream.

Silas got up and walked to the center to kick this thing off. He was going to do what my father had always done.

"How is everyone tonight?" he asked and smiled at the crowd. He charmed them, and they ate it up.

"As you all know, my...my brother can't be with us." Silas paused and looked at the room. It was hard, but I abstained from rolling my eyes. "He loves this gala, and he loves all of you. Hell, I do too—you guys keep us in business."

Some people laughed; others gave a light clap.

"Now, my brother wouldn't want us to be here moping him. He would want us to hope that he will get better. And I have hope fate will give my brother what he needs. What we all need... You see, my brother...he'd shed blood for this family, so I promise to shed mine as well."

As far as speeches went, that was pretty fucking stupid. He then went on talking about our year in business, new branches, and stuff that had me wanting to pull my hairs out.

"For the real reason we are here today...Ember, or should I say the Embers."

As Silas mentioned my name, everyone and their mother turned their head toward the table. I gave a small smile and a wave.

"Come here." Silas waved me over like a dog.

I was walking his way when his words made me sick and want to vomit.

"Since my brother is not here, it's up to me to take care of his little girl."

I did not let his words hurt me, not right now. Yes, they haunted me, but for now, I had to put them out of my mind.

"Now today is also a very special day. My dear Ember turns twenty-five." Silas's hand came to where the jewel rested. "And who better to make her shine on this night than her namesake?"

People cheered and applauded, and I stayed next to Silas

until he gave the last of his speech. When he was done, he put his hand around my waist and led me to talk to the investors. I tried not to think about the way Silas held me and instead focused on the heat at my back. Ren's gaze was heavy like a cloak covering me in darkness.

When the tenth person asked me how I was feeling about my father, I told them I had to go powder my nose. I'm sure half of them thought I meant I was going to snort some coke, which wasn't a bad idea. I held to my dress and walked past everyone, aware that it didn't matter where I went, at least not tonight. I was a prisoner.

"Ember!" I heard Marcus shout.

I ignored him and kept walking to the grounds behind the gala's museum. They were beautiful, flowers everywhere, statues and tranquility, something I wasn't used to. I walked to the tall bushes, ignoring the shouts that came after me.

I ran until I was deep in the maze away from everyone, and it was just me and the darkness. I wasn't like normal girls; the dark didn't scare me. Everyone always showed their real face when they thought no one was watching. What I was scared of was looking in the mirror and seeing how pathetic I looked.

Ren

"Shut the fuck up," I told Marcus, and pulled him back. "You screaming bloody murder isn't helping anyone."

He was pissed, but I was fucking livid right now.

"Well, she's alone with a—"

"You think I don't fucking know that? But you yelling for her to come back will only put her at risk."

"No one would dare come here. We have top-notch—"

He didn't get to finish his sentence, because I punched him. His arrogance was a downfall.

"Fuck." Blood was spilling from his nose.

"Someone is always watching," I spat at him before I left in the direction Ember had taken off to.

With my gun drawn, I made my way in, trying to do it as quickly and quietly as I could. Only Ember could be this fucking reckless. She was the most self-centered woman I had fucking met. I swore to God when I got my hands on her I was going to—*fuck*, I didn't know if I wanted to fucking yell at her or fuck some sense into her.

I stopped dead in my tracks as the emotion—one I only ever read about but never truly felt—coursed through me. I was afraid. It was something I didn't think I'd ever feel, at least not about someone else. Yet here I was in a fucking maze in a thousand-dollar suit hunting down a princess.

I was about to keep going when I saw her. Far in the

corner, seated on a bench, her ridiculous dress too uncomfortable to sit down in, but somehow she managed. She didn't even notice me come; she was too busy staring blindly forward. In her hand was a blunt, and the smell of grape filled the air.

"Save your sermon for someone who cares," she said when I got closer.

"How did you know it was me? It could have been someone else."

She gave a humorless chuckle but didn't look at me. "Ever since you came into my life, you became like a fucking shadow. Following me around, judging me, wrapping around my being like a cloak. Everywhere I go, there you are. Even when you aren't, I feel your stare. I feel your want." She turned to look at me with defiance. "So now the question is, what are you going to do about it?"

The question here was, what wasn't I going to do? I was too busy walking toward her that I didn't notice what I'd stepped on until I felt something under my foot. Upon seeing the blood-like red, I stepped away. I crouched, and in my hand, I held a gem people would kill for. The Ember would solve all my problems and then some.

The chain that held the jewel was broken, from where Ember pulled it to get it off her body.

"When I'm done with you, you're going to hate me," I said, looking up at her.

"When you're done with me, you'll be like everyone who came before you—*nonexistent*."

My jaw felt tense and rigid. She might be right, but I would make sure that once I was gone, she would be ruined. With that thought in mind, I put the diamond in my pocket, and then while I was still crouched, I took out the knife I had strapped on the side of my leg. I moved it up to my sleeve slowly before I rose. When Ember licked her lips, I lost it and the skin I had been wearing shed off me, revealing the man I was within.

I was in front of her within seconds, and she tried to remain still. The rise and fall of her chest was a giveaway of the nerves she was feeling, along with the little beads of sweat forming on her forehead.

"Everything you think you know about me, forget it. You don't know me. What you should know about me—" I leaned toward her, my mouth brushing the shell of her ear, my tongue licking her earlobe. While her eyes were closed and her mouth parted, trying to contain a moan, I had worked my knife at the base of her dress. "I'm. So. Much. Worse."

Her eyes snapped open at the same moment the dress ripped at the seams. She was going to talk, but I held on to her jaw, and I fucking kissed her like she held the key to heaven and I had just been sentenced to hell.

Ember used all her strength and pushed me back. I fell flat on the grass, and she used the opportunity to straddle me.

"You do what I say, *dog*."

Not saying anything, I put the knife to the side, and since the material was fine and already ripped, I finished tearing her dress all the way to her waist. The skirt came off, and she was left in the bodice that snapped at her cunt along with the makeshift garter I'd made her. Curving one of my arms around her waist, I flipped us over, laying her on top of the torn-off material.

"You don't get a say, Ember. Not when it's my dick that's going to sink into your soaked pussy."

My body dwarfed hers, and it turned me on to have the upper hand. She had the world at her fingertips, except for me. With my knee, I spread her legs, leaving her open to my mercy. My cock was painfully hard, and I was going to cross a line, knowing I'd be damning everyone else.

I put my hands on either side of her head and looked at her. She was a rare beauty, and like any man, I coveted it. I bent my head until my forehead touched hers. Her pupils were dilated, and it had nothing to do with the weed.

"You're going to let me own this tonight?" I asked in a gruff voice as I thrust against her.

Ember whimpered as my dick made contact with her pussy. I leaned to kiss her jaw, then sucked the skin on her neck. When she threw her head back, I took that as permission. I sucked all around her neck, aware I was making a collar of my own, marring her neck and rearranging her blood.

"Ren," Ember huffed, but I ignored her.

She seemed to hold her breath when I finally made it down to her center. I gave her pussy a gentle bite, and instead of removing the bodice, I kissed her thigh where she had the scalpel strapped.

Grabbing the scalpel, I removed it from the garter. Ember watched me with wide eyes as I took off the cap, revealing the obsidian tip. She bit her lip but didn't say a word.

"I'd suggest you don't move, princess," I told her as I brought the edge of the knife to where the apex of her thigh met her pussy.

"Ren," Ember whispered, trying hard to lie still.

Slowly I let her feel the sharp edge against the side of her sensitive flesh, laying it flat against her skin. Her soft moan had my head snapping to her face. My nostrils flared when I noticed she was even more turned on than before.

Bringing my attention back to her pussy, I started to slice

the scalpel across the cloth, ripping it off, careful not to cut her. As her center came into view, I could see how fucking soaked she was. Not that the wet bodice wasn't an indication. Once I had sliced across her pussy, I brought my thumb and stroked her slit, then applied pressure to her clit.

Ember moaned, almost jumping out of her skin by the contact.

"Careful," I scolded her. "I might nick you."

She seethed. "Then stop playing with me."

I bent my head to her pussy, holding her stare, and I gave her a wicked grin. "Trust me, Ember, I haven't even begun."

The first taste of her was just as I knew it would be—addicting and forbidden all at once. Her wetness coated my tongue, and I wanted to lap her up and lick away her essence. I wanted to consume her so she would be a part of me.

I didn't want these thoughts. I didn't want her, but I did fucking need her.

I sucked her clit into my mouth, and that's when she screamed, her hand coming to my hair, gripping it, making my scalp burn as she rode my face.

I wanted to cause her some amount of pain, like she was beginning to cause me. She was still riding her high, her pussy still spasming, so I grabbed the scalpel and made a small cut on her thigh.

Seeing her blood spilling seemed to bring us both down to reality. I couldn't let her have control, and she shouldn't trust me. Licking the bit of blood that spilled, I hoped it disgusted her into pushing me away, but instead, she leaned up to grab my face so I could kiss her.

Before I gave her my lips, as I held the scalpel to her neck where my hickeys started to form, I asked her, "Do I scare you, Ember?"

Chapter Twenty-One

Marcus

WATCHING ANOTHER MAN RUN AFTER THE WOMAN I WAS IN love with was hard, and I had to remind myself that it wasn't my job to protect her anymore. Hell, at one point, I would have done it for free. Ember was so much more than what she showed the world. She was all the ugly things everyone knew, but under that, she was also beautiful, and I wasn't talking skin-deep. I meant actions-speak-louder-than-words beautiful.

So yeah, it sucked watching the new guy run after her. I wasn't stupid; I saw the way he looked at her. Just like all of us that got too close to her, he wanted her.

I checked my watch for the tenth time, and neither of them had come out. They'd been gone for long enough, people would begin to wonder where Ember had taken off to, mainly because she carried her family's jewel. Just as I was going to take a step toward the maze, Silas stepped out of the door, looking like death himself.

"Where the fuck is she?"

"She's in there, sir."

Silas's jaw ticked. I didn't like him much—hell, no one really did. He had his own guards. Something about his adoptive trust issues and creating his own family. Except the men he had in his employment all had questionable morals.

"Why the fuck would you leave her alone?"

"I didn't. She's with Ren."

"With whom?" His voice dropped an octave, sounding dangerous.

I stood straighter before I answered. "Her bodyguard."

Rage seemed to come off Silas in waves, and I bit back my tongue to stop myself from saying something inappropriate.

"Take me to them."

Nodding, I did as he asked. I walked ahead of him, scanning the maze in case there was danger.

Silas's phone started ringing, and he fell back a bit.

"Are you sure?" he said. "Don't let the media get a hold of this yet. And start making all the preparations. I want to start making arrangements for the funeral as soon as possible."

My stomach sank from the news that could only mean that Michael Remington had died. Ember would be devastated. Before I could think of ways to be there for her, my blood ran cold when I turned the corner.

Ember was on the floor, her dress ripped off and blood between her legs as Ren lay on top of her with a blade to her neck. I didn't think—I pulled my gun out and aimed.

Ember

They say you see life flash before your eyes before you

die. That somehow hanging in the balance of life and death makes time still, as if time would wait for us mere mortals, but it was true.

I was mesmerized, ready to hand over my soul to Ren freaking Falcon, when I heard a guttural shout. My head turned to the side. I saw Marcus angry, but most of all hurt, and even as his gun was aimed toward where Ren and I lay on the floor, my eyes were on Silas.

Angry didn't begin to cover it. Whatever pleasure I was feeling moments before was now replaced with fear that clung to my skin and clawed at my bones. Looking into Silas's dark eyes, there was no hiding from the truth that Ren was different. Something he knew from the start and I'd tried to deny.

The blast from the gun made my ears ring, and for a moment, I wished it had pierced me, and maybe I'd be free.

I couldn't breathe.

"Are. You. Okay?" Ren breathed in a barely controlled voice.

That was when I noticed he had pressed his weight on top of me. When I turned back toward Marcus and Silas, I saw Marcus was thrown to the side and Silas a few feet away from him. I didn't need them to tell me Silas had stopped Marcus from shooting Ren. One, because he didn't want him to hurt me accidentally. And two, because Silas would want to kill him. *Get rid of him, or I will.* Those words he had said came back to haunt me.

Before I could get myself together and find the words to deny or beg, security rushed into our hidden corner.

"What's going on here?" someone said, but I didn't pay attention.

"This man was raping my niece when we got here," Silas said through gritted teeth. His rage was not in concern for me, but because someone else had touched me.

"It's true," Marcus said, sending a hateful look toward Ren. "He had a knife to her throat."

That's when everyone looked at Ren and me, and I knew it wasn't hard to believe. Looking at Silas's eyes, I knew I had hell to pay if I spoke up. I was going to open my mouth, but when Silas did, he brought a piece of my world crashing down.

"I need you to handle this, Gio. Sammy is dead."

Another piece I didn't know I still had chipped off and disintegrated. Silas was letting me know I was fucked. I bowed my head, not wanting to let anyone see the hurt. I gave myself a moment but snapped out of it when I heard the shuffling of the men coming for Ren. I looked up at him, but he was unusually calm. Either he knew he was fucked or was waiting for me to say something. He didn't even look at me; his eyes were on Silas.

"Tell them the truth, Ember," he said, low and controlled.

"This man raped my niece. Someone take him out of here," Silas said over him.

I looked at Ren, and I begged forgiveness with my gaze. The words he wanted to hear, I could never say. I was nothing but prey in this tangled game. Gio was more than happy to make comply, and when I didn't say anything, I saw the way Ren's eyes became frosty. Moments ago, they burned with lust, and now they were ice. I turned my head to the side, and the metal from the scalpel caught my eyes. I wrapped the tuxedo around myself, bending a bit so I could pick up the small knife.

"Wait," I said, and the men did as I said because we were at a party full of people. I reached for my torn skirt and the scalpel at the same time, hiding it within the shredded material. Slowly, I got up, aware there were some gasps. I couldn't even look at Ren; I didn't want to see his hate.

"He has the Ember," I stated as I reached for his pocket to pull it out. I let my hair shield my face as I tilted it to the side. "I'm so sorry."

My whisper was barely audible, but I knew he heard it because he sucked in a breath. He held it when I put the scalpel in his pocket as I took out the diamond.

"You. Will. Pay. For. This." He spat the words as Gio grabbed him.

I looked up, watching Ren get dragged away from me. Time seemed to go back to normal, making it all go to chaos. People started shouting, and I was in Silas's angry embrace as he led me out of the maze. The yard was full of guests as we emerged, all of them looking at me. At that moment, I realized I was living the thing I most feared Silas would do. I looked left, and I looked right, and there was no sign of Ren Falcon anywhere.

Then there was another silence as soon as gunshots were heard.

I should have told him.

I should have trusted him.

All I did was damn him.

Part Two

"Let your plans be dark and impenetrable as the night, and when you move fall like a thunderbolt."
– Sun Tzu, *The Art of War*

Revenge

Ren

The taste of betrayal still lingered on my lips. The essence was rooted deep in my breath so that with every inhale, I felt it stabbing my ribs. Sounds of pain and pleasure accompanied me at night, barely letting me get any sleep, keeping my misery company. And a thirst for revenge was the only thing that made me go on another day.

Ember Remington was going to watch as I took everything from her, and I would laugh at her as she saw my true face.

Ember

One year later

Remember what I said about a woman not being able to be owned? Yeah, I was wrong. My bad. Everything you did always came back around, and my turn had come, and I was now paying for it.

My hand went to my neck out of habit more than anything, missing the feel of my mother's choker hugging my tender skin. And I couldn't think about it without thinking of Ren. Amid chaos, I forgot he held a piece of my heart with him. Or maybe I didn't forget, and I wanted him to keep it so he wouldn't forget me.

If by some miracle he was still alive, I was sure he'd remember the girl who stuck a knife at his back.

Rolling over, I reached for the tray that was on the nightstand. Grabbing my vial, I made lines and snorted. The coke made its way into my system fast, already numbing me.

When the door to my bathroom opened, Silas walked out wrapped in a towel like he owned the place—and right now, he did. You see, a year ago, everything changed. My fate was now in his hands more than ever. With Sammy now gone and six feet under, there was no one to watch over me.

As for my father? Well, he woke up from his coma, but now he was even more useless than before. I didn't understand why Silas didn't just throw my father in a rehab center and call it a day.

I was sure I was missing something, but the drugs in my system clouded my mind. It was the only way I could escape the bed I had made. Silas took everything from me. If I thought I had it bad before, it was nothing compared to now. He controlled our assets, and he agreed with the board that I was a liability. He moved me to his apartment, where I was now a prisoner with a penthouse view. As for my father, he was in my old home, where he had Dr. W go in and check on him and a group of nurses that watched over him day and night.

Silas smirked at me as he dried his hair, and I turned my face. I was too drained even to move. I didn't have to look at my beat-up body to know how it looked. I could feel the bruises, reminding me of the mistakes I'd made.

"Be a good girl while I'm away," he mocked before he left for work.

My hand shook as I reached for my drugs and numbed myself the only way I could now. Inside my mind, all I knew now was pain and hurt. As I lay stuck deep in my mind where there was no pain, the thought always lingered—to take things further. To go to sleep and never wake up. Either I was a fighter that couldn't give up or a coward that couldn't take her own life.

Once he left, I laid back in bed and stared at the ceiling for a few hours. What would have happened if I'd told Ren the truth?

It was hard to get up when my sore body begged me to keep seated. Step by step, I made my way to the kitchen. There were no servants here, at least none that I could see or who could see me. Only Silas's private security. The world-tough Ember had gone into mourning, and then she went off the grid to a private island and grieved. Silas had a look-alike post on my social media. It was easy to believe a lie when no one got close enough to know you. My father's plan B was of no use to me now that I wasn't in the same building. I was trapped and fucked in more ways than one.

As I made my way to the sink, I saw Gio standing there. If the bruises on my skin repulsed him, he didn't show it. When our eyes met, I mustered all the energy I had in me and smirked at his scar. It went from the top corner of his lip down to his neck.

Truly a miracle that he was alive. I didn't know much because Silas despised Ren, but I'd overheard enough. Ren had killed one of the guards who had captured him, snapped his neck, and then gave Gio a little parting gift. If he survived or not, it wasn't known. I wanted to think he was alive somewhere. I was sure that if his body ever showed up decayed, Silas would find pleasure in rubbing it in my face.

The cold water was like metal down my throat. It was raw from screaming, and with no time to heal, things were not pleasant. As soon as the water hit my belly, I felt queasy. I tried to remember the last time I'd eaten. I was either too strung out, or it had been that long.

After making my way to the room, my prison, I laid in bed and waited to do it all over again.

There was chaos all around us. The guests didn't know whether to look at my battered and dirty body or focus on the gun that had just gone off. Everyone started to run, and I was in shock that I didn't run right away. I was half-naked with not a penny to my name. By the time I decided life was still better that way than with Silas, he was already dragging me to our limo.

"Get every fucking reporter out of here. If they post

those pictures, we will end them. I want every camera confiscated," Silas yelled at whoever was next to him. I clutched Ren's jacket, inhaling his smell.

Please don't let him be dead.

Please let him live.

Please have him come back to me.

Why would he, though? I was a bitch to him.

"You fucked him." Silas seethed once we were alone in the limo.

Tilting my chin up, I mustered my defiance against him. "And I enjoyed every wicked seco—"

Smack.

My cheek turned from the hit he gave me. I'd seen his real face before, and it had scared me, and maybe right now, I was feeling so much that I couldn't feel any more because it made me reckless.

"What are you going to do now? Threaten me? The whole world sees me like a whore right now. You can keep this contained, but leaks happen, and when it does, I will be there, striking the match to watch you burn."

Silas fixed his tie and gave me a smile. "No one tells you anything, do they? I'm in control. The board took a vote and removed your father. It's all mine now. And I won't be giving you a cent. None of it it's rightfully yours. The way I see it, I own everything you have."

I sat still as he touched my cheek, stroking it lovingly.

"I don't care what anyone says anymore. Release the tapes. I. Am. Done."

His jaw went slack, and I saw his eyes darken to the point they looked as black as a starless night. "Because of him?"

His finger came down slowly, and he looked in disgust at

the dirt. His cold hand moved open a lapel, and his lips curled at the sight of my neck.

"I own you now," he stated calmly as he pushed up the sleeves on his shirt.

Before I could give a response, he yanked my arms, throwing me down on the floor of the limousine.

"All you had to say was that you like it rough and dirty," he whispered in my ear as he held my face down from my neck.

"You want to see blood..." His purr chilled my skin. His hand came to my bodice and pulled it up, baring my ass for him. The thump of my heart was so loud, the sound pounded in my ears. "I'll make you bleed."

A guttural scream left my lips, the sound loud enough to pierce the air around me and leave me breathless. Pain burned through my body like a match setting ablaze. It burned slow, down in my back, until it got to the point where I burned all over. The pain was so immense that I opened my mouth and no words came out.

I thought I had lost the ability to cry, that my tear ducts had dried. Something else I had been wrong about.

DRUGS WERE NOW MY COMPANIONS AND MY SAFE HAVEN, something Silas allowed because it kept me numb and accessible. He knew that, either way, I didn't want him, so I guessed he called that a win. Days blurred into one, and in the end, the less I complained, the faster Silas was done with me. I guess this was the downside of having no friends—no one gave a shit about you, and you became nonexistent.

"I don't care what you do, just make her less pathetic."

Silas's voice carried through my foggy brain, and I had barely enough strength to open my eyes.

"She's lost a lot of weight." Dr. Wozniak looked blurry.

He kept looking at me in shock or maybe horror. If I'd had the energy, I would have laughed. No wonder Silas had been careful not to leave bruises in the last few days.

"Doctor," Silas warned.

"With all due respect, Mr. Remington, I have been in charge of Ember since she was a child. I was the one who pulled her out of her mother's womb. She's my patient, and I will ask the questions I deem necessary."

If I wasn't so weak, I might have been awake long enough to hear the rest.

Hours later, I woke feeling better than I had felt since I arrived at Silas house. I tried to move, but attached to my arm was a banana bag.

"Not only were you dehydrated, but also malnourished. Mixed with cocaine, you're just asking to die."

Was I that obvious?

I stayed quiet because I didn't need him to judge me for something he didn't understand. He didn't say anything as he switched the bag and gave me all the vitamins and nutrition I'd lacked in the past months. The more time that passed, the more my hands started to get shaky, and my body jittered.

"You always used drugs, but you were never an addict," he stated.

Hearing him confirm what I already knew wasn't pleasant. If anything, it made me feel even more pathetic. He sat down and observed and looked away when I couldn't take it anymore and reached for my joint paper. It wasn't what my body craved, but it helped numb me a bit. It was sad to depend on something so minimal and unimportant to the point it became your whole world.

He looked down at his smartwatch, and something passed over his features.

"I have to go, but I will be back." He unhooked me and started to put his stuff away. He was about to walk away, but instead, he looked me straight in the eyes. "Are you safe, Ember?"

Before I could answer, Gio was there. "Time to go."

"Thank you," I said, feeling my throat constrict.

I looked away and bit my lip as moisture pooled around my eyes. I didn't know what I thanked him for, whether it was for being here or for caring, and it was fucking weak on my part. Still, that act of kindness got me through the night.

Ember

"I don't care how you do it, but you find out who did this!" Silas shouted as I made my way to the kitchen.

His office was on the way, and I roamed carefully so I wouldn't be seen and peeked into his office. I couldn't see much, just two of his men and some pictures laid on his desk. Deciding it wasn't my concern, I took two steps back and started to walk again. As I passed the office, Silas called for me.

"Get in here now!"

I rolled my eyes and did as he said. It was funny how some vitamins and human contact made a difference. Yes, I still depended on the drugs, but the fact that Dr. W had come five times already made me feel better.

Silas sat behind his expensive wooden desk. He was my master, and I was his helpless subject. He was angry, which was rare nowadays. He had the world at his fingertips, and nothing fazed him much, so it made me a bit worried.

When I got close enough, my stomach dropped at the sight of the pictures on the desk. It looked like me, but it wasn't. It was the woman Silas had paid to impersonate me. As I kept scanning, there was one with a close-up of the girl's face. In bold red Sharpie, it said *Liar*.

I felt a shiver run down my spine. It was probably fear, but it could also be the withdrawal already.

"Stop with your stupid drugs. I need you to make an appearance before people get suspicious."

My eyebrows raised as he expected me to do as he wanted. Go where? What was I even going to do? My eyes caught on the calendar on Silas's desk. One week was more than enough time. I had one shot, and if I did it right, one shot was more than enough.

Last time, I was a coward, but I wasn't the same girl now. I was no longer scared. Silas had stolen everything from me; it was only fair I did the same for him.

"I always go to the Día de Los Muertos celebration." I spoke with a confidence I had not heard in myself since the night it all changed.

I celebrated day of the death as a way to honor my mother. I read in an article she would go to the parade. Once my father even told me she made altars to honor her dead. It seemed fitting, almost like a sign. If it all went wrong, there was no better way to die, I guess.

Silas dismissed it. "Absolutely not."

"I go every year. One year is understandable, but two in a row? Whoever sent those pictures might get even more suspicious. Your perfect little stack of cards is one blow away from tumbling."

He stayed quiet because he knew I had a point, and he didn't like it. It looked like whoever had put a hit on my head was observant. It turned out that the very thing that wanted to kill me could also end up saving me.

"Looks like whoever put a price on my head knows me quite well."

Silas didn't show any emotions. "Get out of my face."

"Gladly," I spat.

As soon as I was out of the room, my hands shook. Nerves, excitement, addiction—who the hell knew. What I did know was I had one shot at making it count and proving I wasn't a coward.

"How's my father doing?"

It was the first time I had asked about him, and it surprised not only me, but also the doctor. My father woke, but he wasn't the same. When the accident happened, my dad had a piece of glass stuck in his spine. They had put him in an induced coma so they could do the surgery and his body could heal. When they tried to wake him, it didn't work. Sometimes those things happen—people die in surgery, or it doesn't go as planned. The Remingtons had money, so they kept him plugged.

"He's doing better," Dr. W replied hesitantly as he worked another round of vitamins through my bloodstream.

I wondered what he thought of all the mess we were in.. Now that my head was a bit clearer, I could see things didn't add up. Sammy was murdered, but it was brushed under the rug. It was contained, so the media didn't know of the actual shitstorm we—*I*—had been dealing with.

"Any function in his legs?"

The great Michael Remington was not only not fully inside his mind, but he was an invalid. I had built up my father to be this great man who was too busy for his rebel daughter, and look at him now. He couldn't even walk or talk.

"He started to have movement below his knees, so that's a good sign."

Yay. Go, Dad.

"He stays in your room."

I felt the doctor's gaze on me, but I ignored it.

"I think it calms him to sleep there."

Silas had moved me out of my home and dropped me

here, and he put my father in my penthouse. It was all about power with him—his way of showing us who called the shots.

"He enjoys being in your closet. I think it's because your essence is still present there."

Yeah, like that wasn't weird or anything.

"Doc..."

I didn't want to, but I turned to look at the doctor. I had never been more grateful for him until now. He kept me from teetering into oblivion.

"Yes?"

Why was it so hard to ask for help? Could I even trust him? What if I opened my mouth and he ran to Silas? Then my one shot would be taken away from me. The world was full of lies, some nicer than others, some tame, some vile, but no one ever said what they felt. It put a mask between yourself and harm.

"I miss my bong. You think you can bring that?" I let out a humorless chuckle.

The sad thing was, I did miss it; it reminded me of home. Funny how you never think about the things you have until they get taken away from you. Sure, I still had a warm bed every night, but it came with unwanted attention. I had food if I wanted it, but it came with the price of knowing that every single thing came from Silas. He was the master of my universe, and I was a flightless bird in a cage.

The doctor gave me a pointed look like he was disappointed in me.

I couldn't stand his gaze, so I moved to grab my coke vial. I was starting to get jittery. And as much as I wanted to pretend like I was strong and could leave it right now, this powder was a refuge.

"Remember, small doses. You have ease yourself down," he said, his voice stern.

I did less than what I was snorting these past few days and let the coke relax me.

"Five minutes!" was shouted from the open hallway.

Dr. Wozniak started to remove the bag at my arm, taking his sweet time doing so.

"Until next time, Doc," I said, pretending that I didn't care he was leaving.

I felt the needle slip from my arm and his cold fingers as he put a Band-Aid over the pierced skin.

He squeezed my arm lightly. "Unfortunately, I don't know when I'll be back."

Because the festival was a day away and I looked healthy, and that was all Silas cared about.

The bad thing about panicking when high? It made you trip out, and I was about to have a bad trip. I looked at the doctor's eyes, full of panic, and wished I could tell him to take me with him, but knowing damn well that would put his life at risk.

"Is there anything I can do?" His hand was still on my arm, and his fingers rubbed it almost soothingly.

Did he want me to ask for help?

"Can you do me a favor?"

He seemed to stop holding his breath, and tilted his head, but his hand remained wrapped in my arm.

"There was a photoshoot that needed my approval," I said, and the doctor looked at me funny at the stupidity coming out of my mouth. "I know a long time has passed, but if you can email the photographer on my behalf. The code to get into my laptop is Reddiamonds420. Once in, you will go to my folders, and once in there, find the one that says shoots. Once in that folder, find the one that says vanity, and then find the one that is labeled ICE. All the info will be in that file."

"After all this time?" he said skeptically as if this was what I was asking help for.

"Please, he will be waiting to hear from me." There was no denying the urgency in my voice.

Before he could reply, Gio was there telling him it was time to go.

"Thank you for everything, Doctor."

His eyes flashed as he noticed that this was me saying goodbye to him. One of two things could happen. I could escape and be free, or Silas would capture me and get enraged and maybe even kill me.

"Any plans for the weekend?" he casually asked as he put away his things.

"Day of the Dead parade."

He nodded with understanding. He'd been with me all my life, and this was one parade I never missed.

I watched him walk away, knowing it was probably the last time I would see him. Before he got to the door, he turned back to look at me.

"There's a tiny little coffee shop across the main street from the parade. It's a serene place, should you need a break from the festivities."

"Out." Gio pushed the doctor out.

He couldn't see me wave goodbye.

The night before the parade, I laid on my bed, twisting and turning, anxious to see what the day would bring. I had a dress brought to me...except this year, I wasn't allowed to wear face paint. It would make me too easy to blend in, and that was the last thing Silas wanted. He did relent and had his assistant bring me a makeup palette and fake black flowers. He even got me some diamond earrings.

After all, who was Ember Remington without her diamonds? I was no one. Plain and simple. I had been reduced to an object in someone's house.

Just then, I heard said someone walking down the hallway. I closed my eyes and clutched the pillow, knowing that it wouldn't matter if I was awake or sleeping. Most of the time, nightmares didn't happen at night or when you were sleeping. Nightmares happened while you were awake, and you remembered every dreaded second and replayed it over and over again in your sleep.

The worst part was, nightmares didn't always start as nightmares; sometimes, they were dreams.

When the door creaked, the blood in my veins froze. My body wanted to quake with fear, or maybe ask for more drugs to numb the pain that was to follow.

Because the pain was a reminder of how far I had fallen from grace.

"I know you're awake," he chastised me as I heard him take off his clothes.

I remained silent, knowing that speaking didn't help my case. I heard the bed creak, and mentally, I tried to brace myself. He moved like a snake, silent but deadly, striking when I least expected. When I met his dark shadow, I wanted to not fight and just let him use me as he pleased for one more night.

But why should he get my complicity? Why should he get my surrender? There was a reason diamonds were created with pressure, and to make a tiny jewel yield, you had to cut it many times. They were indestructible.

His breathing stopped for a second as he waited to see if

I was going to finally give in to his promises. The things a foolish little girl believed. I was weak, looking for love in all the wrong places, and all I found were sins. He wanted to own me without telling me why. I wanted to fly and never be bound to any man.

We clashed.

If this was my last time with him, I wanted him to feel my hate. To feel the rage he provoked when he put his flesh on me. I hit him even if it was in vain. Scratching, biting, and pulling hair, we became savage beasts seeking dominance. He told me I was his, whether I wanted him or not. I told him I'd rather be dead. Through the dark, I saw his sadistic grin. I thought he'd half fuck me to death, but what he did was much worse.

He went soft on me when I wanted him to keep being brutal.

He reminded me that he knew my body as well as I knew it myself.

When I came, I felt hatred and loathing all for myself.

As he walked away, I swore that, one way or another, Silas was going to die.

Ember

THE AIR ON MY SKIN FELT DIVINE, PRICKLING MY PORES AND breathing life into me. My eyes still burned from the sleepless night. And right now, I tried not to think of all the things I had to live through in the confinement of my luxurious penthouse.

"This way," Gio said.

He grabbed my arm, dragging me into the car.

I followed him, trying not to get my hopes up because I didn't think my soul could handle the deception.

This morning as I got ready, Silas came in and reminded me not to do anything stupid.

He gripped my chin and said, "You try to leave me, and I'll do everything shy of killing you."

I bit my tongue, trying hard not to think of last night. When Gio and the other security that was set to accompany were set to take me to the parade, I was happy to follow them.

Now I sat in the back of one of Silas's Explorers. Gio was next to me while one man drove, and there was another in the passenger seat. Every precaution was taken when I was escorted. I looked down at my black dress and played with the skirt. It was a traditional Mexican dress, with red ribbons weaved at the bottom and at the collar of the dress. On my head, I wore a crown of black flowers, with red eyeshadow on my face, and, much to Silas's dismay, I had outlined a Catrina—sugar skull candy as Americans referred to it. I looked like Death's wife, ready to go back to the underworld.

I wanted to relish the feel of the car—the way it vibrated under my skin, the blur of the skyscrapers, and the mindless people walking by. Still, my mind kept going back to Dr. Wozniak.

Everything today depended on him if he could follow instructions to a T. In the folder he would find instructions on how to log into the dark web. He would discover how to navigate it, and lastly, in the notes in bold red, I had put the sigil for the webpage I had accessed months ago.

So if the doctor did as I asked, he would hire the hitman I had talked to months ago.

He didn't care for the motive; he just wanted his money. He did his job, and I wasn't above rewarding him generously.

If all went well, Silas would die, and I would have the last laugh. The only thing that would let me have a shred of sanity in this whole mess.

The closer we pulled toward the parade, the more people dressed with Death's face could be seen—so many colors bringing life to a holiday honoring the dead. When the car finally stopped, I took a deep breath. First, I was going to walk up to the vendors to get a candle for my mother. If it was true and the veil between the two worlds was thin, then I hoped she heard my prayers.

Without fail, I felt eyes on me once again. After being alone for so long, they were welcome. With the world looking at me, it meant Silas was a little out of reach.

I held my head high as I made my way through the crowd, aware of every movement from the two security guys in front of me and from the two next to me. For now, I had to play by their rules even if I hated it.

Every year I hung out at the same vendor, pretending that I was with family just like everyone else.

My hands went to a white candle with an angel helping two kids cross a bridge to safety. Taking it, I gave it to the old lady and handed it to her, hoping she could get the hidden meaning behind my candle of choice.

"Pay her," I snapped at Gio.

As he handed her the money, the lady gave me a look because I was not my usual self, and she knew it. In this place, among the living worshiping the dead, I was not Ember Remington; among them, I was another girl making an *ofrenda* to a dead mother she never knew.

"¿Estás bien, niña?" *Are you all right, child?* she asked.

"En cuando me quite mis sombras, lo estare," I told her. *As soon as I get rid of my shadows, I'll be fine.*

"Let's go, Miss Remington," Gio said, pissed.

Apparently this was one of those things people were surprised I could do. I wasn't ignorant. I went to the best schools and wanted to know everything about my mother, down to her native tongue.

"The dance is about to start," the vendor lady said, and I smiled at her.

"Gracias."

Gio put his hand on mine, dragging me away. "What did Silas tell you? If you tried anything, it would—"

"What, my ass on the line?" I bit back. "I was getting a fucking candle. Let me go before there's a picture of you manhandling me."

He looked at me with hate, but ultimately he let me go because I was right.

I made my way to where they had altars where people were putting out their candles as others said a prayer to walk the poor souls to a happier afterlife.

A day like today, I really missed the diamond against my skin, reminding me that I had a lot to lose. I did the sign of the cross as my heart thrummed faster. My ears began to pound, but it wasn't my own heartbeat; it was the drums from the parade. I made my way to the farther edge from where the parade had already started, having missed the beginning.

The guys were at my back, their presence fueling the fire I'd carried since the day in the limo. I got up on my toes, and across the street far off, I could see the coffee shop Dr. Wozniak had mentioned.

We never talked about coffee or shops, so for him to mention this place after finding out my whereabouts, it had to mean something. Or maybe I was grasping at straws, but I wouldn't know until I tried.

"People saw enough of you. Let's get going."

"Give me a second. This next float is my favorite." I removed my hand from Gio's grasp.

The drums got louder and faster, and the people in the crowd got hyped, me included.

Just then, women dressed in black and red dresses came into view. They twirled their skirts in synch. It was hypnotic watching all these women who looked like death dancing to the beat of the drums. I waited as I felt the beating of my heart in my throat and my hands wanting to shake a bit. Men dressed like charros and Death stepped in front of the sidelines. My eyes met Jorge's, knowing he had probably already spoken to his grandma, and that was when I ran.

I moved fast and in between them yelling, "¡Ayúdeme!."

Help me!

I ran past the women who were twirling and dancing, not wanting to miss a beat, and then pushed against the crowd on the other side. I heard shouts and people yelling. I knew Gio and the men wouldn't care to use their force, but I just needed enough time to pull away.

My lungs were on fire, my throat burned with the breaths I was barely taking, and every cell in my body begged me to slow down. It asked me to get high, but right now, fear and survival dominated.

A car honked, and people yelled, but I didn't care to stop. When I made it to the little coffee shop, I opened the door and ran in. I didn't dare look back, but I ran to the back, and then I locked myself in the men's bathroom—just in case.

As soon as the door was closed, I slid to the floor, my chest heaving, trying to get air back in my body. I felt like I was dying. There were no other doors and no exits this way, so if Silas wanted me, he would have to drag me through the front door. *Not before I sing bloody murder.* Silas changed the game on me thinking he still had the upper hand, and all he'd given me was the courage to do what I had been too cowardly to go through.

Not. Any. More.

He took my home.

He took my life.

My father.

My dignity.

And he left me with nothing to lose.

That was dangerous.

Going over to the sink, I looked at my reflection in the mirror. My makeup had run a bit, making me look more macabre, my eyes a little soulless, and I knew this was not the me I had once loved before, but this was a me I could be in awe of.

Putting my hands in the lukewarm water, I brought it to my mouth and rinsed away the cottony feel I had on my tongue. When I heard someone trying to pull the door, my heart stopped. Looking myself in the mirror one last time, I walked away, ready to face whomever was on the other side of the door.

I closed my eyes and pulled it open.

"Uh, you're in the wrong bathroom." Relief spread through my body at the guy in front of me—one of those hippie coffee-loving guys.

"My bad." I stepped aside, cautious and alert.

The hallways were empty, and I prepared myself for whom I was going to meet in the lobby. With every step, my craving for a hit grew, and my body demanded just to give up, but I didn't want to let my addiction win. The first thing I had to do was find the closest pawn shop and get whatever money I could from this; then, I would try to find a way to get out of this mess.

Where would I go?

Maybe it was time I learned how the other half lived.

The place was empty, just a few patrons sipping their drinks. I was about to walk out when I turned around. There had to be a reason why the doctor had told me to come here.

The woman at the counter looked at me expectantly.

"Sorry. This is going to sound dumb, but does the name Wozniak ring a bell?"

Her eyes seemed to flash with understanding or recognition.

"Yes. The old guy says he's a doctor?"

"Yes," I said hesitantly.

"You Ember?"

"Yes..."

She nodded, then turned around, going to the back.

"He said you left your purse at his practice and couldn't reach it since you live on the other side of the city, but since you were going to be around the area, he left us this."

"Thank you," I said, reaching for it.

"Thank you—his tip was amazing!"

I nodded as I made my way to a back booth, hoping Gio and his men didn't come looking here. There was a reason why I'd chosen the float I had to make a run for it. The vendor lady, her family, ran it. I was hoping her people held off Gio and his men long enough.

With shaky hands, I opened the bag, preparing myself for what I would find.

Dear Ember,

I will not ask questions about what you asked me to do. I may be an old man, but I'm not dumb. At five o'clock, your guest will arrive, and I hope you know what you're doing. I want you to know that your father is in great hands.

Be safe.

I couldn't keep my hands still. I took a deep breath, wanting to believe things were finally looking up, but happily ever afters had never been in the cards for me before, and I didn't know why it would start now.

"Here. The doctor paid for this," the chick said, putting a cup of tea and a sandwich in front of me.

Moisture gathered around my eyes at his generosity, making me feel ashamed, ungrateful, spoiled.

My hand shook as I went to grab the tea. I had thirty minutes. As I waited for the time to pass, I kept digging in the bag. There was a clutch inside with a few hundred-dollar bills and pieces of jewelry inside. My favorite perfume, a pack of gum—and my heart stopped beating for a second when I touched the small pen containing my wax. The need to hit it overrode everything else. It wasn't what I craved, but it was enough to calm the thirst I had. At the bottom of the bag I found a pair of clothes, and in the pocket of the jeans was a small black burner phone.

In this day and age, you never notice how voiceless you are until you go dark. When there's no phone by you. When there's Wi-Fi, but you can't log on. It's a desperate feeling, knowing it's so easy for everyone else to have a voice except for you.

Opening the small phone, I noticed it was three minutes to five. My nerves shot up, my skin went through flashes, and I shot up in my seat, going straight for the women's bathroom this time. My hands started to shake as I brought the dab pen to my mouth. I took one long drag, then another and let myself relax a little.

I was going to remove my makeup, but I figured it would help me blend in to go wherever I went to next. I did remove the dress. Underneath, I had black leggings and my black shirt. The temperature had probably gotten chillier, but I was going to have to survive like this, at least for tonight.

Once the smell of THC had cleared, I opened the door, getting ready to meet the man who would kill Silas.

My hands shook, and I held on to the door for support. The blood drained from my face, and I felt cold. How stupid was I to think I could escape. I looked up again, hoping he wasn't standing there with a dark grin on his face.

"Did you think you could hide from me?"

You Can Run But You Can't Hide

Ember held on to the frame of the door as if that would stop me from barging in and collecting her. She looked like death, and I found it amusing. A crown of black roses adorned her head, and it was just too fitting that she looked ready for her own funeral. She wanted pain. I would give her hell.

Ember

I didn't know what was worse: to die at the hands of Silas or beg Ren for redemption after what I did to him. Betrayal cut deep, and I was past begging any man to let me live.

He stood on the other side of the door, a dark grin on his face. He was the Ren I remembered, yet there was something that was off, and he didn't look like my Ren. Not that he was ever mine, but he looked sharper. Maybe it was the fact that he no longer sported his beard. His face was smooth, exposing a strong jaw. I dug my fingers into the doorframe to stop myself from reaching over and feeling his skin.

I took a deep breath.

I remembered the last words he'd said to me. I heard them on my lonely nights, knowing that if Silas didn't finish me off, Ren would.

"Did you think you could hide from me?" His smoky tone fogged my brain, and I remembered how it felt as I lost a part of myself in him.

Right now, I had no time for him and his vendetta. Without saying a word, I went past him, hoping he wouldn't cause a scene at the cafe. He let me go, but I felt him at my back.

My eyes scanned the shop to see if any newcomers had arrived. I looked at the clock, and it was five past five. As soon as I got to the table, I was trying to think of my next move when Ren stopped right behind me. I could feel his breath in my ear, my back heating with his proximity.

Chills went down my spine as he went to move my hair out of the way. His lips moved against my ear, and then he made my world shake.

"Tell me, princess, are you ready to get dirty and lie in blood?"

I turned around, facing his chest. My eyes slowly trailed up as I remembered the conversation we'd had months ago.

He'd shed the lambskin he wore, and I saw him for what he truly was: a predator, and I was his prey. A prey that came willingly and blindly to him. What I saw of him was only what he allowed, a fraction of the man he was. The edge was still there, but now it was lethal.

I pushed him off me and ran out of the shop. This was not happening. He'd lied to me, used me, and betrayed me.

I was heaving by the time I rounded the corner into an alley.

How?

Why?

This wasn't happening!

Something was wrong. This had to be some sort of sick joke.

"Where do you think you're going?" Ren asked as he grabbed my arm to spin me around so I could face him.

"Y-y-you lied to me," I whispered.

A slow grin spread through his face. It didn't make me feel better because it was sinister. Just because the devil smiled, it didn't mean he'd have mercy. If anything I should be more afraid.

"I did not lie," he smirked at me as he got closer. "I told you who I was."

"You're him," I said, hoping he would lie to me. To tell me he and the hitman I'd tried to hire were not one and the same.

He didn't say anything; instead, he struck so fast before I could move. His hand came to my throat, and he pinned me to the wall. The pressure suffocated me, but Ren had no mercy.

"You had me arrested," he spat at me.

I opened my mouth to defend myself, but I found it hard to speak. What would I say even if I could? I'd stood back while Silas accused him of raping me. I said I was sorry and gave him his scalpel. If anything, I gave him a chance to fight back.

Ren pressed closer, and I could feel his erection digging into my stomach. He wanted me—and I still wanted him. For the last year, I tried not to think about our night in the maze. I tried not to think about his hands on my skin and how his touch would numb my pain, set back my self-loathing. He would make my shitty world a little more bearable.

"I-I d-d-didn't," I managed to choke out. I brought my eyes to meet his icy ones and my hands to his arms, trying to pry him away from me.

"All you've done is lie, Ember, but you're going to pay for it."

"L-i-ike y-y-ou l-i-ied t-to me."

He pressed closer to me, leaving no room to run.

"I should kill you for what you did."

His voice was like a sweet poison that I wanted to drink every last drop of. His hold on my neck loosened, allowing me more room to breathe. The air felt like lava down my throat.

"Maybe in death, I'll find peace," I whispered.

Something in his eyes shifted, and he removed his hands from my neck completely. Instead, he cupped my cheek with his thumb. He removed a tear that had sprung free.

"Who did you want to kill?" He asked the one question I wasn't ready to answer.

I looked down at the floor because I felt so much shame at that moment. It didn't matter who I was or where I came from. I...I should just leave and get myself killed. It would be better—at least that way I'd be free.

"This was a mistake," I said as I pushed him away.

All my life, I'd been alone, not able to trust anyone I didn't know why I thought I could change my outcome. Life was a game you played, or you got played, and I had lost time and time again.

Ren let out a laugh before he pulled me back. "Now, where do you think you're going?"

"Let. Me. Go."

"Who do you want dead?" he stressed.

I looked at him and wondered what would happen if I told him the truth.

"Is it Mattias?"

"What?"

"Because he won't give you your trust fund."

I gave a humorless chuckle. "How well you have me figured out."

"Let's go. I have plans for you."

I let him lead me without saying more. I was scared that if I told him the truth, he would still look at me with disgust. It was easier to let him think about what he wanted. I didn't know where we were walking or why I hadn't run away, yet I just kept telling myself that anything Ren did to me couldn't be as vile as what I suffered at Silas's hands. Knowing Dr. Wozniak was a decent guy and was taking care of my father made me feel better.

Ren made a move to cross the street, but before we did, he grabbed the cash from my purse, pocketed it, and then threw my purse away. I gritted my teeth and said nothing. The disposable phone felt heavy in my back pocket. As far as a weapon against him, it was a damn good one. I just had to find the perfect moment to use it—or so I told myself.

When we crossed the street, the parade was dying down, but there were still people dressed as Catrinas and holding candles, mourning their lost ones. I wondered if Gio and his men were still in the area and if I should mention it to Ren.

Before we could walk very far, he threw his arm over my shoulder and pulled me into his body. He was rock solid but warm, which made no sense, but it was comforting.

"You can't run away now, princess." He kept spitting that nickname, like it was lead on his tongue.

We made our way across the parade grounds with Ren holding me, and we blended in with the dusk. It didn't take long for me to start shivering. My body was cold, but the withdrawals had already begun, each wave stronger than the next, making me seek out comfort in Ren's arms.

The moment I pressed closer, he stiffened for a second. I kept looking straight as I felt his gaze on me. We took a few more steps before he abruptly stopped, removed his jacket, and put it on me. I looked anywhere but at him. As soon as he found out I was going through withdrawals, all that rage would be mixed with disgust, and I didn't think I could handle seeing disgust on anyone other than myself.

Ren stopped holding me to his body; instead, he grabbed my hand and led me to wherever it was he was taking me. I always believed love was a weapon that could be used against you, and right now, looking down at Ren's hand and mine, it made me pity myself for a second because I would never know the feeling. Not from any man, nor family member—no one had loved me, and pretty soon no one would remember me. There was already an immortal Ember; the world didn't need two.

With my fate in Ren's hands, I followed him because I was tired of being the one to mess up my life. Action has consequences, and I had a string of bad decisions catching up to me.

I followed Ren Falcon, giving him the power to destroy me. I wasn't walking into this with stars in my eyes and hope in my heart. I had fear in my veins and thoughts full of hate, but if I had to pick the lesser of two evils, I would gladly do it again. Robbing Silas of a chance to kill me was just a checkmate on my end.

Water droplets started to hit my face, and I closed my eyes toward the sky, relishing the moisture on my skin. One year without rain, without dark skies nor sunny and bright mornings. One year of being a prisoner in someone else's game, and it made you value the little things you always took for granted—the changing of leaves from spring to winter. How time changed and you stayed the same, just withering more each passing day.

"What's the holdup?" Ren turned to glare at me. His jaw ticked, but his eyes softened for a second. I held my breath to see what he would say, but he just turned around and started to drag me again.

We made it to another alley where I could see another car hidden deep in the shadows.

There was no going back now.

Just as I took another step, aware that once I got in that car my life would yet again change, I was dragged back.

"Not so fast." Gio's drawl was pissed.

His hold on me was strong, his fingers digging into my frail arm. I was sure if he wanted, he could fracture my bones.

I was in the middle of two men who couldn't stand each other. Ren didn't look pissed; as soon as he turned, a slow smile spread across his handsome face.

"Nice scar," he smirked as he pointed to Gio's cheek, then cast his eyes past him toward the parade plaza.

Gio's nostrils flared, and his eyes zeroed in on Ren.

"I'd hoped you'd be dead, but I can fix that right now. I'm sure my boss will reward me."

"Why don't you let go of Ember, and we'll settle this here and now," Ren taunted. His hold on my arm was strong but not enough to cause me harm.

Gio seemed to think it over when he suddenly yanked me back, pulling me out of Ren's grasp, or maybe he let me go so he wouldn't snap my wrist. My body hit Gio's with a loud thud. His arm wrapped around my waist while he held onto my forehead, forcing my neck to arch back.

"I'm going to enjoy killing you, and as a reward, I'm sure the boss will let me fuck—" Gio's hand slithered down to cup my pussy.

I froze. My eyes met Ren's, and his icy eyes shone but gave nothing away.

"—her until she begs me for more."

"And you think I give a fuck who this slut fucks?" Ren drawled.

I didn't flinch. I didn't react. Instead, I went to that place in my mind that kept me sane—the place where no one could touch me. There was no pain, just a void of all emotions. Feelings got you nowhere.

Before Gio had a chance to speak, I jumped back against Gio's chest when fireworks started to go off, signaling the end of the parade.

Ren rushed forward, and I flinched when he came at me fast. He went to where Gio was cupping me. Gio howled in pain and let me go. I closed my eyes for a second, scared of what would happen next. I still had my eyes closed when I felt Ren's arm wrap around my waist and pull me toward him. He held on to me as if he owed me.

The problem? He did. When I was in his arms, I opened my eyes. He looked beautiful in all his anger. Beautiful things didn't just come out in the light; they thrived in the dark, full of wicked promises and lies. A violent fantasy—that was what Ren was. His arm was outstretched, pointing a gun with a silencer toward Gio.

"Have fun crawling after me," Ren smirked.

I flinched when he pulled the trigger, my heart palpitating with adrenaline. Gio's hand was bleeding, a nasty gash on his arm, and I didn't feel the least bit sorry for him. As another firework thundered in the sky, one of Gio's kneecaps exploded.

"Time to go," Ren stated as he started to drag me behind him. He pulled my arm, forcing me to keep pace with him. I was weak and couldn't go as fast as he wanted. We rounded the corner, where there was a black car parked.

Ren took me to the door behind the passenger side. He pressed me against the door, his body right behind me, and then his hand came to my hips.

"Nice try," he whispered as he fished out my cell phone.

I closed my eyes as I heard the snap of my phone breaking next to me.

He opened the door for me, and I took a moment before I sat.

"Sorry about this," he said, sounding anything but sorry.

A sharp pain shot up my neck before I lost consciousness.

Ren

CLOCKING EMBER ON THE HEAD WASN'T WHAT I HAD IN MIND when I went to meet her today. This was why I didn't bother with plans in the first place—shit hit the fan with wild variables. And Ember was very much a wild variable, despite her coming willingly.

I gripped the steering wheel tighter. It gave me something else to do, other than to step on the gas. The last thing I needed was to get pulled over. I checked my rearview mirrors, making sure that no more of Silas's men had followed me, because I didn't have the manpower to deal with all of them, and there was no way I was leaving Ember behind. We had unfinished business.

Just as I had unfinished business with Gio a year ago; I barely made it out alive. My mind was clouded by fury, rage, and betrayal, all directed at one person who couldn't even meet my eyes. Reading people was something I was good at. Analyzing them, knowing their patterns, or what choices they would make once I was familiar with their habits was something I'd never had trouble doing. So the moment Ember slipped a weapon into my pocket, I learned all I needed to about the spoiled little bitch.

So I let the men escort me out of the maze, and just like I had a feel for Ember, I also had a feel for Silas. Something wasn't right with him, almost like he was coming unhinged at the seams, but I couldn't figure out why. When he looked at me, his eyes went past mine and at that moment, and I knew Silas had no intention of letting the cops have me, which gave me a small window of opportunity.

The moment Gio led me away from the grounds where the partygoers were starting to come out, and toward a more secluded area, I threw my head back, hitting Gio and allowing myself enough time to grab the scalpel. I swiped it fast against Gio's cheek with enough pressure I knew it would scar. While he was down, I started to run when another of the men tried to shoot me. I neutralized him and brought him to the ground and snapped his neck. I figured his death and Gio's injury were more than enough to hold them back and try to contain the damage done before the media found out.

Gio's pride was something I forgot to take into account. The bastard shot at me three times, the second one hitting my shoulder.

I'd been in pain before, practically raised in it, so continuing to run was a bitch, but I did it. As I managed to get away, I dialed Pam.

Revenge with Gio wasn't as personal as I was going to have it with Ember. I was more than happy to let his pride be his downfall once again. Not only did he lose Ember, but he was now useless to Silas. The loyal dog was about to be tossed on its ass, and that gave me pleasure.

I turned back quickly to where Ember was still unconscious, and now that the adrenaline had died down, I could see changes in her. I turned back to the road and took the exit to drive away from the city.

When plan A didn't work, it was time for plan B.

Now I sat in a chair in the corner of the dark room, waiting for Ember to come awake. I gritted my jaw at the irrational anger I was experiencing. It had nothing to do with my hate for her. She was always a petite girl, but now she was too thin. Frail. Weak. Her hair had grown, but it lacked shine. Her face looked pale, no sign of a tan anywhere.

The moment she whimpered, my head snapped her way.

"Fuck," she moaned.

I continued to watch from the shadows as she came to. She tried to move but only got so far.

"Hey, princess," I chastised her. "Have a nice nap?"

Her head swung toward the dark corner where I hid, and she glared. I bit my lip to stop myself from smiling. God, she looked magnificent. My pants grew tighter, and I was glad the darkness and the angle she found herself in didn't allow for her to see how hard I was.

The haze seemed to wear off the more alert she became. She tried to sit up, only to be held back down by the collar around her throat.

I felt her glare, but she wisely kept her mouth shut.

"I have to go out, but that way, you can stay put," I told her as I got up and left the room without turning back.

◆

Ember

My breathing was coming in shallow pants as I tried to remain composed so the bastard wouldn't know how much he was affecting me. My head was throbbing where Ren had hit me, and it mixed with the insane need I had for my fix.

I. Was. Dying.

I tried to get up, only to be pulled back by my neck.

He'd collared me.

The memory of walking down the stairs came to haunt me. All the times I'd called him a dog, and he silently took it because it was me who had the power. That was the thing about power, wasn't it? Power was always changing.

I glared at him but didn't say a word. Not when his gaze caused more fear in me than yelling from Silas ever did. Silas was never close enough to hurt me the way he wanted, but Ren was there, and I was right—he was going to destroy me.

"I have to go out, but that way, you can stay put," he said as he walked out.

I waited until the door closed before I brought my hands to my neck, confirming what I already knew. Spikes.

One thing was for sure, Ren was a patient son of a bitch.

Moving my hands around my nape, I found the clasps from the leash and took it off. It allowed me to sit straighter. I kept trying to open the collar but found small clasps that seemed to need a key to make it open.

But of course. Ren was the type of guy to think of everything.

Sitting up took effort I didn't have and made me feel like I was seasick. I needed answers, and Ren owed me that much. I'd betrayed him, but he did it first, coming to my house after the conversation we'd had. I closed my eyes briefly to gather strength when I started to feel hot.

Or maybe I was already beginning to burn up and I had yet to feel it.

Everything hurt.

All I knew was pain.

My body was in a constant ache.

My head throbbed. It didn't matter if I was awake or

asleep; it got to the point I couldn't outrun it. My mouth was dry and sour, the bitter taste of desperation on my taste buds.

My body was hot, and my blood felt heavy. My skin itched, and even if I scratched, the sensation wouldn't go away.

Part of me was ready to claw my skin away, to try to find some relief. It was the drugs or the lack of drugs. I twisted and turned, sure that I was going to go crazy. At moments, I was in the room Ren had thrown me in, and at others, I was back with Silas.

"Damn it, Ember," was growled but sounded far away.

My head tried to loll toward the sound, but just the thought of doing that had me drained.

"So stupid."

I woke later, shivering. This was irrational because earlier I was hot, my skin flushed and sweaty. There was a blanket wrapped around me, but that wasn't enough. My head felt full and fuzzy. Pressure all around that had me whimpering in pain.

Make.

It.

Stop.

It was too much.

My body shivered again, a violent wave of coldness rushing over me. I tried to lift my head to see if I could find something to give me relief.

"So fucking stupid."

The shivers didn't go away; they stayed with me the whole night, keeping me company and keeping me miserable. Water was poured down my throat, but it wasn't what I needed. My throat was raw from screaming and begging.

"I'm going to hurt you."

I thrashed some more, trying to get away from Silas.

"I'm not going anywhere, Ember. Remember, you asked for this." He grinned at me.

How did I ask for anything? There were two things I asked for in life, and I never got either of them. I wanted a mother, and she left this world as soon as I came to it. The other was a father, but his empire was more important than I was.

"You're going to regret betraying me."

Silas hated how freely I gave myself to Ren. It took effort, but I smiled at him. If I was dying, I wanted the last word. I wanted to make it count.

"You've done everything to me, and I'm still not yours."

I underestimated him yet again. I saw blurry hands at my throat. He wasn't choking me like he had when he raped me—not this time. This time it was just two fingers at each side of my throat. I didn't fight it all when instead of feeling cold, I started to feel nothing.

I stayed in a state of delirium, hot flashes, and shivers for a few days. With the voices inside my head waging war on me. With the demons that lurked in my mind promising sweet nothings. It was dangerous to be in a state of "in-between"—you never knew what would come out of your mouth. The heart spoke freely when it wasn't guarded.

Ember

I woke up shivering, even though I was under blankets. It felt like a dream, the fact that Ren had taken me. Not like a good dream, but in the sense that it didn't even feel real. There was no sign of Ren in the dark room. I let my eyes wander, trying to find any clue as to where I might be. No windows, barely any homey touches to the place. The only thing this room did smell strongly like was like him.

I tried to sort through my hazy memories, trying to figure out what was real, what was a delusion, and how much time had passed since he'd taken me. Now that I was waking up, I felt the small buzz of a headache. Turning my head to the other side, I saw a door, and it took strength, but I made myself get up. That was when I felt a small thud pulling me back.

The damn fucking dog collar.

So that wasn't a dream. I brought my head back and went for where the leash connected with the collar and managed to open it after several tries.

Getting out of bed was easier said than done, but when I did, I felt wobbly, but not entirely weak, which was odd.

The door wasn't a way out, but it was a bathroom. It smelled like Ren, like his cologne and aftershave. I leaned against the frame, just taking in his smell, and it gave me a sense of familiarity and comfort. Great, I was starting to develop Stockholm syndrome, wasn't I? I was a fucking guppy, I swear.

Chapter 27

As my body shivered, I decided I could do with a hot shower. Maybe that could make me feel more human. Stripping off my clothes, I stood under the shower, letting it warm me. I was so tired I sat in the tub, not caring for anything else. I just closed my eyes and wondered when the hell my life got so fucking complicated.

"You're having withdrawals." Ren's husky tone interrupted my thoughts.

He stood a foot away from me, watching me, his eyes tracing every inch of my body. When I didn't say more, he continued to stare at me before he spoke again.

"Why?"

"I'm a fucking addict. That's why," I spat.

Ren let me soak in the water for a little while longer, and I was grateful for it. I was aware of his eyes as I made a move to wash up. I didn't know what kind of fucked-up I was when I started to feel hot for other reasons other than the boiling water. It was a mix of shame and arousal. When he made his way to me, my whole body became alert. My nipples pebbled, and my pussy ached. *Yep, I'm suffering from Stockholm syndrome.* The only acceptable explanation for why I was acting like a hussy now. As I washed, I noticed dark bruising by the vein in my arm. I turned to look at Ren, but he gave nothing away.

The more I stared at him, the more I desperately tried to think about what happened between him kidnapping me, my delirium, and today. Ren turned off the shower, then grabbed a towel and picked me up. Neither of us said a word as he took me back to the bed.

"You lied to me."

"What?" Ren replied.

"You *knew* me."

Chapter 27

There was silence. Ren sat on the bed, leaning against the headboard, bringing my body between his open legs. My back to his chest, he wrapped his arms around me. It seemed so mundane, so out of place, I almost laughed.

"That's what you want to lead with?" he mocked in my ear.

"You've killed."

"I have. I will again. Can't change who I am."

His words caused a shiver to run down my spine. I couldn't trust my senses, but if I could, I would have sworn he kissed my nape.

"Make no mistake, Ember. Anyone tries to take you away from me, I'll kill them."

I believed him, but I also knew I was now in the middle of a demon and a reaper: both deadly, both wanting to possess me, and both ready to get blood on their hands.

I turned my head to face him, shivering for other reasons now. "Why?"

It was a loaded question, not just why for now, but why come to me at all.

"You believe in fate?" he asked.

I shook my head.

"The dark web is a scary place, princess, and it's full of everything seedy humanity has to offer. You went in there, and out of all the pages and places you could have ended up, you landed in my little dark corner of the world. Normally I don't handle the hits, so it's rarely me you get to speak to. That day it was. I got curious, so I backtracked your connection." He stopped talking to pull a strand of my hair back. Then his hand glided across my cheek. "That was your first mistake. You didn't cover the webcam. Right away, I knew you were a rookie—a scared little girl. It was so easy to see

Chapter 27

you. I saw the fear in your eyes, and it called to me. I wanted to feed off it."

He sat up, but brought me with him as he leaned into the nightstand and pulled out a picture of me taken from the screen of my laptop. I felt chills all over me as I saw the picture. My eyes shone a bit, the pupils dilated. Unshed tears and fear were written all over my face.

"I memorized your face. It kept haunting me, so after a few days, I did a reverse search on you."

I held my breath. Not because he was revealing the truth, but because his hands started to move up and down my thighs, making me feel needy. It evoked feelings I hadn't felt for a year. Want and need for something that was not tainted overtook me. I lived for bad decisions, and when all the wrong ones lately hadn't been my choice, this one was welcome.

"Ember fucking Remington," he whispered against the skin in my neck. "I was doing another job, but fuck, I was obsessed. I knew you'd come back, that you'd seek me out again, and I wanted to be close. I left the west coast and came east. I had no ties; I could do as I pleased. In the meanwhile, I dug up more information on you. That was when I saw the flaw in your security."

I gasped because his fingers trailed up my thigh, slowly reaching my pussy. His index grazed my slit, moving up and down teasingly, waiting to see if I would push him away.

I needed this.

I needed him.

I needed someone else to wash away Silas's touch. I wanted to get lost in someone, even if that someone was Ren. I wanted to forget the abuse and remember the pleasure—even if pleasure came with a price.

Chapter 27

"It was rather easy to infiltrate. I blended in, and as I got to know you, I hated everything about you," he gritted out.

I threw my head back and moaned because he inserted two fingers deep inside me.

"Here, I thought you were a helpless little socialite, and you were a fucking cunt."

Ren started to fuck my pussy, showing me how much he really hated me with the strum of his fingers. He knew my body, he knew my demons, and he was still here. I wrapped my hand around his neck, pulling his hair, and he groaned.

"You were not pure, nor innocent. You were a fucking inferno I couldn't stay away from," Ren said as he used his thumb to play with my clit.

I was beyond caring. I started to fuck his hand as he kissed my neck, sucking on the skin by my collar.

"Ren." I hissed as my hips moved furiously. He groaned, his fingers fucking me roughly.

"Now come like the fucking little slut you are." He bit my jaw, and I came, my pussy gripping against his fingers.

Ren pushed me away, only to throw me on the bed. He loomed over me, his nostrils flaring, and my God, I never wanted to be owned by anyone like I wanted to be owned by him. Ren reached behind me, and then he kissed me like he wanted to taste my soul. His lips clashed against mine, our teeth clanking and his tongue biting my lips, making me arch in pain. He used that moment to snap the fucking leash in place. Ren didn't take off his clothes; he unfastened his belt, pushing his boxers down, letting his dick spring free.

"Are you clean?" he asked as the tip of his dick prodded my entrance.

"Yes," I said breathlessly as I licked the blood from my lip.

Chapter 27

"Good," he ground out as he started to push inside me. "I'm going to fuck you raw, princess."

My answer was to arch my back and spread my legs wider to give him more access to ruin me.

"You're drenched." His husky tone was filled with lust, and his eyes had gone inky. "You came to me, Ember. Now. You're. Mine."

His fingers dug to my hip bones as he fucked me savagely. It wasn't slow and cautious. It was hard and calculating to make me feel just exactly who I had let in my bed. It was a slow burn for me, because he was taking his pleasure, making sure I barely found my own.

"Ren!" I shouted in frustration.

He smirked at me as one of his hands came to my belly, pushing me down as he thrust in and out of me. "I've put up with a lot of your bullshit."

Before I could respond, his mouth came to one of my nipples, and he bit it. I yelled in pain but felt my pussy grip him tighter.

"While I own you, no one else gets you," Ren growled.

He reached for the nightstand, bringing out the black scalpel. I started to pant, remembering what it did to me last time.

"My body…"

Ren let the sharp edge trail from my throat down to my chest, making the blade glide down my breast.

"My pussy—" he said with gritted teeth before he let the metal handle glide over my folds.

"*Fuck*," I moaned.

Ren rubbed the handle of the knife on my clit. The coolness of the metal had me squirming. He wielded the handle like a weapon, using pressure against my clit to the point I throbbed. He then removed the scalpel, and I saw where his

Chapter 27

palm was bleeding from gripping it too hard. He brought the handle to his lips and licked my juices from it.

"It's all mine," Ren stated as he slammed back into me.

He kissed my mouth as I moaned into him and felt his cock pulsate inside me with the warmth of his release.

"You asshole," I spat, trying to hit him. I was still horny and tired, and my body felt hot and cold, my hands clammy. I was a fucking mess.

"That's payback, baby," he replied.

I glared at him as he rose and fixed his jeans. I lay in his bed, my legs still spread, his cum dripping out, and I didn't have it in me to care anymore.

"You're going through withdrawals. It's going to get worse before it gets better," he told me before he left to the bathroom.

I closed my eyes for a second, waiting for that feeling I always got after sex. The one that reminded me of how wrong it was, but it hadn't come. Even though Ren had treated me like a whore, I didn't feel like one.

I closed my eyes, starting to fall asleep when I felt a warm cloth between my legs. My eyes sprang open, and Ren was right there, a joint in his mouth while he cleaned my pussy. I still throbbed from the orgasm I was denied, so when Ren used the rag to clean between my legs, I let out a soft moan.

The asshole smirked at me, kneeling on the bed as he kept adding pressure. He had the joint in his mouth as he rose above me, and his finger moved in circles around my clit through the fabric. My legs spread, and my hips bucked. Ren smiled at me. He threw the cloth away, and he bent his head to give me a shotgun pass. I greedily opened my mouth as he blew the smoke into my mouth. I was an addict, and the hit started to calm me.

Chapter 27

"That should take the edge off," he said before he took another hit and put his head between my spread legs. I was about to rise on my elbows to see what he would do, but I felt him blow the thick smoke at my sensitive clit.

"Ren," I moaned.

He didn't answer me. Instead, he bit my clit gently, making me spasm; then, he sucked it into his mouth, and I screamed. My hand went to his hair as I rode his face. The harder I gripped his hair, the harder Ren fucked me with his mouth. Once I stopped coming, he came back to my face, his lips dripping with my release.

"Kiss me," he growled.

My hand went to his face, bringing him down to me, and I bit his lip first, tasting myself and weed. Ren then took complete control.

"I'm going to take away with your vices and just leave with you with one addiction," he promised.

Before I could ask which one, he got off the bed.

"Rest." He looked at me, still naked and lying on his bed.

I had no idea what he thought, and I didn't want to ask him. Ren closed the door, turning off the lights on his way out, and I fell asleep.

Ren

I was so fucked.

The taste of Ember's pussy was still on my tongue when the door to the main house opened.

"Where the fuck have you been?" I gritted out when Pam strolled in.

"Oh, I'm sorry. While you went to get your little puta, I was out trying to figure out how to get out of our mess!"

Pam was killing my vibe.

"The mess you made, you mean?" I asked, and she flinched.

Pam glared at me, her eyes becoming tiny slits taking in my appearance.

"I hope her pussy works miracles," Pam said before she walked to her room.

"It does enough to take off the edge," I bit back.

I was aware Pam's eyes were on me as I took a seat. I took another drag of the joint I was smoking before I made Ember come on my tongue. That was a mistake, one I couldn't take back, and fuck if I wanted to.

"There's a fight," Pam told me while she grabbed her laptop.

"Who's hosting?" I asked.

I told Ember some of the truth, but not all of it. We came from different worlds, and even though her world and mine often crossed, I wasn't sure how much she knew. In my world, nothing came without a price, and power always did.

Pam and I had grown up on the streets. Our dads were in the same gang, and our whores of our mothers dipped before we could even remember them. When my old man overdosed and Pam's landed in jail, it was just the two of us fighting tooth and nail for a place to rest our heads at night. Since an early age, Pamela was good with numbers and shit while I'd made a name of myself solving my anger with my fists. Blood was fascinating to me, how just nine pints kept us human, alive. Take a little too much out of our fragile bodies, and that was it, game over.

How did someone get as fucked-up as me? Life. Streets. Shitty foster parents, you name it. My first kill was at fourteen. I killed the foster dad I had at the time. You'd think Pam would be the one who would have gotten in trouble, but the fucker preferred little boys. It was a messy kill; if it weren't for his wife helping us clean the mess I'd made, shit would have gone downhill fast for me. She was tired of his abuse and was glad her old man was dead.

Killing was an addiction. It gave you a high that you couldn't get anywhere else, and the thrill of not getting caught, well, that shit, you couldn't get it in any dime bag or shoot it in your veins. It had to be experienced with a blade. Any fucker could grab a gun and kill someone, but to cut them open, letting them bleed—you had to mean it.

"Are you even listening to me?" Pam huffed.

"Who?" I asked again.

"The Estacados."

The underworld was like the one percent. It was exclusive, and once you were in you were in, and we didn't get disgraced if we fucked up—we paid with our lives. If you didn't know someone, you'd heard of them. And in my world, the more people who knew of you, the more power to your name.

Power was never something I coveted. I had my jobs and had enough money to live comfortably. Greed wasn't my problem—it was Pam's. It was the reason we were in exile right now. There was an organization that was not spoken of. The government probably knew about it, but they buried it in files with a lot of red marker.

Once you belonged to them, you didn't have to worry about anything else. They were the crème de la crème. You didn't buy your way in; you had to be invited, and to score an invite, you had to prove your worth. If you failed, then you had to pay a fee for your life, or else it was death for making them waste their time.

So here I was, back to square one, trying to come up with cash to save my life. I was a killer, a hitman, a gun for hire. Pam was good with computers, but she was also a con. The bitch had charisma in spades.

"How much is the buy-in?"

The Estacados had one of the strongest operations in the world. Three brothers, each with their own kingdom to control, and lucky for us one of them happened to be here in New York. It was fortunate because they didn't care for laws other than their own, so the predicament Pam and I found ourselves in was of no importance to them.

"Fifty," Pam said. She at least had the decency to look remorseful.

"I have like twenty stashed here. The rest is back on the west coast."

"I have five," she told me.

I glared at her.

"I could hack—"

"Fuck that shit. You and I both know they'll be searching for your digital fingerprint."

"Well, what are we going to do? You got yourself fired before you could get the—"

"Shut the fuck up. If you weren't such a greedy fucking bitch, we wouldn't be here."

Pam got up, throwing her laptop on the table.

"Fuck you, Ren! I did what I did for us. So we could live the life we always wanted."

I took another hit of my joint as she walked away. I wasn't worried. She was smart and knew how to get around undetected. I didn't have to worry about waking up to her head on the doorstep.

Once I finished smoking, I went back to the room where Ember was sleeping. I walked to the side where she slept and let my finger glide over her face. Her cheeks were too sharp, and I didn't like that. The drugs did a number on her body. My eyes landed on her arm and the bruising that had formed from where I'd put an IV full of vitamins while she went through the hardest part of her withdrawals.

I'd felt rage before, but never like I had those days. Still, I looked at Ember, and I told myself I wasn't getting attached, that she didn't mean shit to me. She was just a means to an end. Ember Remington was nothing special to me.

Taking off my shirt, I climbed into bed with her.

Every night she got chills, and she would beg to make the pain go away. And every night, I would sit in the corner watching and waiting, but tonight I wanted to be close. Not because she was under my skin, not because I had finally fucked the diamond princess. It was so that I could be close when her demons spoke freely.

Falcon's Prey

"Your boner is digging into my ass."

My eyes remained closed, and I found myself smiling. Ember was in my arms, and she made no move to try to get out of them either.

"You could always move," I told her.

She stood quiet, and when she spoke, I almost wished she hadn't.

"I figure I don't have much life left to live, so while I wait for hell to claim me, I'll enjoy all the little things, even if they come covered in lies."

"What little things?"

"Being like this...in a man's arms...it's something foreign to me."

"Bullshit," I spat.

"Do you have family?" She changed the subject

"No. My whore of a mother dipped out, and my old man overdosed."

"That's why you don't do drugs?"

"I don't do drugs because the more addictions you have, the weaker you are."

She went still in my arms.

"You and I have a lot in common, *dog*."

I hovered over her, bringing her body under mine, my hand to her throat as she stared defiantly at me, and fuck, that got me hard. Her hands came to the top of the bedsheet, making sure it covered her breasts, as if I didn't have her naked body plastered all over me last night.

"What did you say?" I asked, squeezing her neck a little and letting go so she could have enough air to speak.

"You a poor boy, and me a rich girl, and we have one thing in common," she said.

"What do we have in common?" I humored her.

Ember blinked, and then she looked away from me. She licked her lips, then spoke.

"No one has ever loved us."

I laughed.

"Love? Seriously, princess?" I gripped her chin so she was forced to look at me. "Love is one of the words that gets thrown around like it's nothing. That word is a weakness—a disease. People say it without meaning it; they use it for manipulation. Love is just a word with no meaning." I bent my head, my mouth millimeters from hers. "A word is just a word. It's actions that give them power."

Ember

I always thought love was power, something that money couldn't buy. I knew it was dangerous, but maybe Ren was right, and I was scared of the unknown. Or perhaps we both had no idea what something we'd gone without meant or how to wield it—two sides to the same word.

Ren kept staring at me, and when I didn't say more, he got out of the bed and went to the bathroom. I needed a moment to gather my thoughts. Hell, to figure out exactly what was going on. I was his prisoner, right? Except being in his arms didn't feel like a cage. They felt strong like pillars, something to give strength to a crumbling structure.

There was no doubt in my mind I was crumbling. Who was I after everything essential to my being got stripped away? No money, no jewelry, no drugs, and no home. I had nothing to hide behind—no place to cower. Everything I'd hidden behind the façade was now in the open, all the ugly parts of me on display, ready to pick apart and dissect. *Who am I now that I have nothing?*

"Get up. Get dressed. We have shit to do today."

Ren walked out of the bathroom, the steam from the hot shower he took coming out like a fog behind him. A towel was draped across his waist. The ripples of his abs glistened with water droplets, and his hair was messy, but he looked divine.

"What are you going to do with me?" I held on to the

bedsheet tight, as if it were a shield protecting me against him.

"That's none of your concern," he said as he made his way to one of the drawers.

"So am I like your sex slave?"

Ren snorted. "You're weak, princess. You couldn't take me how I want you. For now, you're going to be whatever I need you to be."

Right. Because right now, he owned me. He needed his pound of flesh, and I was available.

"I have nothing," I reminded him.

I had been out of it for I didn't even know how long. Except now that I was wide-awake, the craving was there in the back of my mind, a small buzzing sound begging me to feed and give in to it.

Ren didn't answer. He dropped the towel, showing me his ah-ma-zing backside, put pants on, and walked out the door, leaving it open. Where was I going to go naked? The asshole probably did it on purpose.

Not even five minutes later, Ren walked back with clothes in his hands. "Put those on."

He threw the clothes at me and then went to the chair in the corner to tie his shoelaces.

I guess no privacy for me today.

Who was I when everything got stripped back and I was left with nothing?

You are a diamond, and diamonds don't break.

So I swallowed my shame because the one thing I had, one thing no one would ever take away from me, was my pride. I threw the bed shit aside and got out of bed, aware that I had lost weight. I was just skin and bones now. I knew it, and Ren did too. The clothes were big on me, not only because of my weight loss, but they were meant for someone curvier, and that had never been me. I bit my tongue and didn't ask who they belonged to.

Once changed, I looked up, holding my head high. Ren was leaned back in the chair, still shirtless, just looking at me. As I looked at his body, I noticed things that I never had before, like the way his skin was puckered in certain areas with faded scars, all of them a road map to who he was. I didn't want to look into his gaze for fear of what I would find behind his icy stare.

I raised my brow at him, fighting the urge to cross my arms.

You are a diamond, and diamonds don't break.

His eyes trailed from my head down to my toes, making me feel naked in a way I hadn't felt lying down in bed next to him. He then got up, opened another drawer, and grabbed a shirt.

When he walked out the door, I took a deep breath, then followed him. The place was spacious but not very bright. It looked like I was inside a warehouse that had been duped into a home. Small windows were on the top high enough so no one could snoop in and big enough to offer sunlight to come through. The stairs were made from concrete and tile —cold beneath my bare feet.

As I walked down the stairs, I started to close and open my palms, the chills had nothing to do with the coolness of the warehouse. They weren't as strong as they used to be, but still an inconvenience. A reminder of how far I had fallen.

Ren walked to a kitchen—small but practical. Without being told, I took a seat at the table that was by the corner. I was stronger, but nowhere near my old health. Ren was right; I couldn't even take a good fucking at the moment since I passed out on him right after.

I sat in silence as I watched Ren get to work in the kitchen, my mind going to drugs, Silas, and my father. One I was dependent on, the other one got deep in my skin, haunting from within, and the last was someone I wanted to protect even if he never protected me. What would Silas do now that I wasn't his punching bag? Would he take it out on his brother? One thing I was sure of was that family didn't mean shit to him. I was a means to an end who fell for empty words and hollow promises.

I snapped out of my thoughts when Ren put a drink in front of me.

"What the fuck is this?" I asked as I looked at the smoothie in front of me.

"It's a green smo—"

"I know what a green smoothie is. Why are you giving me one?"

Ren grabbed the chair next to me and turned it around, then straddled it.

"You're going through withdrawals cold turkey, your energy is shit, you knocked out right after you got fucked, and you look anorexic. *If* and *when* you die is up to me, not because you were weak to give in to the temptation of fake relief...now drink."

I felt a shiver run down my spine at his words. He thought himself a reaper; I wanted to show him you couldn't even bargain with death. Apparently I should be grateful I was alive.

"Why didn't you kill Gio?" I asked between sips.

"And risk getting caught? No, thanks. Besides, having Silas throw him on the street was more than enough." Ren smirked at me.

"How do you know?" I felt my blood race all over my

body, wondering how closely Ren had kept an eye on my "family."

"Got contacts." He shrugged it off like it was normal.

Taking another drink of the smoothie, I asked a question that was in the back of my mind since I'd found out who he really was.

"Was it the hit?" I licked my lips, and Ren followed the movement. "Did you infiltrate with the intention of killing me?"

My head had a price, and he was a gun for hire. It made sense.

Ren cocked his head. "Had I been after that hit, you'd never have seen me coming, princess."

I shivered from the toxic combination of fear and withdrawals.

"What were you after, then?" I asked, loathing myself for the answer that was in the back of my mind.

"Tsk. Tsk. Tsk." He shook his head. "You don't get to ask the questions."

"Is there anything you can tell me? What am I doing? Are you going to kill me? What do you want from me?" I snapped.

Ren smacked his hand on the table, causing me to flinch.

"Focus your mind on something else other than the damn fucking drugs," he growled. "You're feeding, and you are letting it control you."

He was right. I knew he was right, and I hated it.

"I'm weak, remember?" I bit back.

I waited for his comeback, but it didn't come. Instead, I heard a door—more like a gate—opening, followed by the tapping of footsteps. Ren's head swung toward the newcomer, but I refused to turn to look.

"You won't believe what I found out today—"

A female voice was getting closer.

"I see your little bitch is up," she purred with disdain.

I didn't know her, and I already didn't like her. I lifted my hand and flicked her off. She huffed, and it was small barely there, but I swore I saw Ren grin.

"What did you find out?" Ren asked her.

"I'm not sure I should say in front of your puta."

My body shook with rage at her word, and everything temporarily faded. Slowly I craned my neck.

"Esta puta tiene nombre," I told her. *This whore has a name*.

No wonder the clothes Ren threw at me didn't fit. The woman in front of me was gorgeous, despite me wishing otherwise. My blood boiled the more I looked at her—a lot of tits, curves, black hair with amber eyes, and a golden tan. Compared to her, I looked like a child.

Her eyes met mine, and her hate for me was apparent. Well, fuck her too.

"Pam, speak," Ren commanded.

"The price on her head just tripled," Pam said.

I closed my eyes and took a deep breath. Who could possibly want me that bad? I tuned out part of their conversation, but then I wished I hadn't heard a thing.

"...either we kill her or someone else will. She just became a liability. Anyone who knows shit will be looking for her."

My eyes met Ren's, and I silently questioned what he would do with me, well aware that I was a ticket to a better life.

"About the fight. Did you find out the location?"

"Yes, but without the money, it's no use."

Ren seemed to think about it for a moment before he spoke again. "Can you find any tables that are open?"

I wasn't as dumb as I looked, so I knew he wanted to gamble.

"I'll make some calls," Pam said before she walked away.

My hand came to my neck out of habit when I remembered Ren had walked away with my most prized possession *that* night.

"My mother's choker," I said.

Ren looked at me, confused.

"What?"

"My mother's choker was in your pocket the night—"

"You let everyone accuse me of raping you. I got shot at because of *you*."

Riiiight. Guess someone was still pissy about that. My stomach did tighten at the mention of him getting shot, but since he was still here making my life hell, I filed that away to process later.

"As I was saying," I kept going as I turned to look at him.

I was not going to apologize for the things I had to do to survive. Men stepped on toes all the time and didn't bother to turn back to see if it caused pain, but when a woman did it, they couldn't handle the sharp burn of the heel.

"You have my mother's choker. That alone is worth a couple of hundred thousand."

Ren brought one of his hands to his chin, and his mouth parted in surprise at my suggestion.

"You'd let me sell your mother's jewelry?"

"No. I'd let you gamble it." I looked at him, unflinching. "I don't think you have any intention of losing."

Ren smirked at me. "Point taken. Too bad I already got rid of it."

He shrugged like it wasn't a big deal. As if he hadn't

disposed of the only thing that meant something to me in this world.

My throat clogged, and my lip quivered.

"You had no right," I said through gritted teeth.

Ren got up from the chair in an instant. I held my breath, waiting to see what he would do next. It was fascinating watching his face transform in a matter of seconds. He looked serene one second, and full of rage the next. Like a dark sky right before it lit with thunder. He came to stand behind me, and I exhaled. His hands rested on the top of my shoulders, and he slowly brought them down. His right hand curved to my neck. He then glided it up to my chin and gripped it, forcing me to tilt my head so I could look at him.

"I had every right after what you did to me," he spat.

I turned my head, trying to get him to let me go.

"You survived. Stop bitching," I said to him, but here I was, not sure if I called what I went through surviving—more like faking it.

Ren

Pam and I were talking, trying to figure out which poker game to hit, but my eyes kept going to Ember. After talking to her in the kitchen, I made her stay close—punishment for her, enjoyment for me.

When she started to scratch her arms, I gave her a joint that I had rolled for her earlier. I knew she was in pain, but I refused to give her a fix, not when she was almost over the worst of it

"I mean, with the money we have, they won't turn us away," Pam said.

Ember let out a dark chuckle, smoke coming out of her lips as she did so.

"What's so funny?" Pam bit out. It was safe to say they didn't like each other.

"You're going to show up to a table, uninvited, and then rob them under their noses?" She raised her brow at us defiantly. "I'm no expert, but I don't think that's wise."

Pam glared at her. We both knew she had a point, but it was a risk we had to take.

"You have a better plan, princess?"

She didn't answer me immediately; instead, she took a slow drag of the joint, finishing it off. After she released the smoke, she spoke.

"Zeke."

"Come again?" I said.

"Every Friday, Zeke likes to host poker games. You know, us rich kids get bored."

"You're talking about the dipshit from the docks?" I laughed. "He hates me. He won't let me through the door."

"He will," she assured me.

"How are you so sure?"

"Because you're going to bet me."

Before I could say no, Pam spoke up.

"Your whore is good for something."

"Not happening."

Ember shrugged it off. "He hates you, but he wants me more. You won't even need to use money."

My chest constricted with her words. All I could do was glare at her as she walked away.

"Who is Zeke?" Pam asked.

I told her, and before she could say it was a no-brainer, I left after Ember.

She was sitting on the bed, her eyes closed and her head tipped back, and she was talking to herself. Her lips kept moving furiously. If she was aware of my presence, she didn't show it.

"What are you doing?" I asked as I walked in and closed the door.

"That's none of your business," she said.

I walked to the bed and sat on the edge, observing her. Ember had scratches on her arms, ranging from barely there to deep with a little blood oozing.

"Remember, princess, your life is in my hands."

Ember leaned back on the bed, crossing her arms and softly caressing her skin. "You think that's new to me? My life has always been in someone else's hands. You're just another one in the long list of men who think they own me."

She had no idea that unlike the rest, I did own her. I didn't reply right away; instead, I moved until her soft body was beneath me. She looked ridiculous in Pamela's clothes—messy and unkempt. The thing about Ember was that it was more than her beauty that drew you in. It was the fire that coursed through her skin, her stubbornness, her unwillingness to yield. So, yeah, I got off making her bend to *my* will.

I grabbed her wrist and put her arms above her head. Her chest rose and fell, but she made no move to try to get out of my grip.

"We both know I own you in a way no one ever has," I whispered as I stared into her eyes.

Ember raised her head, and her lips touched mine.

"Are you going to be the one to kill me, Falcon?" She said the words against my still lips, wielding my code name like a weapon.

There was something about her that called to me. It reached into the depths of my black soul, and it fed from it. I closed the distance, and I kissed her. Contained chaos—that was what she was. Her lips molded to mine as her hands tried to move from my hold.

"Focus your mind on something else," I told her, knowing she was fighting the urge to keep scratching.

"It's not that easy," she said, trying to excuse her weakness.

"Shut up," I said before I kneeled so I could flip her on her stomach.

I bunched her hair and wrapped it around my hand, keeping her arms pinned to the bed with my other hand. I pulled it lightly, just enough to get her attention.

"You need to focus on other things so that thirst you feel fades. It's mind over matter."

I didn't need to tell her I knew all about the addictions that called to your soul. How you heard them like sirens in the wind. You needed to keep your mind occupied, or else it would drive you mad.

Drugs called to her like killing cried for me.

"Just small doses. You can do that for me," she begged, frustrated.

"No," I taunted in her ear.

She let out a soft growl. I bent down to put her earlobe in my mouth, playing with the delicate skin with my teeth. Ember moved her neck to the side, allowing me more access to her neck.

"I never got to see my pretty choker," I murmured against her neck. I licked the skin before I sucked it. "Scratch your skin and you'll regret it."

I let go of her hands so I could bring them to her waist. I kissed the two small dimples in the back, something I never really noticed about a woman, but found sexy as fuck right now. I trailed kisses up the curve of her spine, bringing the shirt up as I went. Ember kept squirming beneath me with every stroke of my lips.

"Take your clothes off," I told her as I did the same.

Ember didn't turn around as she undressed. She took off her blouse first, and the pants followed.

"Lie back down, hands on your head," I told her. My cock jumped for attention when she did as I asked. Seductively she kneeled, lifting her ass as her torso flattened. She looked gorgeous: beaten, but not broken.

My hands went to the curve of her ass, skimming her skin with a featherlight touch, up the sides to her curves past her abdomen while I positioned myself behind her. With one hand on the bed and the other on her breast, I pinched her pebbled nipple.

I leaned down and kissed her back. "Focus on this."

That was all the warning I gave as I entered her in one hard thrust, making her put her hands on the bed for balance. She was soaked, her pussy wet and so. Fucking. Tight. It felt like my eyes rolled back in my head.

"Hands, Ember," I growled as I was deep inside her.

Once she did as I asked, I held on to her bony hip, and I fucked her hard.

With every thrust, I drove myself into her soul, or maybe she stole a part of mine.

With every moan out of her mouth, she cemented the fact that she was mine.

The high I was getting from fucking her was stronger than the ecstasy of power I felt when ending a life. Ember wasn't the only addict in this room. My heart wasn't racing from adrenaline and bloodshed; it was racing from the vigorous thrusting in Ember's slick pussy.

"Fuck," she mewled.

I felt her cunt start to get tighter, squeezing my dick, but she wasn't there yet. I curved one of my arms across her waist, causing her to shiver. I pulled back out, and my cock was fucking hard and wet with her arousal. I leaned down, moving her hair from her nape.

"Feel this..." I said softly as I kissed her temple, having no idea why I did that.

I wrapped her hair in one hand as I rose again and slammed into her at the same time as I pulled her hair. Ember screamed, her hands going to the bed and fisting the sheets. Her pussy started pulsating, her release taking me with her. She got off on the pain. It was like she was made just for me.

I collapsed on top of her, making sure I didn't put all my

weight on her. My heavy breathing mixed with her soft pants.

I reached for her arms and held them in mine. "No more scratching. I know you're stronger than you look."

Surprise flashed in her eyes, but she quickly masked it.

"So," she started to say, her voice sounding hoarse from the screaming. "You're just going to fuck me every time I have an itch?"

"I get to do whatever I want," I taunted. Then I rose up and turned her over so she could look at me.

Slowly I spread her legs. My release was all over her pussy. I brought two fingers to her center and moved them up to her clit. The action made Ember roll her hips. I traced my fingers up her stomach to the middle of her chest, trailing up the curve of her neck until I touched her lips.

"And you're going to let me," I told her as I pushed my fingers into the cavern of her mouth.

Ember didn't take her eyes off me as she sucked off our releases off my fingers.

"Because." I slowly pushed my fingers in deeper. "You're." She started to gag. I removed them, putting my hands on either side of her head. "As fucked up as I am."

When I kissed her, her arms wrapped around my head, and she pulled my hair. Her lips moved violently against mine as if she was trying to imprint herself into me.

Her hands were still in my hair when I pulled back.

"We're going on Friday," I said.

"You say it like you had more options," she smirked.

I cupped her pussy. "If I find out this cunt gets wet for someone other than me, princess—"

"You're what?" she said, licking her lips. "Going to kill me?"

There was nothing nice about the smile I gave her, and she knew it by the way her smirk disappeared.

"Oh, baby, that would just be mercy," I said as I leaned down to lick her lips and then bit her bottom one.

"I have to go out, but be good for Pam, and try not to kill each other," I told her as I got dressed.

Ember just rolled her eyes. She got up, cum dripping down her thighs, and I'm not going to lie and say it wasn't hot as fuck. It soothed the part of me that wanted to claim every inch of her. She went to my drawer, grabbed one of my shirts, and walked past me to the bathroom. She stopped before going inside, but ultimately walked in, slamming the door. The action had me grinning.

Ember

Focus your mind on something else.

I was sure the last thing Ren had in mind was to think of my father, but I couldn't help it. It was pretty pathetic because I was sure he wasn't even thinking of me. Yet I couldn't help but wonder what Silas was doing to him now that I wasn't near.

Was he losing his mind? Was it driving him mad? I hoped it did because that year with him had fucked me up, and I had no idea what I stood for. It was all fake bravado.

I didn't go downstairs while Ren was gone. Pam was a nasty bitch, and the farther I was from her, the better. One thing I was good at was reading people. It came with the territory of growing up in the spotlight. You tended to get a feel for leeches, and she reeked of one.

After my shower, I took a small nap. My body was weak, but getting stronger each day. Ren was right; I couldn't even take a good fucking without knocking out. Not that I'd called that a fucking. It was more like a freaking possession. I'd heard that bullshit of bodies becoming one. Something romantic, but Ren wanted to steal my soul, not have it given freely. My body was sore, and I bet if I looked at my hips, there would be small bruises shaped like Ren's fingerprints.

Once I was properly rested, I snooped around. He said not to kill Pam, but he never said anything about not going through his stuff. That's how I found a bag of weed and a bowl along with a lighter hidden under layers of clothes.

Jackpot.

When Ren walked in the door, I was in bed wearing one of his long-sleeves and boxers with the bowl to my mouth, and I was about to light it. He stopped at the door, his eyes trailing over my head down to my bare legs. His icy eyes glinted as he took off a pair of black leather gloves.

"You went through my shit," he said.

"If you didn't want me snooping, you should have let me go."

"Never," he said without missing a beat.

I looked away from him because his words didn't sound like a threat, but more like a vow. Instead, I focused on the inhale and exhale, something other than him. Ren was a force to be reckoned with. Sometimes it felt like I could take him in small doses, but the real him—the one he hid—was intense, and I was sure if he gave me all of him at once, I would suffocate.

He was raw power. He exuded confidence, and he knew what he wanted and how to get it. The problem was that I was what he wanted. I had already been the object of a madman's affection; I wasn't too keen on round two. Except Silas was nothing like Ren. He acquired by brute force while Ren waited patiently, and when he struck, he made me bend.

Violence changed us. For some, it made them cower, fear shadows and loud noises. To others like me, it made us crave violent things. It made us get sucked into other dark things so they hid where you'd already been. I gave my body to Ren so his possessive touch could overshadow Silas's.

I was about to exhale the smoke when Ren put his hands on either side of my head. He didn't say a word as he slowly brought his head down to mine. I thought he was going to kiss me, but he stopped just before our lips touched. His lips parted, and his head inclined a bit. As I looked at him, I exhaled the smoke into his mouth. Ren took the hit, and when he exhaled, he did it in my face, gently covering me in a cloud of smoke.

"How much do you know about your family's empire?" Ren asked.

Out of all the things I expected him to ask, this was not one of them. He extended his palm so I could give him the bowl. I did as he asked while I sat back, putting my knees to my chest. Remington's empire was something I didn't talk about often.

"I already told you my great-great—"

"I know about that and the struggles. What I want to know is why when I search your name, no mention of the scandal surrounding the Ember shows unless you look it up under the deep web. Someone wanted those files buried."

Like all empires, Remington Diamonds was also built on bloodshed.

"Those stories never made it out of South Africa." I gave him a look. "The locals still whisper amongst themselves, our history passed down like some legend. Our real last name is Redelinghuys, which is public knowledge. What is not public knowledge, or people don't like to talk about it, is the fact that when the company was founded, we had a business partner."

Ren sat on the bed. He then reached for me, turning me to face him, and made me straddle him. There was something about the way he commanded my body I found hard to resist.

"What happened to that partner?"

"He tried to claim the Ember as his own."

Ren's hand came to my face, grabbing a tendril of hair and twirling it in his fingers.

"What really happened?"

"My great-grandfather owned most of the machinery, the workers. He was funding everything when his business partner tried to claim ownership to a jewel he got from one of our mines."

"He killed him?"

"No, he stripped everything from him. He took back his company and made it into what it is today...his old business partner, he attempted to kill my great-grandfather."

"So, your great-grandfather killed him."

I shook my head. "Arrested. He later committed suicide."

Ren just looked at me.

"How does it feel to know your castles are built on pillars of lies and glass stained with blood?"

"It's all I've ever known," I said.

His eyes gave nothing away this time. His face was a stony mask. Sometimes he seemed so docile I forgot what lurked beneath.

"Is it easy?"

"What's easy?"

"Taking a life," I whispered.

"Are you asking if it's easy to kill or easy to live with that kill?"

When I didn't answer, he kept going.

"Killing is easy. It's everything that happens after that can fuck you up. Now it just feels like another score to my hit list." Ren put his thumb and finger to my chin. "I'm not a good guy, princess. I don't feel deeply. Emotions can be controlled, and everything is just a means to an end."

My belly dipped in disappointment. "Is that what I am? A means to an end?"

"You are a disaster I never saw coming," he said as he pushed me off him.

He turned off the light to the room when he walked out.

The days leading up to Friday came in a blur. Ren didn't stay with me in those days. I hadn't seen him at all since the day in my room. My door was locked, and food and water were brought to me by Pamela, who was no closer to liking me. If it weren't for her bringing me a bag with clothes, I wouldn't have known what day it was.

The dress was a coral color with spaghetti straps. It was skimpy and barely covered my ass. The material was cheap, and the heels looked like they belonged to a street hooker.

Fucking bitch.

I knew she did it on purpose, but my new mantra was getting me through the days. I didn't break for anyone. So I threw on the clothes and did my makeup. The girl staring back in the mirror was one I knew well. She was a liar, a pretender. She hid her sins in diamonds and covered her secrets with lies.

I was still looking at my reflection when Ren appeared. He stood at the entrance to the bathroom. His appearance took me back to our night in the maze. He wore all black like a boogeyman ready to come out and play. Our eyes met over the mirror. His jaw clenched as his eyes trailed over my body.

"You look like a whore."

"Guess your little bitch was trying to prove a point," I said.

"Let's go." He turned around without another word.

I followed him down the stairs, where I caught a glimpse of Pam. She wore a gorgeous red dress that was classy and nothing like the outfit she had thrown on me.

She wanted to prove a point, but I was not going to let her succeed.

Once we were at the door, Ren stood behind me, his lips by my ear. "Don't do anything stupid like trying to run."

The thought did cross my mind, but every time I thought of running, I got filled with dread. My only consolation was that as long as I was with Ren, Silas couldn't find me. We often fed ourselves excuses trying to hide the truths we were still too scared to admit, and I feared that was the path I was heading toward.

I sat in the back with Pam coming in next to me. Ren was at the wheel. Like I was dumb enough to jump out of a moving vehicle.

Zeke liked to have his parties on the docks. Drive by the harbor at night while everyone had a good time. Make sure his guests didn't go anywhere while he had his fun. We made it to the dock in no time. My door opened, and Ren was there holding his hand out for me.

It almost felt like old times.

A lifetime ago.

The sun was already setting, casting a glow over the water. I stopped for a second to take in the beauty of it all. Funny how you forgot about the little things, and when they smacked you in the face, they made you feel like everything you cared about before was stupid.

"Keep walking, bitch," Pam scoffed.

People were trying to get inside. We formed a line, Pam at my front and Ren at my back. I'd never been one for many friends, but for the last year, I wasn't seen at all. Not unless you counted my social media.

It was a gamble being here today, but most of these people didn't run in Silas's circles, so by the time he heard of my appearance here, it would be a long time from now.

I also couldn't forget the other reason I didn't care. He was over six feet and standing behind me. Ren scared me, he enraged me, but he also made me feel protected. It was weird and probably Stockholm syndrome, but I couldn't help the way I felt. I'd lied to the world, my family—hell, even myself. But this one thing I couldn't lie about.

He made me feel things I'd never felt. I wasn't talking about warm and fuzzy feelings, the stuff all the movies talked about. I was talking about feeling like you were drowning and gasping for air—the dread of falling into an endless abyss of the unknown.

Ren's arm snaked around my waist possessively. I felt the heat of his skin warm me. He pushed me back a bit so my body was flush with his. I didn't try to pull away or give a nasty remark. For the first time in a long time, I felt content.

"Remember what I told you," Ren whispered in my ear.

Before I could answer, he was pushing me forward. I was sandwiched between him and Pam.

The bitch turned back and game me a glare, which I returned. Her eyes then trailed to Ren and then to my hip, where Ren now had his hand rested. She gave us a scowl and looked away.

My breath hitched the moment he started to move his hand lower. I felt the calloused pads of his fingertips on my thigh. His arm went lower, then curved back to the hem of my dress. Since the dress was so short, as soon as he went higher, he made it to my ass.

"You look like a whore," he repeated harshly.

I didn't say anything since I'd had no choice in my outfit. Pam had given me a flimsy thong. One wrong move and people would see my ass. Not that I gave a shit.

"Should I act like one too?" I bit back.

Ren's other hand came to my throat, controlling the air I

breathed. His mouth was on my ear, nibbling. To outsiders looking in, it probably looked like two lovers embracing.

"Careful, princess." He squeezed my neck.

His other hand moved slowly until it traced the curve of my ass to my pussy. He glided two fingers past the cloth. I raised on my tiptoes from the sensation he was causing and felt myself growing wetter.

"This tight little pussy," he groaned as he reached my clit.

I moved my arms until I was holding on to the arm he had at my neck. My fingers dug into his shirt. My lip was between my teeth, trying to hold back a moan.

"Only gets wet for me."

He moved his fingers out after that. And I was left panting, loathing the way my body responded instantly for him.

It was one of my flaws to get off on things I shouldn't.

Ember

The line started moving, and Ren gave my butt a gentle tap so I would walk. He stopped altogether, and I missed the way his body felt against mine. The way I felt the heat he emitted, warming the coldest parts of me. Maybe I was stupid, and I was a pathetic little girl looking for the love she never got from her parents. Look at where that got me—in Silas's bed. Taking his so-called love at the cost of my dignity and tainting my body for something that wasn't even real.

"Your name?" a voice said.

I craned my neck to look past Pam at the man holding a clipboard. I pushed Pam aside, not caring if she fell off the yacht.

"Ember Remington." I said my name loud and proud even though I felt like a total fraud.

He gave a nod, motioning to the side. "Please wait here, Miss Remington."

I squared my shoulders and did as he asked. I knew Zeke would not have taken the humiliation lightly. He was a proud man. That's why I also knew while money was not something he wanted or needed, to have me at his mercy even for a night would be enough to soothe his bruised ego.

Men were predictable. You had to act weak so that they wouldn't feel threatened. As for women, they hid their intentions behind fake smiles and meaningless compliments.

I looked at my fingers, appearing bored. I was aware I

now had eyes on me, so I did what I'd always done and tuned everyone else out.

"People are staring," Pam said.

"Don't worry. They're not looking at you," I said without bothering to face her. "You're no one in my world."

"In my world, I could have you dead in—"

"That's enough, Pam," Ren cut her off.

I turned to face her then. She was hurt but quickly masked it.

I saw Zeke come our way with his security right behind him. He glared at Ren, obviously still remembering the humiliation.

"What the fuck are you doing here?" he spat.

I gave him a smile dipped in poison. "My board cut me off again, and I need some cash."

"I don't take charity." He dismissed it right away. "I want them escorted out, and teach him a lesson."

Zeke was about to turn around, but my words halted him.

"So, you're saying you don't want to fuck me?" My tone was bored.

When he didn't say anything else, I walked up to him, putting my hand to his chest. He watched me with avid interest. Slowly, I let my fingers trail up his chest. Since he wasn't much taller than me with heels on, I pressed up against him and then leaned into him so I could whisper in his ear.

"I want at the table today. I win, I get the cash. I lose…" I let the words hang in the air. "You get me."

I pulled back, looking up at him, hoping it had worked.

"Take them away. She can stay."

"Sorry. Then no deal." I shrugged it off like it was no big deal. "My dog goes where I go."

Zeke gritted his jaw for a second but ultimately nodded. "And who are you?"

Before I could speak, Pam was shaking his hand.

"Pamela Escalante." She spat my mother's name like it was nothing. "I'm Ember's cousin."

Someone tell me this bitch didn't take a name I hold sacred and turn it into a pawn in her game. She smiled at Zeke, and I watched as she charmed him and led him away from us.

"What did I say?" Ren barked out angrily behind me.

I turned around, hitting him in the chest. "Did you know she was going to use my mother's name?"

Something like surprise shone on his face. "No, and I don't care."

My heart skipped a beat. Not from elation or happiness but from a small stabbing pain. Of course he didn't care. I'd always been a pawn in someone's game. It'd been that way since I was fifteen, and it would probably continue to be that way for the rest of my life.

"And I don't care what you said either."

I tried to walk away, but Ren pulled me back. He dragged my arm and pushed me against the rails.

"What did you whisper in his ear?" Ren demanded. His tone was harsh, and his jaw was rigid.

"Are you...are you jealous?" The words left my lips before I could process them.

They were laced with hope. I'd been jealous before of the people who had mothers and fathers who doted on them, but never for someone of the opposite sex. And my feelings toward Pam were just that. I was jealous of her. Of the connection she had with Ren. At the fact that while I was imprisoned, he was with her. She had his respect, his trust, and I had scraps of him.

"No," Ren said, low but steady, and my stomach

dropped. Of course he didn't care. "Remember who owns you."

"Maybe you should remember that while there's a price on my head, the only person who owns me is Death."

I stepped away from him to find...I don't know. Fuck. Some drugs? It wouldn't be hard. Now that the thought crossed my mind, it didn't want to leave. Ren put an arm out to stop me, his fingers digging into my waist.

"Then, I guess I have to take care of that little problem, don't I?"

I shook my head. "I wasn't allowed to go anywhere last year. Whoever wants my head was the only one who noticed."

Once again, I tried to get away, but he stopped me. His finger came to my chin.

"That first picture in Abu Dhabi—I knew that wasn't you. You don't think I recognized your body after spending months with you?"

His voice was docile, a complete paradox to what was brewing behind his eyes. So intense and deadly, and I knew he was telling the truth.

He started to walk us with a hand at my waist, leading us through the mass of people.

Pam was nowhere to be seen, and it was probably a good thing since I was still pissed she'd used my family's last name. Some things were sacred and better left untouched. My last name was one of them.

"Ember, I knew it was never you, and I also knew that if I tied their hands, they would have to let you out sooner or later. So I sent a threat to headquarters with hopes they would let you out. The fact that you reached out, princess... that was just a bonus."

My chest rose and fell rapidly at his confession, and the

rest of the people ceased to exist. It was just me and his words. Out of everyone in the world, he was the only one who knew I was missing. I squashed whatever hope started to grow inside of me.

"To make me pay, right?" I gritted out.

I never forgot the words he said to me or the look of pure rage he gave me as he got pulled out of the maze. There was no hope hidden in his words. If anything, they were a warning that now more than ever, I should be cautious.

"Amongst other things," he mocked.

WHILE WE WAITED FOR THE GAMES TO BEGIN, WE MINGLED amongst the partygoers. Pam? Who the fuck knew where that bitch was? Ren stuck to my side like Velcro. Or maybe it was the other way around, since he had me tucked to his side. People looked, some waved, and I wondered what was going through their minds right now. They drank, got laid, went home, and did it all over again. No real purpose. That had been me too, and maybe that was why I wasn't a pawn. I had no real worth besides the one I was born with.

"I want to get a feel of the players," Ren said. "Let's walk around."

He started to lead me away, which made me roll my eyes. I didn't know why he bothered to ask me in the first place.

"How do you know who's playing?" I gave him a skeptical look.

Ren looked down at me, and something soft passed over his features. He was always serious or angry; sometimes, he was yelling at me, so I was used to his harshness. With this look, he looked more attainable, not so out of reach. He looked normal, and not like he might one day end up killing me.

Ren didn't say anything, but he moved my body so I was right in front of him, my back to his front. His hand came to my belly, holding me in place while his chin dropped to my shoulder. I didn't dare look at him. My heart was pounding in my chest, and it had nothing to do with the state of my sobriety. Rough and calloused touches, I was used to—I'd lived with them—but softness was something foreign. I could count on my fingers the number of times I'd been touched with affection. Half of those touches were calculation dipped in softness.

I was only human, and I was starved for affection. I lapped at any I got. It didn't matter where it came from because I couldn't help it—that sick need to feel loved. As thoughts started to make their way inside my head, Ren interrupted them by speaking.

"You can tell who comes to a party like this to play, who comes to score, and who comes to get laid."

He gently moved my head to the side, where there was a group of guys sitting down, white powder all over the table, with girls hanging off their arms.

"They provide the drugs, and the chicks provide their bodies."

He then turned me to look at the end of the bar where some people were drinking, their eyes lazily scanning their surroundings.

"They came for the game. Drinking because it's a party, but nothing too strong to keep a level head."

Then he moved my face to the makeshift dance floor.

"Most of them are here for something to do. Another party to make them forget about their pathetic lives."

I didn't know if the last part was a dig at me or not. "Why do you want to watch them?"

"You learn a lot about a person by observing them. I'm good at calling people's bluffs, but a little reckoning won't hurt."

I turned my head to look at him. He was right there, so close that all I had to do was lean into him and I could kiss him. Except I couldn't, not really. Every kiss we'd shared was taken or given in anger or a haze of lust. Lips bruising and smashing, seeking dominance, not affection.

"You're really good at it, aren't you?" I found myself asking.

"Good at what, princess?"

It seemed like he leaned even closer, and I felt like I had a lump in my throat, making it hard to swallow or breathe.

"Making you shiver?" His tone was smoky and dark, full of wicked promises that were to come. A small smirk graced his face when my body did as he asked. "Getting your pussy wet for me? You get so fucking soaked for me, I slip right in."

I wasn't the only one affected by his words. The fingers at my hips were now digging painfully as his grip on me turned possessive. That small bite of pain kept me center and leveled.

"Making you come?" Ren's voice turned low and harsh, like it cost him as much to speak as it was costing me to breathe. "Every time I sink myself inside you, Ember, you let out a needy fucking moan. It drives me fucking insane. It's like you've been waiting all day to feel me inside you. When you come, baby...*fuck,* your cunt grips me like it never wants to let go."

I was a mess in his arms. I gave up the pretense that I didn't want him, like I didn't need him, and let go. I let my back fall on his for support because my legs were getting ready to give up on me. The first thing I felt was Ren's hard dick digging into my backside.

"I hate that all these fuckers are looking at you right now. Like they think they have a shot at you. The only way anyone is getting you out of my arms is if they kill me, and I have no intention of that happening."

At that moment, after those words, I knew Ren Falcon was lethal to me. Not because he had no problem staining his hands in blood, and lying or cheating to get what he wanted. He was deadly to me because he made me feel the way I currently felt about drugs. He made my heart race, my palms sweat; he took me high, and when he was done with me, the crash—that, I would never survive.

Before I could panic and lash out at him or do anything to protect myself, we got interrupted.

"Ember. Long time, no see." I swung my head to where Pricilla stood.

She was smiling at me. Not all that fake but not entirely there. Her eyes were glazed, and the pupils enlarged. She was one of the "friends" Ren referred to as coke sluts.

"Hey," I said in return, not really feeling like talking, but also not wanting to look at Ren.

"You want to go have some fun with me?" She tried to grab my hand and lead me God knows where to shoot up, but I didn't want to go.

I felt Ren stiffen behind me, but I ignored him. "Thank you, but I'm good."

Pricilla shrugged it off and walked away. I waited for Ren's taunt to come, but it never happened. Instead, I felt him get closer, his presence like a magnet begging me to give in and get lost in his darkness. Let myself hide there. His touch had never been so soft nor gentle. The feel of his mouth on my forehead was like a stroke of a feather. I closed my eyes, almost pretending like it wasn't happening.

"Don't you two look cozy." Pam's bitter words broke the moment, and I was glad for it. She stood in front of us, glaring our way.

Ren didn't let go of me, but he did stand taller. His hold on me eased a bit but not by much. "Have to make all these fuckers want her if we want a chance to make enough for the fight."

Ren's words were like a knife to my chest.

Sharp.

Acute.

Penetrating.

Reminding me of my place with him.

I didn't break. If I didn't break for Silas, I wouldn't break for him.

"I'm sure I've fucked some of them already, and all of them drilled into me like they were mining for diamonds," I spat at him, pulling out of his hold and closer to Pam.

"Puta." She grinned at me sweetly.

I smiled right back and spoke loud enough for Ren to hear us. "You're not missing much with Ren. It's a hit or miss with him."

Before either could say anything, an announcement was made to go to the top where the game was going to be played. I walked in front of Pam, following the rest of the people who were going to the top, noticing that the men's eyes kept coming my way.

Ren's words and Pam's disappearance made all the sense in the world. My offer to sleep with Zeke was not exclusive to just him. I was fair game for everyone. More bets, more money for Ren.

I was foolish for believing the words he was giving me.

Since I was a child, that had been my weakness. Licking of every scrap of affection, I could find and clawing at it, trying to keep it by my side.

You couldn't keep things that weren't meant for you. Sooner or later they would find a way to escape and be free. I did it with Silas, and now I had to learn that lesson myself.

As I got to the first step to go to the next level of the yacht, I was yanked back by my hair. I whimpered at the tingling burn I felt in my head. Fire—it felt like I had a fire in my head.

"If I were you, Ember, I'd tread real careful while we're up there," Ren growled in my ear.

"Or what? You'll kill me?"

"I'll show you how much I don't miss and drill into your cunt in front of everyone in the room. Show them that I was the one who got the diamond."

My chest was rising and falling by the time he let go of my head. He kept his hold on me as we walked to the top. Before we walked onto the top level, I asked him a question I feared asking. One, because I didn't know what the truth of it would mean, or two, he could be lying to me.

"If you lose, what happens?"

He stopped and looked at me. I always felt so small under the weight of his scrutiny. I was the rich one, the one who had power, but he always made me feel so insignificant, like I was wasting my life away.

His fingers came to my chin. Not harsh, not too soft, but with enough pressure to take him seriously. "Not going to lose."

"You don't know that," I whispered.

"Then I'll kill everyone in this room."

And I knew he meant every word. Maybe he wasn't just a reaper. Maybe, just maybe, he was my angel of death.

Ren

My words shocked Ember—hell, they shocked me too. I'd rather die trying to kill every fucker than watch someone else who wasn't me leave with Ember.

Her words from earlier didn't hurt. I didn't spend all this time with her without learning about her. She was proud, and when backed in a corner, she looked for weakness and attacked. She was a ruthless little thing, and it didn't disgust me as much as I pretended it did. So, no, her words didn't hurt, but they made my blood boil. It was a feeling I never knew nor had time for, but I was now becoming intimately acquainted with.

Jealousy didn't belong in my type of work. Being jealous made you weak. It made the object of said jealousy a target. I told myself that Ember already had a target on her back, so whatever I did wouldn't be much of a difference.

They led us to the chairs starting out at small tables, knocking out the competition one by one. I went to one and Pamela to another. Double our chances at a big winning.

Ember was about to take a seat next to me when I held on to her hand. She looked at it and at me like it burned. As if my touch was causing her pain. My mind immediately went to the night I brought her with me, the first night of withdrawals, and my jaw clenched.

"You're sitting in my lap, princess." I spread my legs,

guiding her to sit on my left side. "Seats are only for the players."

She snorted but did as I said. "I'm sure I could stand behind you."

"I want you right here with me."

"Of course you do," she sassed.

What she didn't know was that the meaning I had behind it was not the one she was thinking about.

Ember had gotten us through the door, but it was up to Pam and me to do the rest, or I'd lose Ember, and I wasn't ready for that. I moved my knee up and added pressure on Ember's waist to bring her body down to grind on my thigh as I put my cut on the table. Poker was all about skill, reading people, and maybe just a little bit of luck.

"You play?" I softly asked Ember as our table started to fill out.

When she started to shake her head, I moved my knee, bouncing it a bit.

"I don't have the patience for these types of games."

She was not the patient type; of that, I was more than aware.

"I'll teach you," I told her.

Pam had worked her charisma voodoo on Zeke and made him think it was his idea that Ember would be part of the grand prize. Not just for him, but everyone. If he didn't win her, there would be more of a chance that I didn't either. This provided more of a distraction for us to earn more money and not have him bitter. The fight was next week, and I needed in on it.

This game needed to be over so we could move on to higher-paying games. A grand was nothing out of all the cash I needed to score.

When I moved to put more chips in, I moved my leg

again and inwardly smirked at the way Ember trembled in my lap.

"Stop moving," she hissed.

I put my nose to her hair, inhaling her, and it smelled all wrong. She no longer smelled like mint, but like generic men's soap, and I didn't like it.

It wasn't her smell.

Pressing my mouth to her nape, I smiled. "Did I *miss* something?"

She stiffened, but didn't say anything. The game kept going, I stopped moving, and that made Ember relax. It got to the point where her head rested on my chest and one of her arms was wrapped around my waist.

"That looks like a shitty hand," she whispered as her hand came to the cards I held.

Her being like this with me, it fucked with my game, my plans, and my head, but damn if I wanted her anywhere else. She didn't notice the effect she had on men—hell, bitches too. She was a diamond in the rough. Sounded stupid to say, but despite everything, she still shone. Jealous stares came from all around us. Ember didn't notice them, and I ignored them. Looking at us now made winning her much sweeter, but I wasn't lying. I would kill everyone or die trying before I let someone else touch her.

Sitting up, I moved my knee again, and this time, Ember glared at me.

"Not shitty if we use it right."

I shifted again, and I felt Ember grind down on my leg.

"Stop."

"What?"

She attempted to look mad but was fighting a smile.

"Full house." I set my cards on the table, still playing weak but not enough to get out of the game.

This time when I moved, I felt Ember's wetness meet my knee.

About damn time.

"Ren," she hissed again.

I waited to get my new cards before I answered her.

"Princess, I'm trying to *hit* this game right."

"Just. Stop."

"Stop what? Rubbing my leg against your wet pussy? You think I should see if I hit or miss in front of all these people?" With my hand to her waist, I moved her again, and this time she let out a small barely there moan. "Before the night is over, you'll be begging me to come."

Her breathing was shallow. "It was a joke."

"I'm not laughing."

I didn't know why I underestimated her. It was like she lived to be challenged. She didn't run scared or cower. She faced it, even if she knew she wouldn't win. Ember leaned on the table as she discreetly rolled her hips.

If I was fighting my dick not to stir to like I was, I was losing the game now.

"Here, let's start kicking ass," I said as I pulled Ember back and sat her between my legs so she could feel me.

She squirmed, and then she did it again, taunting me.

"The faster I get this money, the sooner I can get you home."

Ember turned her head, her eyes staring right at me. She didn't let me see it often, but she was scared right now, and she was vulnerable for me. She was always so strong; this look hit me in the gut.

"Ren..."

I gulped. "Yeah?"

"Don't lose."

My hand came to her cheek. "Never."

Once the word was out, I couldn't take it back. I didn't think, I just spoke, and it was the most real I had ever been with her, and with myself, but I knew it was true.

Ember gave me a nod, then fixed herself on my thigh, her head resting on my chest, and watched me play until it came down to a few players.

Pam was done playing. She was holding on to Zeke's hand and laughing and smiling at all his words as if he were doing a comedy special.

"Last game of the night." The dealer got working on the deck of cards. He then proceeded to lay out the rules and winnings. "Miss Ember, will you please stand up?"

My face stayed impassive as everyone's eyes came to Ember. She turned to look at me, and I nodded. It was all the reassurance she needed. Years of not feeling shit came in handy when I wanted to jump and break everyone who salivated at the sight of Ember. She did a twirl, showing the players the goods, then came to sit down.

"Saw you in Bali a few months ago." One of the guys spoke, his voice directed at Ember. "Called your name, but you never turned."

Ember went stiff at his question. Like me, she wondered if he'd also noticed that wasn't her.

"Sorry, I don't speak to strangers."

Another guy chuckled. "You just fuck them."

"I always wanted to see if her pussy was made of diamonds," someone else added.

Hypocrisy was real. I hated all these men talking down to Ember like this, but somehow it felt okay when I did it, because deep down, I was in awe of her.

"Everything you are thinking about her…" I let my words trail off as I put in my cut for this game, knowing we were one step closer to getting out of here and could afford the cut for the fight. "She's so much better."

Some men chuckled; others were already starting to undress her mentally. Ember's penetrative gaze came toward me, but I couldn't look at her right now. Not when the words I had just said were so much more than sex.

"Well, I can't wait to have your bitch riding my dick tonight, Falcon."

That English accent put every cell in my body on high alert. Everyone knew that the most crucial part of a plan was the unknown. Nothing was ever set in stone, variables were to be expected, but a wildcard fucked you over. My body went stiff, and the only one who noticed was Ember. She soothingly patted my leg.

I was so caught up with Ember, I never saw him play. My head turned slightly to where Pam held on to Zeke and noticed the bitch didn't look at all surprised. I watched with keen eyes as Gideon took the empty seat that was across from me.

In my business, you tended to know everyone or at least had heard of them, and Gideon was someone I knew. He had a fondness for knives like I did. Where I liked to keep it clean and dry, Gideon made art with blood. He was too wild to be tamed. He wasn't just lethal because he could kill a person; he was lethal because he wasn't afraid. He got hired to do some of the most dangerous jobs. He was the person you wanted on your team if you were to do a suicide mission. The fucker never died.

The unhinged look was still in his amber eyes. In a lot of ways, we were similar, both light-skinned with light hair. Where I was a bit more muscular, he was leaner. He wore a suit. You could barely see the tattoos on his neck, but the ones on his hands and knuckles were visible.

In our profession, tattoos made us stand out or traceable if shit ever hit the fan. It was also pride and arrogance that led us to get some, proving to the world we fucked the system and we wouldn't get caught.

"You're a little far from home, G." I gritted my teeth.

The bastard smiled at me. "Missed me, mate?"

Then his eyes went to Ember. Not like everyone else in the room. Not with lust, but with calculation.

"Don't worry, sweetheart. I'm one hell of a ride."

When he winked at her, I reminded myself to take deep breaths. As the game went on, I held on to Ember a little closer and tighter. She didn't say anything; she just leaned back into me like she wanted me to shelter her from the world. For the first time all night, I didn't think I could.

Between me and G, it was hard to tell who would survive.

The more players that folded, the more I regarded Gideon. My mouth made it to Ember's head, kissing her, but I don't know if I was reassuring her or myself. People were starting to leave now that the yacht had made it to the harbor. The game players who lost would begin to leave, and then it would take off again until dawn, and everyone looking to fuck and party would remain.

"Ren," Ember whispered. "I'm scared."

Her words killed me.

I knew it wasn't easy for her to admit. She was proud, and we'd been playing this game for a long time, but I think we both were getting tired of it. She felt like mine, like nothing in this life ever had. I'd grown up in the streets, never having anything to call my own. She'd grown up with everything, but never given her whole self to anyone. Yet here we were. She knew who I was and burrowed closer to me, finding beauty in my shadows. I liked her wickedness, thrived in making it come out. She was a jewel to the whole world, and I was the only one who got all of her.

The dealer looked at me, silently asking if I folded. My eyes stayed on Gideon's; he didn't fold either. I could taste the anguish in the room. It was evident Gideon and I knew each other. I didn't have to turn back to look at Zeke and Pam to know both of them were eager to see who would win.

"Straight flush." I put my card on the table, feeling confident when Gideon leaned back his shoulder and slumped. Ember took a relieved breath.

Gideon jumped up with a smirk on his face, and I felt like I got sucker punched.

"Royal flush, Falcon." He winked at me. "Must be the British in me."

Zeke started to hoot, and Pam was nowhere in sight.

"Take your prize," Zeke said. I was about to get up to get Ember when hands came at me, pushing me down. Zeke's guard from earlier was holding me down to the chair while another ripped Ember out of my arms.

"Don't. Touch. Her." An animalistic growl left my mouth.

"Ren!" Ember screamed, trying to pry herself out of his hold.

Her eyes were coming to me, begging me to save her. I'd never felt more helpless than I did at this moment.

"Mates, not cool." Gideon strolled without a care to where the guards held Ember. "Didn't anyone tell you how to treat a lady? Whore, prostitute, virgin, prude, all the same."

He then pulled his winnings, looking at me and then at Zeke. "Thank you for your hospitality. It was a pleasure playing with you all, but I won't be needing this. Fucking this cold bastard over is more than enough for me."

He walked to the guards. "Come on, love. I have plans for you."

I watched as the guards let her go, and Gideon put a hand to Ember's mouth, stopping her from talking shit to him.

"I would appreciate it if you gave me a five-minute window getting out of here."

"My pleasure." Zeke toasted.

My eyes met Ember's through the sea of people. They begged me to save her. Before I could call out her name, my head was bashed into the poker table, making everything spin.

Ember

Since I was little, I'd learned to master my poker face. I might be in pain and dying inside, but I didn't want the world to know it. Fear was something I could control. I remembered my father sitting me down to talk to me. I was so excited that day; I thought he'd finally taken an interest in me and my hobbies. He wanted to know what I was like as a person and not just the fact that I was his daughter. I was naïve. My father treated me like another business meeting, starting with how had I been to asking about the weather, then gave me some "this is not easy to say, blah, blah" bullshit.

Someone wanted him dead.

Relief—I remembered feeling relived. As if that would make my father want to keep me close and love me.

So, I learned to live with death as a shadow.

Now, pain was another story. I was practically born with it. I tended to put things in nice little boxes in my mind and store them away and pretend they weren't happening or hadn't happened. My time with Silas was in them.

Now all of those emotions I'd neglected and diminished were pouring out of every cell of my body.

The hands that held me were all wrong. They were strong, but not protective. The mouth that kept me from screaming bloody murder was rough and cold, not warm and teasing. My eyes found Ren, and he had a murderous look in his eyes.

"Time for us to go," Gideon said.

Not like I had a choice. Gideon started to drag me out of the boat, which wasn't all that hard since I was basically skin and bones.

His tatted hand still covered my mouth. Since he'd gotten to the room, I knew he and Ren didn't have the best of relationships. I'd been around Ren, and nothing fazed him, but the moment Gideon spoke, he froze.

He was handsome.

Tall, fair, with a youthfulness to his face that no one would dare call babyish by the wicked glint in his gaze. Whiskey eyes that drowned you, and tattoos peeking from his neck and on his hands. There was also something dark and alluring about him. With Ren, it was controlled; you saw it lurking behind his gaze. With Gideon, it was all around him. Pure controlled chaos.

The hand that was on my mouth was the one that had a tattoo so meticulously done. It looked like his bones were over the flesh. The other one had a cracked crown, and on his knuckles, he had tattooed the word *mad* with an anarchy symbol.

As he dragged me away, I realized two things.

The first thing was that I was afraid. I had nothing to my name, no means to survive, and I'd rather be dead than run back to my castle. Not when Silas was currently king. Now I knew that since the moment Ren had taken me, I wasn't afraid, not really. A part of me didn't worry about what happened next—he was there, and he would make everything else fade, and he had.

The second was that I was in pain. The thought of never seeing Ren again made me feel ill. All my life, things had been ripped away from me, without a chance to say goodbye, and now it was happening with him.

No one seemed to care as I got dragged away. The people from the game knew I was being "collected," and everyone down on the lower level was too wrapped up in their own fucked-up states to care.

That was the problem with the world nowadays. No one gave a shit unless it affected them somehow. I was not their problem, so they pretended not to see me.

When we got off the boat, Gideon dragged me into a dark corner. He slammed me to the wall, and with his hand on my mouth, he held me there. With his other hand, he pointed at me.

I wasn't going to break. It had become my personal mantra over the past year.

"Listen, sweetheart," he said with that accent of his. "Things can be easy, but if you make this hard, you will regret it."

When I didn't answer, he took his hand from my mouth. I stared into his whiskey eyes, not knowing what he wanted from me. I knew lust made men fall to their knees like it was a sport, and there was none of that in his gaze.

"Let me go."

He smiled, making his face morph from lethal to docile in a second. Something was not right with him.

"Sorry, sweetheart, I need Falcon, and the only way he will cooper—"

I stopped listening to him and moved to try to get away. I would not be a pawn in his game. Someone always wanted something from me, and I was tired of it. My body shook, trying to get away from his hold, when he grabbed me by the throat, slamming back. I was panting, and he didn't look fazed.

"You..." I managed to get out. "Want..." My throat was on

fire; it was like drinking cheap vodka straight from the bottle. "The...reward."

It was hard to cough as he just held me and cocked his head to the side.

"Money, I have in spades."

His answer did nothing to make me feel better. If anything, he was more dangerous. Which meant he wasn't after me—he was after Ren. I wanted to protect him, which was illogical because I couldn't even defend myself.

I thrashed again, and this time I really pissed Gideon off.

"Hard way it is," he stated.

He then removed his arm, and as I took my first full breath, feeling the burn in my lungs, I felt a cold blade at my throat. With Ren, I was never afraid. If anything, I wanted to push him to see how far he would take things. Now here with Gideon, I was scared.

"Look, I don't want to hurt you. I really don't, but if you become a pain in my arse, I will."

"Then hurt me." I seethed as I pressed my neck closer to his blade. I stayed silent as I felt the edge penetrate my skin.

"Fuck, you're crazy," Gideon said with amusement.

He removed the blade, and then his hand came to my chin, forcing me to look up. My scalp dug into the concrete behind me, and my hair was pulled, causing pain from all directions.

Warm wet heat glided across my throat, licking away the blood spilled. My heart sped up and not from repulsion. When Gideon was done, he yanked my head back down.

Once again, he regarded me with a look. He reached for my hair, feeling it between the tips of his fingers. I could have sworn he said "petals," but I wasn't sure.

"You remind me of someone."

Falcon's Prey

I stayed quiet. His interest was starting to freak me out.

"And now I know Falcon will be fucking pissed at me."

He smiled. Like a psychotic full-on grin that made him look devilish, but boy, was he handsome.

"No more games."

His face became stony in an instant, and he put both hands to my neck. I thrashed, trying to get away, feeling myself losing the battle as he held on to my pressure points.

"Plea…" The words died in my mouth.

I passed out.

◆

Ren

My ribs were somewhat bruised, I could already tell, and this royally fucked me over for the fight coming up. The fuckers fought dirty and wouldn't let me take a shot. This wasn't the first time I'd gotten my ass beat, but it was the first time in a long time. I'd tried to protect myself the best I could and I hoped that was fucking enough.

Once Zeke was content, he had his guards throw me off the yacht. When my body landed in the water, it took all the effort I had to swim out of the cold water.

"Fuck," I gritted out as I pulled myself out.

"Jesus Christ, Ren." Pam's voice came from the shadows. She was now changed into jeans with a backpack on her shoulders.

"Get the fuck away before I wring your neck," I spat at her as I got my wet body onto the pier.

"What the hell, Ren!" she shouted.

I glared at her to stop before she got us unwanted attention.

"We were a team, and then that stupid little bitch comes along and you act pussy-whipped."

Ignoring what she was saying, I grabbed her arm and dragged her away. "Did you or did you not know G was here?"

Her silence was more than enough answer.

"Listen, Pam—"

She pulled out of my hold. "No, you listen. Ever since you brought that bitch to our place, you act like our ass is not on the line."

She had a point.

"How are you supposed to go into the ring like this?" She gestured to my body. I could taste the blood on my busted lip. "I get that I fucked up, but I wanted better for us, Ren. Now don't throw all that away because of some rich bitch who wouldn't waste a second and dump your ass as soon as she gets back on her throne."

I ignored Pamela. I followed her to the car, where she threw the backpack in the back seat.

As soon as I was in the car, I punched the dashboard in frustration.

"Fuck!" I ran my hand through my hair. "Do you have any idea where he's staying?"

Pam shook her head like I knew she would. Gideon was ex-MI6. If he didn't want to be found, he wouldn't. And I was sure the fucker wanted something from me.

"Fuck," I groaned again.

"Do you think they sent him?"

In my head, I tried to go over G's tattoos, but the fucker was covered; it was no use. My days had been numbered since the day after the gala, and I knew it. So did Pam. There were no such things as coincidence in this world.

"Let's go back to the house."

"What happens if you can't find her?" Pam asked.

I turned to look at her as she drove. The weight of my stare pinned her down.

"You don't want to find out."

Ember

The strong smell of alcohol lured me awake. My head felt fuzzy. At least this time it didn't hurt.

"Come on, sweet cheeks. Time to wakey, wakey." The English accent was by my ear, and I felt something—or rather, some*one*—patting my cheeks...and not the ones on my face.

"Stop touching me," I mumbled.

My throat was on fire, mixed with the smell of alcohol. I sat up, coughing up half a lung.

"Shit. I should probably give you some water."

I was gasping for air when a water bottle made its way to my hand. I drank some too fast, and it made me sputter. Once I got my cough and myself under control, I noticed my surroundings. I was in the back of a car. It was dark outside, and I had no idea where we were or if we were even in the state anymore.

"Aw, you're awake." Gideon opened the door to the back seat, smiling at me like he hadn't kidnapped me or choked me until I passed out. "Come on. Let's go before Falcon levels the whole city."

My mind was still a little messed up from the lack of oxygen, so I didn't pay attention to what Gideon was saying. He grabbed my arm and pulled me out of the car. Once I was out, he patted my head, trying to fix my hair, and pulled my dress down so it covered my ass.

"I think I made Falcon suffer enough. I was going to

make him think I took you on a happy, bouncy ride, but if he's mad, he won't listen to me."

What. The. Hell?

I closed my eyes, trying hard to make sense of this guy. He was...there was no word to describe him.

"He won't like that you took me, though," I said.

Gideon put a hand on my shoulder and gently squeezed. "You see, that's where I have my advantage. While Falcon has some sort of code, I sure as fuck don't. It's a dog-eat-dog world, and don't take this the wrong way, but you were just a means to an end. Nothing personal."

Seriously? Nothing personal?

"I hope he kills you," I spat at him as he dragged me across the street.

"I can see the appeal," he muttered with amusement.

Luckily for me, I didn't have to ask for him to elaborate, because he did it on his own.

"Men like us, we don't do easy. There's strength, then there's forged-in-fire strong. We tend to go for the second choice. Your skin is unmarred, pristine—bet it drives him crazy."

I gulped, and I wondered if that was why he was always pulling his scalpel on me.

"Is that what you like?"

"Broken petals and thorns don't scare me. I'll take a body full of scars any day."

Having no idea what that meant, I kept my mouth shut. That was, until I noticed we were at the front of the building Ren and Pam called home.

"Mate!" Gideon shouted as he knocked.

He was certified crazy. There was no doubt in my mind.

"I've found what you lost!"

"Found? You fucking stole me!"

"Technically, I wo—"

As soon as the door opened, Ren aimed his gun at Gideon, and Gideon aimed his at my head.

"Come on, mate. You wouldn't shoot a friend?" Gideon smirked.

"A friend, no. You, I'd have no problem."

Then Ren turned to me, his eyes frozen like the artic. They raked from the top of my head to the bottom of my shoes. He was hurt. That was the first thing I noticed about him. He had changed into jeans and a black T-shirt. His lip was busted, and his hands had cuts on them. They had hurt him.

"You fuck him?"

"You did not just say that to me!" I shouted, pissed that I'd noticed he'd been hurt and he wanted to know if I fucked someone else. I lifted my neck to show him the cut that still burned. "Does this look like we had a grand time? The asshole cut me, then licked me."

One second Ren was still pointing his gun at Gideon, the next he was in front, punching him. When Gideon dropped, I ran into Ren's arms. The first thing that hit me was his smell. I had never had anyone hug me and make me feel like I was home when I was with them, but the way I felt right now in Ren's arms...it felt like finally having a place to call home. His arms wrapped tight around me, pulling me close to his body, and it wasn't enough. I wanted him to crush me into him to make it hurt so I knew it was real.

The way he held me, I knew he cared. I'd known he cared for a long time. I just didn't want to admit it, and neither did he. You couldn't block the sun with a finger, and what we felt for each other was inevitable.

"Fuck, mate. I licked her neck, not her pussy."

Ren went stiff, and I knew he didn't like any part of that

sentence. My heart was beating like crazy as I reached to his face and forced him to look at me. I'd never cared about anyone enough to show them that they meant something to me. Everyone always made the first move, and I made the last one, usually by leaving and never speaking to them again.

I guided his face down to mine, and I kissed him. It was the first time I'd ever kissed someone when sex was not on the table. It was a desperate kiss, burning me from within and consuming my soul. He was like water, food, and air, everything I needed to survive. I may have started it, but Ren took full control. His hand came to the back of my head, holding in me in place as his lips bruised against mine, making the cut on his lip open up. He made it hurt so I knew it was real, because pain was the only thing that left a lasting effect that served as a reminder that you didn't imagine it.

"Ren," I said against his lips.

Pam appeared at the entrance. "Can we take this inside before you idiots cause the cops to stop and ask what's going on?"

"Pamela. Long time no see." Gideon winked.

Ren led me inside the warehouse. As soon as we walked through the door, he turned to Gideon.

"Weapons." He nodded toward a table that was nearby.

Gideon did as Ren asked and started by putting two guns on the table, followed by the knife that was at my neck earlier. He also moved his jacket and pulled out a small needle with a clear liquid.

"Is that T?" Pam asked in fascination.

I wanted to know what T was, but the reality of what kind of mess I was in was now starting to sink in. I mean, I knew Ren was dangerous, but he actually killed people. He hung out with men who carried weapons all the time.

"Are you okay, princess?" Ren whispered in my ear, but his eyes hadn't left Gideon because he was a threat.

I thought about his question before I decided that I was okay. I didn't care what Ren did for a living. I didn't care that what we had had started out as a lie. What mattered was that I wasn't his to protect anymore, and he still wanted to do it.

I'd never had that before, and it was an addictive feeling.

Once Gideon had taken off all his weapons and, for some reason, his jacket, we went to sit down.

"What do you want, G?" Ren asked as he pulled me to his lap.

"Heard about your audition."

Ren went still. "Go wait in the room, Ember."

He was hiding something from me. Fuck that—I wasn't going into the room.

"No," I told him.

"Ember," he stressed.

"What are you hiding?"

"There are things—"

I cut him off. "Someone has wanted me dead for years. I know you aren't exactly Mr. Nice Guy, and this isn't the committee for world peace, so I'm staying. Besides, you didn't get your stupid money for the fight."

"You're going into the ring?" Gideon asked.

Ren ignored everything and stood up, taking me with him.

"Are you with them?" He leveled Gideon with a look.

"The vote to join has to be unanimous. I ruffled some petals, so I don't see that changing anytime soon."

"It's feathers," I told him.

"Oh no, it was most definitely petals."

"I'm fucking wiped. We can talk about this tomorrow morning?" Ren said.

"Aw are we having a slumber party? Wait, we're too old. It's called an orgy now," Gideon quipped.

Ren shook his head, but didn't bother to respond him again. We took the stairs up, and I noticed how sluggish Ren was walking.

"Are you in pain?" I asked once we were in the room.

Ren looked at me first with confusion, but it slowly morphed into awe.

"Am I in pain?" he asked, dumbfounded.

"They hurt you," I whispered.

"Baby, you were kidnapped." His hand came to my face, cupping it.

I would never admit it aloud, but I liked the way he called me baby. He didn't do it often, but when he did, there was a softness to it that calmed me.

"You lost…"

Ren sighed, then sat on the edge of the bed. It took me no time to realize how much things had changed between us. If you had told me a year ago that Ren and I would be here like this, I would have laughed. Darkness always called to darkness, and mine loved his.

"There's a hit on mine and Pam's heads," he started by saying.

I gasped, surprised because that's the last thing I thought he would have told me.

"I shouldn't be telling you any of this, but I figured there's a lot of lies between us." He ran a hand through his face, looking tired. "I wasn't completely honest with you the other day." My stomach filled with dread, and I felt like I wanted to throw up. "You weren't the only reason I wanted to come work for Remington's. I was never supposed to be your guard. I didn't expect you to ditch your old one as quickly. Make no mistake, Ember—I would have still found a way to get you beneath me, but that wasn't my priority. My life and Pam's were. There's an organization, and when you audition for them, you give them what you promised, or they put a price on your life for making them waste your time."

"What are you saying?" I whispered.

"Princess, you're not stupid," Ren answered back just as softly.

I wasn't stupid, but I needed to hear him say it.

"It was a heist to clear your vault to get enough cash to pay back the organization so they wouldn't come after us."

I shook my head, letting his words sink in. I always knew there were secrets he hid, and it made sense.

"This is why you haven't killed me." I looked down at the floor because I couldn't look at him and see that everything that had happened these past few days was a lie to him. "You still need me."

My back hit the door hard. Ren was pissed; his blue eyes had gone inky. His hand was at my throat, and with his thumb he caressed where Gideon had cut me.

"Don't," he growled. "Don't try to twist some bullshit in your head."

I huffed. "You said I would pay. You still need me—"

He bent his head so that we could see eye to eye. The warmth of his face on my cheeks provided a false sense of security.

"That's right, princess. I need you. I crave you. I fucking *want* you. You got under my fucking skin, and I can't make you go away...and I know I got under yours."

Ember

My mouth stayed shut because I couldn't deny it.

"I was so fucking furious at you that day in the maze, but one thing became clear. You were mine, and no one was going to take you away from me. Here you are. You know who I am, and you know what I do, and you still let me into your body. You don't give a shit that I've killed, and you don't give a shit that I will probably do it again. You're as fucked up as I am, Ember, and you want to be owned by me. You want that sense of belonging to someone. For someone to give a fuck whether you live or die, and that someone is me, princess."

I was panting now at his words; they tugged at every emotion I had. Emotions I rarely felt because feelings made you weak and vulnerable.

"I've never been scared before, Ember. When you live by the sword, you die by it too, so I've always known my end would be bloody. But today, the moment they ripped you from my arms, I was afraid. I was afraid to lose you. I was never going to kill you, Ember. I was going to keep you."

It wasn't a declaration of love, far from it.

It was a declaration of want.

He wanted me, flaws and all.

"What happens now?"

Ren put his lips on my own and made a vow. "We find a way not to die."

We were so different yet the same, both of us with a price on our heads, but could we really defy death?

"As much as I love your fucking mouth, when we're out there..." He pointed outside the door. "...keep your mouth shut. When we're alone, you can bitch as much as you want. When we have company, you don't say anything that makes me look weak."

"Seriously?"

"I don't joke about your safety," he deadpanned. "Did he touch you?"

"No, Ren. I didn't fuck him." I pushed him away from me.

"That's not what I asked." Ren was angry again. "Did he hurt you somewhere I can't see?"

My heart broke in places I didn't know it was capable of breaking. What would Ren think of me if he knew what Silas did to me?

"I'm going to take a quick shower." Ren walked away, not waiting for my answer.

I watched him leave and processed everything that had happened. We were both fucked up, and that made us perfect for each other. I could never be with a spineless socialite who enjoyed wasting Daddy's money. That wasn't me. I didn't know a lot about myself, but I did know that I wanted Ren, and I was going to ride this wave until it came to an end. People always abandoned me, so I squared my shoulders. When and if he left me, I would survive that too.

I opened the door to the shower. Steam poured out, and Ren was under the spray, head bowed, but as soon as he saw me walking in, he turned his face toward me. No words were spoken as I closed the door behind me. Not as I removed the heels, the stupid dress, and the thong. I let it all drop to the floor, along with my caution and sanity.

The first thing I said when I stepped in the shower was, "He didn't hurt me... The only person I want touching me is—"

The words died as he pulled me by the back of my head, bringing me to him. The water was too hot, burning my skin, but I didn't feel it, not when all I focused on was his kiss.

"All I've known is hell, but I find heaven in your lips," he told me in a husky tone.

I knew people did stupid things for a pretty face, but they also did them for pretty words. Ren meant them—I knew he did. He was beaten because of me. He was willing to defy death for me. I gulped, and then I dropped to my knees in front of him.

If his gaze was intense before, it was nothing like how he was looking at me now, and there was no ice in his gaze. I was sure the world could come to blows around us and we would be lost in each other.

Ren looked down on me; the water made his hair look darker, beads all over his chest running down his abs. I could see bruises starting to form, and I wanted to make him feel better. He grabbed his dick. It was long, almost angry-looking, the tip leaking with precum, and he stroked it twice.

"Suck, princess," he demanded as his hand came to my hair and gently tugged my head back.

When I opened my mouth, he slowly started thrusting into my lips. I greedily took everything he gave me and asked for more. Being on your knees was supposed to be a sign of submission, but being on my knees for Ren didn't feel like that at all. Being on my knees for someone like him was a sign of power. He trusted me enough not to hurt him while he fed me his dick.

My hands came to his thighs, holding him in place as I took him deeper. I'd never been so turned on while sucking dick. My lips wrapped around him, sucking as the water fell on my back. I grabbed Ren's ass and pulled him toward me, and I gagged. Ren's hold on my hair got tighter, his head tipped back as his chest rose and fell. Between my legs, I felt needy and started to move my hips, trying to find relief, but I didn't want to stop touching him to please myself.

My nails dug into Ren's ass when I pushed him some more so I could deep-throat him. My mouth felt so full, my lips stretched a little too much, and my eyes watered, but when he cursed and he started thrusting furiously against me, it made it all worth it.

He fisted my hair, holding me in place as he fucked my mouth hard. I gagged and moaned, and it wasn't sexy, but it was perfect. Then I felt it, the way his dick started to twitch and spurts of his release shot inside and out of my mouth, dripping down my chin. As he began to pull out of me, I still sucked him, taking every last drop.

"Fuck." He groaned softly as he looked down at me with a tender look in his eyes.

Ren helped me up. With his thumb, he removed cum from the corner of my lips and brought it to my mouth, where I sucked it off.

"Who does your pussy get wet for?" he asked.

"You."

He hummed his approval.

We finished the rest of the shower quietly as he massaged my hair with his shampoo and lathered my body with soap. My body was in front of his as he moved both hands to cup my breasts, pinching and pulling my nipples. Then as he held my waist, his other hand came down between my legs. He moved his fingers over my slit slowly, teasingly. His mouth came to my neck, licking the water, then kissing until he started to suck my skin.

My hips moved against his hands as I moaned, "You're hurt."

He spoke against my neck; the movement of his lips caused me to shiver. "A little pain won't stop me from owning you."

I moaned when he inserted two fingers inside of me.

Ren cursed. "Fuck, right there. *That* little noise."

His fingers kept moving in and out, and then he traced them to my clit, where he gently rubbed it. I threw my hand up, grabbing hair, needing something else to hold on to.

It had never been like this—an all-consuming need to be devoured. Silas wanted to own me, but he never did. It was all about him and never about me. With Ren, even when we didn't want it, I came first. My health, my safety—I was important.

"I'm going to own all of you," Ren vowed. "I'm going to fuck this pretty little mouth." He ran his fingers across my lips. "Destroy this tight little pussy." His hand glided down to cup me between my legs, stroking my clit lightly, making me dizzy.

By the time I felt his finger in my other entrance, I froze. I remembered the pain that came the last time I was taken there.

"One day, I'm going to own this too."

He added slight pressure from his thumb as he kissed my cheek softly. I closed my eyes tightly, trying to prevent my mind from going *there*. Ren removed his hand from my ass and brought both to my waist. He peppered more kisses on my cheeks until I opened my eyes again. When I did, I felt calm. He wasn't going there today, but one day, and maybe one day I'd be ready, because I would love for him to erase everywhere Silas had ever been.

Ren turned off the water. He grabbed my hand and led me out of the shower. It was at that moment that I let everything go—who I was, who I had been. His hands were stained with murder, yet I trusted them completely. It might be stupid to follow the devil, but he was once an angel too.

"Get on the bed and spread your legs." He gave me a push.

I saw him wince a bit as he followed behind me. I wasn't going to ask him to take it easy because that wasn't the kind of man he was. He had a point to prove, and a little pain wouldn't prevent him from doing so.

Once I was on the bed, I spread my legs. I ran my hands from my breast down to my navel, then between my thighs. I could hear him breathing heavily.

"Play with your cunt," he rasped, his eyes were at my sex.

He bit his lip as I used two fingers to tease my folds, my clit, then when I inserted them, he hummed his approval. The fact that he was watching me made it all that much hotter.

I started to grind my hips against my fingers, when Ren snatched my hand away, holding on to my wrist with a vice-like grip. He looked like a bull ready to strike, his eyes with a hint of maniac in them. He brought my wrist to his mouth, licking the side of my fingers, then the rest before he put them in his mouth.

"I've never eaten this much pussy in my life," he admitted before he threw my legs over his shoulder.

He gave a slow stroke from my entrance to my clit. Then he let the tip of his tongue circle my little bundle of nerves. My stomach felt like a coil, so strung out, ready to come apart at any moment. My hand went to his hair, softly running my fingers through his scalp. Ren kissed me down there tenderly, then gave me lashes of his wicked tongue.

"*Oh, fuck, Ren,*" I screeched when he nibbled on my clit.

His teeth gently pulling at it felt divine. I was so close already. I only needed a little more and I would go off like a bullet. I felt Ren smiling between my legs. His mouth moved to the apex of my thighs, where he sucked on the skin. I never knew that could feel so good. Once he was happy, he did the same to the other side, all while I felt like I was burning up. My clit throbbed and my pussy convulsed, tired of being on edge.

"*Ren please,*" I begged.

He let out a dark chuckle. With his thumbs, he parted my folds. I looked down at him as he blew on my clit. The air was cool, a delicious combination utterly different from how I was feeling. My head thrashed back, and I moved my hips only to hump air.

Ren kneeled on top of me, his lips glistening. "Sorry, princess, guess it was a *miss*."

I needed to come, like, yesterday.

"I was jealous, okay?" I gritted out.

That seemed to please him because he gave me half a smile. God, was he gorgeous. He was always so dark, but when he let some of his light shine, it was special. It was more special because when he was soft, it was with me.

Ren didn't say anything; he bent his head, kissing my navel, then licked all the way up to between my breasts. My chest was rising and falling like I had run a marathon.

"My cock only grows hard for you, Ember." He raised his head, making eye contact with me.

He was so honest and real that every word was like ambrosia feeding my malnourished soul. Where I showed weakness, he showed strength; where I was incredibly human, he was merciless and unforgiving.

"Please," I begged again. "Your ribs."

"There is no pleasure without a little pain," he hissed.

Ren's mouth landed on my chest, kissing and sucking as he pinched one of my nipples. He did the same with the other one. I was too lost in the sensation, I missed him pulling something from the drawer. Ren licked on my nipples, then sucked and bit them, each time adding more pressure to the point my hands were on his back scratching and asking for more.

Only when I was squirming and begging for him to let me come did he stop paying attention to my breasts.

"Did I still miss?" he mocked.

Before I could respond, I felt a cool, prickling sensation over my hard nipples. It hurt like little knives, but it also felt good against all the tension that had gathered there. Ren did it again and again on both nipples until I screeched from frustration. My wetness coated my thighs from being on the edge for so long. Ren bent his head again, slowly licking my nipple, then biting it hard. I felt a spasm go over my body, but it wasn't enough for me to come. I wanted it—no, I *needed* it, as much as I needed to breathe. There was a thin line between pain and insanity, and I was on it.

I rose on my elbows, aggravated. In Ren's hand was a black pinwheel that looked scary as fuck—I was going to ignore that for now.

"If you don't make me come, I swear to God I will go find G—"

My words were cut off when Ren slammed me back down on the bed with a hand on my throat. His eyes burned with jealousy just at the mention of another man's name. *Good.*

His mouth hovered by mine. "The only dick you'll ever be getting is mine."

He slammed into me, and I let out a relieved scream. My hands came to his back every time he thrust his hips, and my nails scratched his skin. His body weight was near suffocating, but it still wasn't close enough. His mouth was on my neck, licking, biting, and sucking. I met him thrust for thrust. The only sounds in the room were our labored breaths, the brutal sounds our bodies were making. People thought making love was supposed to be docile, sweet, and slow, but vicious worked just as well. Violent things took passion. I'm talking about scratching so deep you pull skin, biting because you don't know whether to moan or scream. Feeling like you are trying to claw out of your skin to be born again.

Ren pulled out and then slammed back in. I was sure I drew blood when I dug my nails into him as I screamed my release. The orgasm tore through me, destroying me, making me lose a part of my soul in the process.

This wasn't sex. It was something else, something unexplainable. Something so dark, yet so pure, that it scared you.

Ren

VIOLENT DELIGHTS MET VIOLENT ENDS, AND I FEARED THAT was where Ember and I were headed if I didn't get a handle on our situations. My ribs were on fire the next morning when I woke up sore as fuck, but luckily not broken. Pressed against my chest was Ember's head. I breathed through the pain I felt today, but fuck, was it worth it. *She* was worth it.

I wasn't the type of guy to care for a woman. I'd never even loved one. But what I felt for Ember, I couldn't describe. It was intense, dangerous, cruel, but it calmed me. She roared louder than my demons. She was like stars in my dark sky.

Right after we fucked, Ember knocked out. I stood there smoking some weed to dull the pain and just watched her.

What we did wasn't sex or making love. It was a fucking possession. It was a union of souls, handing over everything I stood for and now standing for her. Slowly I removed her from my body, careful not to wake her, gritting my teeth because it was causing my ribs pain.

Showering was a pain, so was changing. As for Ember, she slept through it all. I went out of my room, knowing Gideon would be awake already.

"Morning, mate," he greeted me with a smile as he drank black coffee.

"What do you want, G?"

"Shit, not even because you got laid last night are you mellow. You need to cheer up and stop being such an arsehole." He took another sip. "Kinda regret not collecting my winnings. That scream...I thought you were tearing her in half."

He sighed. I was losing my patience.

"Gideon," I warned.

"They will be sending a message soon."

He didn't have to say who they were. I already knew. I'd been waiting for this message. I didn't know if it would be a bullet coming from the back or the front.

"When they do, I need to send a little message of my own."

"Who do they send to deliver a message?" I prodded.

I knew next to nothing about the organization. The operations weren't stateside, so G heard more about it.

"Their executioner, which leads me to what I want."

I went to the fridge, taking items out to make some breakfast for Ember. "Okay, but first, I need you for two things."

"Falcon, you're not in a position to make demands. I didn't have to bring your plaything back to you."

I continued to make food without facing him. "You want something bad enough that you got on a plane and flew across the world to get it. I'll do it, no questions asked...I'll even let you do the torturing."

This time I did turn to see he was contemplating it. He gave me a brief nod to keep going.

"One, I want you at the fight. Something goes wrong, I need you to come back and get her out of here, set her up, and make her disappear."

"You like this one, don't you? You never cared about Pam that way."

I went on, ignoring his Pam comment. "Second, we need to give a little house visit."

"Those are my favorite kind. Should I go dig up my tool kit?"

"I'm sure what you have with you is more than enough." This last request was somewhat of a push. "You still have contacts in government?"

"Yes," he answered tentatively.

"Can you get me anything and everything on Silas Remington?"

Gideon smiled a different time of smile than the one he had earlier, not playful—this was full of sadistic enjoyment. "If you're doing what I think you're doing, that's fucking cruel."

"Just get me the information, and I will pass along the message."

"Deal," he agreed.

He took the plate I handed him and started to eat. I went back to the room to find an empty bed.

So much for this breakfast-in-bed bullshit.

Setting the plate down, I headed to the bathroom door that was ajar. Ember stood wrapped in a towel, looking at herself in the mirror. Her neck was purple and red all over.

"Morning." I leaned against the door smirking at her. She looked fucking beautiful, a choker of my creation on her neck on top of her breast.

She looked at me through the mirror, and I didn't know if she was happy or sad. Slowly, she turned around and opened the towel. There were little scratches on her nipples from the pinwheel, hickeys going down her navel and the apex of her thighs, and bruises from my fingers on her wrist, legs, and hips. My dick grew hard at the sight. Last night she took everything, silently asking for more.

"You look incredibly gorgeous," I said, leaving all pretense that she didn't affect me.

Ember closed the towel again and made her way to me. When she was in front of me, she got on her tiptoes and kissed me.

Her kiss was timid, insecure. Nothing like her.

"What's wrong?" I asked.

"I don't know. I've never felt like this before. So content with myself. I feel like something is going to happen to fuck it all up."

I wrapped one of my hands across her waist. "Not if I can help it."

"You didn't even get the money for that fight." She looked so worried, what had happened to her wasn't even on her mind.

As she finished drying, I went to the drawer, pulling out a pair of sweatpants and a T-shirt for her to wear. I needed to get her clothes.

"We got the money," I told her.

She gave me a skeptical look as she reached for the clothing.

"I knew Zeke was never going to let me keep the money I won. So while I made slow bets, Pam was working the room. It's why we stayed on the same table the whole night. Make him think I was too cocky, too sure, and let the game come to me, while Pam got everything we needed. In the end, I guess we should thank G. He offered a distraction, and Pam slipped right out."

She opened her mouth, then closed it right away.

"Having G threw me off a bit. They got me before I could get us out of there."

She was quiet as she dressed. While she did that, I went

to the bed and pulled the mattress up and reached for the object I had stored there a year ago.

"You can't hide things from me. Everyone always lies thinking I'm too dumb to handle it or it doesn't concern me. My life is in the balance here too, and I think that deserves full transparency."

"Ember, you're not going to die. I'll make sure of that."

Even if it was the last thing I did. Maybe she was some sort of fucked-up redemption to even the scales.

"No secrets," I lied.

There were some things I wouldn't tell her, not when knowing could put her in harm's way. I walked up to the edge of the bed and sat down, giving my muscles some relief.

"How are your ribs?" she asked as soon as she same me wincing.

"Okay, for now. Pam wrapped them earlier." It was hard to hold my laugh at her murderous glare when I mentioned Pam's name.

"How nice of her," Ember mumbled.

"Would it make you feel better to know that while she wrapped me, she saw how fucking scratched my back was and the bite marks you left on my shoulders?"

Ember's face lit up with a wicked smile. My back had burned when I'd taken a hot shower. I wasn't the only one inflicting pain last night.

"It does make me feel a little better. But next time, I can do it."

"You know how to wrap a rib?" I raised my eyebrow at her.

"No, but you do. You can teach me." She smiled at me, but it wasn't sweet. It was a warning.

I reached out for her, bringing her body between my legs.

"I need to do some things with Gideon, so I won't be around much. It should take one or two days, but I'll make sure you're taken care of."

I grabbed the plate of food that was next to me and handed it to her. It was nothing special, just a breakfast sandwich since I noticed she was fond of them.

"What am I supposed to do? Just stay here and listen to Pam call me names? It's starting to feel like I'm a prisoner."

Slowly I got up, my hand going to her nape. She had yet to notice I clutched her diamonds in them. I brought my other hand around and put the choker on her neck. I heard her small surprised gasp, but ignored it as I worked the clasp.

"You didn't get rid of it…"

"It was the only thing of you I had," I confessed.

"Okay. I'll stay, but I want to go to the fight."

"Ember." Like hell if I would bring her with me.

"No, don't. I've been a prisoner all last year. I couldn't fucking leave anywhere. I hated it, Ren. I hated every fucking second I was trapped. You do that to me, and I swear to God, I'll find a way to leave you too."

"Like hell you are." I seethed. "You leave, Ember, and I swear I will drag your ass out of whatever hole you try to crawl under."

"Then, I guess you're taking me." The little bitch smiled at me as she took a bite of her sandwich.

I ran my hand through my hair as I went for the door. Maybe now was not the best time to tell Ember that if we didn't get answers, our lives would be lived in hiding. Just as I stepped through the threshold, Ember slipped her delicate small hand in mine. I didn't turn back to look at her but gripped her a little tighter.

"It smells like sex down here." Ember scrunched her nose as we made it to the foyer.

Gideon was leaning on the couch in just his jeans. "Is there any part of your body that wasn't claimed?"

"Probably about as much of your skin that doesn't have tattoos," Ember bit back.

"So, tell me. How does an heiress end up with *him*?" G pointed a finger at me.

"He got kinda obsessed with me and sought me out," Ember said as she sat down across from Gideon.

I sat next to her, then brought her to my lap.

"You're trouble. I like you," he told her, then turned to me. "I'll get my shit and we can go."

I needed to get my shit too.

Ember turned around, gently straddling me. "Thank you."

She leaned down to kiss my lips with soft, unhurried strokes.

"I'm going to fix everything," I said.

The smile faded from her face, and I saw it clear as day the shadows that hid in her gaze. "Not everything can be fixed."

I sure as hell was willing to die trying.

When Gideon came out, I gave Ember a quick kiss. "Left you something in the drawer."

I walked out the door without looking back.

◆

"So the rumors are true? The enforcer is a woman?" I

asked Gideon as we waited across the street in front of Remington's headquarters.

"Don't underestimate the bitch. She's like snow: beautiful, but cold."

When we left the house, the first thing we did was find a bookie with intel so I could go in the ring. After that, we came to the headquarters.

"I want you to go to the reception."

"Why?"

I ignored Gideon and kept going. "You'll like Clare. She's your type."

"Oh, so you know my type?"

"Pretty, nice body with a pussy is your type," I replied. "I want you to ask about Ember. Say you're an old friend and it's been a minute since you've seen her. If you see her, get on the phone or send a text, excuse yourself, and meet me where I told you."

Gideon got up. "Is there anything else you need me to do? Take you on a date? Buy you dinner? Suck your dick?"

"How the fuck are you still alive?"

"Don't know, mate."

Gideon was gone for ten minutes before he came out. He didn't come straight to me; he wasn't stupid. He disappeared into the crowd. No less than two minutes later, bodyguards from Silas's personal guard were outside and looking for him. At five minutes, Silas came out pissed as hell and went straight into his car. I got in my car and followed him, trusting that Gideon would know what to do on his own.

Silas made a stop at Ember's place. He got out, slamming the door and rushing inside. I waited about twenty minutes for him to come out, looking not much better than when he went in. I waited for him to leave, trying not to gloat at the fact that Gio was nowhere to be seen. Revenge was good.

Half an hour later, I found myself across town. I grabbed my black cap and put it on as I went to the doctor's office. The place was fancy, with two people waiting in white chairs. I made my way to the desk and asked for Dr. Wozniak.

"I'm sorry," the frigid receptionist said. "He's not taking new patients right now."

"I work for the Remingtons," I spat at her.

Her eyes widened, and she got up and went in search of the doctor. A few minutes later, the old man came out, his eyes wildly scanning the room.

"Doc," I greeted, tipping my head back so he could see my face. When his eyes widened in recognition, I stepped closer. "Can we take this somewhere more private?"

He nodded and led me to the back toward his office.

I took a seat in a chair without him having to tell me and removed my cap. "Why aren't you calling the cops?"

The doctor did have the decency to look scared in my presence, but he still opened his mouth.

"I don't believe you raped Ember."

"Yeah, I don't believe I did either." I sighed.

"I know you helped her escape." His eyes danced with fear.

"Ember is safe; she's with me."

"I...I don't understand."

"You don't have to understand. I need you to tell me everything about that family and everything you've heard and/or know. I also want to know how Michael is doing, and here's a list of things I need from you." I pulled a paper from my back pocket and gave it to him.

I stayed with him for about twenty minutes before reminding him that I would be back tomorrow for the things I requested.

Ren

THE SUN WAS STARTING TO SET BY THE TIME I GOT IN MY CAR. The drive was going to be long, and dark would settle when I arrived at my destination. Gideon was already waiting for me at a park across from a posh community.

"According to what Pam told me, he should be coming this way for a quick jog," he told me, taking a hit of his joint and passing it to me.

I took a hit and waited. He always came like clockwork. Habits were a good thing to have unless you fucked over someone like me that could use them to exploit you.

Five minutes later, I saw a lone man coming, a slow jog getting his body warmed up. I smiled to myself, my blood humming with revenge and thirst coursing through my veins.

"Showtime," I mumbled.

Gideon stayed back as I stepped out of the shadows. I was wearing all black and had my leather gloves on because one could never be too careful. The man was getting closer, and just as he was going to pass me, I greeted him.

"Hello, Mattias."

He stopped dead when he saw my face. He recognized me right away, or he knew more than he let on.

"Y-y-you."

"Come on, let's have a quick chat," I said—it sounded almost nice.

Mattias, however, started to walk back. The pussy was scared. He didn't get very far, because in a second, Gideon was coming behind him, holding a gun to his back.

"Let's go for a quick drive, mate."

Mattias looked around, hoping for someone to save him. People rarely gave a shit about others; no one would be saving him tonight. He got in the back of the car with G while I got in the driver's seat, and as soon as he was in, Gideon put a handkerchief with chloroform on his nose, knocking him out cold. The drive went fast since it was nighttime.

We drove to the shady side of town, where it was full of warehouses. We drove past the ones that were in use, coming to a halt to one that had not seen use in the last three years.

I had scouted this area in the last year, keeping this place in mind to start my revenge. Unfortunately, I'd had to take a step back on Mattias so I could rest, but watching Gideon have fun with him was somewhat worth it.

Between me and G, we carried Mattias to the warehouse. We sat him on the lone chair as we bound his hands and tied his legs together. Uncapping the water bottle I'd brought from the car, I poured it on Mattias's face. He came conscious with a gasp only to be met with water.

I fed off the fear in his eyes. There was something so enticing about how the human body responded to that specific emotion. It was almost the same as it responded to being excited or aroused. Dilated pupils, racing heart, labored breathing, and feeling like your skin was on fire, and you wanted to get out of it.

"You like your life, Mattias?" I asked.

"I have money…" he started to say right away.

Rich prick. They were all the same. They thought that pouring some money on it would make their problems go away.

"Is he calling us broke?" G sounded offended. "Are you broke, mate? 'Cause I'm not."

"It's not about money. You can keep your money." I took a step toward him until I was in front of him and he was looking up at me. "I'm not wearing a mask."

He understood the meaning of my words. When you were kidnapped in hopes of getting cash from you, your kidnappers were masked to keep their identities hidden. I wasn't hiding shit.

I stepped back and gave a nod so G could do his thing. The fucker looked happy like a kid at the park, ready to let loose. He circled Mattias's chair, smiling at him until he walked behind him and held a knife to his throat.

The stench of piss hit the air.

"Fuck, you didn't even last, dick." Gideon groaned. "He pissed himself so soon."

"W-w-what do-do y-y-you w-w- want?"

"Why didn't you give Ember her inheritance?"

"S-s-she's reckless."

"G" was all I said, and he pressed the blade harder enough to pierce the skin.

"Why did you keep cutting Ember off?"

"I-I-I just handle t-t-the accounts. It's my job to make sure she's responsible."

"Do it," I instructed.

Gideon removed the blade he had against Mattias's throat and brought it down to his thigh, making Mattias's screams echo through the warehouse.

"How much pain you get is up to you. Keep lying to me,

and next, you'll find out how it feels to have a knife wedged in your elbow socket."

Gideon gently massaged Mattias's shoulders. "I'm all for you lying again."

Shaking my head, I ignored him.

"Why didn't you want Ember to have control of her money?"

"I-I-I d-d-didn't care. S-s-Si-Silas was the one who told me to do it."

The answer didn't surprise me in the least, but it just added fuel to the burning rage I felt toward him.

"Why?"

"I don't know." Mattias sobbed like a little bitch.

Walking up to him, I grabbed the hilt of the knife, and I twisted it slowly in a clockwise motion as he howled in pain. Blood had already soaked through his pants.

"He'll kill me..."

Mattias spat.

Ignoring the pain in my ribs, I hunched over so I could look him in the eyes. "Do you think I'm stupid? I saw the way you looked at her at that board meeting. You loathe her. Now, I don't know if it's jealousy that a spoiled little bitch has more money than you'll ever have with your fancy degrees. So, you probably got off on cutting her off every time Silas snapped his fingers at you to do so... Now tell me why he voted for her not to get her inheritance."

I believed Silas had something on him. He got control of the board, and I wouldn't have put it past him to play dirty. The only mistake Mattias had made was being more scared of Silas than me.

"Take it out," I instructed.

Gideon added pressure on the knife, then pulled it out, leaving a bloody mess in the process. "Six to eight hours.

That's how long it'll take for you to bleed out. Now, I have no problem leaving you here. Have your throat burn as you yell for help while no one hears your pleas. Or I can drop your ass off the hospital; just tell me what I want to know."

Letting out a defeated sigh, Mattias started to speak. "She was supposed to get her inheritance at twenty-five unless she wasn't ready...but at thirty, she is set to inherit everything. Her grandfather left it all to her."

Gideon let out a slow whistle. I never knew I could be so furious on someone else's behalf, but I felt like I was ready to breathe fire. They treated Ember like a child, a prisoner, and she was going to own all their asses.

"Is there a way for Silas to get it all?"

"O-o-only i-if she dies."

Like I would let that happen.

I got closer again and patted his cheek. "Now that wasn't so hard, was it?"

"Please, please don't kill me."

"This is what's going to happen..."

Mattias hung on to every word I said.

"I'm going to drop your miserable ass at the hospital. Now, if you get any funny ideas of reporting us to the cops..."

I nodded to Gideon, who came to stand in front of Mattias again. From his back pocket, he pulled out a picture of his wife and daughter.

"They look like my type, don't they?" G asked me.

"Sure do."

"I like fucking my victims before I kill them. A nasty little habit, but you know how it is, right?"

Mattias was sobbing again. "Please don't hurt them. I won't say anything."

"I know you won't...but just in case, remember that if

you do speak, what we did to you is a dream compared to what we will do to them."

His eyes widened, and despite the fear and the pain, he got my message loud and clear.

"Can I do it now?" G seemed excited.

"Make it quick."

He took the bloody knife and pressed it to Mattias's pinky, and he cut off the tip. Mattias's sobs made the warehouse tremble; he sobbed so loud that he passed out.

"Do you want to keep this?" Gideon asked me as he held up the piece of meat in his hands.

"No."

"I'll throw it in the river." He shrugged it off.

We carried Mattias back to the car, knowing we still had a few hours before he bled out.

While Gideon waited for me, I brought bleach and poured it all over the floor, washing away any of Mattias's DNA. Once that was done, I got in the car, and we drove to the seediest part of town and dropped Mattias off in the first empty space we found. As I drove away, Gideon called 9-1-1 from his burner phone.

Dawn was beginning to break by the time I was ready to drive back home. I still had a few things to get before I went back to Ember.

THE COFFEE SHOP WAS BUSY THIS TIME OF THE MORNING. I found the doctor shuffled in the same booth Ember had been when she was here.

"Did you get what I asked for?"

The doctor jumped at my voice. He sat a little straighter upon seeing me.

"Can I speak to her?" He held on to a black bag

"No, but only because it's not safe. I assume you know about the predicament she's in?"

The doctor nodded. "I've been with the Remingtons since Michael was a teenager. I saw to him, his parents, and when Silas came along, him briefly."

"Why do you say it like that?"

"He was an angry boy. I suggested therapy, which Mr. Remington did, but there was nothing wrong. It was as if Silas tried to be the opposite of what I suggested was wrong with him."

I bit my tongue so I wouldn't ask the question that was on the tip of my tongue.

"I'll get her out of this alive," I assured him since I could see he was fond of her.

Ember had a way of drawing you in, and once you were in, you didn't want to leave.

The doctor handed me the bag. He looked like he wanted to say more, so I waited him out, staring him down.

"Be careful. Silas was enraged when he heard that you took Ember. He wants you dead."

"How do you know?"

"Michael stays in her room. He misses her, and that's where his at-home care is set up. On the day of the parade, he came to the penthouse to work out his anger on Michael."

Processing the words, I nodded to the doctor and said goodbye. Before I left, I ordered Ember some food. When I got to the car, Gideon was bitching I didn't get him anything, so we had to make another detour.

By the time I got back to the house, I was tired and my chest on fire.

"Whose house is this anyway?" he asked.

"An acquaintance I do business for. He lives in San Francisco."

The guy was a lawyer with some shady dealings. He usually contacted Pam or me to get the information he couldn't always get on his own. Not without arousing suspicion. When we came over here, I told him I wouldn't be around, and he offered his place. I knew he would cash in on this favor when it was convenient for him.

The house was quiet when we walked in. Usually, Pam was up earlier and Ember was probably in the room sulking. I went to the kitchen and grabbed two garbage bags—one for me and the other for Gideon.

"What the hell happened to you?" Gideon mocked as we walked into the living room where Pam was seated watching television.

Her nose was busted, and I knew exactly who did that.

"Next time she touches me, I'll kill her," she spat.

"Come on, Pamela, you can help me shower." Gideon pulled Pam off the sofa and took her away before I could tell her that if she ever hurt Ember, I would kill her.

Slowly I opened the door the room in case Ember was sleeping so I wouldn't wake her. She wasn't sleeping; she was sitting crossed-legged on the bed with a notepad and pen and with papers all around her.

I knew she heard me because she kept sketching, only this time more furiously.

"No good morning?" I said sarcastically as I walked closer to the bed, picking up one of the discarded papers.

The sketch was flawless, the way she sketched the shadows. In the center was a ring focusing on the diamond in the middle. The rest of the page had the same ring, just smaller, all from a different point of view showcasing all the attributes. I picked up another page, and it was much the same with necklaces, bracelets, earrings, and more rings.

"These are amazing." My tone was gruff.

"As amazing as it was for Pam when you fucked her," she bit back.

Seriously? This was what the broken nose was all about? I was not in the mood for this shit. I threw the bag the doctor had given me on the bed next to her and left the food and drink for her on the side table, then walked to the bathroom without a word.

I was putting my clothes in the bag when Ember walked in holding her fancy shampoo bottles close to her chest. She stopped when she saw me. Not because I was naked, but because blood covered parts of my skin.

"You got me my stuff," she whispered.

"Missed your smell."

She took a deep breath, clutching the bottles to her chest. She was trying hard not to break. She didn't want me to see how much this meant to her.

"I know you said the 'who' didn't' matter to you as long as you got paid, but did they deserve it?"

I did this for free and would do it again in a heartbeat.

"Yeah, Ember, he did."

When I got in the shower, she got in with me. Her hand came to my back, tracing the wounds I had received on her behalf. She kissed the hole where the bullet had pierced skin. I might have been pissed as hell with her and had wanted to see her pay, but that all changed the moment I saw her in real pain. We didn't speak any words, not when she cleaned the blood off my skin. Not when I used her minty shampoo on her. There was nothing sexual in what we did, yet it was the most intimate I'd ever been.

"I'm fucking whipped." I broke the silence as we were drying. "I need to sleep."

Ember stayed behind, drying her hair as I got into bed. I carefully picked up her sketches and put them on the chair. Once I was lying down, Ember came out, slipped into one of my shirts, and got on the bed with me.

"I couldn't sleep without you here," she confessed.

It was fucked-up that she didn't run scared of me. But I fucking liked that.

I cupped her cheek and kissed her lips slowly. Something sweet, so I could savor it later. Then I brought her down to my side so I could let my chest rest. After I woke, I would redo the wraps. Right now, I was too fucking tired.

"I was her first," I said.

She froze.

"It didn't mean shit to me. No one ever has...until you. I did it because it was either me, who didn't give a shit, or someone who would want to take it from her savagely."

We didn't grow up in a good place, so taking away the appeal of her virginity only protected her some.

"Well, if she ever talks about fucking you again, I will most likely kill her, and you are going to help me get rid of her body if you want me to fuck you ever again."

My body shook when I began to laugh. Ember turned around so fast, looking at me in awe, and her face had gone soft. I brought her down to my chest, ignoring the pain, and we went to sleep.

Ember

The days leading up to the fight, the place felt tense. Everyone was on edge, and I got the feeling I was missing something, but I didn't know what.

Things between Ren and I had changed. We weren't soft like other couples because that wasn't who we were, but there was an intensity that wasn't there before. Every touch was heightened; every kiss was deeper; every word he said held more meaning. Because Ren knew actions spoke louder than words, and they had.

I was mad the day he left, hearing Pam tell me that she'd been with him. I wasn't stupid. I was a far cry from a virgin, and I knew he'd had his fair share of women before me. I understood sex: the feeling of being wanted for a few hours, then being discarded and forgotten the next day. So it struck a chord in my insecurities. Pam had slept with Ren, and they were still together. It made me feel like I was a distraction, something temporary, and Pam would be his forever. Then it got me thinking that I probably didn't have forever. Sooner or later, my luck would run out and the walls I'd built around my castle would come crumbling down.

Pam could tell I got upset. When she told me how good it felt when Ren fucked her, I punched that bitch hard. It made her fall. She tried to come at me, but I pulled out the scalpel Ren left by our bed.

Our bed.

Where he fucked me last night.

I looked at Pam and saw jealousy soar in her eyes.

"Stay away from me," I spat.

I wasn't going to tell her to stay away from Ren; that wasn't the kind of woman I was. Telling her to stay away from Ren made me feel weak, so I'd rather not say anything at all. She could keep her memories while I got the real thing. On my way to my room, I grabbed a notebook she had been using and her pen and closed my door.

I couldn't remember when the last time I had sketched. It was something that would bring me temporary joy when I was little. One of my early memories was showing my father my designs. As I got older, I doodled my dreams for the company, knowing no one would ever see them.

That day, I drew out of anger and despair. I was feeling so hopeless and scared. It wasn't even about Silas that day; it was about the things that were happening with Ren. The way he made me feel like I was so incredibly alive one second and like I was drowning the next.

Still, I missed him. It was irrational and stupid, but I couldn't sleep without him. Since I was free of Silas, he was always there. Even when he wasn't staying with me, he was in the same house. In ways, he reminded me of Silas. He had a lot of the qualities I'd once found attractive in my dear ol' uncle. Ruthlessness, unapologetic, headstrong, but where Silas made me feel like I was shit, Ren made me feel like it was okay...like I was fine to keep being me.

By the time Ren got home, I was tired of letting my mind wander all night. I was still annoyed; he hadn't told me about Pam. I was so mad I missed the awe in his voice as he saw my sketches like he was proud of me.

The word was foreign on my tongue. No one had ever been proud of me. Then he set the bag next to me and headed to the bathroom. I recognized the purse right away; it was one of mine. It contained some clothes, my shampoos, and my favorite pair of Louboutins. As I rummaged through it, I found an envelope, but left that inside.

There was only one person Ren could have gone to get this from, and it was the doctor. I grabbed the shampoos, holding them close to my chest. No one had ever done something like this for me. He was telling me he was sorry I was in this situation, offering me comfort without saying the words. That was beautiful to me. I had to stop myself from crying in front of him.

I was in the arms of a killer, and I'd never felt so safe. He was covered in blood and my fingers in ink. I got in that shower with him, and the water washed off everything we had been, leaving just him and me bare. We didn't have to make sense. We didn't have to be normal; he was a beautiful nightmare, and I never wanted him to let me go. Dreams were wishful thinking and ended too soon, but nightmares went on forever, and Ren brought delight to mine. I felt like I'd found peace under his dark wings.

Now here I was sitting down on a couch in the back part of the house. The space was empty like it was being remodeled. Ren was shirtless, all his muscles on full display. His face was no longer clean-shaven, but he had a little stubble, reminding me of *my* Ren. In his mouth, he had a blunt. I didn't think it was wise to smoke while practicing, but you couldn't tell Ren what to do. His pants rode low, and the top of his black boxers was peeking out. The V was defined, and I wanted to run my tongue through it. He let out a punch to Gideon. Much like Ren, he was also shirtless. He was more muscular than I had given him credit for. From his neck, all the way down, his body was covered in tattoos. He was a gorgeous piece of art. Pam was nowhere in sight, and I was glad. She was either hiding somewhere else or had found a new fuck buddy.

"I want to see blood!" I cheered.

"She's a vicious little thing, isn't she?" G said as he dodged another of Ren's punches.

I continued to talk smack as their fighting went from playful to full-on competitive, all while I took a hit from my mini little bong. Ren had given it to me the other day while I was sketching.

"I couldn't get you your fancy one, so here's this one for now," he'd said.

I couldn't contain my grin because it was *soo* girly and covered in glitter. I loved it. It wasn't like the bougie one I had, but this one was special.

"That was a shitty move!" I yelled at Gideon as he went for one of Ren's ribs. I turned to Ren. "Are you okay, babe?"

I said the words so casually, not even thinking about them, but Ren did. He noticed them because his head swung my way, and his eyes—his eyes looked like they were glowing. So blue, the ice no longer there. I'd never called him anything other than Ren, Falcon, or dog, but this? He liked it. By the way he was looking at me, he liked it a lot.

"Remember, kids, no fucking."

I raised my finger and flicked off Gideon. He meant it too, saying Ren needed every advantage, and he couldn't fuck before the big fight—he needed to build up testosterone and all that jazz. I thought that was just bullshit, but what did I know? Gideon was adamant about it, going so far as to barge into our room in the morning.

The first day he found Ren with his mouth between my legs, his mouth was right there when he pulled him off. And Ren was selfish enough that if he didn't get any, neither did I. So no sex after the fight.

"Do I have to sleep between you two tonight?"

"Are you trying to jerk my man, G?"

"Probably have to jerk it off you, since he gave you his dick."

I laughed. I didn't know why Ren hadn't killed him. I suspected that he liked him or respected him because Gideon always pushed the boundaries, but you couldn't help but like the guy. He was so easygoing.

"Okay, again. This time, I won't go easy."

And then there were times G was scary as hell too.

◆

THE DAY BEFORE THE FIGHT, THE HOUSE HAD BEEN QUIET. PAM showed up from wherever she had gone. Probably to get laid, because she looked happier than she had in days.

"How's the nose?" I asked as I ate some food.

She glared at me and made a show of looking me up and down before she spoke. "You go and enjoy yourself."

Ignoring her, I went to the room, where I found Ren sitting on the bed smoking. I walked up to him and straddled him. He just looked at me as one of his hands wrapped around my waist. I kissed him as I'd never kissed anyone before, slow with no preamble. I'd never kissed someone just for the hell of kissing, and that was something Ren had that no one else would. People spent time worrying about who was their first, how many people they fucked, but all those things were meaningless. It was the slow kisses that killed the act of being intimate without losing your clothes. Sometimes it was easier to show your body than shed your soul. Little by little, I was losing mine, because Ren kept stealing it.

Ren's mouth leisurely devoured mine while his hands

mapped my skin as if he was trying to commit me to memory. We were a tangle of limbs touching and feeling. We stayed like that until we took a nap.

My hands traced over every inch of Ren's chest, through the scars that marked his skin and the cuts from now-healed wounds. It was rare when I woke before he did. Training with Gideon got him tired because of his ribs, and my body was still catching up on the sleepless nights I'd spent with Silas.

"What are you doing?" Ren asked, and despite waking up, he didn't look drowsy. He still looked alert.

"Molesting you."

He gave me a smirk. "If I can't get pussy, you're not coming either."

"I think that whole testosterone thing is an old wives' tale, or Gideon is just jealous."

I grabbed his tattooed hand, tracing over the forest that started at his wrist and went up to his forearm. He had a compass toward the back of his arm, but the scale was inverted. He had more shading and a monarch butterfly, and in the wings, there was a skull face. The tattoo ended by the elbow with beautiful shaded feather wings, and they finished in sharp blades.

"It's beautiful. Do they have a meaning?"

"Yeah," he rasped.

"The compass is inverted because of your morals." I traced the circle while he nodded with approval. "The wings are kind of obvious, and so are the knife tips…the butterfly is death 'cause you bring it. I don't know about the forest."

"It was the best way I could represent something wild and untamed. A wolf seemed too cliché."

I rolled my eyes at him. "But falcon wings didn't? I should get a tattoo."

"Are you going to get diamonds?" he mocked.

"I should get a falcon tramp stamp," I joked, but kept going when I saw the idea turned him on. "You can look at it as you fuck me from beh—"

Ren pulled me to his mouth. I shrieked with glee as I straddled him. My body wasn't sore anymore from the last time he took me, although the hickeys hadn't entirely disappeared. I wanted him so bad.

"I need you," I begged against his mouth.

Ren's hands came to my waist, removing my pants. "You're going to sit on my face, and after I make you see fucking stars, we're going to a parlor."

"Yes," I agreed immediately.

"Fuck, Ember, you're soaked," Ren groaned as he ran a finger over my slit. He lifted my body, putting me on his face and running his tongue where his finger had been. I moaned, throwing my head back. Then I screamed.

"What the fuck!"

"Wasn't the door locked!" Ren shouted.

"I picked the lock. I had a feeling this was going to happen when you two were eye-fucking each other" was said by my ear.

Gideon had his hands on my waist as he carried me away from Ren. Ren sat up, pissed as hell.

"Can you let her go?"

"His boner is digging into my ass," I mumbled.

Ren shot up off the bed so fast, pulling me away from Gideon.

"You guys wouldn't be interested in a threesome?"

"No," Ren and I said at the same time.

Gideon threw his hands up in surrender.

"What you wanted is ready," he said as he walked out the door, leaving it open.

"Come on, get dressed. We have things to do."

I pouted.

Ren came to closer to me, grabbing my hand and putting it on his erection. "I fucking want to tear into your pussy like no other, make no mistake, but as much as I hate to say this, G might have a point. I need everything to win tomorrow."

He sounded serious, so I got dressed. "Where are we going?"

Forty minutes later, we were in the car heading downtown. It felt good being out of the house joining the rest of the world, but it was also scary. Because when I was alone with Ren in his little bubble, I was safe, and I could pretend nothing else bothered me.

We stopped at a small boutique where Ren told me to be quick and pick up something to wear. Since I had the shoes and jeans, I just grabbed a leather jacket and a top. Ren paid for the clothes, grabbed my hand, and led me back to the car.

"Where are we going?" I asked as my heart started to pound violently against my rib cage.

We were too close to downtown. *He wouldn't take me home, right?* For a second, I felt stupid if he wanted the reward. What if that was the easiest thing to do—collect the money for me and save his life over mine. What if it was all a lie?

"Whatever you're thinking, stop thinking it." Ren grabbed my hand.

"I'm not thinking anything," I lied.

He didn't say any more, and I waited with dread in my veins the closer we got. Ren then took a turn, and I was able to breathe for a second until it became clear where we were.

"I wasn't able to get all the shit you usually get them, but

I think I did okay," he said as he put the car in park in front of the homeless camp.

I always associated crying with being sad, weak, and pathetic. I never knew you could cry from happiness.

Blinking back tears, I asked, "Why?"

"You're not my prisoner, Ember, and I know it doesn't seem that way right now. I know doing this shit makes you happy. I didn't think it was wise to go to the hospital, but this, I could do for you."

"I don't want to go to the hospital anymore." My voice shook.

Ren reached cupped my cheek. "Once things are settled, we can go there."

I shook my head. "I won't... It's been a year, Ren. I...I abandoned them. I know not all of them will be there if I go back..." My chest rose and fell, and I felt sick to my stomach. "What if...*what if they think I didn't care?*"

The last part came out as a choked whisper. We hadn't talked about my time with Silas. It was the only thing Ren never brought up. I never questioned it because I didn't want to tell him about that year. It could be like it never existed.

"Hey, look at me," Ren said as he forced me to meet his eyes. "Yeah, it might suck at first, but you love that. You helped those families more than you let the world see. I saw it that day. The way those kids adored you. The stuff you slipped to the parents. Your money was always tied up, so you gave them your diamonds, didn't you?"

I looked away. He was right, and I didn't tell him otherwise. I didn't care about giving away my jewelry so those families could pawn them. They had sick kids, and they loved them, wanted to be with them. The least I could do was make it a little easier for them to make that happen.

The board would have never approved of me spending my money like that. What I donated to the hospital was more than enough. It would never be enough. So I let the board think I lost merchandise, that I didn't give a fuck about my legacy, because I somehow always knew they would never let me have it.

"You're strong, Ember. And I'm so fucking proud of you."

It was at that moment that I knew I loved him.

I might have suspected it sooner, but right then and there, I knew it, and it completely terrified me. I swallowed back words I wanted to say, trying to forget that I ever thought them.

"Thank you," was all I managed to say.

Ren was by my side as I handed out blankets that weren't as thick as Mrs. Rosales's, but it was better than nothing, and he had bought pizzas.

Actions didn't just speak louder than words; they also destroyed your soul.

Ember

"Everything will be fine, right?" I asked for reassurance.

"Nothing is going to happen," Ren said, and I believed him. "When we're there, you don't leave Gideon's side."

I nodded.

"At all, Ember. No matter what."

His words brought dread deep in the pit of my stomach, making me feel queasy.

I changed into the clothes Ren got me yesterday. I still found it weird that the doctor gave me booties to wear, but I missed my heels, part of my armor, so I didn't think much of it until I felt something digging into my feet. I turned the shoe upside down, and a Visa card came out. No name, one of those reusable ones.

The doctor was giving me help in case I wanted to run. I left it in the bag. I wouldn't need that tonight. I put on a pair of jeans and the crop top from yesterday. Around my neck was my mother's choker. When Ren gave it back to me, it was like getting back a piece of my strength. I never knew my mother, yet I loved her. Kinda pathetic, right? I was not going to cower with fear because of Silas. He'd made me afraid for far too long, and I was done. I was a diamond, and I didn't break.

Ren walked back into the room. He was wearing sweatpants and a white T-shirt.

"You can still see my marks," he mused.

"Aren't you so proud?"

"Oh, I am."

I glared at him.

"You're always carrying weapons. Why not today?"

"Can't go packing to the event."

What did I know? I would have felt better if he brought some weapons.

As if he read my mind, Ren said, "I don't need a gun or a knife to kill."

Right. He could snap a guy's neck.

"Okay, let's go." I took a deep breath and walked out the room. Ren put his hand behind my back as we made our way downstairs. Gideon was waiting for us already. He was wearing dark jeans with combat boots and a black long-sleeved shirt. As for Pam, she was in a hoochie peach dress that looked striking against her tanned skin.

For a second, I wished I had one of my candles. If I needed a little extra protection, today was the day. We all walked outside, where two black BMW motorcycles were parked.

"What happened to taking the car?"

"It's going to get packed. If shit hits the fan, getting out in the car is going to be a bitch."

"How do you even get these things?" I asked as Ren handed me a helmet.

"Cashing markers," Gideon answered as he straddled his bike. He waited for Pamela to get her slutty ass on the back, and he took off.

It was just me and Ren left. He was still not on his bike, staring at me as I put on the helmet.

"When this is over, I'm going to teach you to fly." He straddled his bike and then helped me get on. "Hold on tight, princess."

The motor of the bike purred smoothly, sending a wave of excitement despite the nerves I was feeling. We took off in the night, weaving in and out of traffic until we made it to a popular nightclub. Ren parked next to Gideon in a handicapped spot.

"Um...you do know you'll get towed, right?" I told both of them as they put the helmets away.

"Cops won't be coming this way tonight," Ren told me as he held my hand and led me toward the club.

We didn't go to the line, not even the front. Instead, we went to the side of the club to one of the emergency entrances. Ren knocked three times, then once and three again.

"The first three knocks represent the three brothers. The lone one is for their one kingdom, and the last one is for the brother that is here and his twin sons." Gideon explained the meaning behind the knock. Maybe because we all had been too quiet, and he wanted to break the tension.

The door opened, and there was a beefy tan man in a suit ushering us in. Gideon and Pam went in first with Ren and me behind them. Once in, the security patted us all down, making sure we hadn't brought weapons. After he was content that we weren't sneaking anything, he told us to keep going straight. We were in a dark hallway. The thumping of the music could be heard but not as loud as I would have thought.

"Good luck in there." The guard nodded to Ren, and Ren gave a tense nod.

Gideon walked deeper into the dark hallway, where he made a slight turn. It was so dark that if you didn't know it was a stairwell, you would have missed it.

"I take it you've been here before?" I asked.

"A few times." He didn't joke or tease.

The stairs curved down in a spiral motion. With every step we took, I felt like I was leaving the real world behind. Two red glowing lights could be faintly seen. They illuminated a black metal door. When we reached the last step, I had a sick feeling. I didn't want to be here. I wanted to go back to the house, in the room with Ren. Back to our pretend world.

"You ready?" Gideon turned back to look at Ren.

I got the feeling he was talking about so much more than a simple fight.

Ren didn't answer him. He spun my body around so I could face him. I could barely make him out with the red light, but what I could see scared me. He was all harsh at the moment. Nothing human about his appearance. He looked like he'd crawled out of the underworld, ready to wreak havoc.

His lips descended on mine in an instant. His hand came to the back of my head to keep me in place as he devoured my mouth. He pulled back, breathing heavily, and so was I.

"I'm going to make everything better, Ember."

"I know you will…" I whispered.

In the back of my mind, those words that came to me yesterday wanted to crawl up again, but I swallowed them back.

Ren tilted my chin hard, forcing me to keep eye contact with him.

"Say it," he rasped.

"W-what?" My lips trembled, hoping he couldn't read me, and he didn't want to say those words.

"Tell me." His voice was strained. Dare I say, pained.

I opened my mouth, and I felt like crying. I closed it again, but I couldn't do it. To say those words, it would give him the ultimate weapon against me.

"G..." Ren started to say.

"I got you" was all the tatted bad boy said. Then he turned around and opened the door.

Ren still held me close, even though I didn't say the words he confessed he didn't believe in. I didn't know what I expected to find once we made our way down here, but this was not it. The place was dimly lit with walls covered in red paint, making the whole place look hellish, yet elegant.

It was spacious, the same as the nightclub, except this was happening right underneath the unsuspecting partygoers. People were standing around talking, some on couches, other on chaises that were placed around the room. Guards lined the walls, looking much like the one upstairs, in suits, with bored expressions on their faces. My eyes scanned the room and the people. That was when I noticed what was in the middle of the room: a big wired cage. It came down from the ceiling, creating a perfect octagon.

It fucking terrified me.

Was Ren going to fight in there? A guard made his way to us. Ren squeezed my hand, and when I looked at him, he brought my hand to his lips and kissed it.

"Falcon," the man drawled. "Come with me."

Ren moved to leave when I reached for his hand and pulled him back. Being in here, seeing it all, made it all too real. Slowly, I looked up at him. He regarded me with cautious eyes. I didn't know what the night would bring, but when he was out there fighting, I didn't want the words I'd left unsaid to haunt him. Slowly I rose on my tiptoes, my lips finding his, and spoke against his mouth the words I'd never told a man.

"I love you."

The words were something foreign to me; they came out hesitant and unsure, but Ren didn't care. He wrapped an arm around my waist and lifted me and gave me another bruising kiss.

When he set me down, Ren left with the guy without another word to me. My heart was pounding to the beat of his steps. Each step he took farther away from me was one I could breathe and freak out about what had happened. As soon as he was gone, Gideon threw a hand over my shoulder and led me to the bar as Pam trailed behind us.

"Stay close. I don't need your man to be distracted."

"Yeah, protect her and let me die," Pam murmured.

"This is neutral grounds. If there's any place you're safe, it's here. If they come to get you here, it would start a war with the Estacados, and that would be plain stupid."

"How long until the fight?" I asked.

It was close to nine, so it wasn't that early, and there were people but not enough for it to be considered packed.

"His fight is at eleven. Other ones are starter fights to satiate the hunger."

There were a few stools in the bar. Gideon sat me in one as he put his arms on either side of me, protecting me.

"Barkeep." He signaled for the bartender and got himself an old-fashioned and me some water. "Sorry, sweet cheeks. Lover boy said no drugs and no alcohol for you."

That was when I noticed the men who were walking around carrying trays. And when G raised his hand, one came over. He had a plethora of drugs—dime bags of coke, Cubans, cigarettes, blunts, pills. Old me would have loved the shit out of this place.

Gideon paid for a blunt and then pulled a stack of money from inside his jacket. "Four grand."

With hungry eyes, I watched the bookie-dealer take down Gideon's information. Drugs were right there, and I was not going to lie and say my mouth didn't water. It would be easy to take one, but then in the back of my mind, I heard Ren say he was proud of me, and that...that gave me the strength to look away.

"You need a new addiction," Gideon said. "Something else that gives you the same high."

There was no judgment in his voice, which made me grateful. I wondered if I was that obvious or if Ren had told him.

"What's yours?"

"Adrenaline, blood, and petals," he answered in a heartbeat.

Before I could ask what the hell that meant, there was a voice that spoke our way. I recognized the husky tone with a hint of an accent. It was a voice I hadn't heard since the night I'd given myself to him to fuck with Silas.

"What is the lone wolf doing so far away from home?" He came to the left side of Gideon.

Pam craned her neck with interest. Oh boy, was the world tiny sometimes.

"I'm hunting."

"You're not going to introduce me to your girl?"

Gideon's arm had blocked me from view, and if Gideon was nervous, it didn't show. I took a deep breath and peeked my head behind G's arm.

"Enzo," I said leisurely. He was still handsome, dark, and alluring. Sharp nose, neatly trimmed beard, and wearing a suit. "Long time, no see."

A slow grin took place, showing me those white teeth. *La Principessa dei Diamanti.*

"Where's your boyfriend?" I asked him, referring to his best friend, Ashton Hill, whose family owned the building I lived in—or had lived in.

"Not his scene. I didn't think it was yours either," he drawled. Then he turned to look at Gideon and Pam.

Gideon was taking a sip of his drink while Pam looked as she always did—pissed off at me.

"You two know each other?" Pam bit out.

Enzo smirked at Gideon when he answered. "Last time I saw her, she was squirming under me."

Pam let out a snort, whispering, "Whore."

"Gideon is not my boyfriend," I replied, not having time to measure dicks. "My guy is fighting tonight."

I spoke the words proudly: my guy. Holy shit, I had a guy. Like, I fucking professed he was mine to someone else.

"So it is Falcon who's stepping in the ring tonight?" Enzo's dark eyes went to Pam's, and that was when I noticed there was a familiarity between them.

Pam lashed out on me from annoyance, because I knew someone she thought only she knew.

"I was on a business trip when I heard the lineup, and I thought to myself, what are the odds?"

"You know Ren?" I asked with disbelief.

"Enough that I lent him my pad for him to stay."

If there was ever a time to need a drink, now was it. Sometime between talking to Enzo and now, Gideon lit up his smoke. I removed it from his mouth and took a hit.

"It's a small world," I mumbled after I exhaled.

"You don't even know the half of it," Gideon said.

More people started to enter the floor, all of them making their way to the front where the cage was now lit up brightly.

"Showtime," Enzo said, finishing his drink. "Sit with me, and while we wait for the main event, you can tell me how the hell you ended up with Ren."

Enzo started to walk to the front, and Pam used the opportunity to talk to him, putting her arm through his.

Gideon leaned into me. He wasn't mad, just cautious. Him being serious scared me.

"Stay close and don't trust anyone. I know you may know him, but some people show the world one face and another when they are alone."

I felt a chill run down my spine at his words.

"You don't seem as confident as you did when we got here," I dared to say.

"The only thing I trust in this business is my gut feeling, and since we walked through the door, it's been screaming at me that something isn't right. I just can't put my finger on it."

It was safe to say I was scared.

The table Enzo referred to was a small round table for no more than six people with high stools. To get to this section, we had to pass a small black velvet rope. This was the VIP area. All around the cage were similar tables like this.

Once I sat down, Pam smiled at me and leaned into my ear. "Do you think Ren will finally dump your ass when he finds out you've slept with one of his business associates?"

"Oh, Pam," I smiled at her and patted her head. "Ren turned his life upside down for me. I don't know what he'll say, but I bet it will be a good time."

She was seething, and I smiled at her, despite feeling a little insecure myself.

"So how did you end up with Falcon?" Enzo asked.

"He's trying to keep me alive," was all the answer I gave him.

Less than twenty minutes later, the lights in the room went off, leaving the cage lit up brightly like a beacon. The

MC came out, greeting everyone and announcing the fights that would take place. People cheered as names were mentioned. I was holding on to the edge of my seat, waiting to hear Ren's name being called, and when it did, I wished it hadn't.

"Bets are still being taken for the ring of death. Falcon came to challenge four-time resident winner, Claw."

The crowd went wild.

"Ring of death?" I asked between gritted teeth to the table.

Gideon and Pam stayed quiet. It was Enzo who answered.

"Two opponents go in; only one comes out."

"What happens to the other one?" I asked, looking at him straight in the eye.

He looked at me, unwavering. No pity. No sympathy, either.

"He leaves in a body bag."

And just like that, it felt like my heart had stopped.

Ren

For underground ring fighting, the Estacados kept it classy. Maybe it was just a ruse to prove to the three-piece suits who would be watching that it was okay to enjoy the show. All for entertainment, right?

Make it look pretty, but still, let it kill.

The fights before were clean, or as clean as the players made it. If there was a casualty, well, it was a stroke of bad luck on the player. As for my fight, that was a bloodbath. Two fighters went in, and only one came out.

Now I was feeling guilty that Ember would find out about it this way when it should have been me who told her. Not after I forced her to tell me she loved me. I saw it in her eyes—at least I hoped it was, and I needed to hear her tell me. To let me know that once and for all I owned her. I wanted to, I almost did, but if she asked me not to do it, I would have disappointed her when I refused. This was the only way. The winner not only got an insane amount of cash, they also got a marker. The Estacados granted you one wish per se, and I needed for that favor to come to me.

Now that we were all weighed and read the rules, they brought us to the gym so we could warm up. My ribs were nowhere near healed, but they didn't hurt as much as they had. I didn't chitchat with any of the other players. I wrapped my hands and warmed up while I thought of all the things I was going to do to Ember tonight in celebration. Maybe I'd finally take her ass.

At the thought, I punched a little harder. I needed inside her like a blind man wished to see the sun for the first time. Near desperate. The moment my opponent walked into the room, I knew it. Everyone was quiet for a second until murmurs started to go around. I didn't turn around to look. I'd already done my homework; making him think I didn't give two fucks about him was just part of the mental game.

They would send out fighters two by two for the beginner fights. The winner got some cash with the security of knowing they most likely wouldn't be dying. The emptier the room got, the more I felt the "champion's" eyes on me. They called him Claw because the fucker liked to claw eyes out once he got his opponent down. He was cruel and sloppy, and that worked to my advantage.

Just because he had won the last four fights, it didn't mean he was a beast. He had never faced off with someone like me. He might be bulkier and have brute strength, thinking himself hot shit because he'd made a few kills, but in reality, he wasn't a serial killer. He killed to prove a point. He played it safe and let his prey come to him. That was never me. I didn't give a shit about what was socially acceptable. I killed because after the first time, after the scare went away, I realized that it made me feel powerful. Having someone's life in my hands didn't make me feel like the lowlife piece of shit I was. It became an addiction that I couldn't stop.

So I let him stare me down and think he had me by the balls. For the first time in my life, I had something to lose. I made my hands punch the bag with a little more pressure than before, anticipating moves in my head. It was a mental game as much as it was physical. I knew that once the cage locked, only one of us would make it out alive.

A door opened, and in came Ignacio Estacado. He had his security detail with him and two teenagers trailing after him. I looked at the boys, who looked the same, yet different. One of them had a kindness to him that the other didn't have. They passed by us fighters, going to join the crowd that was outside. Just as they walked to the door, Claw got brave and got up. I kept hitting the bag, taking note of the way the guy walked as if he favored one side than the other.

"What's so special about you?" he said in a groggy voice that reminded me of a frog. "There's a protocol, and you bypassed it."

I kept punching. "I don't make the rules."

"Doesn't matter. I'm still going to kill you, but before I do, you're going to know what it feels to lose sight and have your eyeballs ripped out."

I stopped punching and turned to look at him, giving him my undivided attention. "I hope you at least got your dick sucked, because you're not walking out of here alive."

When I walked away, I prayed that I wouldn't die because I swear I would come back to kill Gideon for his sex ban. I went to grab a drink of water when I noticed it was only two more fights before mine. Part of me wanted to go out and look at Ember again in case it was the last time, but I wouldn't think about that.

Once they took Claw, announcing him to his adoring fans, I removed my clothes, staying only in my shorts. I removed the wrap on my ribs and threw it on the garbage. If I lost this fight, then I deserved to die.

"You're up." One of Estacado's made men called for me.

I took a deep breath and walked out. The place was dark as shit. I made my way to the cage, and as soon as I was in, they closed the door. They made a show of locking us in to make it more dramatic that only one of us would survive.

I tuned out the crowd, the cheering, and the greedy way Claw looked at me. Just like I knew he would, he ran straight to me, trying to take me to the ground.

I stepped to the side, slamming my elbow with force straight into his rib. Like an enraged bull, he started to seethe.

"Should have gotten your dick sucked."

Just like I knew, his eyes went a little wild. He was top dog here, and he wasn't about to let me take his throne. We circled each other for a second when he moved to make a punch, and just as I moved the side to block it, he struck his leg out with an agility I didn't think he possessed. The asshole got me in the back of my knee, causing me to fall to the floor. As soon as I dropped, I rolled, and I heard a thud where he tried to jump on top of me. I was trying to get up when I saw him trying to kick me. I moved my body a bit, and he hit my elbow, knocking me down again.

Fuck.

I needed to get up again because right now, he had the advantage. I closed my eyes tightly, gritting my teeth from pain, and then I saw her face, and I wondered what was going through her mind. I wasn't going to die today. I would make a deal with the devil to keep me here so that I could be with her one more time. I stayed on the floor, knowing he was going to try to go straight for my eyes. As soon as I felt him at my back, I turned around and kicked his balls. It was a low blow, but the moment he tipped over in pain, it gave me enough time to get up.

"Pussy," he gritted out.

Jumping around, I got close to him until I threw three punches, hitting his side, one on his cheek, and before I could land the last one, he got one on my cheek. I extended my arm, striking with the side of my hand to his nose in an upward motion. Blood dripped from his nose, and seeing it turned him in a blind rage. He came at me fast with punches and kicks.

I blocked some and moved out of the way on others. Sweat dripped down my forehead along with some blood. It fucking hurt to breathe, and I took shallow breaths, short of panting. I wasn't the only one who was tired; so was he.

This time it was me who rushed at him, throwing wild punches to get him where I wanted. My chest was taking damage, but I would worry about that later. When I punched the side of his neck, I saw the way he started to blink furiously, trying to stop the dizziness from taking over. Using that as my opportunity, I pulled my leg back and kicked back his kneecap.

The crunch of bone was piercing. I watched him stumbling backward until he fell to the floor. I kicked his side by his kidney when his arm shot out, trying to get enough balance to get up or, in his case, crawl away. I kicked him in his armpit. A hit there immobilized his arm.

Knowing this was a show, I knew I had to make this worth their while. Since he wasn't going anywhere, I circled him slowly, trying to figure out the best way to kill him.

I stalked him as people started to chant, "Falcon," aware that I had my prey where I wanted him.

When I got behind his head, I pulled him into a sitting position by gripping his hair and then threw a blow to his nape, damaging his spinal cord. He howled in pain.

Pulling him up again, I looked at him in the eyes, and there was fear in them knowing he was going to die. He got cocky. He'd killed in here for the first time in one of the other fights. He got addicted to the high, but was too much of a pussy to do it on his own again. So, he did the ring once, got addicted, and kept coming back for more. When you're a born killer, you learn everything you can about the human body. Anatomy becomes a necessity. Because by knowing the human body, you know how to tear it apart. Brute strength didn't do anything against skill.

"I was going to make this painless, but you pissed me off." Still holding him, I pretended to turn around, only to slam my elbow to his throat.

With the force of my elbow, his Adam's apple broke free. His first instinct was to swallow to clear his throat of the sensation, trying to get some air down his windpipe. As he did that, he pushed the bone down, effectively cutting his throat from both sides. I held his head so the fuckers who got their rocks off this little show could get their money's worth. The room was silent as blood spilled from Claw's mouth as he choked to death.

Then, there it was: the applause. I let Claw's body slump to the floor, letting out a relieved breath. They announced me the winner, and as they did, the lights in the room came back on as the cage began to lift from the floor so I could get out.

If you'd asked me a year ago if magnetic pulls existed, I'd laugh it off, but it was the only explanation I had when I found Ember's eyes. After tonight, she might end up hating me, and I'd lose her forever.

Ren

As the cage pulled up, I stayed rooted in the spot I was in. The smell of blood was heavy now that Claw was dead at my feet. I looked at the table where Ignacio was seated. He was with his two boys. The one with the kinder eyes now looked at me with curiosity, while the other looked bored.

Ignacio gave me a nod before he got up. I waited for someone to give me the go-ahead to follow him. I had questions, and he had the answers. Looking across to Ember, I was shocked at who was at the table with them. Gideon was standing protectively around Ember, and across from them was Enzo Toscano, the guy whose home I was staying in. I'd heard the rumors about him, and the fact that he was here only confirmed them.

"Falcon, go back to the room, and Mr. Estacado will be there shortly."

I gave a tense nod, wishing I could go to the table where Ember was, but I was so close to getting answers now, and I would not blow it. My eyes met Ember's, and I still heard the echo of the words she'd said to me. No one, absolutely no one, had ever said them to me. Did I feel guilty for making her say them? No, because at the end of the day, they were just words. But to Ember, they meant more. She needed that admission if I wanted to stand a chance after the betrayal I was about to make.

My eyes bored into hers, noting the way she looked at me with relief and wariness. She'd just watched me kill a man with my bare hands, and there was no trace of repulsion in her gaze—all her problems and deceptions, all her worries and heartbreaks, she was molded to be the perfect woman for me.

I looked past her at Gideon, a warning to keep watching her. It wouldn't be long now before we got to go back home. Hell, that wasn't even home; it hit home when the owner of the place was across from Ember.

My eyes met his too, and he smirked at me and raised his glass in a toast. Nodding, I turned around, starting to feel better. As I walked back, I felt a prickle of heat on my skin. I got the feeling I was being watched. My eyes did a quick scan of the room but found nothing. I shook my head, telling myself I was paranoid.

Still, my end was near.

The thing about hiding in the shadows was that as soon as someone shed some light, that was it—no more places to hide.

I washed my bloody hands in the sink and looked at myself in the mirror, and I smiled. I missed the way the adrenaline pumped in your veins, the slight brush with death. Tempting it and saying, "Is this my end?"

When the door opened, I was already dressed and somewhat cleaned up. In came the guards protecting their New York king. The guards pointed at me to follow him. We went to the back from where he had emerged from before the fight. Inside was a black office desk with a matching chair that had a red cushion. Fit for a king.

"Ren Falcon," he said as he took a seat, and the accent of his native tongue was strong. "You've made me a lot of money tonight. No one thought you would win."

I smiled at him, watching his two sons stand behind him. "You left out my resume. I'm sure that would have changed a few minds."

"It's simply business, boy." He grinned.

I'd never seen any of the other brothers, but the vibe I was getting from Ignacio had me on edge.

"Now, what can I do for you, Falcon?" he asked as he signaled for one of his guys to get him a drink.

"Just a favor."

Ember

The fights started out small, like something you'd watch on TV. Just guys trying to prove a point. With every couple that went in and out of the ring, my heart beat a little louder, and my hands would get shakier.

Gideon wouldn't let me out of his sight, Enzo watched the fights with mild interest, and Pam disappeared for a little while.

Now all the lights had dimmed entirely.

"Ladies and gentlemen, please give it up for your four-time champion, Claw."

I watched with avid fascination as men dressed in suits and women in their fanciest pearls cheered like they were in some sort of game. Everyone had shed the skin they showed the world, and in here, they were their true selves. A man stepped into the ring, and I gasped. He was not as tall as Ren, but he was bigger and had a murderous grin on his face, making a show of waving to his adoring fans.

My breathing got ragged, because now I wasn't so sure I would see Ren again, and I hated him a little less for forcing me to say words I wasn't ready to speak.

"His challenger, standing at six feet five inches, weighing two hundred and twenty-pounds, Falcon."

The room hushed with the anticipation of the challenger. Then he came out walking tall and proud, no emotion on his face whatsoever. He looked like Death, and one thing was clear: he would not go down easily. He wore shorts, his chest bare with no wraps, showing no weaknesses, just feeling them.

I was on the edge of my seat watching Ren circle his opponent. When he would get close enough, I would flinch. I gasped, and I felt Gideon holding my head to his chest as Ren fell to the floor.

Get up. Get up. Get. Up.

I whimpered when Claw came behind him. Then Ren turned around, kicking his balls, and it gave him enough time to rise to his feet. Hit after hit and seeing his blood spill, I knew I didn't regret the words I'd said.

I didn't know how it happened or when, but I loved him. Every piece of my tattered soul called to him. He was the first person not to run scared of me. He was the first person to not give up on me. He was the first person I'd ever loved, because love wasn't heart, flowers, and perfection. Love was rage, betrayal, and deception, things that made you feel so deep, you know that what you felt was real. Love was a beautiful nightmare, a double-edged sword that killed.

At one point, Gideon relaxed, and Enzo said, "He's incapacitating him."

Ren made it so the guy couldn't move; then, when the guy was fully paralyzed, he killed him.

Repulsion was the furthest thing from my mind. All I felt was relief that he was okay and that nothing was going to happen to him.

When our eyes met, I knew I was fucked. There was no

other man for me but him, and I would follow him everywhere blindly.

Enzo raised his glass to Ren, then turned to us and grinned. "Thank you, Falcon. You just made me a bit richer."

"Like you need the money," I murmured, then turned to Gideon. "You bet on him, too, didn't you?"

"Be stupid not to. Barely anyone did."

"So, what now?"

"Now, you wait," Enzo said. "He'll meet Ignacio, ask for his wish, then you leave this place and go back to your lives."

It sounded simple enough. Now that the anxiety had worn off, I needed to pee. I didn't know how long this meet would take.

Just then, Pam came back.

"Where were you?" Gideon asked.

"At the bar. Fighting makes me queasy."

Figures.

"I have to pee."

"Really?" Gideon said.

"I'll take her," Pam offered.

"No, thanks."

Just then, Gideon stood a little taller, his neck arching and his eyes trying to find someone. "Be quick."

I watched him take off in the other direction. Enzo pointed me toward the bathrooms, leaving Pam behind.

Once in the bathroom, I was quick, and while I washed my heads, some airheads came in talking about how hot my man was.

"He's hot, isn't he?" I grinned at them.

One of them nodded. "We're going to stick around until he comes out and offer him a good time."

Weren't they lovely?

I laughed. "You guys are cute, but I don't share him."

Leaving them gaping, I turned around and left only to collide with a hard body.

The first of my senses to react was smell because I smelled his cologne the second I was in his arms. The second sense was touch the moment he grabbed me. I felt sick. Hearing him call my name froze me in place.

"Hello, sweet niece." His voice was docile, a fake bravado hiding hate.

My eyes trailed up his body, and the sight of him enraged yet pained me.

He found me.

"Let. Me. Go." I seethed as if I was breathing fire.

I hated him. I hated myself for falling for him, but most of all hated that he manipulated a little girl who wanted to be loved and twisted her up.

"I've been so worried about you." He smirked at me, his eyes trailing down my body.

"I swear to God, if you don't let me go—"

"What?" Silas answered smoothly. "Your little boyfriend is going to come after me?"

That's precisely what he would do.

"How do you think I knew you'd be here?" Silas's hand came to my cheek lovingly, but his eyes were burning with a rage he could not show in public.

"You're lying," I said, trying to pull away.

Silas laughed, pulling me to the side. "You're so naïve and pathetic, wanting to be *loved*. You know what he is, what he does. Do you really think he came to con the company? It was never about you, Ember." Silas chuckled. "Well, it was, but the Remington Ember. He wanted to steal your family jewel."

This was not real.

"You're lying," I said, trying to pull away.

I needed Ren. I needed to find him so he could tell me that everything Silas said was lies.

"Oh, God. You really are pathetic." Pam came out behind me.

Her smile was victorious, and for a second, my heart faltered, refusing to believe what was being said to me.

"Did you really think Ren loved you? He said you would pay for what you did to him. It was so easy. He made you believe he wanted you because we still needed you."

"You're lying!" I tried to pull away and hit her.

Pamela laughed. "He couldn't even be bothered to make the arrangement himself; that's how little he thinks of you. Right now, he's asking the Estacados for protection. He's going to negotiate the money we just claimed for returning you safely back home for our lives. He might have liked fucking you, but he likes living more. Why do you think he was so adamant you tell him you loved him when he didn't say it back? It was just another form of payback... You were never anything more than his next target."

With that, Pam just looked me up and down. Then she turned to Silas and purred.

"It was a *pleasure* doing business with you."

Silas smirked at her. "The money is transferred."

I felt so fucking stupid. A part of me refused to believe what Pam had said. *I'm so much worse.* The memory came alive, echoing in my skin. *You will pay for this.* His hatred for me was always there, and I chose to believe he cared when no one in my life had.

Stupid.

Pathetic.

Little girl.

"Whatever," I seethed. "I'd rather be dead than go with you."

Silas pressed me to his chest, his hand at the back of my nape. "You don't come with me right now, I'll kill your father."

I should have fought harder or maybe tell him to go fuck himself. To kill a father I'd never known, but in the end, I couldn't.

"I. Hate. You."

"Not as much as I do," he spat back as he led me out.

I didn't look back to try to find Ren. I didn't ask for help. I wanted to be loved, and I never got that. I wanted to love, and it fucking burned me. As I walked out of the club, I didn't have it in me to care anymore.

Deep down, I always knew my life was not my own, but it was time I gave in to it fully.

Pawn. Princess. Prey.

It was all I'd ever known.

Ember

Every mile that was put between Ren and me felt like a stab to the chest. I think it was the adrenaline and betrayal that didn't let me process what was being said and not reason. The farther I went away from him, I realized one thing: I would never let another man hurt me as he did.

"Where are we going?" I asked Silas.

"Back home."

Right, back to my penthouse prison.

A few minutes later, when it became clear that we weren't going to his place, I sat up, trying to stay alert. Think of a game plan. I was so stupid to leave what the doctor had left for me behind. This was what I got for putting my life in the hands of a man. I lose my control and self-preservation.

Silas got a call, and I pretended like I didn't care. "One hour. We'll meet you in the pad."

It didn't make sense until we arrived at the Hill. The hotel had a helipad that was accessible for the Hills, and I was more than welcome to use it, but I'd never needed it.

"Where are we going?"

"Back home," Silas repeated.

Once parked, he got out of the car as his men came and dragged me out. I kicked, and I screamed, but they wouldn't let me go. One of them put their hand in my mouth. I bit it hard until the metallic taste of his blood coated my lips.

"Someone shut her up. I don't want to hear her," Silas commanded.

"Stupid bitch." The guys whose hand I had bitten smacked me, smearing his blood on my cheek.

My skin throbbed, but sadly, it wasn't anything new.

I kept quiet as we made our way up to my floor. I needed to buy enough time. I could escape; I could break free. I didn't care about the money, the fame, or the glory. I just wanted to stop feeling this fucking despair that came with feeling and caring. I wanted something for myself, because it was evident no one else would.

The doors to the elevator opened, and Silas dragged me inside the house. He pulled me up the stairs to my room. As I walked through the corridors, I saw Ren everywhere: glaring at me by the kitchen, walking down the stairs shirtless, and it fucking killed me.

The pain—I wanted it gone.

Silas barged into my room, and the first thing I noticed was my father in a wheelchair. His eyes seemed to widen with the shock of seeing me here.

"I told you I would find her again, Michael." Silas smiled triumphantly, coming behind me. "Get a good look at her, because this is the last time you'll ever see her again."

"You said that if I came here, you wouldn't kill him." I swung my head back, hitting him the mouth. The pain in my head was the least of my worries.

"You fucking bitch." Silas gripped my hair and threw me across the room so I landed by my father's feet.

Like a scared little girl, I hugged my father. A part of me broke because this was the only time I'd felt him close to me. He'd neglected me for years, and I wanted to protect him.

"Pack your shit, Ember, or I will kill him and make you watch."

Before I could ask why, Silas was slamming the door

shut, making me jump up. There'd always been something dark and alluring about Silas, until that allure went deadly, and it hurt me. After the last year I'd spent with him, I knew he would do it. I let go of my father's legs. He may not have been able to move, but his eyes were alert.

"Did you miss me, *Dad*?" My voice cracked on the last word. "Or did you barely notice I wasn't here?"

Going to my closet, I started to pack a bag, grabbing enough that I could survive on my own until I figured out my next step. I took the simplest of clothes, and all the jewelry I could fit in it. I needed money, and trading diamonds was easy.

As I raided my jewels, I came across a little bag full of pills from my party days. I looked at them and shook my head. It would be so easy to take one right now and let my life fall apart yet again in another man's hands. I grabbed the bag too and brought it with me, putting the pills in my back pocket. I could make some cash from them also.

With the bag in my hand, I went to my father, who watched me with keen eyes.

"We don't have a lot of time, but we have to go out now." I went to the back of his chair to try to push him. "I have better chances if I escape on my own, but you see, Dad, I'm not like you. Despite everything, I love you. So either we both get out of here, or neither of us does."

"I tried to do this the easy way." Silas's low voice had me snapping my head up.

I held on to my dad's wheelchair as Silas came for me in a fit of rage. He dragged me out, throwing me at the foot of the bed, letting my father watch. When I looked at my father, I realized his eyes were moist. I closed my own, not wanting to look at them because my father didn't get to cry for me, not when he'd never been there for me.

"What do you want?" I screeched, finally gathering enough air in my lungs. "Haven't you taken enough from me?"

Silas laughed. "It will never be enough. Now grab your bag. We're going home, back to where it all began."

Nothing made sense anymore.

"What are you talking about?"

"Your family. They took everything from mine."

"My family gave you everything!" I screamed.

Silas slapped me, making me fall to the side.

Pain radiated from my skin.

I was a diamond, and diamonds don't break.

Rising to my feet, I looked at him. "You were a nobody. A poor little orphan boy! We gave you a name, we gave you money. We. Made. Y—"

Silas started to choke me.

◆

Ren

"Before you ask it..." Ignacio sat a little straighter. "...let me tell you I've heard about your troubles, and my family, we care not for that organization, but we also won't make enemies out of them. So, if what you came to ask was for protection, then you are on your own, boy."

This I expected, and I would never bring anyone into the mess Pamela had made.

Clearing my throat, I spoke. "I know sooner or later they will come to collect what was promised, but the favor is not for me..."

"For Michael's daughter?" Ignacio asked.

I nodded.

"I recognized her as soon as you two walked through the door. Her father designed my wife's wedding ring."

At the mention of their mother, one of the boys let out a small grin and the other a scowl.

"Tell me, are you planning to stay in the city for long?"

"I don't know yet." I had no place to hide, so running would only prolong my life for a little while.

"I like you, and I could have some use for someone like you, so before you waste your wish on something that I cannot give, let me tell you this. Michael came to me a long time ago. This hit is a birthright. When her grandfather passed away, it transferred to her. Just like when Michael's grandfather passed away, his hit passed on to him. It ensures that one day the line will die. It might not be today or tomorrow, but with it being passed down, it ensures that one day someone will come along and fulfill a job that was started almost a century ago. This curse has followed them their whole lives, hailing from their homeland. So, I can't do anything about it, for the man who created it is now dead."

Chills went down my spine. I knew it. The hit on her head was dodgy. She was a spoiled bitch, but she hadn't lived long enough to make enemies like the ones I had. It all came back down to her namesakes. Empires were built on blood indeed.

"And offering my protection will be useless since she's already been claimed. Her mother was not an oil heiress, but a cartel princess. She had to renounce her familial ties when she married Michael. That's why nothing is known of her nor her family. Not because they like privacy but to ensure this doesn't follow the girl around either. Her grandparents protect Ember in the way that if someone touches her, they, along with their family, will be eliminated. Now tell me, is there something I can do for you?"

I wasn't easily blindsided, but I could admit I was just fucked over by what he said. That left me with no options and back to square one. It left me with one thing to do, and that one thing would have to be enough.

"No blowback." I spoke the words loud enough that he heard them.

He knew what I was asking, and he thought about it for a second before nodding his head. I was going to paint this city in red, and I would not have to worry about it landing back on me.

"Just let me know when, and it's done." He finished his drink. "Any chance you'd be willing to step in the ring again?"

"I'd rather not tempt fate again." Yet I was about to push it. "But if you lend me some men, I'd be willing to do a job, no questions asked."

I let the offer hang out casually as if I was joking.

"Three men. Three markers."

"Deal." I didn't hesitate to make a deal with him. He was a devil, but I already knew hell.

"You may go now." He threw out a dismissive hand my way.

I did as he asked, making my way scarce, and went to find Ember to get us the fuck out of here so I could sink into her pussy.

Nothing could have prepared me for what I would find. No sooner was I out the doors than Gideon was walking toward me.

"She's gone."

I let the words sink in as ice seeped through my veins.

"What. The. Fuck. Happened?" I seethed.

"Fuck, mate," Gideon was pissed. "She went to the bathroom with Pam."

"Where's Pam?"

"Gone," he clipped out.

My jaw felt heavy. I couldn't even speak with how enraged I was. No phones were allowed here, so I couldn't exactly call Pam.

"You were supposed to watch her."

"Fuck," Gideon cursed. "I thought I saw someone."

I grabbed him by the collar and pushed him against the wall. "If anything happens to her—"

"They're here... Fuck, I know what I saw...I know who I saw."

Nothing should shock me, but if there ever was a worse time for them to collect the debt I couldn't pay now, this was it.

"I hate to break this little lovefest." Enzo's dry tone was on my right. I turned to look at him, and he just blankly stared at Gideon and me. "I saw your little girlfriend leave."

"Where?"

"I was about to head out when I saw her get in a blacked-out SUV. Didn't think much of it when I saw Pam get picked up and neither of you two around."

My ears were ringing.

One thing I was sure of was that one of those two had betrayed me.

"We need to get out now," I said through gritted teeth.

I walked out with both Enzo and Gideon at my heels. I ran out to the bikes, and just as I knew they would be, they were fucking trashed.

My priority was getting Ember back. Pam would get what was coming to her. She did not get to live a new life after fucking me over twice. I felt some sense of loyalty, having grown up together. She was the closest thing I had to family, but family didn't betray you. Jealousy was one hell of an emotion, and she let it get the best of her.

Pulling my phone out, I called one of my contacts. I told Ember I had people keeping an eye out on her family. I had one contact, and I called him.

The phone rang three times before he answered. "Where is he?

"He's at the Hill... Listen, man, I don't know what's going on, but he was pissed. He tried to get the Ember out of storage, but he couldn't do it. After the gala, it was stored in the vault inside a fail-safe, and the only person who knows the code is Michael."

A desperate man will do just about anything. This was not at all the news I wanted to hear, but at least it gave me a starting point. I just hoped I wasn't too late.

"I'm heading over."

"I'd hurry if I were you. He requested the company heli about ten minutes ago."

Fuck.

"Marcus..." The line was silent. "Thanks."

He didn't say anything back, and I didn't expect him to. Before I grabbed Ember, I'd gone to Marcus. I explained a few things, and he was already wary about Ember's whereabouts. He cared about her, and I exploited that to my benefit.

"I'm going to need to cash my favor sooner than I thought."

Enzo, who was still with us, smiled. "I'll make a call."

Ember

"Shut up." Silas seethed as he held on to my neck. The choker dug into my skin, making it even harder to breathe.

"No...bo...dy."

Silas laughed and then let me go. He yelled for one of his guards.

"Bring them to the living room. I want Michael there too. I want him to watch me take his precious little girl." Silas looked at my father with disgust.

The further they took me from my room, the more the hope I had moments ago deflated. How was I supposed to escape now? I looked at my father as they carried his chair down the stairs. Our eyes met, and I could have sworn he tried to tell me something, but I didn't know him enough to communicate without words. He was my father in name, but in reality, he was nothing but a stranger that DNA told me to love.

"Why do you hate us so much?" I whispered as they threw me on the couch.

Silas's dark eyes bore into mine. "Hate you? If you remembered well, Ember, I loved you. I was never supposed to want you, and you made me fall for you."

He spat the words out like they were nothing. The guards put my father next to me, and I had never felt so ashamed in my life.

"I was just a kid!"

Silas laughed, then took a step forward, but he didn't

come to me, but to my father. "She was the sweetest revenge I never knew I could have. Defiling your little girl, *brother*, was a delight."

"Stop!" I choked out.

"I told you, Ember, it could have been the easy way, but you chose to be a whore. I would have given you mercy, and you didn't want to take it."

"For what?! What did we ever do to you?!" I cried.

"I'd start saying goodbye to your father. You're never going to see him again."

Moisture hit my eyes. I didn't want to cry; I didn't think I was still capable of feeling this way, yet here I was. I could remember all the times I'd spent with my father because they weren't many, but they were precious but too painful to think about. Now knowing I might never see him again saddened me.

"Where are we going?"

"Back home." He said it like it was the most obvious answer in the world.

"We are home." I shook my head, trying to understand what he was talking about.

Silas was unhinged. He sounded maniacal.

"We're going back to Africa. I'm finally going to take my birthright!"

"What birthright? You aren't even a Remington. You get nothing of ours," I spat at him.

"Yeah, and whose fault is that? Your family took everything from *mine*. They left us out cold. Cut us out and threw us in the streets." He stopped and looked at me. "I see I've stunned you. Your grandfather fucked up. All these years, he felt guilty for what his father did. He knew the way he took the Ember was dirty. He didn't want that sin on his. He took me in, a poor orphan boy, giving me a better life to pay for his father's mistakes. Except I wasn't an orphan. And my family, we have hated yours since. We've stayed in the shadows waiting for the perfect opportunity to bring you all down."

I opened my mouth and closed it. Nothing made sense.

"Before my great-grandfather took his life, he gathered all the money our family still had, and he placed a hit on your great-grandfather and his son. He wanted your family gone. That money—*our* money—was put into a bid to bring yours to their knees. Your father and mother lived over there, trying to escape your mother's family. Did he tell you that? Did daddy tell you why he never speaks of your mother?"

My chest was rising and falling.

"She was a kingpin's daughter. They ran to the other side of the world to leave her life behind. Then your great-grandfather died, and the hit was passed down to your dad. Your father loved you enough to come running back to America so he could be safe."

Silas came to me, bending down, and I flinched.

"You poor little girl, thinking your father didn't love you. He did everything for you. He begged your mother's family to protect you. He tried to move heaven and earth to make sure that this curse never caught up to you, and what did you do? You fucked the person responsible for this curse... again...and...again...and again, getting off on it even when you hated it."

I tried to hit him, but he was there, grabbing my arms, stopping me from doing so. I thought I hated before, but that was nothing compared to how I felt right now. My skin was lava, hot and molten, trying to incinerate everything in my path.

I spat in Silas's face.

He threw me on the couch, my head slamming against the wood in the back.

"It was all me, Ember. When daddy had business meetings, it was me pulling strings, treating him, trying to isolate you. The car crash was meant to kill your worthless father, but it didn't work out that way." He turned to give my father a pitying look. "Look at him. He can't talk or walk. I sure as fuck hope he can hear me."

"Sammy..." I managed to get the words out.

"Ah, yes...Sammy. He got too suspicious. Looking in places he shouldn't have. Hiring people who didn't pass a basic check. Did you know he hired your little boyfriend knowing his résumé didn't add up? On the day of the gala, he found out I had something to do with the accident. He was not going to stop me from having my revenge. I vowed I would see your family crumble, and I finally have. Everything else I do will just be a bonus."

Hatred like his wasn't born; it was created. Sooner or later, we all pay for our sins, but it's fucked-up to pay for the sins of your father. I watched Silas leave, knowing what I would do. I didn't have the strength to get up, so I slid down the couch, reaching into my back pocket as I did. Once on the floor, I crawled to my father.

I kneeled at my father's feet, and after everything Silas said to me, I felt too ashamed to look him in the eyes. I put my head in his lap and cried. I cried for everything I'd missed out on with him, and the future we would never have.

"I love you, Daddy...I love you so much it hurts. I'm sorry for everything..."

I had to stop because I couldn't keep talking from the sobs that were leaving my body. It was painful, and it was raw. It was the acknowledgment that what you felt was real.

"I was your biggest disappointment; I just didn't know how to make you look at me long enough to feel proud of me... It was easier to pretend like I didn't care," I sobbed into his legs, knowing that my end was near.

One last time. I could look at him one last time.

Slowly, I raised my head.

I was a diamond, and diamonds don't break. But hit them long enough, and they sure as hell cracked.

My father was crying, and that killed me. The man he once had been was now trapped in a body that failed him.

"Daddy...can...you...hold me one last time?" I knew asking the question was useless, but I didn't it anyways.

Bringing the pills to my lips, I started to swallow them, forcing them to go down past my sobbing and dry throat to the point they felt like they were cutting me. Committing suicide was supposed to be an ultimate sin, but I didn't think God could be so cruel to not grant me this out.

I laid my head on my dad's lap, holding on to his hands for strength. "I love you, Da—"

The words failed me as my body started to shake violently. This seemed like the perfect end to Ember Remington, the princess of diamonds, wild party girl who didn't give a fuck about anyone else. No one would ever know that she loved too deep and cared too much. They say you see life flash before your eyes, but I didn't see anything as I laid there waiting to die, but I heard it.

A gut-wrenching, soul-crushing yelling of my name.

Then it was all silent.

MICHAEL

Being trapped in your own body was the equivalent of

being buried alive, except you could very much still see. I watched as Silas, the man who was raised as my brother, manhandled my daughter. Looking at her, beaten and bruised, I knew I failed her. In staying away for her protection, I'd lured her into the arms of the person who wanted to harm us all these years.

Everything he'd told her, I already knew. The only reason I wasn't dead was that he wanted the code to get the Remington Ember out of the vault. I was the only one who had it. My daughter didn't even know she had the code all along. A bit before the accident, I'd taken out the Ember to get it polished and ready for my daughter to wear on the celebration of her birthday, where I would proceed to hand her the reins to the company. She thought I didn't see what she did, but how could I not when I loved her more than my own life?

Before Sam was killed, he brought to me his suspicions, and it was thanks to him that I had managed to stay alive, if only to see my daughter safe and sound. God, the things he did to her. I would never forget everything he told me. I felt like the biggest failure. Loving our kids blinds us sometimes. We want to give them everything when all they need is for us to be right there, holding their hands, and I couldn't remember the last time I'd held my daughter's.

"Did you miss me, Dad? Or did you barely notice I wasn't here?"

God, those words killed me.

I wished I hadn't taken the medication Dr. Wozniak left me for emergencies. I would have happily risked what I was trying to accomplish just so I could tell my daughter I loved her, to beg her to run away through the secret tunnel and leave me behind. Instead, when I heard Silas coming, I injected a neuromuscular-blocking drug, making sure I was paralyzed for when he got here so he could keep believing the ruse. The accident did make me invalid. I would never have use of my legs again, but my cognitive function came with time. I just kept getting drugged when Silas was near so he could think otherwise.

Despite everything, I love you.

My beautiful daughter. I didn't deserve to be called a father, not after everything she'd suffered because I couldn't protect her. Watching her get beaten in front of me was hell when I couldn't do a thing to stop it. I couldn't move, but I could see, hear, and feel. This was my cross to bear for all the pain I'd caused her.

"Daddy...can...you...hold me one last *time*?"

When the words left her lips, I panicked. I looked down at her knowing what she intended to do, and I couldn't do a thing to stop it. I was yelling inside my body, and she couldn't hear me when she grabbed my hand...fuck. My eyes burned with tears that were too stubborn to come out.

No! I willed my body to move, but the effects of the drugs were too strong.

Baby, don't!

"I love you, Da—"

The words died on her lips. My little girl was dying in my arms, and there wasn't a damn thing I could do to stop it. When her body started to convulse, I wanted to die right there with her.

"*Ember*!" A guttural scream echoed throughout the house.

It came from the second floor. I closed my eyes, praying for a miracle. The emergency tunnel was the only way someone other than Silas and his man could get in here. It's how Dr. Wozniak had been keeping me company, more than Silas allowed.

Shots rang through the penthouse. They were quick, aimed to kill. Silas's men dropped. Footsteps could be heard coming down the stairs, and I wanted to shout for them to hurry. My girl was now on the floor; her eyes rolled back. If I died tonight, that image would follow me to hell where I would relive it for eternity.

"I don't care what you do to them...but Silas? He's mine." The voice was harsh, unyielding, and lethal.

My late wife was religious; she prayed and did it often. I never bothered, but today I did.

The man came into view. He was tall, fair-skinned, and he looked desperate. His eyes met mine, and they were cold. They slid to the floor, and just like that, I watched that coldness crack and break. He breathed heavily as he dropped to his knees. His hands came to Ember's before he cradled her head.

"*Ember*," he croaked. "Fuck, princess, stay with me."

He pressed his mouth to my daughter's lips and breathed into her mouth. He kept repeating the action every five seconds, keeping her alive.

"*Someone get me a fucking ambulance!*" He screamed the words, and it felt like the floor quaked.

I watched him repeat the action again and again until someone else said help was on the way.

"Damn you, Ember," the man hissed. "I told you no one would take you away from me."

I watched the man press a kiss on her forehead as help came for her. I didn't know anything about him, and I didn't care about the things Silas told me. This man loved my daughter, and that was more than enough for me.

Ember

Three months later

HAVE YOU STOPPED AND SMELLED THE FLOWERS?

That's one of the first questions my therapist had asked me, but I ignored it. Now, as I sat here in the garden of the rehab center, I couldn't remember the last time I had done it. To stop and marvel at Earth's beauty just for the hell of it. For the first time, the unknown didn't sound so bad.

I sat with my legs crossed on the bench and inhaled. You couldn't have it all in life, and even though I was at peace, I was broken. My life had been lies after lies, making it easy to be manipulated. When I woke up in the hospital, Ren was at my bedside. The words Pam had said to me lingered. He had been honest, or so I thought. I didn't want him anywhere near me. I wanted no one here.

I wanted to be alone.

I had been ready to die.

Ren went still when our eyes met. Everything Pam said came crashing back, everything Silas did was glaring, but all the half-truths and pretty white lies killed me.

"Ember," he breathed my name.

"I told you I loved you and you didn't say it back."

He stayed silent, just staring at me. "I told you, it's just words."

"Words that meant everything to me," I gritted out. "You knew that, and you took that from me."

"Listen—"

"You can't even say it back!" I shouted back, a small part praying, wishing he told me he loved me, and he didn't.

My chest was rising and falling, and the machines I was hooked on started to beep like crazy.

"It was never about me. It was always about the fucking diamond."

"Miss. Miss, you need to calm down."

"Ember," Ren warned, looking at me much like he had the first time I met him. He was mad, and I didn't care.

"Get. Him. Out," I shouted. The nurses were telling me to keep calm, and Ren looked at me, walked out the door, and never returned.

It was for the best; my life was now at peace without him. Except when it wasn't, because Ren was like a damn tornado. Pure chaos, dark, twisted, beautiful, and destructive. I was too mesmerized. I got caught up in his path, and now that he was gone, I was not the same.

A part of me felt stronger, like I could conquer the world. I survived what Silas did to me, and I was surviving with a broken heart. Other parts of me felt weaker. There was a need that wasn't getting fed, and I ignored it, pretending it wasn't at the back of my mind calling his name.

I pulled my legs up on the bench, resting my chin on them, and I smelled the flowers. Tomorrow I would be getting out and rejoining the "real" world. My dad's accident, my so-called uncle going AWOL, pushed me over the edge, and I finally sought help.

I was a diamond, and diamonds don't break.

It turns out I didn't pull that out of my ass. It was something my father used to say to me when I was little before we moved to America. My therapy sessions were intense, especially the first one I had with my father. There was a lot of crying, apologizing, feeling ashamed. He cried, I cried. We both lied to protect the other, and at the end of the day, he didn't judge me, and I couldn't do the same. After our first session, I told him I needed a smoke, and he just laughed and said I had to wait until I got home.

I always knew my problem wasn't that I needed the drugs. I just did them to party, to have fun, to be what everyone already thought of me. When I was with Silas, they were a crutch, but now the only thing I craved was pot. Well, almost the only thing.

"May I sit next to you?"

My head snapped up at the soft lull of the woman's voice. She had black hair and pale skin and was about my height, maybe just a tad bit taller, but that wasn't saying a lot.

"Go ahead," I said, getting ready to get up out of the way and let her have the bench.

"I love daphnes; they're my favorite," she said in the same low tone, almost like it was being controlled. "I'm sorry...I'm probably freaking you out. I come every week to visit my brother, and I see you sitting here looking so alone, I couldn't help myself."

"My father came already; he gets tired easily," I mumbled, trying not to be rude to her.

"Ah, fathers. They can be a big blessing or the biggest of burdens."

Wasn't that the damn truth? I sat there with the weird goth chick until we got talking about other life things. She had a way of coaxing things out of you. She told me things about life, and I told her about mine without going into detail.

She went to play with her hair, and the tattoo at her

wrist caught my eye. It was simple yet elegant, just the letter S, and I wonder if it meant something to her.

"Boyfriend's name?" I asked her with pain because I was pathetic, and tattoos reminded me of Ren.

"It's a family tattoo. We all get them." She smiled, but it didn't reach her eyes.

"How about you? A boyfriend waiting for you once you're out?" she asked, and if she knew if we were meant to wait before going into a relationship so soon, she didn't care.

"There's no one," I mumbled.

"You have fire in your gaze," she said as her silver eyes pierced me. I found it hard to keep looking into her eyes, so I looked away.

"My time is up," she said as she stood up. She might have been short, but she carried herself with confidence. Before she left, she turned to me one last time. "You can often tell the measure of a man or a woman by simply looking at those they've given their hearts to."

What a weirdo.

Even so, as I watched her leave, her words stayed with me.

REN

Hidden in the shadows, I waited for the gates of the rehab facility to open. I was too far off that Ember wouldn't see me, so I wasn't worried about that. Leaving her in the hospital was the last thing I wanted to do, but she had almost died and didn't want me there. So as mad as it made me, I left. I had shit to take care of, so I would give her time to get her pretty little head on straight, and then I would go for her.

I didn't believe in coincidences. From the start, Ember was meant to be mine. Everything kept adding up. Out of all the people who lived next to her, it had to be Ashton Hill. Thanks to Enzo, I was able to gain access to the emergency tunnel. I lit a cigarette and brought it to my lips, not wanting to think about what would have happened had I killed anyone who stood in my way just to get to the top floor. I would never have made it to Ember on time.

She was my ultimate addiction, and I knew I was hers, so no amount of rehab was going to take that want away. I watched the gates open and her Maybach leave the grounds, and I knew her days of pretending she didn't need me were numbered.

You never really let your addictions go; you pretended like they were irrelevant by making a new life where they are forgotten, to find something new to sink yourself into to forget that one craving you had. It would be a cold day in hell before I let Ember forget me.

I took a drag and exhaled. "You can run, princess, but you'll never hide."

So I watched her leave in her car back to her pretty little tower, and I stayed behind because, before I could go back to her, there were a few things I had to take care of.

Watching my surroundings, I made my way to my motorcycle. I was laying low in one of Gideon's safe houses. The Estacados had done enough, and if I lived long enough, I owed them three favors.

The only reason G had been sticking around was that he was waiting for the day they came for my head. Last two months, I was busy tracking a scared little Pam all the way to Mexico. The bitch didn't make it very far.

The only mercy I gave her was by killing her easy and making it clean. I didn't know why she was surprised I had found her or why she thought her begging would mean dick to me.

Walking into my place, I pulled out one of my scalpels and went to the basement.

"Hope you didn't miss me too much," I said despite the smell of piss and feces.

One month later

In every newsstand in the city was Ember. I felt my chest constrict at seeing her picture. She was fucking gorgeous and took my breath away. She looked healthier; her skin glowed. Her hair was a little longer, but her smile didn't reach her face.

"Just this," I told the guy, buying a copy.

"I didn't take you for the sentimental type."

Ignoring Marcus's comment, I turned around to look at headquarters.

"How's she doing?"

"She's good... She won't say it, but she fears Silas will come back." Marcus gave me a look that I ignored. If he suspected, he didn't say or give any indication he cared. "I put in my resignation already."

Marcus left shortly after telling me his plans. I looked up at the sky, trying to see all the way to Ember's office, and then I left.

She got her so-called happiness, yet she wasn't happy. She had her peace of mind, and yet she lived in fear. The time for waiting was over, and it was time I went back to her, but before I did there was just one little thing I had to take care of.

I went back to my place but left the lights off this time.

My footsteps were slow and low; I didn't want to give any warning that I was home. As I made my way down the steps, my heart pounded with excitement, and my dick grew hard. Because after this, I was going to go fuck the hell out of Ember.

I heard the rattle of chains now that he knew I was in the room. Once I was in the center of the room, I raised my hand and reached for the chain, turning the light on.

"Silas." I smiled as I said his name.

He whimpered and cowered, trying to get closer to the wall. One day in the dark and you're scared. After a week, you start losing your mind. But after four months, you forget you're even human.

He had a chain around his legs, preventing him from going very far. I liked to monitor his every step, just as he liked to monitor Ember's. He'd always been a pale-looking fucker, but now he looked gray; it was the lack of food, water, and blood. His body was frail, ribs showing, the skin marred and scarred from the cuts I'd given him, then wiped away with saltwater.

I got closer to him, and he started to whimper like a puppy trying to get away, pushing himself to the wall. I patted his head, and it seemed to ease him. That little spark of humanity that wanted affection thrived.

"This is where we part ways," I told him. "I won't be coming back, and you won't be seeing me again."

I took out my scalpel, and his eyes went wide with fear. He opened his mouth to scream, but you couldn't do that when you had no tongue.

He was weak and no match when I went for his left hand.

"You should never have messed with what was mine. You hit her." I gritted my teeth. "You controlled her."

I pressed the scalpel to his wrist.

"You manipulated her."

I started to cut the skin across, his blood spilling down and into my clothes.

"You defiled her," I spat at him as I grabbed his other wrist. "While you stay here, exsanguinating, I am going to go to her."

I pressed the blade to his other wrist.

"I'm going to erase everything you ever did to her."

I moved my blade slowly this time, taking my time.

"She's no pawn or princess. She's a fucking queen."

I finished slicing as I held onto this wrist, aware that I was a bloody mess too.

"So as you stay here dying, alone, I'm going to go own all of her. Then tomorrow, when dawn breaks, whatever is left of you will get put in an acid tub, and you will be nothing but a fucking memory, and if I have anything to do with it, not even that."

I spat at his face and made my way out, grinning.

No blowback was all I asked the Estacados, and Silas was never to be reported missing. People disappeared all the time, and he was just another one.

I didn't know how much of a future I had, but I hoped that with Pam dead, I would be left alone. And whatever I had left, I wanted to spend it with Ember.

She was the job I never saw coming.

Ember

"Fashion week hit the streets of New York, and yesterday was the first collaboration between powerhouse—"

"Miss Remington," my secretary said.

I waved a hand, shushing her so I could listen to the television.

"The new collection was gorgeous, but the real gem in this was the collaboration they did with Remington Diamonds."

I felt a sense of giddiness course through my body. I leaned back in my chair and put the volume up on the television in my office.

"Many were wary when Ember took over her father's company after her uncle's disappearance, but after yesterday's show, I don't think there's a thing to be worried about. The new merchandise is stunning."

My secretary was as engrossed as I was with the footage they showed from yesterday's show. It was me walking a runway—short-as-hell-me on a catwalk. I wore a black dress with little jewels all over it and a blackish veil, and on my neck was the Ember. When I approached one of my favorite fashion houses here in New York for a collab, they jumped at the idea. Their only stipulation was to have the Ember featured and have me model it. It was scary, and I wanted to back out, but my father was right there, front and center, cheering me on. Tears streamed down my face at the way he looked at me like he was proud. Our relationship wasn't easy, but it had improved.

"I say she's doing just fine. She has a vision; the media loves her. She truly looks like she can take the world by storm. She's the happiest we've ever seen her."

I turned off the television when they started to discuss my happiness. Happiness was a state of mind, and I was in a good place. I was clean and finally had something that set my soul on fire, but there was still an emptiness that I couldn't make go away.

"What were you saying?" I said, turning to my secretary.

"Oh yeah, I have the designs you sent over yesterday. I just need your approval before we send them to production."

Grabbing the papers from her, I went over my new collection. People loved gothic things, and they were all over the feel of them yesterday when they were featured on the catwalk. Black steel with rubies, diamonds, and sapphire, and it was already a hit. My eyes landed on the stupid piece that I almost didn't let go through to production, but my father saw it and sent it over. It was a pendant of a falcon. The bird was in flight, preparing to attack, wings upward and body starting to angle down. The whole design was onyx with the sharp wings covered in red jewels, and the eyes were blue diamonds.

Before I could back out, I handed over the designs. "It all looks good."

When she left, I opened my desk, pulling out my dab pen. I'd gone to rehab, got my shit together, but since pot was a flower, I told Dr. Wozniak it didn't count. I needed it with the stress of running a fucking company. Besides, people loved my bong so much that I'd partnered with one of the biggest head shops to make affordable glitzed-out products for girls. My favorite was the pen I currently held in my hand. I took a drag and turned my chair around and stared out the window at my prime view. The day after I got out of rehab, I put on my heels and my mother's choker, and I made my way to work, calling a meeting.

The first one to kiss my ass was Mattias. He said Silas had threatened them, but I cared not for the excuses of weak men. He usually fought back, called me names, but before he could, it was as if he remembered something and thought better of it. I caught him looking down at his hand and noticed the imperfection on his pinky. If you didn't pay attention, it wouldn't be noticeable, but someone had wanted to leave a message.

Not letting myself get caught up in that, I fired him, and all the ones who had wronged my father. It was a loss on my part, buying them out, but it had to be done.

Looking out the window, it never failed to make me feel insignificant and small. The view from the top was somewhat lonely. I put my head on the window, just staring down at the city, knowing I loved it here but wishing I could be somewhere without the memories.

After the hospital, Ren never tried to see me again, and I think that's what hurt the most. He had given up easily, not that I wanted him to fight for me. Shaking my head, I grabbed my purse and walked out, locking my office. I hated myself when I got like this, thinking of things I should let go of.

As I was making my way down the hall, I saw Marcus.

"Hey, boss," he said, giving me a small smile.

"You sure you still want to quit? I can triple your salary."

I needed people I could trust, especially since I had no idea what had happened to Silas. I was determined to live my life out of his shadow, but I knew the threat of him returning was real. The only thing that we were able to do was trace back the money he'd used to triple the price on my head. Hopefully, that gave people enough incentive not to do anything stupid.

"Change is good, Ember, and it's way past time I got some."

I smiled sadly at him. It was for the best. He needed to move on, and I needed to take a page from his book and do the same. Ren Falcon was not coming for me. Why would he when I'd told him I never wanted to see him again?

"I know, but now I have to go over all the applications and find a head of security." I groaned. I reached out to him and hugged him. "Thank you for everything, Marcus. Thanks for seeing me even when I couldn't."

I stepped back and turned around without looking back at him. Nice boys like him weren't for me. Hell, at this point, I didn't think anyone was. As I passed by the lobby door, I was greeted in all directions. Smiling at the employees, I made my way outside. Instead of going to my car, I opted for walking.

Stop and enjoy the little things.

Except walking got old fast in heels and when my eyes seemed to zero in on every couple walking by. The walk home was going to suck.

◆

"Daddy, I'm home!" I shouted as soon as I walked into my penthouse. My father had asked me if I wanted to move out, but I didn't...I couldn't. Doing so proved that Silas and Ren broke me. The house was full of good memories and bad, and it was time I made new ones.

I put all of my work files on the kitchen island and took

off my heels. Today was the day I gave my staff off, only keeping my father's nurse.

Going to my couch, I grabbed a few fashion magazines and looked through them. Next to them was my blinged-out bong. I smiled when I looked at it. Some things didn't change, and that was okay as long as the rest of you did grow.

The house was quiet, but it was expected on days like today. My plans consisted of a hot shower and sleep.

When I opened the door to my room, I faltered at the figure that was sitting in my bed, yet I wasn't afraid.

"Close the door, Ember, and get undressed."

I felt chills go down my body at Ren's tone. My body came alive at the command in his voice. He was a rush of adrenaline that went straight to my core. I wanted to scream at him and run toward him at the same time.

"Ember," he warned.

Standing straight, I closed the door only because I didn't want my father to get scared.

"I don't listen to dogs."

"Oh, princess," Ren mocked.

He stood up, his height towering over mine, but that's not why he made me feel small. He was pure lethal power.

"I'm going to enjoy reminding you just exactly who you belong to."

I scoffed, but it came out weak. "I can't be owned."

Ren removed the hood from his face, and it was like I forgot how handsome he was, how much he took my breath away. I could turn on the lights and see him better, but this way, with the lights off, I could still pretend he wasn't the one thing I couldn't stop missing.

"I told you, Ember, I would take away all your vices and leave you with one..."

He moved so fast, and all I did was walk back until my back hit the wall. His hands came to mine. He entwined our fingers and brought my hands up over my head, making my breasts press against his chest.

"Don't lie to me, Ember. Don't act like every fucking second you were away from me you didn't think of me, 'cause I know I did. Like you didn't wake up in the middle of the night, reaching out for me."

He wedged his knee between my legs, the skirt I wore today hiking up.

"And every night when you reached to touch your pussy, you wished it was me touching it, stroking it, licking it, and fucking it."

I was heaving. I was pissed as hell at him, but I was also turned on.

That was when I felt he was wet.

"You're wet," I said, trying to pull away.

"No, princess, you are," he said.

He let go of my hands, and his came to my waist, his lips crashing against mine. He was everything I missed in the world. All the dark things I craved, because there was beauty in darkness, and I had always been attracted to his. His hands moved over my body, gripping and feeling, but he was over my clothes, not touching me where I needed him the most. His lips moved to my cheek, and he buried his face in my neck. He licked the pulse from my tendon before he kissed it and sucked it.

"I'm so fucking mad at you, Ember."

He bit the side of my cheek, and I whimpered.

"I'm going to fuck your little cunt and remind it just who it belongs to."

He grabbed me by my ass and kissed my lips as he walked us to the bathroom. He sat me on the counter, his cold, wet hands coming to my shirt, slowly lifting, leaving a damp path as he went. My head fell back as his hands moved over my midriff and over my breast. His mouth kissed all over my neck. His tongue licked me from my collarbone to my chin.

"Fucking missed you," he groaned as he took my lips again.

His hands were tangled in my hair, keeping me in place. My hands went to his face, cupping his cheeks softly. That was enough to make him pull away.

Ren put his forehead to mine, our breath mixing... entwining. He was the night sky to my diamond stars, making it balanced and better.

"Do you still love me?" he rasped.

I stayed quiet, and that was enough for Ren to pull back. He turned on the bathroom light, and I gasped.

He was covered in blood. Crimson stained his white T-shirt. Then I looked down at myself, and I was covered in blood as well. My heart seemed to want to beat out of my chest at that moment.

"I knew love meant everything to you, princess, when the word means shit to me."

Despite how scared I was, my stomach sank at his words. I thought I had come to terms with them, but they still disappointed me.

"Love doesn't mean shit, but actions do. And yours, Ember, didn't mean shit... The first sign of a struggle, you fucking left me."

I squirmed in my seat as he got closer. He put his hands on either side of my hips, and what he was saying made me forget that we were covered in blood.

"Love doesn't mean shit to me, but you, Ember...you do. I'd lie, cheat, and steal for you."

His hand came to my cheek, caressing me sweetly. Then his eyes went dark with a mixture of anger and lust as his hand came to my neck, choking me.

"I've killed for you, and if it fucking came down to it, princess, I'd die for you too. Love doesn't mean shit to me, but I'd worship any altar in your name."

His mouth hovered over mine, our lips almost touching.

"You say it was all about the fucking diamond?"

He let go of my neck only to move his hands back and unsnap my choker. Once he removed it, he grabbed my hips, moving me off the sink and forcing me back to look in the mirror.

"Did you ever wonder why there was a pattern inside your necklace?"

My eyes met his through the mirror, and at that moment, I realized three things. One, there was no way that he knew. Two, I never hated him. I was just scared because I loved him when I had never felt this way before. Three, he was rock hard behind me. When I didn't answer, he kept going.

"It's a code, and I bet it opens the safe where the Ember is kept."

My father had admitted the same to me; that's why he hated that I wore it, for fear that one day someone would discover his secret. My father showed his love for my mother by trusting her to his most prized possession. Without the Ember, our company was nothing.

"So no, Ember, it was never about the fucking jewel. You want to know what changed?"

I could only nod. Slowly, he turned me around, sitting me on the countertop again so I could be at eye level with him.

"The day after I took you, you were so fucking delirious

with withdrawals you said something to me...something that put everything into perspective. You never have to worry about *him* hurting you again."

My eyes widened, and my lips parted as I tried to speak or maybe get away.

"I know what he did to you, Ember. I know that he hurt you, and for that, he didn't get any fucking mercy. He took something from you..."

Ren stepped closer to me, and I gulped air, not able to meet his eyes because he knew the darkest part of me. His fingers came to my chin, tilting it.

"Tonight, you're going to give it all to me. Because I'm going to fucking ruin you in the best way, so when you think of pain, you'll think about the pain I give you that makes your pussy wet... Now tell me, do you love me?"

"Silas is dead?" My lips wobbled as I looked at my body and his.

"You think I'd let him live after what he did to you? No one, as long as I fucking breathe, will hurt you." His words were vicious, violent, brutal, but they were honest.

Ren was like air. He was everywhere at once and not at all. He was the most basic necessity I needed to survive, except I also wanted him. He never hindered me as Silas did. He made me stronger. He took a broken girl and made her withstand fire.

I didn't answer him. I grabbed his cheeks and pulled him to me as I kissed his lips. It was a vow covered in the blood of my enemy. A warning that if he lied to me again, I might not come back, and a promise because he might never tell me the words I longed to hear, but he promised them with every single thing he did.

"I love you." I bit his lip into my mouth and sucked it.

Ren took off his clothes, and I marveled at the body I

missed so much. I got off the counter, removing my bra, skirt, and panties. I walked to the shower and turned it on. I had barely turned the water warm when Ren came behind me, his bloodied hand coming across my waist. He pushed us into the water and kissed my neck as the water washed the blood off our skin.

A few minutes later, when Silas's blood no longer stained the tile red, Ren's hand came to my pussy, cupping it.

"Who owns this, Ember?"

"You," I moaned as his finger worked my clit.

"*Fuck*, I missed that sound."

Ren pushed my body against the cold tile as he trailed kisses down my neck, my back, on the top of my waist. He opened my legs, and his mouth was right there. I didn't have time to freeze like last time as he kissed the puckered skin before his tongue dove into my wet folds.

"Ren!"

He gripped my ass as he ate me from behind. Just as I felt like I was coming, he got up. He turned me around and inserted three fingers inside me, stretching me. I needed him now.

"Fuck, I missed you," he murmured as his fingers worked my clit. "Relax."

His thumb and index finger worked my clit, and I started to shake, and just as I began to come, I felt an intrusion on my backside. I didn't have time to register because Ren was making me scream by the way he played my pussy.

I felt myself coming down, my walls still convulsing, and one of Ren's fingers was in my ass.

"You're so fucking tight. Fucking perfect. Mine."

I let out a little whimper when he removed his hand.

Then he gave me the slowest of kisses against my lips. "He'll never hurt you again."

He knew my ultimate sin, and he was still here.

I threw my arms around him, kissing him back as he lifted me in his arms and took me to bed. We were wet, and there was still blood in the room, but I didn't care. Because in Ren's arms, nothing could touch me. He was my ultimate high, and I never wanted to come down.

Ren laid me on the bed, his body coming on top of mine. He tilted my hips, then slammed into me, and I screamed. I held on to him, letting him give me everything he had to offer, and I gave it to him right back to him.

"I love you," I whispered in his ear.

Love was not perfect. And making love didn't have to be sweet.

Queen. Knight. Soldier

Ren

My eyes sprang open in the middle of the night. I had a gut feeling I was being watched. Without moving, I did the best I could to look around the dark room, trying to find any danger. It sounded stupid, but I trusted my gut. Just like every night, one of my arms was around Ember's waist, her body molding against mine, seeking protection and comfort, something I no longer fought against but fucking lived for. I bent down and smelled the mint of her hair and kissed her forehead lightly so I wouldn't wake her.

The door was closed, but something felt off. I reached for my nightstand, trying to grab my gun, when my hand met the cold wooden surface. My heart thumped, knowing I left it there last night. My head whipped to the right, my eyes adjusting to the darkness. That didn't matter because there was no denying that the Glock I always left there for protection was missing.

Shit.

Carefully I laid Ember on the pillow, trying not to wake her—at least not yet. My blood ran cold when I saw what was on her side table. Fear was not a word I used lightly. When you played devil's advocate, you became desensitized to emotions. Fear was an emotion that that came with caring for someone other than yourself. Not too long ago, I called myself fearless, but wanting someone so fucking bad you'd die for them—it made you human.

I got off the bed, slowly walking to the other side. I turned on the lamp just to verify that what I was seeing was real and not a figment of my imagination. In my world, it was a calling card. Only one person used this, and it was known from east to west from the Pacific to the Indian Ocean. This flower symbolized death. Silently, I checked the room until I was sure no one was in here. I kneeled at the side of the bed and grabbed a Glock I had stashed and moved my pillow, grabbing a knife.

The only thing that kept me rational was the fact that if they wanted Ember and me dead, we would already be. I opened the door slowly, my Glock in front of me ready to shoot first and ask questions later as I checked the hallway. Arrogance was a downfall, and right now, I was falling.

Since I now took Ember's safety personally, I was the only one in the house with her—to give us a sense of normalcy. I figured that with guards outside, it might have been enough. No one was in the control room, so there was no one to watch my back while I searched the house.

The hallway was dark; the only light I could see was that of the windows. I faltered for a second the moment I saw a shadow on one of the sofas. I could feel eyes boring into me, but I ignored them. Straightening myself, I made my way down the staircase into the living room.

The city lights illuminated the living room. Sitting on one of Ember's sofas was a woman I was sure was a myth. Her legs were crossed, and she watched me like *I* was her prey. Funny how the tables had turned. Her hair was black and shiny like feathers of a raven. She had pale porcelain skin, and her clothing blended with the night.

"Are you lost?" I told her once I stepped foot on the floor.

"Just needed a place to rest." Her voice was gravelly but pleasant with a mild Russian accent. "What are friends for, right?"

Her eyebrow raised, and I felt her gray eyes pierce me, trying to get a rise out of me.

"What are you doing here? You hurt her, and I swear to God I will make you—"

"I bow to no kingdom, and I kneel before no man. You're not going to make me do anything." She uncrossed her leg and sat straighter as she glared at me. "Did you not think we would come to collect what was promised to us?"

"I never made—"

"It matters not who made them, but that they were made."

"Kill me. Take me. Call it even," I growled, pissed because I should have known it would have come down to this.

"You killed your partner. The one who had been with you since the beginning."

"If there's no loyalty, there's nothing."

Killing Pam was the easiest decision I'd ever made. I

gave her mercy by doing it quick and clean. The woman seemed to think about it, her head cocking to the side. I felt the slow presence of death at my back, ready to strike, and I was afraid. Not for me, but for Ember.

"I came here to offer you a deal," she said.

I raised my eyebrow for her to keep going.

"Her life for your servitude."

My body chilled. I never thought I would be separated from Ember this soon. This would crush her, and the thought fucked with me because she was a part of me. I never wanted to see hurt.

"Fine," I gritted out.

She tilted her head to the side.

"You'd throw your life away for her?"

"I'd kill you right here if I knew your fucking people wouldn't come after her."

"And if I let you stay with her?" Her voice dropped to a softer tone, much gentler.

I knew what she wanted from me at that moment. "I'll give you my gratitude, and maybe one day, even my loyalty."

"War is coming, Falcon, and I started to place my pieces on the board. I need soldiers, but most importantly, I need loyalty. Now, I know loyalty is earned and not bought, so I want you to remember my mercy. I want you to know that I will not collect what we were promised. I will make sure the organization does not come after you. The blame will lie at my feet, and in return, I want you to be ready."

"Ready for what?"

"For the day I say jump."

I thought about it for a second, letting myself think about what this could mean. In the end, it kept Ember safe, so I'd sell my soul to the devil if it meant I could stay with her another day.

"You have my word."

"Until we meet again, Falcon."

She gave me a nod as she rose to her feet. She was a lot shorter than I would have thought. Her presence alone made her appear taller.

As she made her way to the elevator, she said, "Let's go."

I tried not to make a move.

"Boo," was whispered by my ear.

I turned my head and finally saw the other person who had been in the room all along, ready to kill me had she given the order. He was my height, making it easier to look him straight in the eyes with a face anyone would recognize in plain sight. He was on all the magazines and tabloids. If Ember was the princess of diamonds, he was the oil prince. One day, he'd dropped from the face of the earth—turns out, he had been residing in hell.

"She's a pretty little dime," he taunted me.

I whipped my gun out so fast, the barrel touching his forehead. The fucker smiled at me, his white teeth gleaming.

"He's kinda mouthy, but I need him."

Both our heads swung to where the lobby door was now open, and it illuminated her as she spoke. She was like Snow White, if that bitch was gothic.

"Bas," she warned.

The asshole took a step to the side and followed her. He was in a suit while she wore a commando getup. I made my way after them, making sure that they got on the elevator and left Ember and me alone.

Just as the woman pressed the button to the elevator door, I passed on Gideon's message. And all I could hope was that the fucker didn't get me killed. Because I knew the pale woman with the face of an angel was a demon. One of their deadliest members. No one knew her real name, just her alias.

"Petals don't last long on their own."

There was no emotion on her face, which was still as impassive as it had been earlier. She put her hand in her back pocket, and just as the door started to close, she brought her hand out like a cobra. I heard a loud thud behind me, but I didn't turn around.

I put my gun down as I watched the elevator make its way down, knowing I'd be meeting them again. Once the numbers showed that the elevator had made it to the first floor, I turned around.

On the floor was a canvas bag, and inside was an obsidian dagger with rubies adorning the hilt. I took it out, observing the craftsmanship. It was a beauty of a knife, no denying that. In the middle of the handle, it had a scripted S.

There was a reason G called her petal, why her calling card was the same flowers she used as her alias, Daphne's were toxic, and so was she.

You could run from everyone in this world except for the organization she worked for.

The Sect: feared by all and bowed to none.

Epilogue

Ren

The monitor room was quiet and peaceful, unlike the rest of the house. I never knew the Day of the Dead could be so chaotic. Checking the camera feed, I found Ember right away as she smiled at whatever her makeup artist told her. She looked beautiful, full of life, different from how she had looked the first time I saw her.

My dick got hard just looking at her. Something that had also happened the first time I laid eyes on her through my computer screen. Her rookie mistake of not covering her camera lens had probably saved her life. If I had never come along, who knows what would have happened to her?

Now when I looked at her, there was no sadness in her gaze, but I did see fire. She was full of it. She ran her company with a passion that enthralled you, and I noticed it every time she spoke about it.

I stopped staring at her and checked the rest of the cameras in the house. The maid was making food, and the guards were posted by the front entrances. Ember's dad was on the terrace, reading a magazine.

He would not be joining us today. He wanted to spend the day alone. It was obvious he'd never gotten over his wife. I moved the screen again so I could put Ember's room on the big monitor. Since fashion week, we had been going solid. Fights here and there, nothing major, just mostly stress on her part at the fact that we were both a bit fucked-up and I didn't do a nine-to-five job. Except somehow I got roped into being the Remingtons' head of security all while doing a favor at a time for the Estacados.

Something Ember wasn't allowed to ask about. If something ever happened, I wanted her to remain clean.

Having the Sect's enforcer come gave me peace of mind that no one else would be coming for me. I finally had a future. It never felt like I'd had one when I was living my life one day at a time, but this time I was making it count.

A little while later, there was a knock on my door.

"Come in," I said even though I already knew who it was.

Ember walked in, smiling at me. There was mischief in her eyes, and right away, I sat straighter.

Death had never looked so good.

She was wearing a tight leather halter top with a long red tulle skirt, and her face was done in full skull; the white wasn't heavy, just a lot of shadowing. She looked fucking hot. She loved this holiday because it reminded her of her mother. I didn't understand it, but she asked me to go to the parade with her, and here I was wearing all black and a face full of skull makeup.

"You look hot." She grinned at me.

I extended my hand to her, and she took it, letting me drag her toward me, and then she straddled me.

"Are you ready?"

"Yeah, came to get you. I want to get there early, walk around a bit through the vendors, and then watch the parade and the fireworks and come back home."

My hands came to her waist, pulling her to my body as she ground on me.

"You're feeling better?" I asked.

She'd been bitching a lot in the past days, and she might not have known why, but I did. Ember was one of the hottest jewelers right now, and all the celebrities and socialites wanted her to design their wedding or engagement rings. I didn't think she knew what she was saying when she bitched about it, but I did.

"I am. I think I just needed a break, and lots and lots of pot."

"You're crazy," I mumbled, kissing the top of her breast.

"No hickeys," she whimpered as she pulled my face closer to her chest. "I'm a businesswoman."

"Princess, I barely get my mouth on you and you start begging me to show the world you belong to me."

She stayed quiet because it was true.

"Well, you're supposed to have self-control."

I started to lick up her chest and her neck as she kept grinding against me.

When I made it to her lips, I mumbled, "When it comes to you, I have none."

Ember kissed me as she started to undo my pants.

"If you're going to fuck me right now, Ember, you're going to be walking around with cum leaking down at the fest."

She seemed to think about it, which I found amusing.

"Come on, let's go," I said because it was apparent I had to be the one who showed restraint.

She rolled her eyes, but I had plans for her, and I didn't want to be late for them.

Once I was up, I put the code into the computer system so the feed could go to someone who was at headquarters and they could keep an eye on Michael. Even though the threat of their hit was minimal, there was always someone looking for a quick score. Not that I thought anyone would want to mess with me.

When that was done, I hugged Ember from behind, my lips brushing her ear, causing her to shiver. The way she loved everything I did to her got me high.

"Tonight you're going to climb on the pole and strip for me while I jerk off, then you're going to get on your knees, suck me off until you feel like they're bleeding, then will I let you choke on my cum."

She made that little noise that drove me mad. I kissed her neck and led her out of the control room. Hand in hand, we were a couple forged in hell, and in each other we found paradise. To everyone else, she was no angel, but to someone like me, she was the most angelic thing I'd ever seen.

"Bye, Daddy!" she called out as I walked up to the elevator.

I took a second to marvel at her beauty. My hands went to the crown on her head; it was black, adorned with red and white diamonds.

Come tomorrow, she would be in front of another magazine cover, and I would be along with her. The media was obsessed with her, and in return, they were obsessed with me. I stayed out as much as I could, but it was hard, so I just went along, feeding a sorry past to the paps and praying they never dug too deep.

Then again, no one would expect Ember to date a killer.

As the elevator made its way down, she pulled out a joint.

"Ember."

She turned to look at me as she lit it up.

"Never change." I kissed her nose.

We made our way to my new car, a gift from Ember's father. I'd refused it, but the fucker was persistent.

"I know who you are and what you do. He hated you."

He didn't have to tell me who "he" was.

"I don't care because you saved my little girl. I heard you in the hospital. You wanted to wake up so you could show her how to soar... Let me do this for you, for her... Take it, because what you've done for my family and for me I could never repay."

I'd grown up with nothing, learning to claw my way out of the gutter, and now I was fucking a princess every night and driving a crimson matte Ferrari Spider, and my life was somewhat my own.

Life was fucking perfect.

Once at the parade, I made my way to where the floats were kept and parked there knowing the crowd would watch over my car. Not that I cared about materialistic things. They didn't get me hard like they did other people.

As soon as I grabbed Ember's hand and we started to walk, I felt people pointing their phones at us. Ember didn't even notice anymore, and she never made an apology about it. I knew what I had the moment I decided I wanted her.

For it being the Day of the Dead, Ember looked happier than I'd ever seen her. She was full of life, talking to Mrs. Rosales and her nephew, Jorge, as they asked her about the new homeless shelter she was helping build.

Keeping her in my sight at all times, I gave her the space to talk without me hovering around. I put my hand in my pocket to pull out a cigarette when my fingers met the round object.

Michael had been all too happy to help me with my request.

When the parade started, I held on to her waist as she watched the dancers. When the fireworks began, I bent my head so I could kiss her lips.

"Let's get you home," I whispered in her ear.

She grabbed my arm and rested her head on my chest. As we walked to the car, she pulled back, held my hand, and walked toward the alley where I had shot Gio.

"It all happened so fast."

Her words were low, but I heard them.

"You asked me once if I believed in fate. I do."

She turned to me, her hands cupping my cheeks.

"I had been praying for so long for someone to save me, and then stopped. Instead I asked God to give me strength, and that's you…" Her head tilted to the side. "You're the steel in my spine, the strong arms that have held me at my weakest. You're the redemption I didn't know I was looking for. Because you saw something in me when I could barely look at myself in the mirror and not be disgusted."

Fuck, I felt those words in the pit of my stomach.

I grabbed her hips and pulled her to me. "You stood by me, Ember, when everyone else ran from me." With one hand wrapped around her hip and the other on her chin, it was now or never. "I've never had anything that's been just mine. All my life, I have had to fight, lie, cheat, and steal to make ends meet. We made our vows in blood already in your shower…I'm not going to get down on one knee because I think that's stupid. A tradition of men feeling like they need to kneel when they feel superior. You're my equal, a fearless fucking queen, and I'm in awe of you."

Ember blinked furiously, and her mouth parted and then closed until she whooshed out, "What are you saying?"

"For the first time, I want something that's just mine, something that when everyone looks at it, they know they can't ever get it."

I let go of her chin to grab the ring from my pocket.

"I'm not asking you, princess. I'm telling you that you're never going to get away from me," I told her as I slid the ring on her finger.

Tears were sliding down Ember's face, messing with her makeup, but to me, she'd never looked more beautiful. She marveled at the ring on her finger. There was barely enough light for her to see it properly, but she was smiling. It was a black emerald-cut ring with a ruby in the middle and small rubies in the band. The design was perfection, Michael's best work.

Ember threw her arms around me, and I lifted her to kiss her.

"Yes," she breathed.

"I didn't ask," I said against her lips.

"I need you." She did that whiney high-pitched voice that went straight to my dick.

With her in my arms, I walked us back to the shadows and pushed her against the wall. My hands came to her tulle skirt, lifting it slowly, savoring her.

"Fuck," I groaned against her cheek as I felt her soft pussy. "You're bare."

"I need you right now," she breathed again, knowing what her begging did to me. I undid my belt quick, then lifted her using the wall for support and thrust inside her hard. She was wet, tight, and forever mine.

I fucked her cunt hard and raw, watched as her head slammed back from pleasure, and when we came, we did it fast.

"'Til death do us part," I vowed against her lips.

A Few Months Later

Daphne
Location: Colombia

The warm summer breeze hit my skin, caressing. It was almost comforting. The ocean was deep; although it was a thing of beauty, it was also deadly...like me.

"You're exquisite, love, but you already knew that. Too bad it's just another weapon in your arsenal. So beautiful, yet deadly."

The wind seemed to mock me, whispering words in my ear I didn't wish to hear.

"How are you holding up?" Bastian barged into my room with a small briefcase in tow.

He had already showered, his hair slicked back, that three-piece suit that cost as much as the view I was paying for wrinkle-free. You could take the socialite out of the spotlight and teach it to live in hell, but the roots of his upbringing would never go away.

"Why wouldn't I be?" I started strapping my weapons on.

Twin knives on the inside of my leather boots. A small

survival bracelet at my wrist next to my coiled snake saw bracelet. Two small Glocks, one in the front compartment of my leggings, the other in the back, and my small rose pendant that contained a deadly vial of T. Nothing too alarming—we didn't want our host to get suspicious or anything. We were in Barranquilla today for a small gathering; depending on how things went, we would move things to the jungle.

"It's not like I'm scared they're onto me or anything."

"Not funny. You die, I die with you. Your head and mine on neighboring spikes."

I rolled my eyes. Bastian was a drama queen, something no amount of torture managed to take away. I guess that was his tell that he was nervous. Mine, well, I didn't think I even knew them. Being the devil's pawn for so long, you got used to living in hell, and your stomach was a bottomless pit of despair.

"Do people still use spikes?" I humored him.

"Even worse, we'll be in some unmarked cooler in the middle of the Siberian tundra," he deadpanned.

"You're foolish if you think they'll bury me anywhere near home. They'll probably cut me up into tiny little—"

"Okay, enough," Bas shouted. "Do we have time for fun right now?"

I stopped braiding my hair long enough to glare at Bastian. "Keep your dick on a leash."

"Just 'cause you're allergic to some vitamin D doesn't mean other women should have the same deficiency."

If looks could kill, Bas would be dead at my feet, but what good would that do me? It took years of training to mold him into my right hand, years of breaking the chains of his righteous pedigree upbringing. It took blood, sweat, tears, and lots of bone breaking to make him into the beast

A Few Months Later

before me. Well, I broke everything but that pretty face of his...and his dick. He begged me not to break his dick.

"So beautiful yet deadly."

It was much easier to follow an angel into heaven than the devil into hell—too bad looks could be deceiving.

"Let's go. We don't want to be late. You know how temperamental these men can get," I said.

I walked out of my room, leaving Bastian to lock up. If he wanted to have a key to my room, he might as well be of use.

The sun was out full blast, the hot rays burning me through my gear. I hated warm locations. It was such an inconvenience to cover up just to hide all my weaponry. When I got to the last step, years of training was the only reason why I didn't gape. There, tall, slim, hair as dark as mine, stood Damian.

Damian had a scowl on his handsome face, looking down at me from head to toe. "Why aren't you dressed in something more appealing than your commando getup?"

I guess he meant something like his. He was in a pair of Bermuda shorts, loafers, and a light white shirt.

"You can tell them I'm your bodyguard."

"Speaking of guard dogs, where is yours?" Damian fell into step with me, his sunglasses blocking the sun's glare.

I didn't wear them, especially not on a day like today. I didn't need my eyesight hindered.

"I'm right next to you, which you would have noticed if it weren't for the glasses," Bas said, coming from out of the shadows.

A small smile passed between us.

"Good thing I have the Sect's top two dogs," Damian spat.

There was no point in answering him. One day, he would get what was coming. Revenge was a dish best served cold, and mine had been freezing for years. If I closed my eyes, I could still see droplets of blood in the snow.

"*Mis amigos.*" Damian opened his arms in greeting at the men seated at the table.

Casting my eyes over them, I saw Sergio at the back with his most trusted mercenary, Robinson, who was an expert with scissors—he liked to take out the trachea.

Next to Sergio was a man who'd recently taken over for the old Chihuahua cartel. Julian Rivera. Seated next to him was his son and behind them Lobo, his son's second-in-command.

Next to them was a man I hadn't seen in a year. He wasn't Latin like the rest of them, nor Russian like me; he was English. There was a cruel smile on his face, making those amber eyes light up with wicked delight. I didn't have to turn to Bastian to know he was smirking at me. My eyes left Gideon's as quickly as they landed on him, effectively dismissing him.

"Hello, Petal. You can't deign yourself to say hello?" he quipped with that smooth accent of his. "Or can you only do that if I'm chained up?"

The men at the table all looked at me, some with more interest than others. Sergio always looked at me like I was his next meal. Rivera was a piece of shit who thought women were better left in the kitchen, and his son looked like he wanted to give me a wild ride. With one quick look at Bas, he pulled out the chair in between Damian and Gideon.

"You wouldn't know what to do with me otherwise."

I threw a carefree smile, crossed my legs, and didn't say a word as these men planned on how to take over the world. I caught sight of the intricate *S* tattooed on Damian's forearm.

A Few Months Later

The Sekten—an alliance, a shield, and a warning. A mockery of what it once was.

"Por que tan calladita?" Julian Jr. teased. *Why so quiet?*

I couldn't let them know that while they discussed their biggest rivals, all I saw was potential allies. So I smiled and gave them what they wanted.

"With the Sect at your back, no one will be able to touch you. Daran mas miedo que ni el mismo Diablo." *You'll be feared more than the Devil himself.*

All the men nodded in agreement. Damian didn't even bother to look at me while I felt a slight touch on my knee. The reaction caused me to sit up straighter. Turning my head to glare at the man responsible, he was already grinning at me.

"What are you doing here?" I asked, turning to the man who made my blood boil.

Rivera and Sergio, I knew they wanted to expand their cocaine empire, and we had the resources to bypass any government. *Feared by all, bowed to none.* But Gideon was a mercenary, a lethal one. One who was crazy enough to do the contracts no one else dared touch. They called him the lone wolf because he had no alliance. No mob, cartel, or government was watching his back. It was rare to survive in this world on your own.

"I did a little job for Sergio; he asked me to stay."

Alas, Sergio wanted more manpower in this meeting.

"Petal," he murmured.

My skin broke out in hives.

Gideon's eyes went molten, and a seductive smile flashed from that pretty mouth of his. "Why won't you look at me? Is it because the last time we saw each other those pretty thighs were wrapped—*fuck.*"

My little scalpel was lodged between his middle and

index finger, a small clean cut staining the white tablecloth red. Everyone was looking at us, a smile on most of them, thinking I was cute.

Leaning into Gideon, I ignored the smell of his cologne. "Yes, handsome. It was just a fuck."

Bastian pulled my chair out for me so that I could get up. My hand was resting on the table for support...and then I heard the loud thud and felt sharp metal between my index and middle finger. I looked at the black dagger—my black dagger—that was now lodged between my fingers. Unlike me, Gideon didn't pierce skin.

"Did you not like my message?" Gideon mocked.

"Los veo mañana para irnos a la selba." *I'll see you tomorrow so that we can go to the jungle.*

I ignored Gideon and walked away. Bastian kept a distance from me, appearing to be aloof like he was just my guard dog and I his master. In reality, he was my crutch; he just didn't know it.

And he never would.

That dagger was from early imperial Russian and worth millions, and now it was missing the fucking rubies, and I'd just left it behind because I couldn't stand the English prick. I'd seen him from afar the day of the Estacado fight. I'd kept a reasonable distance as I watched Ren Falcon and tried to gauge what kind of man he was.

As soon as he lost his job and went off the grid, I was sent to kill him. Damian was not happy with me, but what use could we have with the Ember? Other than having another thing no one else could. It was nothing for us. So I was punished by doing all the shit work, but I liked it better that way.

"I need a favor," I said as soon as we walked into a room and checked it for bugs.

A Few Months Later

"You know my offer to give you a good dicking still stands."

I rolled my eyes at Bas. That was his thing—humor and sarcasm to cover up the fact that we were knee-deep in shit.

"Come on, Gideon couldn't have been that big... He's not bigger than me, right?"

"I need a meeting with Franco," I told him.

Bastian started coughing.

"*Estacado*?" He gaped. "The man who they were just discussing—*that* Franco?"

"Yes." I opened the balcony doors, looking out at the ocean.

"So beautiful, yet deadly." Gideon's words rang louder than before.

"Why?" Bas glared at me.

What I was doing was reckless; to set foot in Italy to go see the king of the Estacado's was suicide.

I made a vow covered in snow and dripping in blood. That I would burn down the pillars in which our kingdom stood. Watch the ashes blow as I laid the foundation for something new—something better. I vowed I was going to make them all pay. The time had come.

"It has begun."

The Sect does not forgive.
The Sect does not forget.
Keeper of secrets and dealers of lies,
We bow to no king, nations, or men.
Crossing us is certain death.

Want more Gideon? **Add book one of the Sect's series on Goodreads-** http://bit.ly/Sekten1

Join my Reader Group: Claudia's Coffee Shop for all the exclusives.

And for an extra scene of what happened when Ren found Pam make sure you are subscribed to my Newsletter

If you liked this book, I would be forever grateful if you left a review :)

Acknowledgements

I want to start off by thank you, the reader, for picking up Ember and Ren. When I started writing this story, it was for another project, but these two did not fit that mold. When I added them as an intro in the Sect world, it felt like coming home. I love all my books, but the Sect series has been a work in progress for the last five years, and I am so ecstatic to finally share it with the world.

Thank you to Becca Steele, who is not only my work wife but one of my best friends. Who has been through every mental breakdown and managed to cheer me up. If you loved the epilogue, thank her. She dragged me back to do this book justice.

Jenny Dicks, thank you for braving the rough waters of my alpha file lol. Seriously you two made this book shine. When I said this shit just got darker, you two psychos cheered.

To Katherine Lopez, who has been so fantastic with all her help and input. Thank you for making me go back and add more depth.

Andrea, Mercedes, Shonte, thank you so much for taking the time to beta this baby. This meant so much.

To all the girls in the promo group, I adore you all. You're all fantastic, and I can never say thank you enough.

My Coffee Shop babes, you guys make my day.

To my Chaddettes, thank you for always being in my corner. It takes a tribe, and I am glad I am part of yours.

Sandra, thank you for kicking ass at editing and making my baby be the best.

Carmen Richter, you are an amazing proofreader and a great friend. I know my books are always in great hands.

My fabulous cover designer, Jeannette from Net Hook & Line Designs, you fucking rock.

To my family, thank you for being patient with me when I was focused on my writing.

Brenda Hawkins, you waited for the man when he was just an idea. I hope I did him justice, and your man is everything you hoped for.

Xo

About the Author

Claudia lives in the Chicagoland suburbs, and when she's not busy chasing after her adorable little spawn, she's fighting with the characters inside her head. Claudia writes both sweet and dark romances that will give you all the feels. Her other talents include binge-watching shows on Netflix and eating all kinds of chips.

Want to know more about me?
Stay up to date on my Facebook
Join my Reader Group: Claudia's Coffee Shop
Instagram account: @C.Lymari

Printed in Great Britain
by Amazon